# SPOILS OF WAR

## BOOK THREE OF THE EXCALIBUR KNIGHTS SAGA

## LUKE MITCHELL

*This one's for Rick.*

*What can I say, but that he was a loyal and thoughtful reader, and that—from this author's limited perspective—he seemed a truly amazing father, husband, and all-around person as well.*

*Thank you for everything, Rick.*

*You will be missed.*

# CHAPTER 1
# AS YOU WISH

*What fresh hell is this?* Nate Arturi couldn't help but wonder, as he turned away from the hazy swirl of crusher space in the *Camelot*'s viewport, thoroughly flummoxed.

"She wants to do *what* now?" Jaeger asked, before Nate could open his mouth.

"Uh, pick… asteroids?" Over at the bridge entrance, Snuffy scrunched his face up, like he was questioning the accuracy of his own report. "She wants to go pick some asteroids. Sir. Demands it, actually." He dropped Jaeger's gaze to frown at his feet instead. "She called me an Yggdrasian slum monkey. I don't even know what that means."

Neither did Nate, exactly. Even if the general sentiment was easy enough to intuit. Either way, though, that pretty much settled it: He was never escorting Eldari royalty again.

*So long as good Master Priatus doesn't yank the leash and MAKE us,* Ex muttered in Nate's head. Which, much as he would've liked to argue, was probably more than fair, considering just how much he was starting to feel like the shiniest lapdog in the Alliance Council's yipping menagerie.

"We're not stopping," Jaeger said, before kicking his feet off the control consoles and shooting a surly frown Nate's way across the bridge like he'd forgotten whose ship this was.

"We're not stopping," Nate confirmed.

"That's what I told her," Snuffy said. "Tried to tell her, I mean. It's just that—"

"Just that your blubbering slum monkey fails to understand that this is not some whimsical request," came the elegantly frosty orator's tone of Princess Elsavataryllianna Priatus as she strode in for a grand entrance behind Snuffy, shadowed as always by the two Eldari merchants of death that were her bodyguards. She'd changed outfits. Again. Though, to her credit, this one seemed at least marginally functional—either some kind of base layer or maybe even a survivable space suit in its own right. Nate couldn't tell. Like everything else she wore, it was still plenty shiny, and probably worth more than pretty much anything else aboard, save for Ex and Cammy themselves.

"I'd appreciate it if you'd stop calling my crew monkeys," Nate said.

"As would I, if only I could do so honestly."

Nate just happened to meet Tessa's eyes in time to catch the full quirky payload of the pilot's reaction. He suppressed a grin. Just over a year holding the fort in Alliance space, waiting to be called up to the Big Leagues culling Synth protoswarms on the outer rims, and yet here they remained, pampering hoity-toity royalty like a bunch of interstellar chauffeurs.

At least they still had their humor.

"I require a sample of that celestial belt," the princess said, with just slightly less acid. She shifted in her glitzy space suit, looking almost vulnerable for a moment. Almost. "It is of great personal importance, and I will likely not be passing through this system again anytime soon."

It wasn't exactly an apology, but something about her tone sparked a tiny bit of empathy in Nate. Personally, he would've sooner dived into the nearest star than be betrothed to Prince Phaldissus Kelkarin, and in what limited interactions he'd had with their royal passenger, he kind of got the impression the princess might've felt the same way. But still…

"Be that as it may," he said, gesturing to the golden-armored Hurch and Lurch behind her in a gentle appeal for some backup, "I think all of us here can probably agree that stopping anywhere short of Vanaheim is an unnecessary risk to your safety, your highness."

"We exist to serve her royal highness," growled the Hurch of the pair, in a way that made it clear he would've gladly thrown down with Nate for his insolent tone alone, Excalibur Knight or not, had his lady willed it.

"Fine. *I* agree it's an unnecessary risk," Nate amended. "And—"

"And doth my brave Knight truly doubt his ability to protect me?" The princess' demeanor was positively vampish as she leaned in, all arched brows and pouty golden lips, slender neck angled just so, and—

*Keep your squishy human hormones to yourself, will you?*

Nate hoped his irritated grunt was quiet enough to go unnoticed. Judging by the looks around the bridge, it wasn't, but most of them—the old hands of the 501st Space Aggressor Squadron, at least—were fairly used to him making odd noises at the voice in his head by now. If any of the "new" crew hands—those few Council reps and Terran specialists he hadn't managed to refuse outright—had anything to say about his Knightly quirks, they'd kept it to themselves.

"I doubt the wisdom of willingly stepping into a situation where anyone *needs* protecting," he said, carefully slipping his composure back on. "Accidents do happen, even to brave Knights."

In truth, stopping for some impromptu asteroid mining was probably about as risky as trusting Cammy with the toaster—or to not scare the crap out of a new crew member in the bathroom at some point, either literally or metaphorically. It was more just that he didn't *want* to stop. Didn't want to drag out this "mission" any longer than necessary. On some level, he supposed some part of him just wanted to see their royal Princess Elsa *not* get her way, for once.

Or so he thought, as he began, "And seeing as we're aboard *my* ship..." only to find himself trailing off at the look in those damned puppy dog princess eyes and shifting to a reluctant, "How long would you need to... pick your rocks?"

He should have known better by now.

"Celestial bodies," she corrected evenly, that soft vulnerability evaporating from her eyes with disturbing speed, replaced by some predatory pleasure—like he'd given her everything she really wanted just by simply confirming she was indeed still the master of her own little galaxy, and of all the poor peons roaming within. "And what does it matter, what time I require? My father bade you—"

"Your father asked me to see you to Vanaheim *unmolested*," Nate shot back, insides curling at the smug look on her face, and at the memory of the Supreme Chancellor's exact choice of words. "He didn't say a thing about stopping for souvenirs."

He was being petty, he knew, and almost certainly inviting more long-term headaches than this was worth. But dammit, he was tired of being yanked around like a freaking prize pony. Tired of being nothing but a shiny errand boy while his fellow Knights—if they'd even allow him the use of such a level word as *fellow*—were out there doing their duty. Doing something, *anything*, that actually mattered.

"Maybe once you're Queen, you can send a nice armada of cargo haulers out here to cart the whole damn asteroid belt back to you on Vanaheim," he continued, earning himself a fresh layer of serpentine ice from those royal golden eyes. Hurch and Lurch actually reached for their lances. Nate didn't give a shit. "But until then, I'll ask you to kindly return to your quarters and —Oh, what the shit..."

The words were still leaving his mouth as the raw data came pouring into his head from Cammy's sensors, shaping answers to the still-forming questions rattling up his nerve endings from underfoot, where the *Camelot's* decks had just shuddered like...

Like they'd fallen out of crusher space. Yanked clear by—

"Pirates," Tessa said, just as Nate felt the ship register on Cammy's sensors. An ID-scrambling corvette slinking around out in the belt coverage, waiting to see what booty fell into the grav traps they'd apparently sprinkled across the system.

"Goddammit," Nate muttered.

"Oh, *protect* me, Ser Knight," the princess cooed, her face deadpan, practically bored half to death as she turned to glide off the bridge. "I shall return to my quarters and await news of your pending heroics like a good girl. My poor heart simply cannot handle the trepidation."

They watched her go in silence, Hurch and Lurch backing off the bridge at her flanks as if they expected one of them might actually open fire or something. And that could've been that, if her royal highness hadn't insisted on pausing just long enough to add over her shoulder, turning to show Nate the upturned razor's edge of her devilish smile: "Do my father proud, Ser Knight."

She glid off down the corridor in all her Eldari grace, not bothering to look back and gauge Nate's reaction. Instead, that honor was left to all the other sets of eyes on the *Camelot's* bridge. He let out a slow, calming breath, trying to play his quick, customary round of *What Would Iveera Do?*

*Well, I doubt even an Eldari princess would dare to show Ser Katanaga such flagrant disrespect,* Ex pointed out, in a tone that suggested he was genuinely trying to be helpful. Somehow, it only made the point burn that much deeper.

"I need a new job," Nate muttered. Then, just to get the bridge moving again: "Can someone please shoot them, by the way? I mean, not *them*," he added, glancing after the princess and her bodyguards, then back to the others. "You know. The pirates."

"Why not both?" Tessa murmured, still frowning in the general direction of Princess Elsa's royal departure as her fingers began to dance across the *Camelot*'s controls. At an unimpressed frown from Jaeger, she shrugged and turned back to her task.

"You know the drill, people," Jaeger said, slipping easily into his usual role as battle commander. "Slag the engines. Cue the stern warning message. Yada yada."

"Love to, Boss," called Ramirez over at one of the gunners' bays, "but—

"They're being coy out there," Tessa finished for him. "*All* up on that belt. Pilot knows what they're doing."

Nate sighed, calling his armor down from Ex's e-dim stores. "I'll go say hi, then."

"Wait." Jaeger caught him by the shoulder. "Something's off."

Nate looked at the hand on his shoulder, maybe a tad more aggressively than intended. "What's off?"

Jaeger frowned at the displays, shook his head, and focused back on Nate. "Could be more ships drifting dark out there. I'm not sure. Maybe we just blow the traps and get a move on."

It sounded much less like an order—much more like a suggestion—than it would have a year ago, when they'd just been getting their start as the Council's prolific errand squad, post Avalon shit storm. Nate shook his head anyway. "They'll just try again later. It's not like it's any secret where we're headed. You remember what happened back at Triton?"

"Ah, Triton," sighed Snuffy, who'd just so happened to have found himself locked planetside during that particular mishap, passing the time with their three Atlantean charges in what he'd later called "life-changing sexcapades." The frazzled mechanic returned from his fond memory to realize they were all staring. "What a shit show, right?" he added, quickly pretending to busy himself on his tablet.

The rest of the present bridge crew—namely, the two UN science officers who'd returned from Earth with the first Atlantean outreach a few months ago—looked a lot less certain about *all* of this, but no one spoke up.

"So, let's just put the old fear of god in 'em here and be done with it, right?" Nate concluded.

*Hear, hear,* Ex chimed.

Jaeger didn't quite look convinced, but Nate didn't dwell on it. The grumpy old bastard never looked convinced anymore. And much as Nate knew Jaeger was probably just doing his best to help him along, he still couldn't help but get a touch more annoyed each time the colonel second-guessed his every decision. He was the Knight here, after all.

So, he phased his way smoothly through the *Camelot*'s hull, gunned his gravitonics, and set out across the vast blackness of space to go show them.

# CHAPTER 2

# DRIVE

Nate was pretty sure he'd never forget his first solo dive into an asteroid belt.

It'd been about a month after Mordred LeFaye's defeat and their so-called victorious return to Forge Station—back when Iveera had still been flying with them. They'd been hunting a group of suspected Blackthorne cultists, hoping to shake lose a lead about the mad Atlantean pirate queen herself—or, at the very least, some clue as to what the hell she'd done with Iveera's stolen Knightship, the *Kalnythian Wilds*. Instead, they'd gotten one holy hell of a smuggling ring mess, and little in the way of answers, but Iveera hadn't missed the chance to find a nice "teachable moment" in sending Nate racing straight through a densely packed quagmire of speeding rock, ice, and debris into the cultists' cleverly hidden outpost cache.

"Just don't lose your head, Nathaniel," she'd told him. Which had almost felt like words of encouragement, until Ex chimed in.

*Literally. I'm reasonably certain that's the only bit I CAN'T regrow.*

As was often the case, Ex's pep talk had left something to be desired that day—as, admittedly, had Nate's own resolve and focus whilst drifting into the swirl. The first moments had been more or less controlled, albeit tensely. A wild gravitonic dance that rode the knife's edge between jubilation and sheer panic. For a minute, he'd managed to sit back and simply marvel at his and Ex's combined motor reflexes, and at just how far he'd come in a few short months. On some level, it'd even felt silly and irrational that the same dude who'd faced down Troglodan armadas and the Black Knight Mordred LeFaye (twice) should still find himself quaking in his space boots at the sight of big, speeding rocks at all.

But then, it was kind of hard to overstate just how damned *big* and *speeding* those rocks had felt as they'd whipped by in person, dwarfing him *and* the horse he'd rode in on. He remembered nearly shitting himself as two small mountains of ice and rock collided nearby, practically detonating in the eerie silence of space. Silent, at least, until the resultant cloud of debris had come pelting over him like a *crack-crack-cracking* choir of supersonic hail.

Thoroughly distracted by the mess, he'd made his first real navigational blunder and found out what it felt like to be struck by a speeding skyscraper. He'd come back to consciousness still pinned to the asteroid's surface some indeterminate blink later, Iveera waiting patiently on comm standby to offer her detached input, as was her way.

"Do not let fear defeat you even before your obstacle has had its chance," she'd said.

"Pretty sure it had its chance just fine," Nate had groaned, peeling himself painstakingly off the craggy face of said obstacle and trying not to pass back out as Ex made some casual comment about how most of his internal organs were only *partially* liquefied.

"Some obstacles you may not dodge. Some fights you may not win. Yet countless paths will always remain, so long as you do not allow fear to strike down your first steps."

Nate had scoffed it off at the time, dismissing it as the arm-chair quarterbacking of the Gorgon Knight who'd already had a good six-hundred-plus years to conquer such petty chestnuts as *the fear of speeding, giant-ass rocks* and couldn't possibly be expected to empathize with his headspace. And maybe that last bit *was* true. He didn't especially get the feeling that Iveera remembered what it was like, to be where he was now. But her words had still echoed back to him in the weeks and months following that lesson. Because he *had* been afraid that day, soaring into that asteroid belt. He'd been terrified. Terrified of what would happen if he crashed. Terrified of what he'd find on the other side if he didn't. Terrified of pretty much everything, looking back on it.

He wasn't terrified any longer.

If anything, he was probably too *eager* as he tore out of the *Camelot* in the present, racing for their coy pirate friends—more than a little ready, after tiptoeing around Elsa Priatus for the past few days, to rev the engines and give someone *else* a proper bad day for a change. He shattered through the first few truck-sized asteroids like brittle sugar candy. With the lance-shaped barrier charge Ex was putting off, he barely felt it as anything more than a spot of in-flight turbulence. He could've been more agile, as he'd tried to be on that day back in the Separuu system, under Iveera's watchful eye. He could've sought to match their coy sneaking with his own cunning maneuvers to catch them unawares.

Bursting through the drifting wall of ice and rock seemed to work just fine, though.

Countless paths, and all that.

Nestled away as the pirates were among the belt, they didn't see him coming. Not until it was too late. The ID-scrambled corvette barely had time to fire its thrusters before Nate caught its slender nose with a furious plasma blast and punched right through the slagged hull. He hit the bridge deck like a vengeful god. Or so he imagined, as the pelting bits of decompression debris and the howl of venting atmos gave way to the sharp clap of activating hull sealant and a chorus of spat curses. He rose to his feet, fixing on the few pirates fleeing the bridge for the short shot back to the corvette's cargo hold, and to the escape pods contained within. He actually felt a small rise of satisfaction at the sight.

*Wait*, Ex snapped, quite unexpectedly. Nate was already most of the way through the connecting corridor, soaring on a hard gravitonic burst. He hit the cargo hold deck at speed, skidding to a halt, discordant details slamming into place even before Ex could explain himself. A pair each of black-clad Hobdans and Atlanteans, scrambling into escape pods across the bay. The fact that those fleeing pirates wore Blackthorne insignias in plain sight, and that there weren't nearly as many of them aboard as there should've been for a corvette of this size. The conspicuous emptiness of the cargo hold, and the way the scarred Atlantean in the leftmost pod smacked a raised middle finger to the porthole, grinning a shit-eating grin as the pod jettisoned.

*The crusher drives*, Ex growled, right at the same time Tessa's voice burst into his helmet with something of concern in her tone, something about more ships powering up out there. *Inverted.* Nate's mind was scrambling, trying to weave the pieces together, parse it all out through the filter of Jaeger's bad feeling.

Crusher drives. Inverted. Turned inward on—

He started to move. Felt the charge already building, cresting.

Unbidden, Nate's mind flashed to the scene in Watchmen where Adrian

Veidt had lured Dr. Manhattan into his Machiavellian intrinsic field subtractor.

*Think big thoughts,* Ex snapped.

*Bastards just Dr. Manhattaned me,* was about the only thought Nate managed.

*BIG thoughts, Nathaniel.*

Then the crusher drives engaged, and space itself collapsed.

## CHAPTER 3

# POD 7

"**D**id… Did they just…?"

Back on the *Camelot*, no one seemed willing to even try to fill in the blank of Snuffy's reaching question. The answer was at once blatantly obvious and totally mysterious. All they really knew, staring at the suddenly crumpled shell of the unmarked pirate corvette, was that Kalders had still been mid-sentence with Nate when the whole damn ship had spiked off the gravitonic charts and started going all… all *wobbly* before their eyes, like the freaking thing was melting in the quantum microwave even as something at its center was trying desperately to hold it all together.

*Nate*, Jaeger felt them all hoping, right up until reality reasserted its control, and the entire ship imploded like a Coke can in the hand of god.

Jaeger pried his eyes away from the dead ship, forcing himself to compartmentalize the internal explosion of questions and focus instead on the most pressing concerns that lay within their control—namely the eight ships that'd been running dark until the moment their corvette friend had sprung its trap.

*Told you so*, Jaeger thought bitterly at the darkness.

The kid better have survived out there, dammit.

He opened his mouth to start doling out engagement orders and ask Cammy for a sit rep. An alert pinged on the displays before he could: "Escape pod launched."

"What the piss?"

Jaeger took in the bridge crew's reactions and found nothing but more questions in their collectively confused expressions. His gaze drifted aft, thoughts churning from malfunctioning pods, to pirate sabotage, to…

Son of a—

"Cammy, tell me you have eyes on the princess."

The ship's response was immediate, scrolling across his display in blocky green text.

"Princess Elsavarataryllianna Priatus - last seen boarding Escape Pod 7."

Jaeger didn't need to look—he did anyway—to confirm that it was indeed Escape Pod 7 currently drifting across the tac display, bound for that damned asteroid belt.

"I'll be damned," Ramirez said over in his gunner's bay, connecting the dots himself. "She must *really* want those rocks, Boss."

"Goddamn royalty," Jaeger muttered.

The first targeting lasers swept over the *Camelot*'s hull, the full brunt of their pirate ambush swooping in to do their worst.

Jaeger traded a grim look with Kalders, and they went to work.

# CHAPTER 4

# HICCUP

**S**hit got weird.

That was about the only solid fact the diverging branches of Nate's brain were willing to agree upon for the next few... *however longs*, once the crusher drives fired. The rest was left to a chaotic maelstrom of impossible dualities. The pain, he'd expected. It seemed to go without saying. But it was kind of shocking, how much that pain didn't seem to matter. He was a mountainous colossus, orbiting the nucleus of a single atom—limbs stretched for kilometers, smashed down to a vacuum-pressed blob. Time rushed by, creeping like molasses. A voice shouting in his ear. The faintest whisper, booming like a cannon.

*Focus.*

Iveera?

The world rippled with sight and sound across a pulsing web of nanoseconds condensing down to eons.

*Bigger, Nathaniel.*

The words struck him like a tsunami of existential realization, from somewhere beyond the overwhelming crush of it all. Part of him, a part that couldn't seem to recall the meaning of such words, latched onto them all the same. Latched on and *believed*. Strained against the unrelenting rush of expansion and collapse.

*Bigger.*

A flicker of something else. Something far removed from the pressure.

Something almost peaceful. Soothing, unassuming music. A rustic yet shimmeringly sophisticated place, endless and not, stretched out behind—

"No, not *here*, Nathaniel," growled the silk-vested, severely mustachioed man suddenly staring him in the face with wild eyes, jabbing a finger. "Out there!"

Something shoved him as he turned to follow that finger. Shoved him straight back into the shit. Howling expansion and collapse. Crushing pressure. He saw some distant flicker of Todd Mackleroy's sneering face staring down at him on the floor of a Penn State gym. Felt something tearing.

*Push, damn you.*

He did, as best he could without knowing which way was up or down.

Then, with a world-wrenching rush, disparate realities all collapsed into one smoking wreck of a cargo bay—head spinning, nose burning with the acrid bite of scorched electronics. The lazy hiss of the last venting atmos, giving way to the still silence of vacuum.

*—ot so bad, see?* Ex was saying.

"'The fuck just happened?" Nate groaned.

*Spacetime hiccup, in simpleton speak. As I was saying. Credit where it's due, though: that WAS a borderline competent use of your full gravitonic suite. Well done, Nathaniel.*

"Was that...?" Nate started, grasping for some coherent replay. All his spinning head could manage was the stark afterimage of the mustachioed man shooing him out of what could've been—must've been...?

*Yes, and no,* Ex said. *And also—*

"You... have a mustache?"

He wasn't sure why those particular words came tumbling out. He hadn't meant to say them, and couldn't quite seem to *understand* them, even as some part of Ex's exasperation made itself clear. Reality wobbled like a drunken mess, blurring the twisted cargo bay and Ex's reply about sad monkeys and pertinent details.

*Speaking of which,* Ex was saying, as the world lurched and buzzed back into something like focus, *it appears our wayward princess has been captured. The horror.*

Nate blinked a few times, waiting for those words to make proper sense, then gave up and shook his head, reaching for the *Camelot*. He felt her out there, dancing through the asteroids by some loving combination of Tessa's hand and Cammy's will, trading fire with six—no, seven—pirate vessels that must've been lying in wait all along. Clearly, Jaeger's gut had had a point. But as for the princess... He tracked Cammy's report, felt the unexpected launch and subsequent capture of her seventh escape pod by an eighth pirate vessel, which was currently…

"Shit," Nate grunted, setting aside the long string of *hows* and *whys* for the moment in favor of screwing his head on tight and getting a move on.

"Guys?" he asked over the comms, as he dropped out of the nearest rupture in the cargo hold's hull and took off after Pirate Ship 8.

"Nate?" Tessa's voice was momentarily tight, like she was mid-maneuver. Then she let out an even breath. "Nice of you to join us, Mr. Knight. What the hell happened over there?"

"Spacetime hiccup," Nate relayed, trying to comprehend the course and intercept times Ex was throwing up on his HUD. His tongue felt funny. Christ, his *everything* felt funny. "Long story," he added. Or tried to. His lips didn't quite seem to comply.

*Ex?* Something was wrong.

*Just some minor hemorrhagic aphasia. Nothing to worry ab—*

*Wait, some WHAT?*

*Well, YOU try keeping a squishy noodle bowl in one piece through catastrophic spacetime warpage, Nathaniel. You mightn't believe it to listen to you speak, but your brain tissue is rather complex.*

Nate wrinkled his nose, smelled light tingles up his spine, corroded batteries on his tongue. Outside, space wobbled strangely. Inside, on the oddly distant ringing of the comms, Jaeger was doing his *unimpressed Jaeger* thing and wrangling them all back to the point.

"—need to get her royal highness back here before she gets us all in deep shit."

"Thought you were gonna say before she gets hurt," Tessa chimed in, sounding a tad amused despite everything.

"Well, that too."

"I'm on it," Nate said, pushing the gravitonics a bit harder, and feeling the sizzle more than he should've. "And what the hell was she doing, leaving the ship like—"

"Going to pick her damn space rocks, for all I know," Jaeger cut him off at a low growl. He didn't sound too happy about any of this. Nate could practically taste the colonel setting aside the looming *I told you so* for the after-action report. "Doesn't matter now. Just—"

"I've got it," Nate said, firmly enough to send an unpleasant ripple through his aching head. His gravitonics sputtered like they felt it too. Minor brain bleed. Jesus Christ. "You guys just keep those ships busy and worry about yourselves over there."

Jaeger was conspicuously silent.

"Sounds like my kinda party," Tessa filled in, half-heartedly.

Nate didn't have time to dwell on it. A minute later, he was closing on Pirate Ship 8, a mid-sized, heavily modified Seventh Star frigate, ID-scrambled like the others. This time, he at least waited for Ex to complete an initial scan, determined to stick with a cautious approach. Determined, that was, until Ex's efforts revealed a spectral outline of the cargo hold, where a dozen-plus well-armed killers were taking aim as the lead pair slapped breaching charges on the captured pod's hatch locks.

Shit.

*No Crusher Drive Surprise,* was all Ex needed to say.

Nate gunned it. But he was already too late.

The charges must've detonated at the same moment he breached the frigate's hull. He came down in a confusing mess of smoke and weapons fire—plasma bolts and a few slugs splashing against his armor as Ex modulated the HUD spectrum to something a bit more smoke-friendly. Nate moved without hesitation, thrusting his hand toward the first foe... only to watch as his wrist cannon sputtered and died mid e-dim deployment.

*Ah,* Ex said, like he genuinely hadn't seen that one coming. *Damned hiccups. Just a moment.*

Nate was already leaping forward to do the job the old-fashioned way. He caught the unfortunate Hobdan with a chest kick that cratered his armor plating, then sprung right and brought an Excalibur-powered fist down on his friend's head. He launched for the next target, trying not to think in terms of killing blows or otherwise. He'd tried for his stunner. No time to worry beyond that. Not as a heavy plasma bolt punched into his side past the barriers he'd thought he'd raised, sending him staggering for balance. He spun and tore the offending weapon free from the Troglodan shooter's grasp, distantly aware that his ribs were on fire, then grabbed the stunned Trog by the arm, and flung him at the densest cluster of enemy tags on his HUD, not stopping to watch, already whirling at incoming on his left.

He drew up short, fist cocked, as one of Princess Elsa's guards came charging through the smoke, lance raised. They both froze. Then a ghostly violet tracer tore through the Eldari's chest armor, and he collapsed in a slack heap. Nate turned to follow that tracer, raising energy barriers and a physical shield even as recognition dawned and he realized it didn't matter. The next three disruptor rounds tore through him, connecting the fiery dots from thigh to chest. He hit the deck on hand and buckled knee, free arm raising toward the threat of its own accord.

This time the wrist cannon didn't fail, nor did Nate hold back. His shot bore a smoking half-meter hole in the fully-armored shooter and passed on through with enough fury to scorch the arm off the Atlantean behind him and leave the bulkhead behind an oozing red-hot mess. Nate turned for the next mark on his HUD, grunting through the pain. Both Eldari guards dead, he dimly noted. Most of the pirates, too. And the princess…

There. Right at the leveling end of the last pirate's gun. An *Asgardian*, some corner of Nate's brain registered with a flicker of surprise. Too late, he reached for his gravitonics, thinking to throw himself forward, or yank the shooter closer, or maybe to even full-on flash step like Iveera did. He wasn't sure.

Then Princess Elsa caught the Asgardian's gun hand like a striking viper and came off the deck, twisting around her attacker with a dancer's grace. Twisting until the towering Asgardian—who must've outweighed her by at least two-fold—went flying across the deck like a lawn chair caught on the wind. He hit messily, clearly having not expected a fight from her highness, but came up neatly enough as his training took hold. Nate was already there, close enough to have reached out and knocked him back down for good, but some part of him was too captivated as the furious Asgardian rounded back on the princess, realized too late that he'd lost his weapon in the fray. Realized a second later that their shiny, fashionable Eldari princess had in fact stripped it from his hand mid-throw.

Her royal highness shot him dead without a shadow of hesitation. One ghostly violet disruptor round, straight to the pale golden forehead.

Silence settled through the bay, broken only by the crackling rush of the spreading fire, Princess Elsa glancing curiously at the weapon in her hand before tossing it aside. It clattered to the deck as she looked around the hold, presumably for her guards. Her gaze only found Nate instead.

"You good, Nate?" Jaeger's voice crackled over the comms.

Nate held the princess' golden eyes, panting harder than he should've been as Ex began knitting his injured flesh back together. Too close. Two Eldari royal guards dead. The princess alive only by a lucky shake and her own intervention. Way too fucking close.

"All good," he lied evenly, positive that *good* was about the last thing they were.

For once, the look in Princess Elsavarataryllianna Priatus' eyes said she couldn't have agreed more.

## CHAPTER 5

# NO, IN YOUR HONOR

Whatever else one wanted to say about the Eldari, there was no denying they were fiercely diplomatic.

Almost *lethally* so, Nate couldn't help but think, as Prince Phaldissus Kelkarin and his band of well-groomed sycophants approached, glaring daggers at him from across the golden architectural wonder of the landing platform causeway.

Warm and friendly, or anything else of the sort? Hell no.

But diplomatic? No doubt.

Nate breathed steadily, focusing on the itchy heat of his freshly healed gunshot wounds and resisting the urge to make like a hermit crab and call the Lady-blessed cover of his helmet back down from e-dim. The city of Vanaheim (capital, vainly enough, of the *planet* Vanaheim) had really rolled out the welcome mats for the triumphant arrival of their soon-to-be princess.

Tired as Nate was of feeling like nothing but the shiny stamp of Alliance power that the Council loved to smack down here and there, it actually had been kind of gratifying, to see such a vibrant welcome parade massing on the *Camelot*'s descent like, at least to the people of Vanaheim, this escort mission had been more than just another pointless Council-mandated errand.

Of course, after everything that'd happened out there, it felt like more than that to Nate, too. It was hard to imagine how it couldn't have, with two dead Eldari royal guards stashed in the cargo bay freezer and an unreadable princess locked away in her quarters, quite possibly ruminating on just how close her brave Knight had come to letting her die. Not that she would've needed any saving at all if she'd just stayed aboard the damned ship. Still, there was no getting around it. He'd overextended himself. Dismissed Jaeger's gut feeling and rushed in too carelessly. And much as he wanted to blame it all on the princess' rash actions, not to mention the fact that those "pirates" had been suspiciously well-prepared for a Knight, and had exhibited far too many signs of being an orchestrated hit squad rather than opportunistic kidnappers—and a hit squad eager to lay blame at the feet of an easy target like the Blackthorne cultists, at that…

But that was all beside the point.

At the end of the day, there was just no denying it. He'd fucked up. And now he didn't know what the princess was going to do about it.

*You worry too much,* Ex said. *Do you think Iveera would sit around fretting over what some Eldari princess might say about her?*

Of course she wouldn't have. But that was kind of the entire point, wasn't it? He *wasn't* Iveera. Wasn't Zedavian, or Dalnak, or Viktos. Not yet, at least. And they all knew it, just like the Council knew it. Which was exactly why *he* was here playing Shiny Errand Boy, and *they* were out there beating back Synth protoswarms from civilized space. And what were the chances anyone was going to ask him to step up and go join the real fight once they found out he'd nearly been bested by a few petty criminals?

*I'm more interested in the chances that we can skip the sniveling and get on with our lives,* Ex grumbled. *You must learn patience, Nathaniel. You've barely been Knighted for a year, and the Synth threat is not going anywhere. This is part of the journey.*

Coming from Ex, they were unusually restrained words. He tried to take them to heart. But he still couldn't help but worry about what havoc Princess Elsavataryllianna Priatus, daughter of the Supreme Chancellor of the Alliance, might wreak on his life should she choose to make a point of it. He caught Tessa studying him from where she'd gathered with the crew at the base of the *Camelot*'s ramp, and for a moment, he forgot about the rest. For a moment, he could think only of the way she'd looked at him in the aftermath of the battle, as the others had all been busy thumping backs and carrying on. That vivacious energy he'd all but felt bouncing along the uncanny bond between her and his ship, spilling over to him in the light of her eyes. Bright and alive. Inviting him to join the party.

He dropped her gaze back in the present. Did his best to focus back on the flashy welcoming march of the Eldari.

He hadn't told the crew about their close call back on that pirate ship. Hadn't even let on that the crusher drives had been more than just a minor hiccup. At first, he'd told himself it was just that he didn't want to diminish their high at having won out over seven enemy vessels while he'd been busy "saving" Princess Elsa. But it was more than that, if he was being honest. Because, even if no one would've said as much out loud, he'd felt the changes in the way they looked at him in these past months. Somewhere along the way, they'd actually started to believe he was the Knight he still felt at times he was only pretending to be. They'd started believing in *him*. Trusting in his growing power.

The last thing they needed now was to know how nearly that power had failed in what should've been the equivalent of a routine traffic stop.

So, he'd let them focus on their victory, kept things vague when the subject had turned to the deaths of Elsa's royal guards, and hoped the princess herself would stay locked away in her quarters with no need to correct him. Soon enough, they'd arrived to Vanaheim and to all the welcome distraction of pomp and circumstance awaiting them there. And what an impressive display it'd been.

With the exception of Old Man Jaeger and their medic, Carter, who as a rule seemed to be emotionally pair-bonded with whatever the colonel felt and thought, they'd all gathered around to gawk like children at the grand reception marching out to meet the *Camelot*.

Without even counting the hundreds of guards now lining the grand causeway, sporting pulse lances and royal banners, it was clear there must've been at least four- or five-thousand Eldari out there. Maybe more. Definitely more than Nate had ever seen gathered in one place. Most of them dressed in rich silks, ancestral treasures, and expressions that conveyed some masterful balance of jubilant reverence and dignified reservation, like they wanted to make it clear that, while they were happy to greet their soon-to-be crown princess, they weren't really beholden to anyone.

*Classic Eldari*, Ex said. *Natural politicians.*

It wasn't a compliment.

Nate continued scanning the oncoming procession, noting the various furry familiars that accompanied many of the nobles, including a few big, fox-like kitsunes like the one that'd taken a meaty bite out of Jaeger's arm back at Zedavian Kelkarin's home palace on the Forge. Judging by the frown etched across the man's brow, Jaeger must've been recalling the same episode. Throughout the procession, a few of the Eldari were mounted on large, vaguely equine creatures Ex identified as sleipnir. Others were accompanied by more sentient familiars, aides and servants, scampering faithfully along beside their masters. Hobdans, Androtta, the odd Atlantean, and even a few Gorgons and Svendarians—though the latter were hardly capable of *scampering* with their seven sturdy legs and powerful upright torsos. And as for the mighty Prince Phaldissus himself...

"I still can't believe that's a thing," Snuffy whispered, echoing Nate's own thoughts rather astutely.

"Man, you've met space vampires," Ramirez said, equally quiet.

"Yeah, but—"

"Space goblins," Ramirez added, like he was ticking off fingers. "Atlanteans. Asgardians. Freaking space centaurs, man."

"Still..." Snuffy mumbled, frowning at one of the Svendarians in the crowd.

Nate couldn't really blame the mechanic. Even with the prior knowledge of their allegedly rare (but extremely real) existence, even after everything they'd seen in their travels so far, it was still pretty damn bizarre to watch Prince Phaldissus Kelkarin marching down the causeway astride an honest-to-Christ griffin—its gleaming white wings tucked back along its muscular sides, nestling the prince's golden-armored legs in place. Nate considered the sharp beak and feline eyes, wondering whether the creature was more or less sentient than Ser Zedavian's kitsune, Zartan, whom the First Knight had somehow taught to speak.

Unbidden, he thought of Copernicus back home, corgi tongue lolled and panting, and felt a rare pang of homesickness. The thought of Gwen wasn't far behind—of her ever more distant looks and elusive smiles. Of hers and Marty's decision to suddenly join the fledgling Earth Defense Force—or the EDF, as they'd taken to calling it—without so much as a heads up. Acting out their frustrations at having been left behind? Maybe. Probably. He still wasn't sure. Still wasn't sure how he felt about any of it.

How long had it been since they'd last spoken?

He shifted his weight, telling himself he'd call them soon, and tried to focus back on the welcoming party. Somehow, his gaze found Tessa near the base of the *Camelot*'s ramp instead. She wagged her eyebrows and tipped her head front and center, like *pay attention, Mr. Knight*. He nodded acknowledgment and glanced over to check on Princess Elsa, who awaited her incoming procession with a kind of grim dignity, standing close to Nate and his crew, but also unmistakably apart from them.

The absence of her towering twin shadows tugged at Nate's conscience. *Hurch and Lurch*, his mind provided, accusatorily. Haughty as the two royal guards might've been, it didn't seem to make up for the fact that he hadn't even bothered learning their names. If the princess was thinking similar thoughts, she didn't show it.

Hopefully, the good people of Vanaheim didn't find out how very close she'd come to joining her loyal guards.

Hell, he would've preferred they didn't learn of the attack at all, but that was almost certainly too much to hope for.

News had yet to hit Vanaheim's channels. That much, he already knew thanks to Ex's background monitoring. There was nothing of the attack on the local bands, and the princess herself hadn't contacted anyone, her father included. But it was only a matter of time.

*You did nothing wrong*, Ex reminded him, as the royal vanguard drew to a halt ten meters out.

Nobles, aides, pets, and assorted royal posse all waited in brimming silence—the city bustle below only a distant hum up here in the rarefied air of the palace landing pad—as Prince Phaldissus dismounted from his majestic griffin and strode forward to greet his betrothed. They met with a bow on his part, and a kind of curtsy on hers. For a species that was arguably the central foundation of the entire sprawling, hyper advanced Galactic Alliance, the whole thing felt rather medieval.

"Princess Elsavataryllianna Priatus," he said, taking her hand and drawing it smoothly to his lips. "Your beauty and grace are just as I remember. I trust you were well-tended on your voyage to Vanaheim?"

The question set Nate on edge, but it was nothing compared to the look on Elsa's face as she turned from her dashing prince to look straight at Nate, a cold smile etching its way across her lips.

"*Quite* well-tended," she finally said, after an uncomfortably long pause. Phaldissus definitely didn't miss the way her gaze lingered on Nate, nor did he especially seem to like it, but the Eldari princess remained calm as she turned back to him and added, casually, "I only wish my brave companions needn't have perished to see it so."

Murmurs and whispers dancing on the Vanaheim wind. Nate tried to relax suddenly tensed shoulders.

The prince's voice was tight and demanding. "Explain."

Behind him, his pet griffin scratched curiously at the pale causeway stone, then inspected its foreclaws.

"We were set upon just shy of your kingdom borders, my prince," Princess Elsa said, like she was a little surprised he hadn't already somehow heard the news. "By Asgardian assassins, lest I miss my guess."

Gasps and sharp curses, spreading like wildfire.

Prince Phaldissus sucked in a long breath through gritted teeth, then finally blew it out, turning to look for someone among the crowd. One of the Eldari that'd walked in by his side—a slightly older, rather grim-looking fellow with tightly-braided hair and more than a few scratches and dings on his heavy golden armor—straightened to full attention at the prince's gaze, like he expected he'd be called upon. Nate was still busy wondering when Elsa had hatched this pet assassination theory of hers—not to mention whether she'd been planning to tell him at all—when the prince's boiling attention strayed from his approaching man to spill over and address the crowd instead.

"Assassins and treachery, here on our very doorstep!" he cried. "Is it not exactly as I have warned you, my beloved people? Symptoms of an ailing kingdom. Of hands grown too old, too weak and cautious to wield the lance and the shield at a time when it is clear that strength, above all else, is what we require."

The words stirred more than a few whispers and looks.

The prince's enraged eyes rounded back on Nate.

"And you. Where were *you* whilst my lady was set upon by these cursed fiends, Excalibur Knight?"

"Well…" Nate glanced at Elsa, uncertain about the dynamics at play here. Not sure whether to start with what he *had* done right, or with the fact that she'd been the one who'd gone and willingly jettisoned herself away from the safety of the *Camelot*.

"He saved my life, my prince," the princess said before he could make up his mind. "I owe him my highest gratitude."

A natural diplomat, Nate most certainly wasn't, but in the past year, he'd at least learned how to keep a steady face when the shit was going quietly sideways. His Iveera Face, he'd taken to calling it. It almost failed him now, shocked as he was by the conviction in the princess' tone. Her sticking up for him had been about the last thing he'd expected. So much so that, amidst the rest of the rabble-rousing, it immediately raised his hapless political hackles.

The look Elsa shot him, as Phaldissus gave an unprincely scoff and stormed off for his mount, seemed to confirm that those hackles weren't completely off base.

Nate barely even registered what the next few Eldari nobles said, as they stepped forward to fill the empty space and shower their new princess-to-be in all manner of official, high-tongued greetings and compliments, only slightly deterred by the sudden and awkward need to add their condolences and righteous outrage to the list. He was too busy watching Prince Phaldissus pause beside his restless griffin, one hand on the saddle, to have a word with that grizzled Eldari warrior, who nodded gravely along. Both their eyes flicked back to Nate, wary and—

"Ser Arturi."

Nate pried himself back to the moment to find an Eldari waiting for his attention. A herald, he thought, eyeing the man's high quality but comparatively simple robes, and the meticulously silken-stitched emblem at his breast. Nate was pretty sure it marked the ruling house of Vanaheim— which was apparently *not* the same as the Kelkarin family crest, despite the fact that they'd allegedly been more or less running the planet since their great-great-great-great-to-the-nth-degree grand-relative Zedavian had ascended to Excalibur Knight some 3,000 years ago.

"The gratitude of the Eldari people cannot be overstated for your aid in this matter," the herald was saying, with about as much apparent gratitude as a tired scribe reading back another's words. "Especially in this time of war, when so much weight lies on the conscience of your order. Accordingly, High King Phallinor has decreed that you and your crew shall be welcome guests and recipients of any hospitality you desire of Vanaheim, for so long as you choose to remain."

The words struck him as decidedly disconnected—maybe dangerously so—from the sentiments of the High King's own son, Phaldissus. Nate laid a flat hand across his abdomen and bowed his head in the customary Knight's salute anyway, in no rush to spit upon the good graces of the first person to be courteous to him, even if it was only at his king's royal behest. Phaldissus and his wary friend were still watching.

"Your generosity is much appreciated," Nate said to the herald, glancing at Princess Elsa and wondering if maybe they shouldn't just make like a tree and blast the hell out of here anyway, before things went any more sideways. The small question of how the King had even known to extend such gratitude alighted in the corner of his mind like an irksome butterfly. If Vanaheim hadn't yet heard the news of the attack... Probably, it was just standard boilerplate hospitality.

"It is also my duty," the herald continued, in a voice like drying paint, "to inform you of your invitation to the official welcoming ceremony of Princess Elsavataryllianna Priatus this afternoon."

Nate, as he so often regretted doing, reflexively glanced a question at Jaeger. The colonel, as he so often was, was wearing one of those expressions of his—professionally attentive with a strong undercurrent of personal boredom. The man might've made a decent Eldari, if he hadn't been lacking their smug superiority. Nate looked back at Elsa to find her watching him with an inscrutable expression, and made up his mind.

"We'd be honored to attend."

He needed to have a word with her before they left this planet.

Ahead of him, the Eldari herald bowed his head and spread his hands, managing to look both gracious and also just a smidgen like Nate had gone and spiked a rancid ham at his feet.

This was going to be great.

The nobles were swarming forward en masse now, several of those who hadn't yet kissed Elsa's royal cheeks—posteriorly speaking—all vying for their chance to do so. Several offered gifts, or invitations to their respective estates for tea and other more foreign recreations. Nate scooted closer, intending to get her attention before she was ferried off on a wave of superficial adoration. He caught himself just shy of reaching for her arm. Causing a stir was the last thing they needed here. And yet, whether he liked it or not, he had a feeling that was exactly what he'd already accomplished. Especially as Prince Phaldissus appeared above the swell, climbing atop his restless griffin, angry eyes sweeping the crowd to land back on Nate.

Nothing for it now.

"May I speak with you in private, your highness?" Nate asked the princess, as quietly as he could.

Somehow, the question seemed to make it to every golden ear on the causeway. Princess Elsa made no effort to hide her demure surprise, which itself wasn't much of a surprise, considering he was pretty sure it was a complete act anyway. *Whatsoever would you need to speak to* me *about?* that look said. Almost like she was enjoying this. He thought of the two men —*her* men—who'd died protecting her back on that ship. Behind her, Prince Phaldissus the Indignant was approaching by griffin, paying no attention to the startled nobles scrambling hurriedly out of his way. He kept his glare fixed on Nate, looking about as affronted as if Nate had just loudly and publicly asked his betrothed for a pre-wedding roll in the hay.

"Jaltethen will show you to your quarters, my princess," Phaldissus said as he drew up to them, his eyes never leaving Nate's. He tipped his proud golden head pointedly in the direction of the grim-faced warrior who must've been Jaltethen, his griffin mount shifting anxiously beneath him, like it was eager for flight. "Do not leave the palace without adequate protection. Not until I have unraveled the mystery of your attackers."

The order might've seemed a bit more genuine on the *concerned fiancée* front if Phaldissus had bothered to even look at the princess as he spoke. It did, however, succeed at shifting something in the calculus on Elsa's face, momentarily clouding her sweetly demure smile before warping it into something sharp and dangerous.

"Come then, Ser Knight," she said, turning back to Nate as if the prince hadn't even spoken. "Let us speak *privately* in my quarters. I trust you'll protect me."

That, at least, finally earned her the prince's full attention.

Nate could only watch the drama unfold, wanting to wash his hands of the princess then and there, but painfully aware that—even if he could've comfortably left Vanaheim without worrying about what Princess Elsa might tell her father—there was nothing he could say right then to disperse the cloud of righteous, princely rage that Elsa was weaving him into here. Probably deliberately. There seemed to be very little about Elsavataryl-lianna Priatus that *wasn't* deliberate.

Deliberate or not, though, Prince Phaldissus looked about one twitch shy of slapping Nate with a golden glove and demanding a duel as he recovered from Elsa's comment and remembered that half of Vanaheim's nobility were staring at them with rapt attention.

"I *will* defend your honor, princess," he practically hissed, leaning down from his griffin to enunciate the point. Then, straightening and crying out for the whole crowd to hear: "This attack on our kingdom shall not go unpunished. This, I promise you all. Be they the lowest dregs of pirate scum, or the ill-tempered machinations of Asgard itself, the culprits will pay."

For a fleeting moment, Nate couldn't help but think the prince looked very small up there, atop his mighty griffin. Somehow, it only made the silent threat in Phaldissus' narrowed golden eyes that much more poignant as he looked back down to Nate and Elsa. He glared at them both until his betrothed gave him a stiff curtsy. He waited a moment longer—probably for a Knight's salute, Nate realized, in hindsight—then he spoke a scowling word to his mount, and the crowd watched in their dispassionately superior Eldari admiration as the creature bounded forward and leapt from the high causeway, mighty wings shooting wide to carry their golden prince off into the rising Vanaheim sun.

Or off to wherever Eldari princes went to plot the murder of those who'd slighted them, possibly.

"Well, then," Princess Elsa said, all of her cavalier chipper returning like sunlight after a passing cloud. Around them, the Vanaheim nobility continued watching breathlessly, like they hadn't seen such delectable drama in years. Elsa held an expectant hand out, utterly unconcerned, waiting, it seemed, for Nate's arm to be offered. "Shall we, my brave Knight?"

*Nothing for it, eh, Little Hobbit?*

With a stiff jaw and one last glance back at his crew, Nate offered out his arm and set off uneasily down the causeway with the princess, moving under the weight of a thousand gawking eyes and one very determined resolution.

He was *definitely* never escorting Eldari royalty again.

# CHAPTER 6
# DIRTY LITTLE SECRET

"Okay. What the hell was that?" Nate growled the moment the golden doors of Princess Elsa's royal bed chambers clacked shut behind them. He shook his arm loose from her warm grasp, scowling at the obscenely decadent living quarters, letting go of the polite composure he'd held under the watchful eyes of Jaltethen and the rest of the Phaldissus Posse that'd followed them through the palace like angry shadows.

"Are you *trying* to get your husband to kill me?"

*I'd like to see him try*, Ex said.

Truth be told, much as Ex's big-dick battle lust might've exasperated him in a past life, Nate kind of would've liked to see the same. Not that that made it wise to speak to the current crown princess of Aesirheim/soon to be crown princess of Vanaheim as he was now. But it was kind of hard to care right that moment. Especially as the princess studied him, maddeningly unimpressed by his words, then turned instead for the neatly arranged stack of belongings the palace servants had hurriedly delivered from the *Camelot* ahead of their arrival.

"He's not my husband, technically speaking," she said over her shoulder, stooping for one of the blocky containers from the pile. "And no," she added, her voice slightly strained as she hefted the container up and turned for the wide table beyond the entryway, "not particularly, to answer your question."

Lady curse his misguided sense of chivalry. He was rushing forward to help the pretty golden damsel with her heavy object before his brain could step in and remind him that she was at least a *little* bit terrible, and definitely manipulative ad infinitum. Still…

"Here, let me—"

But she shouldered off his reaching arm with a flash of contempt like he'd never seen. For a moment, an odd silence stretched between them, like she was as surprised as he was to realize there was in fact a living, breathing reactionary person beneath her carefully controlled exterior. Then she pulled it together, and he was staring at The Princess once again.

Nate watched her cart the heavy crate the rest of the way over to the gleaming onyx table, not really sure what to make of her reaction other than that, for a split second, he was pretty sure he'd glimpsed something of Elsavataryllianna Priatus that she hadn't meant to show him. That was definitely a first. He followed her into the lavishly adorned living room, looking around without really paying attention to anything he saw. Mostly, he was trying to figure out how to quickly get to the point and get out of here.

Curiosity brought his attention back to Elsa's box as she cracked the seals and lifted the lid. He watched with a deepening sense of uncertainty as she began to unpack her precious asteroid samples with careful, almost reverent movements.

She'd ventured back out without a word in the aftermath of the pirate attack—or the assassination attempt, if that's what it'd truly been. Either way, with her two loyal servants dead at her feet, mere minutes past her own brush with mortality, the princess had gone out to pick her rocks. By that point, with the rest of the enemy vessels either destroyed or fled from the system, and with Nate floating patiently at her royal side, no one had bothered to argue.

"I don't get it," he said, taking one of the smaller rocks from the table. It was dark and porous. Rough against his fingers. "What's so important about these rocks? Seemed like pretty much any other asteroid belt in the galaxy."

"Celestial bodies," she murmured, plucking the dark porous *body* absentmindedly from his hand, like she might've been irritated about it if she hadn't been so distracted with her work. "And just so. Perfectly ordinary."

He watched her methodically organize her samples, trying to parse it. Was this merely some eccentric hobby? Or maybe some kind of grounding practice. The highest of all royal highnesses, so bored with her eminent wealth and power that she'd moved on to collecting perfectly ordinary space rocks just to feel… what? Normal? He didn't know. But two Eldari were dead because of these rocks. Not to mention Lady knew how many of their unlucky attackers. And Nate… Nate still wasn't sure where he stood.

"About what happened out there…"

He waited to see if she'd step in and fill the blanks with whatever she was thinking, but she just carried on, drawing some kind of handheld magnifying device out of the box and settling in on one of her samples. All things considered, it kind of irritated the shit out of him.

"What were you thinking, leaving the *Camelot*'s protection?"

She didn't look up from her lens. "Perhaps I was thinking my brave Knight would protect me."

Nate felt his jaw muscles clenching. Felt the sudden, overwhelming itch to call on Ex's power and incinerate the damned table out from under her precious rocks. Instead, he listened to the voice of cool reason in the back of his mind. The one that sounded oddly like Iveera's. That voice dispassionately pinched the head of the rage slithering its way to the surface, and let the tension out on a slow, quiet exhalation. He unclenched his jaw, releasing the rage along with the indignant urge to point out, yet again, that she never would've been in any danger at all if she'd just been reasonable and stayed on the damn ship.

"I'm sorry about your guards. I… should've been there sooner."

That caught her attention for sure, but there was no flash of self-righteous *damn right, you should've* as Nate had half-expected. Instead, it was just a kind of tired assessment. "You wish to know whether I intend to tell my father what happened. That I would've died if not for taking matters into my own hands."

He tried to match her detached air. "What is it you want, Elsavataryllianna?"

She showed him a pale ghost of that predatory smile. "Very good, Ser Knight. You do begin to learn."

He said nothing, pretty sure he'd only dig himself deeper into her machinations if he spoke before knowing her game. She watched him for several seconds, waiting, perhaps, to see if he would anyways. Finally, she nodded her quiet approval.

"I wish to come aboard the *Camelot*. Permanently."

That, of all things, he hadn't seen coming.

*Blackened hands*, Ex agreed.

"I… doubt Prince Phaldissus would be pleased to hear that."

"Mmm," she agreed, her smile coming forward, going a touch feline.

"You also presuppose that I should *care* what would and would not please such a man."

"He *is* your betrothed, isn't he?"

"A sacred bond," she agreed, nodding with dramatically grave reverence. "One that is nigh unbreakable for Eldari of our respective stations, but for a few esoteric exceptions."

"Exceptions?" he asked, before he could stop himself.

This was it, he was suddenly certain. The grand scheme she'd been stoking since they'd touched down.

"I assume, despite your lack of any such allies, that you are at least aware of the politically privileged station of the Knight Envoys."

"You… can't be serious. You're—You're royalty. That's not—"

"Ah, but it is," she cooed, waving away his protests. "It is, and I am. And you, my brave Knight?" She set down her magnifying lens and rock sample and turned to face him in full. "You would do best to simply go along with it. Unless, of course, you'd rather continue this dance and explore with me what would happen were my father to learn of our… *close call* aboard that shit-stain of a pirate ship."

*You ARE still alive,* he wanted to point out. Shortly followed by, *I thought you said they were assassins,* and about a dozen other protests.

"And what would your father say," he finally went with, "if he were to find out his daughter had stooped to trying to blackmail an Excalibur Knight?"

Her lips quirked. "'That's my girl,' I'd imagine. Or something to that effect." Her golden brow creased delicately. "Though I do expect he will be slightly… dismayed by your decision to take his eldest daughter as your shipmate."

"Well, it's a good thing I'm sure as shit not doing that, then."

He glanced toward the door, thinking that might as well be his cue. It wasn't like he'd be all that missed at the welcoming ceremony. Before he could say a word, though, a holo pane winked to existence in front of him. His stomach sank as the footage began and he recognized *that shit-stain of a pirate ship* approaching the recorder—or the other way around, he realized, as he got his bearings. He watched the camera perspective approaching the ship's cargo bay magseal, noting the log record details set in green text in the corner of the holo pane. She must've grabbed the footage from the escape pod's automated launch records.

*Maybe don't let strangers access your system records in the future,* he thought irritatedly in Cammy's general direction, trusting Ex would make sure the message got there. It did, judging by the mournful touch of acknowledgment he felt from the ship at the edge of his mind, but he was a bit too distracted watching the shit show of Elsa's holo vid unfold.

It hardly painted Nate in the best light as he blew into the cargo hold and lurched about like a drunken bull, looking even more unsteady than he remembered feeling in the aftermath of the crusher drives. He flinched as that hulking armored shooter—probably another Asgardian, now that he got a closer look—put three disruptor rounds through him, his mostly-healed wounds aching in sympathy. And then the crowning moment: Nate, fresh off of coring his shooter with a brilliant lance of energy, just kneeling there dumbly, watching as the last Asgardian leveled his gun at the princess, offering no more than a helpless reach of the hand and then a drunken stagger to his feet as the Princess of Aesirheim went to work defending herself and dispatching her attacker.

Elsa paused the holo vid, watching him.

"No one ever needs to know."

His jaw was clenching again, reaching for every logical argument only to draw up short each time. It was preposterous. Just downright shitty. They both knew he hadn't done anything wrong—both knew she'd been the one who'd thrown herself into the crosshairs to start with. And yet, he'd seen enough of the way the Council operated to know those details would hardly matter. Because adept as they might've been at holding the Alliance together, keeping trade routes functioning, and even quelling the odd uprising here and there, when it came to things like reputation and nepotism, the Alliance Council was worse than a group of gossiping school children.

The Supreme Chancellor would not be happy about this. And as much as Nate wanted to believe that that shouldn't matter for a Knight of the Order Excalibur—which was technically *supposed* to be a free agent where Alliance power hierarchy was concerned—he knew it'd be naive to think Priatus couldn't make his life a living hell. More bullshit errands. More Council bureaucrats "requesting" assignment to the *Camelot*, watching his every move. He doubted the Merlin would intervene on his behalf. Not when he was preoccupied thinking about the real war facing the Alliance.

Elsa had moved closer, snaking around his frozen ruminations. She raised one elegant golden hand and touched his cheek.

"Your secret is safe with me, Ser Knight."

He stared numbly into her eyes, his mind riding the similarities to Zeda-vian Kelkarin, imagining how the First Knight would scoff at Nate's amateur errand boy cock-up here.

"Provided I say yes, you mean?"

She just smiled and slithered off, letting her fingers trail across his cheek. They were warm and smelled irritatingly sweet. She stalked across the room and waved up the wall holo display beside what appeared to be a walk-in closet—shopping for a welcoming ceremony outfit, he assumed, either from the room's current armaments or for short order delivery. An unpleasant thought occurred to him.

"Did you hire those pirates?"

She paused from her browsing to look back at him for a stretch, her golden face unreadable. "I assure you, there is no shortage of those who would delight to see my violent demise. Such is the blessing of royalty."

"That doesn't answer my question."

She smiled. "No. I suppose it doesn't."

With that, she turned her attention back to her holo dress shopping. Nate watched for a few more seconds, somewhat sickened as she apparently reached the end of the on-hand items and he saw the exorbitant price tags begin to appear beside each new scrolling item.

"I'll talk it over with my crew," he said, turning for the door.

He needed time to think. Maybe even time to bounce this off Jaeger and Amelia.

But the princess fired back before he'd taken two steps. "Splendid. I'll talk it over with my father. Meet back in five?"

For the first time since he'd met her, the smile she shot him might've actually been genuine. It made him want to spit more than a few hot words at her, none of them kind. He reined the scalding emotions in, trying to think. This was exactly the kind of shit Iveera had tried to warn him about —the never ending game of political cat and mouse that no one ever mentioned when they talked about the glory and might of the Excalibur Knights. The sickeningly petty game that should've had no place in a galaxy at war. And he was pretty sure he'd just lost this round.

*You could do worse than to have Eldari royalty for an envoy,* Ex pointed out, in his version of a supportive tone. *Even if she IS a conniving pixie of a bureaucrat.*

It wasn't the worst point. Even if it did make them both want to punch a hole through the carved onyx wall art.

"Fine."

She watched him evenly, perfectly nonreactive. "Fine?"

Nate shrugged, feeling sick. "Fine. I mean, *not* fine. But fine. For now."

"Oh, but Lady's Light," she said, pleased as goddamn punch as she glided forward to take his hands in hers. "What fun we are going to have together, my brave Knight."

## CHAPTER 7
# CRITICAL RECEPTION

"**S**he wants to do *what* now?" Snuffy coughed out, looking up mid-slurp from his ampule of liquefied Eldari children's candy with a horrified expression.

Nate couldn't really blame him. It seemed to be a recurring question wherever Princess Elsa was concerned. But that didn't make it any less exasperating as he pinched his brow and restarted from the beginning. Again. Luckily, the crew was mostly gathered by that point, so he figured this would be the last time he had to walk through the spiel.

"But she's, like—"

"Royalty?" Tessa offered.

"That's what I said," Ramirez said.

"That's what *I* said," Pierce muttered, from over in his usual brooding corner.

"That's what we all said," Nate confirmed. "But that's"—he took in their expressions, feeling dirty for what he was about to say—"also kind of the point. She's royalty. She gets what she wants."

Which was more or less the truth of the matter, even if he had left out a few of the awkward details in his spiel—like the fact that, in this case, the princess was getting what she wanted because she was royalty *and* because he'd screwed the pooch back on that pirate ship. And that this wasn't *really* a team meeting to discuss the decision so much as it was a triage to cover up the fact that he'd already been blackmailed into saying yes.

*Nothing like a good lie for team morale, I always say.*

Ex's comment settled like bad sushi. It wasn't that it was any more catty than usual. Just more below the belt.

Maybe this had been a mistake.

"So the chancellor's on board with this?" Jaeger asked, too astutely, from the battered orange armchair where he sat in his classic grumpy colonel pose, arms crossed, boot heels kicked up on the center table. In the chair beside him, Emily Carter mirrored his crossed arms and resting skeptic's frown.

Nate glanced at their two Council reps. Amelia Sundercaste showed him a supportive smile, polite and disconcertingly gorgeous as usual. Nepotism or not, he was glad their mutual friend Calum Statecaste had managed to pull his limited weight and get the Council to grant Nate at least one friendly-faced watchdog out here. Gendra the Gorgon, on the other hand, was distant and impassive as ever, though the flittings of her jin expressed hints of doubt.

"I get the impression it's a bit of a contentious point with the chancellor," he admitted, "but…"

"But Elsa's got daddy wrapped around her little golden finger?" Tessa suggested.

Nate shrugged, figuring that excuse was as good as any. Then, feeling the need to add something more: "It'd only be for a little while. I think… I think she just wants to see the galaxy through our eyes for a bit. Maybe do some good out there before she returns to take on the burden of leadership here."

*Laying it on a bit thick now, aren't we?*

*It could be true,* Nate mentally replied, remembering the way the princess had obsessed over those perfectly ordinary asteroid samples of hers. Maybe she really did just want a chance to be a part of something that she'd chosen for herself—something that wasn't forced upon her by the mere fact of her royal-blooded existence. Maybe deep down, she actually had a heart to match that fine golden skin of hers. But then again, maybe not.

He felt another wave of the *bad sushis* as he looked around at the crew —*his* crew—processing this new development. Elmo and Ramirez shooting each other thoroughly unimpressed looks. Tessa looking much the same as she met Nate's eyes like *Why now? Why her?* Even the two newish brainiacs they'd been leveraged into taking on from the UN a few months back—Drs. Friedrich Lundquist and Anitha Ramachandra, PhDs to the infinity power —seemed to have found their crew-status footing enough to look politely mournful about the news. And then there was Hannah O'Sweeney, their third Terran add-on. She'd never introduced herself as "doctor," despite carrying multiple PhDs in economics and political science. As far as he understood, she was mostly there thanks to her rugged track as a wartime journalist. Maybe that's why those icy blue eyes of hers made him want to squirm. Cool, and collected, and—he couldn't help but worry—thoroughly immune to the thick slice of liar's pie he'd just tried to feed them all.

And here he was, pretending like the Council were the school children.

"Does anyone have any thoughts they'd like to share before we do this?" he asked, against his inner dictator's better discretion.

There was something almost comforting about the way everyone in the room automatically looked to Pierce on that one. "What?" The moody pilot asked, looking around like he couldn't imagine why anyone would possibly expect him to be anything but a ray of sunshine. "I've got nothing."

The room pondered that for a silent moment.

"You think she's hot," Tessa declared.

"She *is* hot," Pierce said, glancing sideways at Amelia as if the Atlantean would've cared on account of the fact that they'd been casually *coupling* each other for months now. "But mostly, I just don't give a shit."

Nate looked around the room, waiting for anyone else to speak up, but no one did. His gaze settled on Jaeger. The colonel met his eyes, quietly assessing, then finally shrugged.

"Your ship, isn't it?"

That seemed to settle it for the moment, albeit uncomfortably.

The conversation turned more casual after that, bouncing around from the golden splendor of Vanaheim and what to expect of the welcoming ceremony that afternoon back to all the things they hadn't yet had time to unpack in the after-action scramble of what the crew—or Snuffy, at least— seemed to be settling on calling "the attack of the pirate-assassins."

Nate had half tuned out—was beginning to feel like he was somehow intruding on the gathering—when the sound of his name drew him back to the room, where Snuffy had just asked him something.

"Hmm?" he asked, looking around.

"He asked—" Ramirez started.

"Indelicately," Tessa added.

"Indelicately," Ramirez agreed.

"They say," Pierce muttered, loudly, "preparing to ask the same damn thing."

Nate tried to shake himself loose from his haze, searching their faces for some hint. To his surprise, it was Dr. Lundquist who spoke next.

"I think we are all very curious," he said, in his pleasantly Swedish accent, "what it was like, being, how do you say…"

"Crushered, or whatever," Snuffy finished. Delicately.

Nate looked around again, realizing Jaeger had done his Jaeger thing and excused himself from the room, as he usually did once the proper business was taken care of. Carter, as she often did, had gone with him. The room was still waiting for his answer.

"Kinda like having an underwater city collapsed on my head, I guess."

"Hmm," Snuffy said, nodding sagely, like that actually made perfect sense.

Over in his brooding corner, Pierce just waggled his fingers like *oh, look at me, I'm so tough.*

Nate wasn't sure he blamed the pilot. It wasn't much of an answer—not where factual accuracy was concerned—and he supposed it had sounded like something of a humble brag. He found himself standing, closing the door on the topic. No reason to start kicking any other troublesome stones loose. Especially not after he'd just spent so much effort lying to them like he *hadn't* almost lost control of the situation back there at the Attack of the Pirate-Assassins.

"I'm gonna go workout," he supplied to their questioning looks.

"Yeah, I think you're starting to shrink," Pierce said, pointedly eyeing Nate's arms.

Nate glanced down and felt a familiar ripple of disorientation, like some part of his brain was still attempting to reject the fact that the body it found there was indeed *his.* Understandable enough, in his brain's defense. The feeling had come less and less frequently as the months ticked by, but it was still frankly a bit ridiculous how quickly Ex had helped build him up from the scrawny Penn State senior he'd been a scant year ago. Now, half a meter and some hundred-plus kilos of solid muscle and bone later… *Hulkish* was the word Snuffy kept using.

Nate would've been lying if he said he hated the feeling.

Unbidden, his mind flashed to thoughts of Todd Mackleroy. Gwen was only a moment behind, right along with the whole confusing doom spiral of his friends' EDF enlistment. Freaking Earth Defense Force. He realized he was watching Tessa, some part of him half—or maybe fully—expecting she'd ask if he wanted a spotter. Practically speaking, the idea of a spotter had become somewhat superfluous ever since he'd started counting his gravitonic resistances by metric tons. And Cammy could always kill the loads anyway, if anything ever got out of hand. It'd simply become something of a customary routine for him and Tessa to hang out during his training—the only time that really felt safe and above the table for them to hang out anymore, even if some part of him knew damn well he was becoming more attached than he should've, considering the situation at home.

Tessa didn't seem to notice his gaze, anyway, caught up as she was in some thought of her own.

"I'll catch you guys later," he said, turning for the door.

A workout did sound good right about then. Anything to clear his head, get him centered. Except he'd barely made it a step into the corridor before he found Jaeger and Carter waiting nearby, talking in that sort of arms-crossed, unfocused way that made him think they'd been waiting for him.

"What's she got on you, Kid?" Jaeger asked, before Nate could drop so much as a *my, what lovely weather we're having.*

He sighed, first at the question, then at the title of address. Jaeger hadn't called him that—kid—in a while. Under normal circumstances, it might've simply irked him. Now, though, coupled with the discerning look in the colonel's eyes, it just made him feel like his act had fallen completely flat.

"Just a long list of *my father* this and *my father* that," Nate said. "Didn't seem worth the political capital to fight it."

"C'mon"—Jaeger was watching his face for some reaction—"I recognize the look of a man who's got his balls caught in the vise. I'm sure you noticed that that prince was sporting some serious murder wood for you back there."

"Elsa says she'll handle it. After the ceremony, once things have had a chance to cool down."

Carter's face didn't hide what she thought of that. Nor did Jaeger's mouth.

"Elsa," he muttered, shaking his head. "Nate, if this is some kind of puppy dog, butterfly bullshit…"

"It's not." Frustrated and sickened as he was with the entire situation by that point, Nate more than resented the implication.

"Fine," Jaeger said, spreading his hands like he was washing them of the whole deal. "Your ship, your headaches. You decide you need a hand prying those sad little raisins of yours loose, though…" He cupped his hands back toward himself and Carter, as it to say *we're your people.*

Nate regarded the two of them, a flicker of amusement pushing up against his irritation. "Got a lot of experience extracting balls from vises, do you?"

The colonel huffed one of those black chuckles of his. "Not enough, apparently." His gaze darted briefly to Carter before settling back on Nate. "Just check my first wife's mantle."

~

THAT AFTERNOON, on the way to the welcoming ceremony, they had the delightful misfortune of stumbling into Elsa's royal entourage. At least fifty or more extravagantly-dressed Eldari, many accompanied by pets and servants. The sight of her serpentine smile fixing onto him from across the open courtyard turned Nate's stomach a bit, and *a bit* turned to *a lot* when she made a point of stopping the entire procession just to come greet Nate personally with a warm embrace and a royal kiss on the cheek—a funny little bit of Terran culture she'd picked up from the archives, she laughingly informed the gawking crowd.

Even after having gotten everything she'd claimed to want, Nate still couldn't help but think the princess simply enjoyed stirring the pot. *His* pot, he amended more precisely, as he somehow managed to wiggle his way out of escorting the princess on his arm again.

Still, by the time they were marching down the illustrious path toward the cathedral-esque hall of ceremony and the deepening roar of the crowds, some part of him was also starting to wonder if maybe this whole arrangement wouldn't be so bad after all. Occasionally annoying, maybe. Okay, *probably*—and frequently, to boot. He doubted Princess Elsa was going to be winning any popularity contests aboard the *Camelot*. But the benefits wouldn't be entirely nonexistent, either.

The Excalibur Knights weren't exactly chop liver to the worlds and people of the Alliance, but it did get kind of tiring, having most of those people treat him like the Council's personal lawman—or their dread executioner, come to collect on debts owed. And while there *had* been a fair share of mythic awe and Knightly ass kissing worked into the mix as well, that attention always seemed to come with its own set of problems. Ambitious assassins, he'd quickly come to learn, were only the tip of the iceberg. Far trickier were the non-lethal complications. Disingenuous supporters hoping to win a questionable favor. Shameless opportunists willing to do anything—and he did mean *anything*—to get some juicy (and profitable) dirt on a Knight.

Amelia had taken great care to warn him of the prevalence and resourcefulness of such reputational predators—nearly as often as she'd reminded him, in just the kindest, most friendly-natured way he could've imagined such an invitation being made, that he was not only welcome but highly encouraged to use *her* to keep his baser needs in check, whenever and however he so desired.

Atlanteans and their freaking coupling…

Those were usually the moments he found himself running to go crush himself with a workout—or calling home to see Gwen, back when that hadn't felt so… he didn't know what. The word *estranged* felt too stuffy and legal for people of their age. Too severe, as he pushed the thought aside to focus back on the here and now, and on all of the vibrant, ceremoniously dignified culture around him, marching beneath the grand palace arches to the pace of Princess Elsavataryllianna Priatus' royal grace.

Maybe it wouldn't be the worst thing in the world, having an Eldari princess around to divert the attention away from the Council's Dread Errand Boy. Hell, maybe her presence would even convince some of the more uncertain worlds to roll out the royal welcome mat instead of the cautionary tarp. Garner them the royal treatment, so to speak. That actually sounded kind of nice, right up until they reached the edge of the covered section of corridor, and Nate got a good look at that royal treatment in all its manifest glory.

It all seemed so unnecessarily *big*.

Maybe grand was the word. Opulent. Freaking majestic. The golden causeway stretched ahead into open sky. Huge, periodic arches of intricately-carved crystal running the rainbow gamut, gleaming in the bright sunlight above all the proud royal jewels that'd gathered to bear witness to their march. All of it framed by the pulse pike tips of the guards lining the way behind them. The entire palace perched upon its mountain base, bolstered through past generations by permanent gravitonic engines and other additions, all seemingly intent on reminding the "commoners" of Vanaheim of their collective station below the Lords and Ladies of Vanaheim.

Those Eldari commoners—who themselves would've been treated as something close to royalty throughout much of Alliance space—roared on below anyway. It was at once the most- and least-dignified behavior Nate had ever seen from the Eldari. On the way down, the view of the palace from the *Camelot* had been breathtaking enough, but now, standing there at the edge of that gleaming skyway, listening to the crowds chant for their new princess…

It was impossible not to feel the power in that place. The ancient roots of wealth and strength and pure pride that'd slowly stretched their way out to the stars from this very spot. Suddenly, it wasn't so hard to understand how the Eldari had come to practically rule the galaxy.

And there, at the far end of the grand skyway, stood the focal titans of all that majesty—the High King and High Queen of Vanaheim, unmistakable even to an outsider in all of their golden splendor. Their royal children lined the dais behind them, all proud and regal in their own rights, but none quite so bright and towering—albeit largely thanks to his ceremonially gilded griffin mount—as their brightly-bristling crown prince.

Nate didn't need Ex's optical magnification to feel Prince Phaldissus' eyes lock onto him. He felt it like an inky weight settling across his chest. Instant low-grade nausea, tinged with a chaser of deep dread. It was startling, how heavily it hit him—a sudden, grave certainty that Nate had stepped out of his galactic lane, fucking with Eldari royalty, and that the prince *would* do everything in his considerable power to...

*Blackened hands*, Ex murmured, right about the same time that that nausea spiked, sending Nate clutching at his knees for support.

*Ex, what the hell is...* he started, mind flicking from secondary strokes, to poisons, all the way to focused sonic weapons. But he felt it there, at the edge of his mind, even as Ex came to the same impossible conclusion.

"Nate."

Tessa sounded concerned beside him. But not for him, he realized, as he glimpsed her wide-eyed fix on her omni tool and felt Cammy's message.

"Kid?"

"Get back to the ship," Nate hissed. "Now."

To his credit, Jaeger didn't waste more than a single uncertain glance with Carter before he turned and barked the order to the crew. Nate was already calling the rest of his armor down from e-dim, rushing forward into the bright sunlight. He cleared the shadows of the underpass right as the first alarms rang out over Vanaheim, confused Eldari all looking down to their omni holos for answers. Nate looked skyward, to the true source, mind reeling, grasping for answers that wouldn't come.

*Be careful what you wish for, I think is the imperative lesson here*, Ex growled.

Right as the first tendril of a Synth protoswarm came bursting through the clouds, racing for the city.

# CHAPTER 8

# PARTIAL MATCH

As fast as Nate could fly these days, he was no match for the devastatingly brilliant lances of Vanaheim's massive anti-aircraft batteries. Pristine as the Eldari gunners' reaction speeds were, he wasn't at all surprised to watch the leading tendril of the protoswarm vaporized from existence well before he was even halfway there.

The surprising part, after a long minute hanging near the top end of the troposphere, was that the rest of the swarm was nowhere to be seen.

He waited there, feeling Vanaheim's bated breath far below. No dense, swirling heart of the swarm descending from the heavens. No racing tendrils of inorganic death. Even for a larger protoswarm, the leading edge shouldn't have been more than a few klicks—maybe even a few dozen— ahead of the pack. And yet...

*I don't feel them near,* Ex confirmed, in answer to his unformed question. *But there is... something.*

Nate felt it too, even if he couldn't quite put a finger on what the hell *it* was. An amorphous, sickening darkness nursing on the edge of his mind. More Synth presence scattered throughout the system, maybe—or maybe even farther out, in nearby systems. He couldn't tell. Iveera would've scolded his dull senses.

He needed to go have a look.

He felt Ex's unspoken agreement and was already reaching for Cammy when the rest of his brain caught up and reminded him it'd probably take

Jaeger and the crew at least another ten minutes to make it across the palace and back to the *Camelot*'s landing pad on foot. Briefly, he thought about calling Cammy up to meet him anyway. But he'd already lied to his people once today. He wasn't in any hurry to add *abandonment* and *involuntary bench-riding* to the list of his transgressions.

Plus, he might end up needing them out there.

Whatever was happening, something sure as shit didn't add up.

So, he sent a concise update to Jaeger and Tessa, acknowledged their recommendations to be careful, and leaned on the gravitonics. A quick in-flight mind-clearing exercise to focus his senses, courtesy of Iveera. A double-check with Ex to confirm they had the e-dim oxygen stores for an extended scouting flight, just in case. And then they were clearing Vana-heim's atmosphere, the hissing rush of altitude-thinned air giving way to the perfect outer silence and the cold, vacuous embrace of space.

No Synth protoswarm.

He drifted there for a moment, allowing Ex to complete his system sweep, pulling—either politely or not—from the Eldari fleet ships and outsystem colonies as needed. There was something calming about facing the situation now that he was out here removed from Vanaheim, staring down the void that once would've sent him into a panic but now just felt an intoxicating paradox—at once infinite and yet somehow also close enough to touch. He felt more connected out here, his senses sharper. He felt that oily presence fading from their proximity right about the same time that Ex started talking, and a burst of powerful plasma flares lit the darkness out near Vanaheim's moon.

No Synth protoswarm, but the fleet *was* still tracking a few unidentified, tendril-sized masses throughout the system.

*How the hell did they get this far into Alliance space?*

Ex was too occupied chewing on the local and Alliance networks to bother with an answer. Nate wasn't really expecting one anyway.

It should've been impossible. *Was* impossible, according to anyone with any say in the matter.

Zedavian and Dalnak, out there on the outer rim, striking at the heart of the enemy force. Viktos on the way to join them. Wave after countless grad-uated wave of Alliance warships pushing out to reinforce their efforts, adding as they went to the already breathtakingly elaborate gravitonic detection system that was demonstrably able to track, quite accurately, the flow of any swarm-sized mass throughout most of the settled galaxy, and much of the outer regions as well. The detection system that *absolutely* would've seen a protoswarm coming light-years before it reached Vanaheim.

That was the entire point. The mere fact of the detection grid's continued existence was proof enough of its efficacy. Without hard evidence that it worked, the grid surely would've long ago fallen to the vocal Synth skeptics among the Council, who'd apparently been lobbying for generations to recoup the considerable upkeep costs and just let the damn thing die once and for all. Even *with* hard evidence of the Synth resurgence staring them in the face, a few of those stubborn bastards had held onto their beliefs, muttering into their hats that the grid was an unnecessarily expensive use of resources. But Nate had noticed that even those councilors had stopped using words like *pointless* and *waste*. Even Zedavian and the Merlin believed in the system's efficacy.

The Synth couldn't be here.

Another onslaught of Eldari dreadnought fire made it's disagreement known somewhere off the dark side of Vanaheim. In the back of his mind, Nate fleetingly pictured Eldari children looking up to the distant fireworks in the night sky, pointing and asking their parents what *that* was. Fair damn question. It idly occurred to him he hadn't seen more than a handful of children since they'd arrived on Vanaheim.

They must've been there, right?

There, but out of sight.

Hidden.

How?

One last flash of heavy artillery fire, deep outsystem, and that foul presence at the edge of his mind evaporated from their proximity, lingering only distantly. Almost like the swarm had somehow been scattered not just throughout the system, but across the entire sector.

It didn't make any sense.

And yet here lay the vaporized micro-remnants of at least part of a Synth swarm.

Nate eyed the darkness warily, wondering about the threat of reassembly, half-expecting to see the heart of the swarm simply appear out of thin air.

"Where the fuck did they come from?" he heard himself whisper.

*This is not an isolated incident,* Ex said, finally rousing from his dive into the nets.

*Where else?* Nate wondered, stomach sinking. *How bad?*

*Unclear in total, at present. Updates are all preliminary, and quite scattered.*

A slight pause.

*It seems there were casualties in the Endarion system, most notably on one of the outer colonies. Details are sparse, but I gather the fighting is still underway.*

Nate flexed his fingers, itching for something useful to do. The Endarion system was close, relatively speaking, but it was still over half a light-year away.

A quick jump for the *Camelot*'s q-drives.

He was reaching for the comms to check on his crew's status when Ex's systems chimed with another incoming request. He almost brushed it away reflexively. Then he registered what channel it was coming by, and accepted the request with a silent curse.

"Supreme Chancellor."

"Ser Arturi." Priatus said the name like he was testing the edibility of decidedly spoiled meat. He looked... not quite ragged. Outwardly, the Eldari looked as well-groomed and put-together as ever. But there was something in the lines of his face. Something fraying. "Well, what do you see out there? Report."

*What do YOU see in THERE, asshole?* Nate wanted to fire back, glancing beyond the overlay of Ex's HUD to the gold-blue glow of Vanaheim below, painfully aware that every second he floated here waiting for the *Camelot* was potentially another life lost in the Endarion system. Maybe more than that. He thought uneasily of the Beacon relay there—the sole gateway from Eldari space to Forge Station and the rest of the Alliance.

"I don't know how," he said, "but it sure looks like a fragmented proto-swarm just dropped into the sector out of nowhere."

"Impossible."

"That's what I thought."

"You are certain this is not some... misunderstanding?"

"Uhh... Yes?" Nate's mouth replied slowly, his mind elsewhere, tugging at its own threads. Maybe the detection grid couldn't have missed an entire protoswarm slipping by. But *fragments* of a swarm?

Priatus was speaking to someone off camera, looking irritated.

Nate was opening his mouth to ask what else they'd heard on the Forge, and where in the sector his help was most needed, when the Merlin butted into the holo frame, eyes a bit squinty, like an old-timer trying to figure out if the webcam was on. Or like he was drunk off his ass.

The wizard sniffed a few times. Wiggled his nose. Probably drunk. Squinted again. Definitely drunk. He'd started drinking again. Not that he'd ever really *stopped,* as far as Nate knew. But started drinking *heavily* again, by the looks of it. That didn't bode well.

"Nathaniel?" For a second, the Merlin looked genuinely confused to see him. "No, that can't be..." Then something seemed to occur to him in a rush, and he staggered back out of view like he'd just realized he'd left the oven on. Gone, just like that. An extremely sour-looking Priatus replaced him a moment later, muttering something about confounded this or that.

"Is he...?"

"Irrelevant," Priatus snapped, before regaining his usual composure. "At any rate, that will be all. You are to aid the Vanir in cleansing the system and then return to the Forge for debriefing."

"What?" The word fell out of Nate's mouth before he could think better of it, but once it was out there, he didn't see any reason to stop. "With respect, Supreme Chancellor, I think it's prudent I—"

"Prudent?" Priatus drew fully upright, composure slipping again, catching fire. "You wish to speak to *me* of prudence and respect after your behavior with my daughter?"

Nate froze, mind blanking to short circuits. Had Priatus already heard about their agreement? Had she told him? Or could it be that he'd somehow found out about—

*Is this REALLY what we're worrying about right now?* Ex asked. *Synth sneak attack? End of the world? No?*

Fair point. Not that Supreme Chancellor Priatus looked all that likely to care.

"Clear that system and get back to the Forge, Ser Knight," he said, his tone leaving no room for argument. "Ser Katanaga will be dispatched to handle the proper investigation once she's returned from her current duties."

Some part of Nate wanted to point out that, technically speaking, he took his orders from the drunk-ass wizard in the corner—or, failing that, from Zedavian Kelkarin, or any of the other senior Knights of his Order. But he knew it was pointless. Especially as a message pinged at the corner of his HUD from Tessa via Cammy, flagged urgent: "Griffin Boy's giving us trouble at the landing pad."

*Goddammit.*

*Phaldissus,* Ex muttered with distaste. Then, with a bit more cheer: *More like Phallic-ssus, am I right?*

On the in-helmet display, Priatus killed their connection with a prickly scowl and a pointed lack of polite farewells.

*Cute, Ex. Really cute.*

He felt Ex's mental equivalent of a shrug and let out a sigh. "Just once, it'd be great if someone trusted me to do my *actual* job out here."

*Blackened hands, how do you think I feel?*

Again, probably a fair point.

Nate looked from the vast expanse of suddenly not-so-safe space down to the brilliant gold-blue stretch of Vanaheim, thinking of that confused look on the Merlin's face. Not for the first time, he wished the wizard would just get his shit together and tell them all what to do, as it'd so seemed like he would back in those first weeks after they'd returned from their clash with the Black Knight on the ruins of Avalon. Apparently, even the resurgence of the Synth wasn't sufficient incentive to keep the wizard off the sauce for long. Ex bristled at Nate's train of thought, just as he always did at any critique of his precious Merlin. At least they'd gotten past the point of bickering about it.

As far as the Knights were concerned, the Merlin did what the Merlin did. Apparently for reasons no one understood. Reasons that often looked like drunken annihilation but very, very occasionally somehow ended up yanking the whole of the goddamn galaxy back onto its axis. And that was pretty much that.

But none of that could seem to wipe the wizard's confused look from Nate's mind, or quell the inky unease resting at the edge of his senses.

Something was going on here. Something they needed to get to the bottom of. Whether that was his off-the-books concern or he was going to go slinking back to the Forge with his tail between his legs like a good boy while Iveera swept in to take over, he wasn't yet sure.

Either way, they probably weren't going anywhere until he'd dealt with Prince Phallic-suss.

*Catchy, right?*

Nate shook his head, refusing to concede the point.

*Just give me a flight solution, will you?* he asked, reaching for the gravitonics.

# CHAPTER 9
# PHALLICSSUS

Much as Jaeger balked at the thought that he would, or even *could*, ever feel *bad* for Princess Elsa Priatus (AKA "that glitzy, stuck up space fairy," in the words of Lt. Tessa Kalders), he had to admit, standing there at the heart of the royal peep show: If ever he *was* going to feel bad for Princess Elsa, it was probably right then.

The woman's fiancée was, for lack of a better word, a raging cock head, and a domineering tyrant, to boot.

Maybe there was a better word for it in Eldari. Whatever it was, though, the palace court was absolutely eating this shit up. They watched like starving wolves. Riveted. None of them saying a word to help. All of them just watching their new soon-to-be princess face down Prince Phaldissus. Or vice versa, considering the noble prince's sizable griffin-mounted height advantage.

Jaeger wondered if it was time to step in. The fact that the royal A-hole even had the time to come swooping in on them in person seemed to suggest that the initial surge of the Synth attack was at least somewhat under control up there, but that didn't really change the fact that they had less than zero time for this bullshit. Then again, it *also* didn't change the hard fact of the several dozen lance-happy royal guards currently caging them in. Or the additional waves pouring out onto the landing platform behind them at a brusque, boot-smacking march, stern glares and humming pulse lances at the ready.

It felt like they'd found themselves in a freaking episode of *Cops: Royal Eldari Edition*.

He wished to high hell the princess would've just stowed the *my fathers* and listened to reason when they'd tried to quietly slip back to the ship without her. He still wasn't sure why she'd gotten it in her head that *now* was the time to come racing for the *Camelot* alongside Jaeger and the rest of the crew, stirring up all the gossipy palace hens in their wake. Then again, considering how Prince Phaldissus was taking the news, even here in the middle of a potentially world-ending attack, maybe it wasn't such a mystery.

Princess Elsa was afraid they might leave her here. With *him*. With the man who hadn't even bothered dismounting his prized space griffin to address his betrothed. The man who'd in fact seemed to derive some sick pleasure in letting the big cat-bird *thing* prowl in closer and inspect the princess with its sharp-looking beak as she spoke. In her defense, Elsa hadn't so much as flinched. Or didn't, at least, until Phaldissus spoke up again.

"No," his royal highness finally said, breaking the stark silence that'd been stretching too long.

Elsa's posture remained strong. Defiant. But Jaeger could see the fine cracks spiderwebbing through her psychological armor. "No?"

"No. You are never to set foot on that filthy Terran's ship again."

That was as good a cue as any.

"Well, pardoning that filthy Terran's friends, your highnesses," Jaeger said, keeping his hands where the guards could see them, "but maybe you can let us pass while you two discuss this matter. Ser Arturi has urgent need of his ship up there. Order Excalibur business, I'm sure you understand."

Christ, now who sounded like a cock head?

"Think Nate's on his way," Kalders whispered at his ear. Jaeger wasn't entirely sure whether that was good news or not, given how few fucks Phaldissus Kelkarin seemed to give about their Order Excalibur business. The prince didn't make any sign he'd even heard Jaeger speak.

"Well," Jaeger replied quietly to Kalders, eyeing the guards' tense stances and thrumming pulse pikes, and settling tentatively on the *good news* column, "maybe tell him to hurry his ass up."

A freaking Synth sneak attack in the heart of Alliance space, and *this* was what these people chose to focus on.

"My fleet has already crushed the invaders," Phaldissus said, with a dismissive glance in Jaeger's direction. Maybe he *had* heard, then. "Vanaheim has no need of your aid, Terran." He focused back on the princess before Jaeger could offer so much as a *fuck you kindly, then*. "You may go. Go, and tell your Knight he may hereby consider Vanaheim's hospitality revoked, and his invitations rescinded."

"My lord?" murmured one of the royal ass-kissers—or heralds, or whatever—who waited at the griffin's right flank, nervously drumming downward-steepled fingers beneath his flowing robe sleeves.

"Phaldissus," Elsa added, in the kind of *be reasonable* tone that set the prince's hackles on edge about as fast as a good slap right to the face.

"I will *not* have *my* bride"—the prince's mouth gave an ugly twitch searching for the words, practically frothing—"*spoiled* by some dirty, unchaste Terran *boy* whilst I labor to lead this kingdom."

For the first time, Elsa broke stares with the prince to take in the gawking crowd. She seemed to shrink a little as she remembered where she was, and to whom these royal gossips had all sworn their oh-so-loyal allegiance.

"I am not your property Phaldissus," she said quietly, focusing back on the prince. "You have no right to govern me so."

The sneer that twisted the prince's lips was as ugly as it was familiar. There was hatred in that look. Hatred that transcended species lines. The same kind of vain, poorly directed vitriol Jaeger had observed in the worst, most self-aggrandizing of dictators back home.

She *was* his property, as far as this haughty bastard was concerned.

Jaeger didn't mean to step forward, then. He certainly didn't *intend* to open his mouth and point out that he'd absolutely known pig farmers back home with better manners and nobler hearts. Somehow, he found himself several steps closer to Prince Cock Head anyway, the crew tensing behind him, three thrumming lance tips leveled warningly in his face. He couldn't bring himself to care.

Beside him, Princess Elsa was shooting him a look he couldn't make heads or tails of.

Then someone cried, "Look!" and after a wave of rustling fabrics and courtly gasps, Nate came slamming down to the landing pad with all the grace and poise of a full-grown Newfoundland who still thought itself a lapdog. Fancy stones cracked. Eldari recoiled. Nate's expression—doubtlessly surprised or apologetic—was mercifully hidden behind his emotionless faceplate as he straightened and looked around, taking in the situation.

"We have a problem?" he asked, fixing his attention on the prince.

Maybe it was the helmet filters talking, but he didn't sound like some meek Terran tourist anymore. Lingering rough edges aside, Jaeger had to give it to him: the kid really *had* come into his own out here. At least compared to the whiny shit he'd been back when all this had started on Earth. Jaeger found himself relaxing just a tad, shoulders easing, like some undisciplined part of himself figured the day was saved.

Probably, he was just relieved he hadn't gone and blown diplomatic relations himself.

Not that that outcome looked any less likely, as Phaldissus set his snarl on Nate.

"You," the prince growled. The griffin flexed its claws as if acting out its master's barely contained rage, leaning in, threatening—

Only to recoil with a strange, mewling yip as one of Nate's unseen energy barriers crackled and singed its probing beak. A smell like badly burnt hair filled the air. Several things happened at once, then—all in about the time it took Jaeger to mutter, "Oh piss."

Prince Phaldissus Kelkarin leaping from his affronted steed on a wave of pure, indignant rage.

Princess Elsa, attempting to put herself between them.

The beak-singed griffin, giving over to its primal instincts, lunging forward to attack.

A gray-blue blur of motion later, Nate was in front of the princess, one arm thrown protectively out, the other extended outward to where Phaldissus' griffin had just cannon-balled into the raised lip at the edge of the causeway twenty meters away, leaving a trail of dazed Eldari guards and noble scattered on the ground in its wake. And there, right in front of Nate and Elsa, sat Phaldissus, gaping up in disbelief at the brazen Excalibur Knight who'd just knocked him on his royal ass.

"Sssorry," Nate said slowly, showing his open armored hands to the rest of the guards with even slower motions. "Let's all"—stepping toward Phaldissus like molasses, offering a hand up—"take a breath and reset?"

Phaldissus' lips curled with more of that vitriol, rising with his visible shock at having been unexpectedly pushed—unexpectedly *assaulted*—maybe for the first time in his proudly gilded life. Jaeger was certain the prince would start spitting insults and threats. A *you'll pay for this*, maybe, or an *I could have you killed for that*. For a second, it seemed Phaldissus would, at the very least, scream for the guards to seize them. Then something strange happened. A sudden, disconcerting dampening of the rage in those golden eyes, almost like someone had slid a blinder over the open flames.

It was freaky in a serial murderer sort of way.

The prince stood without a word, straightening his armor.

"We need to sweep the entire system for any trace of Synth presence," Nate said, tentatively seizing the opportunity to move on. All around him, the royal guards waited with lances primed, waiting to see what their venerable prince would do, but Nate paid them no mind. "If we can establish the trajectory of their appearance throughout the system, we might be able to—"

"As I already told your servant," Phaldissus interjected, expression flat, "your aid is not required here, Knight. No more than it was required to deal with these invaders."

Something about the way he said that last word. Invaders.

"There could be more where they came from," Nate said, "which—"

"Which, as you can plainly see, is not an issue for the people of Vanaheim. I'm told my fleet eradicated the entirety of the threat before you cleared atmos, Ser Knight."

"Your fleet destroyed a *fraction* of a protoswarm," Nate corrected, a bit stiffly. "And we have no idea how it got here, or where the rest of it might be. That's a problem."

"Then I trust you'll see to it your masters hear of this *problem*," Phaldissus said, turning as if he intended to mount his griffin, which was only then beginning to stir over by the parapet. A brief flicker of irritation crossed the prince's face, then he gathered his royal dignity and turned to depart the old-fashioned way. "Until our next meeting, Ser Arturi," he added dismissively, not bothering to look over his shoulder as he gestured to his guards and royal posse to fall in with him. "I have important matters to attend."

And for one hopeful moment, that really did seem to be that. Then Phaldissus paused beside Princess Elsa, not directly looking at *her* either, but clear enough in his intent as he offered her his royal arm. Elsa looked from Phaldissus to Nate, expression guarded, eyes racing. Something seemed to pass between them. Then, to Jaeger's surprise, she bowed her head and took the prince's arm.

"Wait."

Nate's voice, like the first ominous crack of pond ice underfoot.

Phaldissus paused but didn't turn.

"If it's your decree that I should leave Vanaheim, I'm afraid I'm going to have to finish my business here first."

Jaeger swore he saw a few courtly onlookers licking their lips, like they sensed delectable gossip nuggets were imminent.

"Princess Elsavataryllianna Priatus of Aesirheim, Daughter of Selvondar Priatus, Supereme Chancellor of the Galactic Alliance…"

Elsa's lips quirked almost imperceptibly at Nate's formal words, Phaldissus turning just enough to glare at her. Jaeger couldn't decide whether to groan or smile. His insides tried both.

"… I hereby request your presence aboard the *Camelot* as an acting envoy of the Order Excalibur."

Almost sweet. Mostly incendiary.

The crowd was stunned. Phaldissus stood frozen, shoulders tensed like a jungle cat. For several mute seconds, no one seemed certain what to do, where to look. Then all eyes turned to Princess Elsa.

"I accept," she said, quietly, her eyes never leaving Nate's.

This wasn't how Jaeger had seen the day going.

Phaldissus' jaw worked its way back and forth, lips parted, like he'd momentarily forgotten how to speak. For a few seconds, Jaeger half-thought the prince would snap under the clear blood lust boiling beneath his surface and challenge Nate to a duel right then and there. But even riled as he was, the prince wasn't that stupid. Royalty or not, mortals didn't challenge Knights to fair fights and expect to live.

Of course, that didn't really preclude *unfair* fights.

Maybe that's why Nate looked as oddly calm and collected as Jaeger felt at that moment. They both knew the knife would come later, in the dark, and probably when they least expected it. Beside him, Carter also seemed to intuit as much, as did Ms. Hannah O'Sweeney, interestingly enough. Or *Dr.* O'Sweeney, he mentally corrected himself. He still didn't know what to make of the guarded journalist. But their little island of calm did nothing to stop the rest of the crew from tensing up again, or the guards from shifting yet again—almost tiredly this time—to more ready combat stances, all of them preparing for the shit to hit.

"Very well," Phaldissus finally said, sliding his arm free from Elsa's hand and taking a pointed step back from the princess. "I shall see to it the contracts are liquidated."

"My lord?" asked the same herald who'd questioned the prince earlier.

Phaldissus waved down the protest, but the herald was adamant.

"My lord, your father will not—"

"My father will not care which Aesir whore opens her legs to this kingdom, so long as the deed is done."

The words hit like a sobering slap of ice water, drawing a sea of gasps from the crowd, some as seemingly horrified as others were delighted. The herald fidgeted beneath his robe sleeves, looking mortified. Elsa stood unmoving, chin held high.

"This one has several sisters," Phaldissus forged on, pretending not to notice—or maybe just completely oblivious to all of it. "Perhaps one of them might possess a scrap of dignity." He started to turn with all the airs of a man who didn't give half a shit how his words landed, only to falter when it seemed they hadn't landed at all. "Perhaps next time you might consider the consequences of your inane whimsies, *Princess*," he added over his shoulder, "before you bother wasting the time and resources of an entire kingdom."

"I shall take that to heart, Phaldissus," Elsa said, touching lightly at her breast to emphasize the point. "More so than I ever would've taken you, I suspect."

This time, the giggles and chatter of the crowd felt decidedly at the prince's expense.

Phaldissus' strong jaw worked, his eyes searching for something—probably a viable, dignified exit plan—and settling, finally, on Nate.

"Vanaheim will not forget this day, Knight."

This time, the prince didn't wait for cheeky remarks. He spun with a whirl of his short, silken cape and marched off, golden boots stomping across the stone with purpose as a cadre of royal guards fell in around him. The crowd made way, those closer bowing and otherwise genuflecting while those farther away chatted animatedly on, some behind raised hands, others quite openly. Back toward the ship, a commotion over on the periphery of the causeway drew Jaeger's attention—the griffin finally shaking itself off from its tumble and padding after its master. It snorted at Nate as it passed, then hurried along, beak held high, claws clacking all the way.

"Sooo, what just happened?" Jaeger heard Snuffy ask quietly behind him.

"Pretty sure our boy just started himself an itsy-bitsy galactic blood feud," Ramirez said.

Jaeger was pretty sure Ramirez was right. The real question was just how far Prince Phaldissus would be willing to go, and at whom he'd take aim when it came time to avenge that smarting ego of his. Maybe Vanaheim would simply issue a stern *poo-poo*ing at Nate and the Knights. Or maybe they'd erupt into a new era of bloody war with Aesirheim, right smack in the middle of everything else going on.

He glanced at Princess Elsa, read absolutely nothing from her expression, and decided they'd better figure this out elsewhere regardless. Nate turned to them, helmet peeling back from e-dim to show his face. Jaeger met the kid's gaze, half-expecting him to spout a stupid grin, all giddy at having held his ground against a prince of Vanaheim. But Nate just looked tired, and more than a little bit concerned. That was good.

"Let's get the hell out of here," Nate said, just loud enough for the crew to hear over the chatter of the slowly disbanding crowd.

"Amen," Kalders said, giving his armored shoulder a friendly knock-knock as he passed, like *well done*.

Princess Elsa traded a few private words with Nate before turning and drifting after the crew toward the *Camelot's* ramp, moving with a kind of somber grace that somehow looked as light as it felt heavy. Nate looked equally heavy as he glanced back toward the palace and Phaldissus, like he was wondering if this had all been worth it. Not for the first time, Jaeger wondered what had transpired between the two of them on that pirate ship, and then again in the princess' short-lived quarters here on Vanaheim.

The thought faded to background as his senses pinged incoming in his peripherals.

Two broad, towering figures dressed in dark armor half hidden beneath woolen travel cloaks, stepping forward from the milling crowd. Atlanteans, Jaeger was pretty sure, though they were bigger and far less aesthetically perfect than the average Atlantean fare. Almost like whatever Castors had coded this pair's genetics had deliberately intended for their faces to be as forgettable as their bodies were built for war.

A strange tension stretched the air as Nate turned to face them. It built, the silence lasting too long as the Atlanteans squared off with Nate, eyes held conspicuously low beneath their woolen hoods. Then the two warriors dropped to their knees, cast off their hoods, and bowed their heads at Nate's feet.

"My lord," they both said in unison.

"We are Tristan and Tor," the male boomed, indicating first himself then his partner.

"We have come to serve, my lord," Tor added, her dark eyes fixed somewhere below Nate's knees as she rifled in her pack for something.

Understanding dawned on Jaeger right about the same time Nate shot a sideways glance his way. It was plain enough in the kid's face that he'd forgotten all about their planned rendezvous with everything else going on. In his defense, though, so too had Jaeger, right up until the moment Tor bowed her head again and offered up a battered but well-serviced shield bearing elaborate runic designs of copper and silver hues that flowed into concentric circles around a roaring dragon's head.

"Please accept this token of the Round Table's fealty, my lord," she said, as a stupefied-looking Nate accepted the shield from her hands, "and know that I hereby swear to serve you by my life and death, in whatsoever manner you should require."

"As do I, my lord," Tristan said, head still bowed.

"That's not—I didn't—" Nate eyed the shield distractedly, still trying to process, then finally looked up to the sky and back to the palace, like he was remembering everything else. "Ah, why the hell not?" he murmured to himself. He waved a hand toward the boarding ramp, beckoning to the two kneeling Atlanteans. "Welcome to the *Camelot*, Tristan and Tor. You picked a hell of a day to join the party."

# CHAPTER 10

# GUIDELINES

"That was incredibly stupid."

Back aboard the *Camelot*, with Vanaheim safely behind them for the moment, Nate set his frown on the princess who was either their newest resident time bomb or, thinking bigger, the striking spark of a whole new era of Eldari civil war—or hell, maybe both—and tried to parse that.

"I thought this was what you wanted," he finally said.

"I didn't say otherwise."

"So you're saying it was incredibly stupid *and* welcome?"

Her lips—still silvered in keeping with the rest of her ceremonial makeup—twitched. "Perhaps I merely seek to fulfill my duties as envoy and inform you of the political yield of your recent decisions."

"Clearly we're lucky to have you." Nate considered the room, thinking of the palatial living quarters she'd so abruptly left behind. "Hope you can get used to living in squalor, Princess."

She followed his gaze absently around the tidy-but-small quarters and finally wrinkled her nose at the thought of living here for more than a couple of days. "It *was* refreshing, though," she said, "seeing Phaldissus Kelkarin knocked to his insufferable ass."

Nate grinned a little at the memory despite himself. At least until the second half of the thought caught up. Refreshing... *and* potentially catastrophic—at least where that political yield of theirs was concerned.

Luckily, Ex chose that moment to speak up and declare that he'd finally collated enough data from the aggregated Alliance reports to begin calculating likely origin points for their mysterious protoswarm attackers.

He turned to go, reaching out to Cammy's awareness to locate Jaeger.

"Ser Knight."

He paused at Elsa's tone and looked back to find an uncharacteristic hesitation etched across her brow.

"Thank you," she finally said.

They didn't sound like words she said all that often. At least not in earnest. But he was pretty sure that's what they were now, despite the near-death-blackmail mess and the rest of the collective dumpster fire that'd led them to this moment. Maybe it wasn't as simple as the binary question of whether he was being manipulated or not, used or not. Maybe, setting all the rest of the politics aside, along with the fact that she was probably rich and powerful enough to buy an entire civilized planet... Maybe he really had done something to help the woman in front of him escape a life she hadn't wanted. Maybe that was worth something on its own. He filed the thought away in the ever-growing *it's complicated* drawer of his mental galactic hierarchy, nodded his quiet acknowledgment to Elsa, and turned to leave.

The Atlanteans were waiting in the corridor just outside. Tristan and Tor, he reminded himself, after the initial jolt of surprise settled. They stood at passive attention like a pair of meaty sentry bots.

"You two don't have to follow me, you know. Especially not on the ship."

"It is our duty, my lord," Tor said, not quite meeting his eyes.

It was the oddest thing, having someone that big and clearly deadly avoid his eyes. Then again, after a year of Ex's tweaks and his own rigorous training, Nate *did* stand level with the hulking, genetically-engineered Atlanteans—equally massive, and probably about ten times as strong, even without his battle armor. Still. He'd gotten somewhat used to the covert stares and rubbernecking attention of the crowds. But this? This was something different. A loosely centered attention that was somehow almost more intense than any open stare could've been. Almost reverent.

"Can I get you two anything?"

He couldn't quite decide how their attention made him feel, but he was pretty sure he didn't need it right just now—as emphasized by Ex's pointed throat clearing and the waiting data map he jangled at the periphery of Nate's mind. The Atlanteans just looked a little uneasy at the question. Warriors of the freaking Round Table.

"Would you like to eat or sleep?" he tried again. "I'm sure it's been a long journey from Olympus."

"In shifts, my lord." A moment of hesitation on Tor's face, like she was thinking about adding something more. "One of us will remain by your side—"

"Within convenient proximity," Tristan amended, in his deep voice.

"—At all times," Tor finished.

That probably explained why they'd wanted to send more than two of their warriors for this little... whatever it was. A *trial run*, Nate had thought, back when he'd given in and agreed to Calum and Amelia's prolonged urgings to take these two on. But maybe sworn guardians and sacred oaths didn't mix all that well with trial runs.

"You needn't concern yourself with us, my lord," Tristan added, in what was probably supposed to be a reassuring tone. It fell kind of flat in the wake of all the *by your side* business.

What the hell had he agreed to, here?

He didn't know. On some level, he was still just trying to wrap his head around the idea that there was apparently an entire small academy's worth of Round Table acolytes back on Olympus who, just like Tristan and Tor here, had spent their entire lives training to serve Arthur Pendragon's successor, just as their ancestors had been doing for generations, on the off chance that that successor might happen to be Atlantean (or Terran, as it were) and to come along in their lifetimes. He didn't really want to think about how many generations of Tristans and Tors had lived and died waiting for someone to take up Ex. And now that he *had* taken up Ex, it kind of felt ungracious not to welcome these Round Table people with open arms. But there was good reason he and Jaeger had done their darnedest to keep the crew small.

It certainly hadn't been for lack of options. In the past year, they'd turned down hundreds of requests from all manners of world governments, private militaries, public charities, and more than a few eccentric sole proprietors. Whether it was political leverage, Ex-level tech secrets, or just Nate's favor, everyone wanted *something*. Most of them packaged their requests behind diplomacy. Some even claimed simple and innocent desires to fulfill childhood dreams of Knighthood. But it was impossible to vet them all, and given how many times he'd already been stabbed in the back out here—both literally and metaphorically—it just didn't make sense to take on the additional risk.

The decision to refuse additional personnel from the newly-christened

Earth Defense Force had been a particularly contentious point with his friends back home. Marty and Gwen had taken it as a sure sign he was never going to let them join him on the *Camelot*. And maybe they were right. He still didn't know. But, with the exception of a couple of Council reps and three of the brightest scientific minds Terra had to offer, they'd kept the *Camelot*'s roster as tight as possible. And now, in a single day, they'd gone and added a shiny envoy-princess and two Round Table… acolytes.

The huge Atlanteans were still watching him with those off-center stares —waiting, he guessed, for some command.

Still not the worst situation he'd stuck his foot in today.

"Maybe we should lay down some guidelines, here."

Honestly, that probably went for the whole damned ship right then. They'd spent the past few hours cruising outsystem from Vanaheim on the sublights, all earlier urgency having evaporated along with any evidence of the Synth swarms. Or swarm, singular. Nate still couldn't tell. All he knew was that something was seriously off about all of this, and that Supreme Chancellor Priatus was expecting him back at the Forge anyway—where Priatus would no doubt be thrilled to learn about his daughter's recent life decisions.

The Atlanteans obediently fell in step with him as he set off for Jaeger's quarters on the upper deck, trying to lay a few basic ground rules while also skimming through the data Ex had collected. News was still trickling in at a frustratingly slow pace. The attack on the Endarion system had been quelled by the time they'd made it off Vanaheim. A few neighborhoods beyond that, Asgard had apparently come under moderately heavy attack but had routed the enemy with exactly the kind of brutal fury that everyone seemed to expect from a planet of ex-Atlantean war mongers.

The hiss of an opening door drew him out of his walk-and-talk multitasking in time to see Amelia striding out of Pierce's quarters, looking vibrant and rejuvenated. Inside, a thoroughly ruffled Pierce practically limped out of the shower unit, a towel wrapped at his waist, and scowled at Nate before waving the door shut. Amelia just smiled and raised a hand as she passed by, greeting them without a single iota of awkwardness on account of her tousled hair or reddened throat.

Atlanteans.

"So, uh, how was the flight to Vanaheim?" Nate asked his hulking shadows, partly to fill the silence that was probably only awkward in his mind, and partly because he hadn't yet managed to coax more than a *Yes, my lord* from either of them.

Tristan gave a rumble of a grunt as they began to move again. Then, seeming to realize that wasn't quite a full answer, grumbled, "Civilians."

"The journey was sufficient," Tor said, like that was all there was to say about that.

In their defense, Nate hadn't heard the most glamorous things about traveling by Alliance passenger liner.

"Though we did not expect our services might need be rendered upon Vanaheim itself," Tor added unexpectedly, with another one of those hesitant non-looks.

Nate blinked. Had that been a joke?

*I do believe she's joshing you, yes. Now, if we could focus on the potential collapse of civilization...*

"Right," Nate said, half to Ex, half to Tor.

The Atlanteans took up posts nearby as Nate approached Jaeger's door a short way down the corridor from the bridge. Not for the first time, Nate wondered if he shouldn't move his own quarters to the upper deck, too. It wasn't like it was much of an issue for Cammy to shift things around, and the spatial distinction from the rest of the crew on the lower deck seemed somehow significant to Jaeger, though not at all in a lording, *upper class passenger* sort of way. And now that they were starting to look at Nate as something more than just the de facto owner of this ship…

Again, he was drawn up short from his thoughts, Jaeger's door hissing open even as Nate reached out to sound the chime. Jaeger stood inside, leaning on the door frame, arms crossed like he'd been waiting for Nate all along. Or not, Nate realized, as he took in the rest of the room and spotted Carter sitting on the edge of Jaeger's bed, sliding on her boots and pulling back her dark hair like she'd just been getting ready to leave. She met Nate's stare like she would've loved for him to say a damned word about any of it.

Mostly, Nate was just busy wondering if he was the only person *not* having sex on this ship.

*I feel like you DON'T want me to answer that question.*

*I feel like you shouldn't be ABLE to answer that question.*

*Yes, well that's probably because ONE of us is clearly being playful and coy, while the other is poorly attempting to conceal his longing to accept the pilot's standing invit—*

*That's not—*

*Is—*

*Isn't—*

*Isn't NOT—*

*Why don't you go—*

"You talk to Ivy yet?" Jaeger's voice broke in back in the real world, where he was still watching Nate with that air that seemed to suggest that Nate was here at the colonel's orders, rather than of his own volition.

Nate declared truce with Ex long enough to frown at the colonel. The routine air of authority, he was pretty much used to by now, but it always chafed a little, hearing Jaeger call Iveera by that little nickname of his. Probably because Nate had a pretty strong feeling that the Gorgon would never have stood for *him* calling her anything so casual, despite her not seeming to care when Jaeger did. But regardless.

"Not yet."

He couldn't say exactly why he suddenly felt so reticent to reach out to the Gorgon Knight. Something in his gut, he supposed. He couldn't help but think she was somehow going to sniff out everything that'd happened between him and Elsa the moment she saw his face. Or maybe it was just that some part of him balked at being ordered by the Council to call anyone.

Probably, he was just pissed that they were flying in the A Team—and flying *out* their shiny Terran errand boy—in order to deal with "the incident," as everyone seemed to be unanimously agreeing to call it. Even after the trouble he'd taken to confirm it with Nate directly, the Supreme Chancellor was being oddly reticent in officially placing a proper name on what had happened out in Y-Sec. The net feeds had willingly taken up the slack and produced their own explanations. Spontaneous asteroid events. Mysterious radiation storms and unidentified celestial phenomena. They'd even seen one particularly colorful feed line claiming it to all be some backhanded wartime land grab attack by "those damned dirty Svartalfs."

It was a problem. Maybe a serious one. But right now, he needed to focus on the task at hand.

"Ex has something to show us," he said, waving for Jaeger to join him as he turned for the bridge. He felt Jaeger's side-eye, that odd look he still got from most of them whenever he mentioned the voice in his head, but the colonel fell in step with him. It was different with Cammy, who at least communicated with the crew indirectly via her scrawling green letters on the displays. Ex, though… Nate still didn't quite understand the full extent of the communication embargo between an Excalibur and anyone else but their beloved Knight, but the fact remained—

*I only have words for you, my sweet.*

*And aren't I a lucky lass for that,* Nate thought back, waving a hand toward the forward displays as he and Jaeger marched onto the bridge. Ex obliged wordlessly, projecting the fruits of his data mining labor up for the rest of the crew to see.

*Clear directionality,* Ex said, as a speckled nebula of protoswarm bits lit up the Y-Sec map, stretching from Vanaheim to Asgard, with the densest cluster focused toward the latter. *And the entire spread seems to have appeared almost simultaneously across systems, based on transit-corrected timing of reports from q-adjacent worlds. As for the projected origin, though...*

Snuffy's voice broke in.

"Am I the only one who thinks that sorta looks like—"

"A reaching arm?" Tessa offered from her flight rig, hammering home the strange feeling in Nate's gut.

*Ah,* Ex said, like that meant something to him, as well.

Snuffy, meanwhile, looked dismayed. "Well, I mean, I was gonna say a flipper. But I guess an arm works too."

*Ah, WHAT?* Nate thought back, as the bridge collectively set in on Snuffy about how in the hell he'd gotten *flipper* from that bundle of dots.

*Anthropometrics.*

*What?*

*No, you're right. It seems unlikely.*

*That's not what I—Look, maybe just pretend for a moment like I don't know what you're talking about.*

*A hand, Nathaniel. A reaching arm. Follow the proprioceptive chain. If I were a vast, system-sprawling synthience, reaching out with my giant arm-flipper...*

*Then... where's... my brain?* Nate hazarded.

*Rest assured, I wonder the same thing every day,* Ex replied, chortling to himself as a new region of space came alive with a gently glowing highlight on the map.

"What's that?" Jaeger asked.

"Uhh," Nate started, still trying to process. "Working theory. Anthropometrics."

"Sure, sure," Tessa said, drumming on her console. "Sooo, we gonna go check this out, then, or what?"

As one, the entire bridge traded a look. They all knew about Priatus' orders to return to the Forge. Jaeger, especially, looked less than thrilled by the prospect of so openly defying the chain of command—even if that chain was admittedly more of a leash on a rope on a rubber band, and rife with gray zones and technicalities to boot.

"You assume handedness?" asked a lightly-accented Indian voice they weren't used to hearing. They all turned to Dr. Ramachandra, who was still staring intently at the star map. "And, well, *anthropo*metrics?" She looked to Nate, and seemed to wither a little as she realized the bridge's collective attention was now fixed on her. "You're looking for the reaching arm's head, yes?" She glanced at Snuffy. "Or the dolphin's." That got a few snickers. "But why assume any particular morphology to this... spatial entity?"

"It's a, uh, proprietary algorithm," Nate said, roughly translating Ex's resultantly indignant outburst, sans the select curses and rather extensive jargon. "Just a ballpark guesstimate, really."

*Guesstimate*, Ex growled, disgusted. *Bah.*

"I see," said Dr. Ramachandra, nodding like that was good enough for her just now.

"It seems quite thin," Dr. Lundquist said, stirring beside her like he felt some pressure to contribute. "But I like it."

For some reason, that drew eyes to Hannah O'Sweeney, like everyone expected their third Terran genius might as well take her turn to weigh in, too. "Don't know what you're looking at me for," she said. "I'm just here to write it all down." She tapped her pen thoughtfully on her thigh, only drawing attention to the fact that she hadn't actually seemed to have written a single word since coming aboard, despite always having a pen handy.

"That said," she added, "if we're all set on the Giant Reaching Flipper hypothesis, I will say I can't help but wonder what the hell it was reaching for."

They all turned back to the display, lost in their own silent thoughts, the strange feeling that'd been creeping through Nate's gut finally climbing up to the surface as they considered O'Sweeney's words. It set him on edge. Because whatever their *it* was, and wherever *it*'d come from, it seemed to have been reaching straight for something on Vanaheim.

# CHAPTER II

# SOMETHING IN THE WAY

Nate's fears about Iveera, it turned out, were absolutely warranted.

He barely made it through his cordial, "Hey, how's it going?" before her serpentine Gorgon jin took critical poise in the comm holo, like he'd just confirmed everything she'd already suspected.

"What have you done, Nathaniel? What leverage does she hold over you?"

As it so often did, that piercing electric blue stare left him fumbling for words.

*I'm fine, by the way,* thought some sarcastic corner of his brain, *thanks for asking.*

"I didn't do anything wrong," his mouth said instead.

Merciful Sith, he sounded like a child, caught at the scene of the crime.

"And yet something *did* go wrong amidst the ambush, did it not?"

"Well, I was a little stroked out after getting caught in a—"

"Crusher drive trap," she said, supremely unimpressed. And that's when it clicked. It wasn't just her freakishly acute perception at work here. Someone must've told her at least part of what'd happened.

Freaking Jaeger.

"You should have seen that coming, Nathaniel," she said. "So, what was it? A moment of primal weakness after sweeping in to the rescue?"

"What?"

"No. I thought as much. You nearly got her killed, didn't you?"

He sputtered through a few choice starts and stops, let out an irritated hiss. "*She* nearly got her killed, Iveera."

"Royalty," she murmured, like she understood perfectly well. "Nonetheless, it *would* be extremely unwise to engage in any sexual recreation with Princess Elsavataryllianna, Nathaniel."

"Well, I wasn't planning on it, so you don't have to worry about... you know, *that.*"

"I do not worry. Only advise. You've placed yourself in a very precarious position, agreeing to take on the crown princess of Aesirheim as an envoy."

"Well, I didn't exactly have a—Look, can we just focus on the actual news here?"

Her jin remained poised with skepticism a moment longer, then rippled into a thoughtful pattern as she considered his question.

"What can you tell me?"

He hesitated, suddenly reticent to give up what little they knew—or what little they hypothesized, at least. Apparently, he hesitated a moment too long.

"Where are you bound right now?" she asked, like she already knew it wasn't the Forge.

"We have a rough idea where the swarm might've snuck in from."

"Snuck in," Iveera echoed, like she was trying the words on for size.

"Originated," he said. "Freaking *teleported*. I don't know." He studied her non-expression. "What the hell is this, Iveera? How did they get here?"

Her jin swirled, calm and thoughtful, and just a little uneasy. "I don't know."

"It's... I mean, I thought this was supposed to be—"

"Impossible," she agreed. "As far as the civilized galaxy is concerned."

Silence stretched between them.

"So, is this the part where you tell me to hand over whatever I know and get back to the Forge like a good boy?"

"There will be consequences, should you choose to ignore a direct request from the Supreme Chancellor."

"That's doesn't sound like an order."

"I needn't remind you from whom we truly take our orders, nor by what channels that authority flows." She watched him for any reaction. He watched right back, until she finally tipped her head, like maybe he'd passed some test. "It is not my place to tell you what you must do."

"Only to advise?" He felt his lips pulling into a shallow grin. It wasn't the answer he'd expected.

She didn't deign to respond verbally, but there was definitely a flicker of amusement from her jin this time.

"Are you already on your way out here?" he asked, eyeing what little of the *Crimson Tide*'s interior he could make out through their connection. "How's Malfar doing?"

"He remains…"

"Malfar?" Nate offered.

Was that a flicker of amusement in her jin? Or affection?

"Very much so."

Something about the way she said it made his insides wriggle a little, but he was ashamed to find that the words also brought him a touch of peace. It wasn't that he'd *enjoyed* seeing Malfar continue to struggle with his new identity as the Sixth Excalibur Knight—and as direct successor of his bastard broodfather, Ser Groshna—in the months since the Merlin had finished cleansing the corruption from Groshna's old Excalibur and cleared Malfar for his Knightly duties. It was more just that it was kind of nice, knowing he wasn't the only newbie the rest of the Knights were snidely scoffing at any chance they got.

He actually kind of liked the Troglodan, as abrasive and impossible as Malfar could often be. It seemed like maybe Iveera did, too.

"Nathaniel." The tone in her voice brought him back to reality. "Whatever you do, do not underestimate our foe."

He studied her grave expression, nodded his acknowledgment. "Talk soon, then?"

She just gave him one of those unreadable looks and signed off with a farewell flick of her jin.

He was quiet for some time after that, staring through the bulkhead.

*You wonder if we should not wait for Ser Katanaga,* Ex observed.

*I wonder a lot of things.*

*I'm painfully aware.*

"Ex," Nate whispered aloud, mind churning. *What are we dealing with here?*

He didn't bother giving voice to the rest of the questions bouncing around his head. Didn't need to. Ex could feel them there, just as surely as Nate could feel his companion's lingering uncertainty. Neither of them knew for certain whether they should call Zedavian, or maybe even try to contact the Merlin again. Either way, it would probably be a humiliating report. Maybe Jaeger was right. Maybe they should just head straight back to the Forge like they'd been ordered to do.

But not *ordered*, he thought, remembering Iveera's words. Asked. A direct request. Probably, the distinction didn't make a single lick of difference. But if the entire front line was somehow compromised out there... if this was merely the prelude to something bigger...

The Synth didn't *do* sneak attacks. Didn't employ clever tactics. If they possessed any true *synthience* at all, as Ex liked to call his own inorganic sentience, that intelligence seemed thoroughly consumed with the quest to devour anything they could and proliferate their swarms across the galaxy.

And yet here they were, scrambling in the wake of a... a what? If not a sneak attack, then at least a sneak appearance.

*Keep it up*, Ex said, *and you're going to begin infecting me with your squishy superstitions.*

Nate blew out a long breath, easing his racing mind. For the first time in a while, he felt the urge to call his friends back home. But what was the point? He wouldn't find answers there. Marty and Gwen were probably busy with their EDF duties, anyway. They'd been considerably harder to reach ever since joining up. Or maybe it was him who'd been less apt to try. He thought of Copernicus sitting in the Penn State house with Kyle, both of them together alone.

Maybe he *should've* requested Marty and Gwen be transferred out to the *Camelot*, as they'd clearly both been hoping for. But then again, he thought, as he checked in with Cammy's sensors, maybe not.

They were about to arrive at the outskirts of the Asgard system.

And according to the chatter on the net, they weren't the only ones.

"WHAT THE PISS," Jaeger was muttering, as Nate stepped onto the bridge.

A few of the crew turned to look his way before directing their attention back to the main displays, which were currently telling an interesting story of a coming galactic shit storm.

Two sizable fleets squared off a few light-minutes outside of the distant traffic and chatter of Asgard's main planetary perimeters. One plainly Eldari by the prevalent gold hues alone, and the other Asgardian. Nate had never actually seen an Asgardian warship in person, but he recognized the builds easily enough—some hard, mildly frightening cross between Atlantean ingenuity and Troglodan brutality. They stood in stark contrast to the slender thrust and elegant curves of the Eldari hulls. The fleets themselves looked to be about evenly matched from Cammy's and Ex's initial assessments.

As to what the hell they were all doing out here, on the edge of Asgardian space…

"Maybe our boy Phaldissus sent his goons to find out who took a shot at his bride?" Snuffy suggested.

"Doubt it," Tessa said. "In no small part because—"

"Because I am not his bride," Elsa interjected, from where she'd just appeared in the bridge entryway behind Nate. "And because those are not Vanir ships. They hail from Aesirheim."

"Right," Tessa said, jutting a thumb in Elsa's direction without looking. "As I was saying."

"Any idea *why* they hail?" Nate asked the princess quietly, his mind grasping almost hopefully for several interesting possibilities before settling down to worriedly gnaw on the two most likely answers: Either the Supreme Chancellor had found out about his daughter's recent life choices and had somehow divined where he should send the fleet to head them off and bring her home, or he'd learned of their Asgardian pirate-assassin run-in and had sent in the troops to demand answers—or blood.

"I expect my father is less than pleased about the recent attempts on my life," Elsa was saying. Nate only half-heard her, occupied as he was trying to recall what it was Priatus had said when they'd spoken just after the attack on Vanaheim: something about speaking of prudence after what had happened with his daughter—which… shit, but—

"Did she say *attempts*, plural?" Snuffy asked.

That got Nate's attention. Right along with everyone else's on the bridge.

"It's complicated," Elsa said, as the looks all turned her way.

Somehow, the answer didn't seem to satisfy.

She looked to Nate. "You honestly believe my father would've conscripted an Excalibur Knight to escort me for naught but pomp and circumstance?"

"Yeah," Nate answered, before he could filter himself. "I guess I kinda did."

He wasn't sure whether she was telling the truth, or even how he felt about the revelation that maybe Priatus actually *did* consider him something more than a shiny errand boy. Mostly, he was just wondering how the hell the Supreme Chancellor had forgotten to mention that shots had already been fired. Except, thinking back, maybe it was Nate who'd failed to listen. Maybe he'd just been too miffed after all that "see my daughter to Vanaheim *unmolested*" business.

*He DID say there were many who would not wish to see the Crown Princess of Aesirheim delivered safely to Vanaheim,* Ex pointed out.

Christ, how vague could you get? Would it have killed him to just say *A-holes already tried to kill her once?*

*Politicians,* Ex grumbled in agreement.

"So what do we wanna do about *them?*" Ramirez asked, tilting his head in the general direction of the squared-off fleets.

Tessa looked from Jaeger to Nate and back again. "You want me to tell 'em we're looking for the dolphin's head?"

Nate was just busy wondering—pretty much for the first time—if maybe Priatus hadn't actually had damn good reason to recall the *Camelot* to the Forge. If he was willing to play his cards that close to his chest with his own daughter…

"I'd rather we didn't tell them anything at all," he said, pulling himself back to the bridge and setting the rest aside for now. "We're cloaked?" He could feel through his bond with Cammy that they were, but he still liked to ask, even when he wasn't just stalling for time.

"Aye aye, Mr. Knight. Shall we slip on by?"

Jaeger was watching him like this was one of those test moments of his. Or maybe like he should've just left well enough alone and gone back to the Forge in the first place. Sometimes it was hard to tell.

He turned back to Elsa. "Does our new envoy have any strong reason to believe these fleets *won't* just compare dick sizes and walk away?"

It was only as the words left his mouth that he fully remembered that he was speaking to a princess of Aesirheim, and that such potty-mouthery *might* be frowned upon. But Elsa didn't bat an eye. Just fired back, deadpan. "That depends. Have you ever *seen* Asgardian genitals?"

"Unfortunately," Jaeger muttered, rubbing at the kitsune scars on his forearm in memory. "I think the more pressing question is whether we should risk stirring the pot at all. We don't know what's happening here. And unless you want to uncloak and *ask*…"

"So we slip by," Nate said. "We sweep the area quietly and go from there."

"That's a lot of area to sweep."

Nate was opening his mouth to point out that it was a good thing they had a pretty big broom when a cold wave washed over him—through him—electric sensations crackling from his insides to his fingers and toes. For one infinitesimal moment, space—reality itself—seemed to flicker.

"Maybe we could get those fleets to come help us look," Snuffy was saying, like he hadn't noticed a thing.

"Yeah," Ramirez chimed in. "Giant angry genitals, and all."

No one had noticed the flicker, Nate realized, as the rest of the crew began adding in their collective two cents.

Probably just some lingering effects of his minor little stroke.

*It wasn't*, Ex said, already tapping every system-wide telemetric he could find.

No one but Ex, then. And maybe Gendra the Gorgon, whose jin warily sampled the air as she looked around the bridge like she'd felt a disturbance in the Force. Finally, though, she gave it up, crossed her arms, and settled her attention on Nate.

"I would be remiss were I not to reiterate that, in the interest of maintaining healthy Alliance relations and, ultimately, serving the mission of your Order—"

"We should get back to the Forge," Nate finished for her. It came out sounding a bit less fill-in-the-boring-blank and a bit more tense than he'd intended. Confused looks turned his way. He crossed his arms to match Gendra's, still trying to shake off the disorientation, and forced some calm into his tone. "Duly noted. And we will. But first, we're gonna have a look around and make sure the sky's not about to come falling down on Alliance heads."

Which sounded well and good, apart from the prickling edge of intuition now whispering that whatever he'd just felt was most certainly *not* nothing, and that he'd best pump the brakes before they found themselves walking into another crusher trap, so to speak.

"Tess," he heard himself murmur. She was already watching him, the faintest hint of concern touching at her usual cavalier expression. The rest of the crew was watching, too. Gendra looked less than pleased but wasn't going to argue.

*I think maybe we should get out of here*, some part of him suddenly wanted to say. But that was just nerves talking. He pushed the jitters aside, reminding himself that this was exactly what they'd come here for, exactly what he'd wanted—a chance to actually *do* something. Something more than chasing pirates and escorting royalty.

"Take us into the dolphin's head," he said.

Or was in the middle of saying, at least, when something happened that no one missed.

*Mysterious radiation storms*, that prickling corner of his mind suggested sardonically. *Unidentified celestial events and damned dirty Svartalfs.* Whatever it actually was, it was *big*—a raw, incomprehensibly enormous crash of energy that left Nate hunched over, staggered for balance, senses making a loop-the-loop back to reality, where the bridge had gone dark, lights and critical systems sputtering, unharnessed crew suddenly floating in the air, scrambling for purchase in the sudden absence of Cammy's gravitonics.

Nate reached instinctively for his own gravitonics in the darkness, thinking first and foremost to get the crew safely down to the crash couches. Then the *Camelot* lurched back to full power, and the crew hit the deck with an extra g and a chorus of curses and indignant groans.

"Whaaat the fuck," Tessa breathed over at her pilot's rig, right about the same time Nate's brain caught up and started making sense of what he was feeling from Cammy and Ex. Except *sense* wasn't quite the right word, because they'd definitely just jumped halfway across the system without so much as an extra push from the main engines.

*That wasn't a jump,* Ex said. *More of a transdimensional, um...*

*If you say hiccup...*

*A transdimensional kerfuffle, then. We didn't move.*

Nate gaped at the displays, silently daring Ex to explain that one.

*Fine. We didn't move EXCEPT in every four-dimensionally measurable meaning of the word.*

*What the fuck does that even mean?*

*I'll be sure to let you know when I figure that out.*

Tessa was staring at him with the kind of open-faced shock he'd only ever seen from her a handful of times, the rest of the crew scrambling to order around them, strapping into their couches, snapping harried updates back and forth. Nate was stuck just swiveling his dumb stare back and forth from Tessa to the displays to the viewport beyond—which he only then noticed was peppered with faint cracks. He dimly noted the ship's cloaks had failed. Dimly noted Princess Elsa gaping at the small *celestial body* she wore as a pendant like the thing had just sprouted two heads. The consoles pinged with incoming comms requests—likely of the *what the fuck* variety, Nate figured, as he realized how close they'd just *not-jumped* next to those two bristling fleets. But pissed off Asgardians and Aesir hardly seemed the most pressing of their problems at the moment.

Something had pulled them.

The thought struck like a sledgehammer, knocking the rest into place. Something was nibbling at his side like an army of angry fire ants. Elmo clutched at a bloodied shoulder, Gendra at her leg. Nate looked down at his burning side, brain stutter-stepping to connect the dots between the cracked viewport and the blood welling beneath his torn tunic. Like someone had fired off a flechette cannon through the bridge.

His eyes snapped back to Tessa—that shocked look of hers clicking into final, horrible place in his mind—just in time to see her sag in her pilot's chair like she was going to sleep, eyes half open and unfocused, face too pale.

"Tess," he gasped, starting forward.

Then another wave hit, and reality disappeared again.

# CHAPTER 12
# A GOOD CAPTAIN

When they blinked back to existence, they'd moved again. Nate couldn't quite register where, in the mash of things. Only that Asgard was nowhere to be seen, and that a vast, dark planet filled the viewport, and that—

"Tessa," he hissed, the rest rushing back with cold horror.

Jaeger was already springing from his crash couch, snapping for Pierce and Cammy to take the controls. Nate hurried to Tessa's side, calling down his armor, bidding Ex and Cammy to prep the first aid. Cammy was already on it, setting aside many of her other processes with a kind of fierce, maternal urgency that made Nate's stomach ache for both of them.

"Hey," Jaeger said, as they reached Tessa on opposite sides, her pilot's chair morphing under Cammy's care, gently leveling her out onto something more like a bed. Tessa didn't seem to hear him. "Hey come on, Kalders."

Nate reached for the bloody shreds of tunic just below Tessa's sternum, mind racing, howling, not at all liking the tone in Jaeger's voice. She caught his wrist quite suddenly, her grip surprisingly strong for the state she was in. Something passed through her expression as her shocked eyes found Nate—something he couldn't understand.

"Should've..." she whispered weakly. She almost looked like she was trying to smile.

Then she flopped back to the gurney with a wet-sounding sigh.

"Shit," Jaeger hissed, so softly Nate barely heard.

Carter was there the next second, elbowing the colonel aside.

"Guys." Over at the secondary pilot's rig, Pierce's voice was tight enough to tell Nate pretty much everything he needed to know. They weren't alone. Not if the resumed pinging on the comms was any indication. Nate kept his focus on Tessa, carefully peeling her bloodied tunic aside, distantly aware first of Carter's iron-clad stare then of the medic's skilled hands moving in to help, clearing the blood, guiding his hands as he and Ex began to fill Tessa's wounds with enough regenerative biofoam to at least tamp down on the internal bleeding. He prayed to the Lady it'd be enough.

*"Guys."*

They turned at Pierce's tone, biofoam still flowing, and Nate realized he hadn't gotten the full extent of it. They *weren't* alone—that much was true. At least a few Asgardian ships seemed to have been yanked cross-system along with them. But that wasn't it.

Something was coming. Not plainly visible to the naked eye against the dark side of the planet below, but clear enough on Cammy's scanners—a roiling cloud of mass and motion, rushing toward them from the planet. A swarm.

The air hissed and hummed beside them as Cammy shifted the gurney's structure yet again, sealing Tessa into an improvised hermetic med pod, vital displays winking into existence, ticking orange. Nate's gaze flicked back to the main display, grim and vacant.

A swarm—but not like any swarm he'd ever seen. It was finer. More like a wild desert sandstorm than the bulky churnings of ice and rock he'd come to expect.

It vanished without a trace.

"What the—"

And reappeared a moment later, closer, coming in at a new angle.

"Light it up," Jaeger called, stone-faced as he rose from Tessa's side and moved for his rig.

Ramirez and Elmo must've been sitting on the triggers. The words were barely out of Jaeger's mouth before the viewport blazed to life with a hail of plasma fire and the deck vibrated with the *whoomph whoomph whoomph* of launching torpedoes. Jaeger was snapping at Cammy to get their uninvited Asgardian neighbors on the horn when the swarm vanished again. This time, Nate caught the fine misting across the mass scanners, like it wasn't actually disappearing so much as rapidly dismantling. Untold trillions of extremely fine particles, dispersing like a pressurized gas to the vacuum. Controlled by what?

He had no godly idea. Distantly, he heard Jaeger conversing in rapid fire on the comms with whoever else had gotten yanked along with them— something about unexplained shrapnel and systems down. It hardly seemed to matter as the *Camelot*'s opening salvo tore on through empty space, and the unharmed swarm reassembled itself, coming for them with a cold, mechanical vengeance.

"Say again." Jaeger's voice was tight at the comms.

Nate didn't catch the full reply, but he picked up the only three words that seemed to matter.

"—drives are dead."

For some reason, Jaeger looked to Nate at that. "Well, shit."

Outside, the swarm rushed on.

No commands were needed. The *Camelot* unleashed hell, deathly quiet gripping the bridge as they redoubled the onslaught. Jaeger kicked loose the antimatter munitions. Nate had Cammy open up with the point defense lasers. The Asgardian ships, the ones that could, opened fire. Thousands— maybe millions—of Synth particles annihilated in the space of seconds. But it was futile. Whatever the hell this was, it was too fast, too impossibly numerous, and diffuse.

It kept coming. Exploding out and collapsing in on them, unrelenting.

Nate looked around the bridge. Everyone's faces, tight with concentration or outright fear. Allied ships dead in the water. Unknown enemy closing. Amelia gripping hands with Lundquist and Ramachandra. Elsa was wide-eyed, still holding that pendant of hers. Gendra the Gorgon, hand-to-chest, jin pulled in like a too-tight hoodie. Hannah O'Sweeney surveying it all with that freaky, almost bored calm of hers, like she was just trying to think of a good headline. She caught him looking and raised a questioning eyebrow like *well, are you just going to stand there?*

Fair point.

"Get those ships back to Asgard," he called, turning for the bulkhead. "Tell them what's happening here, and—"

He drew up short as he nearly ran straight into Tristan and Tor. He'd forgotten they were even shadowing him. They held their ground. It occurred to him they might try to stop him.

"Protect the crew," he said, as his helmet unfolded down from e-dim, cradling him for what came next. "Colonel Jaeger's in command."

The hesitation was barely perceptible. "Yes, my lord," they said in unison, stepping aside with heads bowed.

Jaeger was less convinced. "Nate, you don't know what—"

"We don't have time," Nate snapped. "We can't let these things slip away, and apparently, we don't have the firepower to stop 'em, so get those ships out of here, rally those fleets, and call Iveera. Tell her we found our Synth leak." The first edge of the swarm swatted against the *Camelot's* prow with a *crackle-hiss* of foreign matter on energy shields, drawing all eyes forward. "And that I might be needing help," Nate added, considering the thickening Synth sandstorm.

"Nate!"

But he was already darting past the Atlanteans, launching for the bulkhead, phasing neatly through the solid hull. He plunged out into too-turbulent space with something considerably less than a plan. Felt those things harassing his shields the moment he left the *Camelot's* protection—a thousand-thousand imperceptibly tiny fire ants, dinging against him like a full-on sandblasting in the middle of empty, airless space.

And that was just the leading edge.

He angled into the coming storm and blasted away from the *Camelot* and their vulnerable allies, keeping his speed moderate, raining what he hoped was sufficient plasma fire to catch the swarm's so-called attention. His mind was churning, comms pinging, side throbbing where he only then remembered he'd taken a hit back on the bridge.

*It's nothing,* Ex said. *The particles passed straight through. I've already closed the wounds.* But Nate was stuck on that word. Particles. Stuck on the mysterious flechette fire that'd raked the bridge—and apparently other bridges, too—in the wake of whatever had yanked them cross-system. The look on Tessa's face. The look on *Elsa's.* Celestial bodies and—

*Might I recommend we circle back around to this later?*

It was more than a fair point as the swarm thickened around them, ripping like a tornado, Nate's heart pounding in the muffled suit interior even as his mind frantically attempted to jump ship, like maybe it could escape even if he wouldn't. Still.

*Did you just become a 'let's circle back around to this' guy?*

The swarm enveloping them.

*I don't know what that means, Nathaniel.*

A giant, silent storm swallowing them whole, to the steady *crackle-hiss* of laboring energy shields. The *Camelot* barely visible behind, angling toward the first listing Asgardian cruiser.

*Seems kinda like bureaucrat talk, Ex.*

*I hope you get eaten.*

Nate waited until that seemed all too likely, insides bubbling with some wild mix of sheer panic and terror giggles...

Then he made like a Super Saiyan and unleashed everything he had in a full spectrum, multimodal blast that must've atomized everything within several hundred meters, at least. He didn't stick around to see. He jetted off on tightly-clenched gravitonic thoughts, trailing plasma fire and leading the way through the undulating storm with a shimmering, lance-shaped energy barrier.

He tore free with a gush of relief, angling toward the light side of the unidentified jungle planet below, praying to the Lady the swarm would simply follow him away from the *Camelot* and her allies. As long as he could keep their attention. As long as they didn't catch him in full.

He wasn't sure what came next. Maybe he could whittle this nanoswarm down, blast by blast. At least hold it at bay until Jaeger got those ships clear, or more firepower arrived. Assuming it was even close enough to arrive, he realized, noting the clear absence of Asgard on the visuals. He felt from Ex that they still seemed to be somewhere in the ballpark of the Asgard system. But even then... He didn't know what. Wasn't even sure whether destroying this swarm would be the end of it. What would happen if these things just started showing up all across the Alliance?

He didn't want to think about it.

*Circling back to how I hope you get eaten...* Ex murmured.

Nate checked the tac display on his HUD, saw with some easing in his chest that his brash move seemed to be working, the swarm by and large forgetting about the larger ships to chase the tiny little bugger who'd just gone off like a small sun and slipped their squirmy clutches. He loosed a bright column of plasma back at the leading edge of the swarm, along with a few antimatter torpedoes for good measure. The swarm ate the losses, no longer seeming to care—seeming, somehow, to be growing despite the damage. Nate kept moving, keeping the fire up.

He didn't know how they were going to solve the mystery of where the hell this thing had come from, or how it had managed to scatter its friends clear across the sector. For now, it was enough to just survive and—

"Shit!"

The course correction was so sudden, so violent, that he almost didn't have time to register what his eyes had seen. A double-take verified what Ex's sensors were already telling him. A solid wall of swarm had appeared out of thin vacuum right in front of them—almost like their pursuit had pulled a teleportation act to jump ahead.

The swarm was on him before he could begin to wonder how, leading edges sizzling at his shields like so many flies to the zapper, the more substantial roots closing in, driving him back toward the main mass of the swarm they'd left behind, like an ocean-sized nutcracker.

*A Knightcracker,* Ex declared, sounding entirely too pleased with himself. *What?* he added, when Nate—veering onto the only clear course left to them, toward the planet below—proved unamused. *You should just be happy I'm warming to these ridiculous puns of yours.*

Nate flew on, blasting away any tendril that came too close, trying to keep his cool and weigh his options. Trying not to panic as the far edges of the closing swarms began to curl in like a closing fist—or to falter at what he saw below. At first he thought he was imagining it, but the dark side of the planet was definitely coming alive with a faint sheen of reddish energies, and whatever it was seemed to be growing, swirling with a kind of bioluminescent vitality.

*Well, that doesn't seem normal,* Ex said.

Nate's half-hearted quest for a suitable *no shit* died as the growing storm began to shift more rapidly, the diffuse energy suddenly coalescing into an erratic network of glowing ruby nodes that stretched across the planet, huge brilliant arcs crackling back and forth like some giant, arcane circuit.

Nate, having been thinking of dropping into the atmosphere in hopes of burning off his pursuit, slowed to reconsider, searching for the *Camelot.*

*Any idea what the hell we're looking at?* he thought at Ex, as he spotted his ship tethering to the first stranded Asgardian cruiser.

*Well...* Ex started thoughtfully.

Then the planet burst with a thrumming rush of light and energy—that arcane circuit discharging, firing off enough electromagnetic flux to scramble Nate's HUD and, and—

He gasped as the force of gravity took hold of his stomach, the sudden sound and tug of rushing air where before there'd only been cold vacuum.

*Atmosphere,* some shocked observer pointed out from the back of his mind, right as his eyes and clearing HUD caught up and he registered the twisted treetops of an alien jungle racing up to meet him.

# CHAPTER 13

# ESTRANGED

*I think we might have a problem, Nathaniel.*

Nate grunted his general aching agreement and pushed himself up from the respectable little crater they'd just punched in the damp jungle soil.

*Might that problem have something to do with why the hell you just cut the jets and let me eat dirt?*

*It might.*

He waited for more, but Ex seemed to be crunching something or another. He cupped his ringing head in his hands, beckoning the tac display up on the helmet HUD. Nothing but static. No sign of the *Camelot*, no sign of *anything*, except...

He turned, following some flutter of intuition, and frowned in the general direction of the distant, mountainous blip he'd caught on the dark horizon, just before the gravitonics had kicked out completely. Nothing to see now but shadowy jungle all around—yet some dark weight hung there in the distance, on the edge of his senses. Dusk was falling, he noted, trying to parse the fact against where he'd been relative to the planet's dark side when that last strange wave had hit and... and what? Plucked him straight out of space on another transdimensional hiccup?

*Ex*, he thought, resisting the urge to speak out loud. Something about the silence of this place. He waited for his companion's explanation, mind churning with questions, grasping for any clue as to where the hell that swarm might've gone—not to mention the *Camelot* and the rest of the Asgardian ships.

Was this even the same planet he'd been flying over a moment ago?

He waited for Ex to chime in with an *obviously*, or an *it stands to reason, Nathaniel*, or even a *calm your squishy superstitions, will you?*

*Ex?* he wondered again, starting to worry now.

*I'm... rather maddeningly blind, here*, Ex finally admitted, plainly still distracted by whatever he was up to. *This entire planet is... do you feel that?*

Nate frowned at the growing darkness pressing in from the tangle of spongy foliage and strange trees. Pressing in all around. An emptiness. An eerie stillness in the air. Like someone or something had sucked the life out of the place. And that's when he understood.

*The Light.* He looked around, heart beating faster now, some useless part of his brain hoping he simply wasn't looking properly, even as the rest of him accepted the cold, hard truth.

*So, it's not just me, then*, Ex said, sounding about as barren as Nate suddenly felt. There was a long moment of silence, both of them unpacking the full implications of this development.

*What have you gotten us into this time, Nathaniel?*

Nate thrust his hands wide at the darkening jungle. *How is this MY fault?*

*Well, you were the one who was all, 'Get those ships back to Asgard,' and 'Tell Iveera we found our Synth leak,' and 'Let's go defy the Council and run off on the Quest for the Holy Dolphin's Head' in the first place.*

That last bit felt especially rich, coming from the synthient companion who'd spent their first several months together doing nothing *but* goading Nate to step up and take the bull by the horns, but Nate was caught on the one word Ex had just said that sounded remotely like hope.

Iveera.

*We can't reach anyone*, Ex replied, before Nate could even ask. *This entire planet is...*

*Is what?*

*Cut off, somehow. I'm not yet certain what we're dealing with.*

A distant howl split the night, sparking at the growing tightness in Nate's chest. *Where the hell's the Light, Ex? Where ARE we?*

*I JUST said I'm not certain. Pay attention, Nathaniel.*

The familiar scolding was oddly comforting. More comforting than anything else out here in this foreign, possibly hostile landscape, at least.

*How bad is it?* he wondered more calmly, trying to recall Jaeger's limited lessons on wilderness survival situations as he looked around at the ominous jungle. It'd been hard to imagine he'd ever need such lessons, with Ex on his side. And now... Was he imagining the subtle movements, the uneasy feeling of being watched? He couldn't help but wonder what kind of beasties might've made their home in this place. *What am I working with if it turns out we're not alone out here?*

*Only the most powerful weapon ever known to mankind,* Ex grumbled.

"Batteries not included," Nate muttered aloud, then wished he hadn't as another howl answered the first, closer this time.

*I have other methods of energy production, Nathaniel.*

*Comparable methods?*

*Other methods,* Ex said carefully. Then, quicker, half under his breath: *Most of them currently tied up in e-dim to be called on in emergencies, but that's neither here nor there. And need I remind you that you're not exactly a defenseless little Terran anymore? I think you can handle a few wild predators.*

Nate didn't disagree, per se, but that didn't stop the sudden trapped rat feeling from closing in around him. He needed a breath of fresh air. Even if it was a bit thin by the HUD readings. He started to release his helmet back to e-dim, then realized that even that functionality might be lost to them without the Lady's Light.

*Not lost,* Ex corrected. *Just... Oh, I'm working on it. So boo-hoo, you're stuck in the finest power armor ever—*

*Ever known to mankind or to anyone else,* Nate finished for him, pulling the manual seals and yanking the helmet free the old-fashioned way. *Yada freakin' yada. Can we fly?*

Ex hesitated. *How far?*

Nate frowned at the darkening jungle foliage. *I don't love that that's your first question.*

*Well, perhaps if...*

Nate didn't need to ask what'd caught his companion's attention as Ex trailed off. He caught it himself through the tangled mess of strange branches, there in the night sky—the ruby flash of something like the arcane pulse that'd pulled them down, momentarily illuminating the clouds in the distance. He gaped at the spot as the light vanished, scared to even ask, senses straining until his brain caught up, and he jammed the helmet back on, coaxing the optics out to their max.

There was something wrong with the air here. Some unnatural *thickness* that hung like an oily film, thwarting any attempt to see much of anything at distance, even with the helmet's extended spectrum. But there. The faintest blips of red, trailing lazily down in the distance. Flares, maybe. The *Camelot's?*

*I don't know,* Ex replied, before he could even consciously ask.

*Well can you—*

*I'm trying, Nathaniel. I've never experienced so much interference on a habitable planet. I think maybe...*

A burst of static filled his earpieces, broken by staccato syllables, like a poorly tuned radio. Jaeger's voice? Maybe. Too distorted to tell. Whatever it was, something told him it wasn't coincidence that the lightshow seemed to be headed in the direction of that mountainous darkness he'd glimpsed from above.

*You asked how far,* Nate thought, sealing his helmet back on and preparing for flight. *How about that far?*

Ex sounded grim. *I'll see what I can do.*

~

THEY CRASHED about five minutes in.

*Come now,* Ex grumbled, as Nate picked himself up for a second time. *That was hardly a crash. I'd barely even call it a patchy landing.*

*Pretty sure my wrist is broken,* Nate noted, resisting the futile effort to brush his armor free of the clodded mud and silt that would only smear anyway.

*BARELY broken, Nathaniel. Barely. And I'm working on it. So, you know... Cool your jets.*

*Interesting choice of words from the guy who just dropped me out of the sky for the second time.*

Ex just grumbled something about appreciation and working with what he was given—and what exactly had Nate accomplished in the past five minutes, anyway?

Smarting wrist aside, Nate didn't see much reason to push the matter. For one thing, Ex had a point: He hadn't done jack shit throughout their short flight, aside from confirming the location of that foreboding mountain a few hundred klicks away. There'd been no more arcane flashes, no sign of anything. And while he should've been busy taking the lay of the land—searching for water and distinguishable landmarks, or attuning his senses to the mysteriously absent Light—he'd mostly just wasted what precious airtime they'd had, uselessly fretting about the *Camelot* and her crew.

Of course, he hadn't *known* their airtime was precious. And the unnaturally thick darkness hadn't exactly helped on the scouting front, either, even if the visibility had been markedly better up above the stifling jungle air.

Ex, to his credit, had tapped what sensors and systems he had available to draw up a limited map of the surrounding terrain as they went.

*You're welcome,* Ex chimed, rather pointedly.

But still, even with a map of sorts, this was thoroughly uncharted territory. No crash survival courses on what to do when the Light dried up. Because it *didn't*. The Lady's Light was ubiquitous. Everywhere. Freaking all-pervasive.

Except here.

Wherever the hell *here* was.

*About that,* Ex said, offering up a new suite of data on Nate's HUD. *After parsing what I borrowed from the Asgardian fleet and cross-referencing against what little I was able to see of that dreadful sun and our surrounding stars before we fell into this... muck, I BELIEVE we may be on the lost planet the Asgardians once referred to as Ginnungagap.*

*You believe?*

*I'm sorry, I couldn't hear you over the sound of my doing everything, Nathaniel. Triple-star systems are a bit tricky.*

Triple-star systems. Nate tried to imagine what that would look like for planetary orbits but didn't get far before his head started spinning. He felt his cracked wrist warming with the itchy flurry of Ex's accelerated healing. *Point taken. But a lost planet? How's that even...?*

*As I said. Tricky. The planet's been unobservable from Asgard for over a thousand years. I take it it's become something of a legend.*

*All right. That's... something,* Nate thought, still trying to wrap his head around the basic mechanics, and the more troubling question of how the hell they'd ended up here. *Wait. Why a legend?*

*Probably largely on account that its actual location seems to have been deliberately expunged from all records.*

*Creepy. So, what do we actually know about Ginnungagap, then?*

*Only that it's absolutely forbidden and allegedly extremely dangerous.*

Nate eyed the surrounding jungle, suddenly and acutely aware of the feeling of being watched. *You might've opened with that.*

This place was too quiet.

Ex gave a noncommittal grunt. *It's probably nothing. The mandates were issued over a thousand years ago, back when Asgard was still recognized as belonging to the Atlantean Empire. And besides, such classifications are often nothing more than heavy-handed ploys to keep the Little People away from juicy discoveries—rare resource deposits and such.*

*Except when they're not?*

*Except when they're not,* Ex agreed. *The exact details ARE conspicuously absent, even from the classified records. But let's not assume the worst until—*

*Until a freak energy storm kidnaps us from across an entire solar system?*

*A TRI-solar system, Nathaniel. Pay attention. But also, yes.*

Nate let out a long breath, mind turning with mythic legends, mysterious forces, and vengeful gods. He found himself staring in the direction of that damned mountain again, gauging distances, weighing options, wondering what had become of his people. Maybe they'd gotten those Asgardian ships clear. Maybe even now, they were rallying Iveera and a whole fleet's worth of reinforcements to come find him and exterminate that bizarre nanoswarm, wherever the hell it had gone. He and Ex weren't even really sure those had been flares they'd seen earlier—much less that it had been the *Camelot* in the sky, or Jaeger's voice on that burst of static. All he really knew was that, whatever it had been, it seemed to have been drawn toward the mountain, and that for some reason—probably just some stupid human instinct to steer toward the big and mighty—he was, too.

Off in the brush, something cracked. The first sign of life he'd heard. He didn't realize he was holding his breath until Ex cleared his throat.

*It IS a jungle,* Ex pointed out, though he didn't sound so certain himself.

Nate took the point anyway. They needed to move. Needed to find the Light. Find his people. Maybe, with a little bit of luck, they could even figure out what the hell was going on here—and what the Synth had to do with it.

*There's one more thing.*

Something in Ex's tone.

*It's probably nothing,* Ex added quickly, in a way that made it sound like anything *but* nothing. *Just a choice curiosity I happened to stumble across in an archaic Asgardian data log. A note, as it were. One that seems to have slipped the black bars of whomever wished to keep the affairs of Ginnungagap quiet.* He hesitated. *It was a warning, of sorts,* he finally said. *A warning penned, oddly enough, by someone claiming to be 'the last LeFaye.'*

Nate stiffened. *What?*

*I don't know,* Ex admitted. *But it's dated right around the time the Asgardians put the kibosh on the planet, and whoever wrote it seemed to be under the impression that this place was damned.*

*Damned?*

*Oh, you know. Prowled by terrible beasts. Haunted by tortured, misshapen souls. So on and so forth.*

*Sure,* Nate thought. *That old chestnut.* He could hear it in Ex's voice—there was something more. *What is it, Ex? What else?*

*Well, whoever this last LeFaye might've been... they called this place New Avalon.*

The words hung in the unnatural darkness, ringing with the echoes of memories Nate had tried to set aside. Cold ash and the thunderous crash of titans. The ruins of Avalon. The ghost of Mordred LeFaye hovering over his shoulder, suddenly here, staring alongside him at this void of a planet. The shadows watched them right back. A cold sheen of sweat had appeared on Nate's brow.

What the hell was this place?

What in nine hells would've ever merited a warning from Mordred freaking LeFaye?

*We don't know it was Mordred,* Ex pointed out. *Or even a genuine LeFaye. It could've been anyone.*

But they both knew, somewhere deep down, that it hadn't been just anyone.

*Besides,* Ex pushed on, like he didn't see the writing on the wall, *we're not going to find the answers just standing here, and fifty percent of us already have quite enough on their plate without the added burden of flight so, umm... happy trails?*

Nate stared through the foliage with unseeing eyes, and a sudden, terrible certainty as to exactly what he might find waiting for him in that dark mountain. And yet... *What would Iveera do?*

As was sometimes the case, he wasn't positive whether the thought had been Ex's or his own.

He blew out a heavy sigh and started running.

# CHAPTER 14

# GHOSTS

Something was following him.

*What,* he couldn't begin to say. The presence was entirely too ghostly, too silent. Maybe it was the actual freaking ghost of Mordred LeFaye. Or maybe it was nothing but Nate's own growing, irrational sense of dread. Whatever it was, it wasn't backing down. And power-armored superhuman or no, bit by bit, he was.

He'd been running for about three hours by the time he tuckered out—some two-hundred jungle kilometers later, by Ex's count. In a past life, that number would have left him speechless. Now though, he just plopped gratefully to the dirt, pressed his back up against an enormous tree, and tried to keep his senses halfway alert as he thought about what came next.

Even with the enhanced night spectrum of his helmet vision and the relative ease with which his suit had allowed him to plunge straight through the smaller bramble and vines of the jungle, the going had been tough—the terrain fighting him every step of the way, the nighttime darkness nearly absolute. And as for the wildlife…

He closed his eyes and listened, sinking into the silence between heavy breaths.

Something was out there. He felt it in his bones.

He opened his eyes, thought about calling out to whatever it was. *Halt, who goes there?* Maybe he was cracking. He couldn't remember the last time he'd been this hungry—or hungry at all, for that matter. Ever since Terra, Ex had seen to it he was always sufficiently nourished, whether he'd eaten or not.

*Yes, yes*, Ex grumbled. *Working on it, working on it.*

He tried not to let his mind go anywhere unduly harsh, knowing Ex would more or less hear the general sentiment of his thoughts, regardless of whether he intended it.

*Your diplomacy is deeply touching*, Ex said. *Honestly.*

It sounded anything but honest, but Nate was relieved to feel the edge of his hunger dulling just a tad, the deadened weight ever-so-slightly lifting from his tired limbs.

*Thanks, buddy.*

*Bah*, Ex grunted. Then, a few moments later: *You might as well sleep a wink if we're merely going to get all mushy, here.*

It didn't sound like the worst idea. At least not until he remembered that he may or may not have the Phantom of the Black Knight on his ass. And that, regardless, he was definitely running from *something*, toward some indeterminate *something else*. And that, even if he hadn't had his crew to worry about somewhere out there, nowhere on this damned planet felt safe. But even so, he hadn't slept in… Christ, had it really been that long?

*It has*, Ex confirmed. *And I'll keep watch.*

It was kind of impressive, how quickly those last four words added weight to his drooping eyelids.

*Provided you say pretty please*, Ex added, the suggestion of a malicious grin in his tone.

Nate snorted half-hearted rebellion and promptly fell asleep.

STRANGE DREAMS GAVE way to humid darkness. Rough tree bark at his back. Heavy silence in the air. For a split second, he couldn't remember where he was—right up until Ex asked quietly, as if not to startle him, "If one were looking for a casual way to say, 'I think there's something out there that may want to eat you…'"

Nate sat up, trying to shake the sleep off, wondering how long he'd been out. Some sensible part of his brain reaching to call his sword from e-dim, only to remember that might not be an option.

"I'd probably start with, 'Good morning,'" he grumbled back, eyeing the ghostly outlines of fronds and foliage. He froze when he saw the wiry apparition of Ex beside him, decked to the gills in cartoonish woodsman garb and a raccoon skin hat.

"Superb," that apparition replied almost cheerily as he turned from the jungle, tweaking his mustachio. "Well then, good morning, Nathaniel. I believe something's coming to eat you."

～

STRANGE DREAMS GAVE way to humid darkness—this time with the marked bite of waking reality. The smell of damp earth. The achy muscles of a shitty sleeping position.

The unsettling hiss and crackle of something moving in the darkness.

Nate planted his hands in the soft soil, tense to the max, hesitant to make any sudden movements, to even stand for fear of what was out there.

Silence.

The night pressed in on him from all sides, constricting tight lungs—the moment stretching, stretching. The terrible void of not knowing.

Then four speeding shadows came exploding out of the jungle straight for him.

# CHAPTER 15

# MYRR

Jaeger snapped awake to cold darkness and a pounding headache. He cracked his eyes open, stifling a groan—sharp pain in the side—trying to remember… what? Nothing. He blinked again, just to make double sure his eyes were open. Nothing at all. Pitch black darkness. Dripping water. Hard, uneven ground beneath him. A cave?

He tried to sit up. The groan escaped, sharp pain doubling. Low voices nearby. And closer still, more voices. Whispers. Snuffy, he thought. Snuffy and—

"Carter?" he whispered. It came out rough and dry. Pieces tumbled back. Mismatched flashes. The *Camelot* breaking atmosphere, ripped downward by… by that freak swarm. And something else. Another storm wave. And escape pods. He'd ordered everyone to the escape pods. Set the rendezvous for—

"Don't move," came Carter's quiet voice nearby.

Nearby, those low voices stopped. Not human, he registered. He heard rustling. Careful movements. Hands found him in the dark, coaxed him firmly back down to a supine position on the cold stone. Steady hands. Carter's. He stowed the urge to resist. Turned his attention to more important things.

"Where are we?"

"Don't know," she said, her hands methodically working their way across his torso. "Subterranean, obviously. Under a mountain, maybe. Thought I saw a mountain."

That jarred something. Escape pods. A bisected Asgardian cruiser, trailing them on the tethers. Cammy warbling something about the mountain on the forward scanners. Escape pods, and then what? He'd stayed with the ship. Hadn't he? Stayed with Kalders. Couldn't leave her behind. Except...

"Kalders," he breathed, recalling the pilot's injuries with a sickening twist in his gut. He felt the silent *negative* hanging in the darkness—maybe a shake of the head he couldn't see but somehow felt.

"I don't know," Carter said quietly. Grimly. "Shut up a second."

Something pressed up against his chest, distracting him, hyperalert senses reconciling the shapeless pitch black into Carter's head, her ear to his chest, her hair tickling his chin. Listening to his heart, he supposed. He was thinking of Kalders, thinking of just how badly fucked they might be here, trying not to notice—despite it all—how damned good Carter's hair smelled, or how she'd just slackened against him, just a bit. Hugging him? Hugging without hugging.

Of the many things they did to each other, hugging wasn't one of them.

Any other time, the gesture might've left him glibly satisfied—and probably begrudgingly aroused. Any other time, he would've glanced around to make sure no one had noticed, before allowing the professional colonel voice to come out and nix the moment, remind them both that anything beyond the physical was a bad idea. Instead, he found his hand reaching for her in the dark.

She was already pulling away from him. "Few bruised ribs, I think," she said, sounding a touch pinched but otherwise perfectly clinical. "Maybe cracked. I can't see shit. Anything else bothering you?"

He tried to put a grim smile in his voice. "You mean aside from crash landing and waking up under a mountain?"

"Aside from that," she agreed.

"Peachy as fuckin' pie. Maybe you'd better fill me in on the rest, though."

He listened, glad to be able to drop the brave face in the darkness, as the others joined Carter in the rundown. Most of the crew was present and accounted for in the cave, most of them having awoken much like he had—groggy and frustratingly lacking in the memory department. A third, though, were still missing between Pierce, Amelia, and the Round Table Atlanteans. And Kalders, he reminded himself with another pang of worry. Nothing like having a soldier go MIA to show you just how much you'd started to think of them in all the ways you weren't supposed to. It might as well have been his daughter missing out there. And then there was Pierce, too.

Something about the thought rankled his insides, something scratching at the door of his hazy memories. He forced himself to focus up as Carter and the others moved on to describing the creature—or maybe creatures, plural—that seemed to have brought them all here. Details were as disturbing as they were scattered. The one thing everyone seemed to agree on was that it had been some terrifying, black-furred biped.

"Like an upright panther," Snuffy insisted. "Or a black tiger. But, like, also with a bear's body. Like a black tiger bear. Or a sasquatch."

"A black tiger bear," Jaeger echoed numbly, the scratching more insistent now, demanding his attention.

"Or a sasquatch," Snuffy repeated, as if the distinction were important.

"Two in one hand, three in the other," Ramirez muttered, humorlessly.

"Thing's strong," came Elmo's deep voice, strained like he'd taken a good hit or two. "Damn fast, too."

But Jaeger was caught in a blurry fragment of memory, unfolding with maddening slowness. Escape pods. Dark beasties and escape pods. He'd stayed with the ship. Stayed despite Cammy's frantic warnings. He'd *stayed* with Kalders. Hadn't he? Couldn't leave her behind. Couldn't.

Right up until Cammy had gone and jettisoned him straight out of the bridge in an improvised crash pod.

"Shit," he heard himself whisper, insides twisting up. The shocking impact of a hard landing. The wrenching of metal and crunching composites. Hot breath, and fear, and—

"Boss?"

"I… think it bit me," he finally said, pulling himself together. He couldn't remember even seeing the thing, but somehow he knew the words were true as he grimaced down at the hot yet oddly anesthetized ache he was only then really noticing in his forearm, subtly distinct from the rest of the aches and pains. Practically the same spot that damned kitsune, Zoltan, had gotten him back on their first involuntary visit to the Forge.

"It must have some kind of venom," Carter said. "We're all still feeling a bit shaky. Might also explain the patchy memories."

"Delightful." Jaeger was scowling into the darkness, sudden guilt threatening to overwhelm him. He allowed himself one more crushing moment of indulgence, then forced his Colonel Face back on. Nothing to do for Kalders and the others now but to get their shit together, get out of here, and find them. "So, we vaguely know what it looks like. But what the fuck *is* it? And what does it want?"

Uncomfortable silence.

"It calls itself Myrr," someone said quietly. Gendra the Gorgon, he realized after a moment. It was the first she'd spoken.

"How do you know that?"

"She felt it," Carter said quietly in his ear, as if everyone in the blind huddle couldn't hear her anyway. "When it—When *Myrr* was dragging her in here."

Jaeger wasn't entirely sure what she meant by *felt* it. The art of Gorgon empathy, as far as he'd gathered, was mostly reserved to sensing and sometimes influencing raw surface emotions rather than actual explicit mindreading, and Gendra claimed she wasn't much of an empath anyway. But something in the way Carter said it told him it wasn't a topic to linger on, for the Gorgon's sake.

"Don't suppose anyone has any idea what this Myrr is after?" he asked instead.

"You mean assuming we're *not* food?" Ramirez asked.

"Assuming we're not *just* food," Jaeger corrected. "Seems like a lot of extra work to gather us all here if all it wanted to do was eat us."

"Well," Snuffy said, hesitantly, "unless it's planning to, you know, ration us out. Make us last, or whatever."

There was a pleasant thought.

"I mean, maybe we're just, like, the stockpile for the winter mon—"

"We get the picture, Snuffy," Carter cut the mechanic off. "Maybe we wait until any of us actually knows what the hell we're talking about before you start scaring the civilians."

Grateful for the backup on the team morale front, Jaeger silently reached out in the dark, found Carter's hand, and gave her a thumbs-up. She felt the signal out and gave him a middle finger in return. He almost smiled. Low voices elsewhere in the cave depths drew his attention instead.

"Great," he heard someone—maybe Ramirez—whisper nearby.

One of the Elsewhere Voices, seemingly emboldened by the lull in their conversation, spoke up louder—loud enough that there was no missing it from what sounded like maybe ten meters away.

"Give them time, brother. The little Terrans will eventually come to understand."

An Asgardian voice, some corner of his mind intuitively guessed, right before Carter leaned over and murmured as much in his ear. The cruiser, that corner of his mind decided. The forward half of the bisected Asgardian ship dangling along on the *Camelot*'s tethers like some oversized just-married can, cleaved clean in two by whatever the hell had yanked them into the atmosphere when that spooky ruby charge had gone off. They must've crashed when the *Camelot* went down. *If* the *Camelot* had gone down. He shut those thoughts down before he could get swept away in unknowns. Right now, the most pressing question was how many people were in this cave, and what they all had in terms of productive common interests.

"Maybe we can skip the foreplay," he said, "and get to the part where we all figure out how we can escape, together."

There was a bark of harsh laughter. Multiple barks.

"Escape?" Asgardian or not, the derision in that tone was clear.

"Unless I missed something here," Jaeger said, "that does seem like the move."

More bitter laughter.

"We have come to Ginnungagap, Terran," called one of the Asgardians. "There is no escape from this place."

"Well, maybe not with *that* attitude," Ramirez murmured, half-heartedly.

Jaeger glanced uselessly around in the darkness, wishing to Christ he could see his crew's faces and gather whether or not they'd already heard about this Ginnungagap.

"What are they saying?" someone else whispered—Dr. Ramachandra, he thought. Had the Myrr creature taken their translator discs, then? That hardly seemed like the act of some mindless predator.

"More fire and brimstone stuff," Snuffy whispered back. "We'll keep you posted if anything changes."

Not for the first time, Jaeger was glad he and the SAS crew had decided to go ahead and get permanent translator implants a few months into their Alliance soldiering.

"Listen," he called toward the Asgardians, deciding to try a new angle. "The Eighth Excalibur Knight is out there right now. He'll be coming for us. He can deal with this Myrr thing, but the least we can do is get our shit together and make things easier for him."

In truth, Jaeger had no idea what had become of Nate, but his voice was steady, his promise confident. Hell, maybe he really did believe in the kid. The Asgardians, on the other hand, were thoroughly unimpressed.

"Fools. From the deepest of nine hells was this place born. It has birthed abominations longer-lived and more fearsome by far than any of your precious Excalibur Knights. Demons and dark gods the likes of which would see your Terran Knight soiling his breeches in his haste to leave you here."

"You don't know Nate." That was Snuffy, having Nate's back with the utmost faith. "He'd never leave us behind."

It was actually kind of touching, right up until the mechanic's mouth had to keep running.

"Well, you know, except for that one time on Separuu. And that thing out in the Triton belts, too, I guess. And then I guess it might've been a close call back on Vanaheim, too. But that was like, a—Well, you had to be there. He'd never leave us behind for good. Like, to get eaten and stuff."

By the time Snuffy finished, Jaeger didn't bother even trying to pick back up the momentum and agree with the basic sentiment. He could practically smell the Asgardians' derisive sneers in the darkness, and he was caught anyway on the thought of these so-called demons and dark gods, thinking warily of the way they'd all arrived at this planet. Spooky ruby flashes, and warping space, and demented particle swarms. And that damned mountain. All of it somehow wrapped up with the inexplicable appearance of Synth protoswarms in the heart of Alliance space. And now this Myrr.

He thought uneasily of the Black Knight, Mordred LeFaye—the only other living being they knew of who'd apparently shared some kind of union with the malicious, so-called synthience. "If this planet's such a dark place," he started, deciding to sidestep the demons and gods for the moment, "then what the hell's it want with us?"

When the Asgardian answered, there was a grim satisfaction in his tone, like Jaeger had finally asked the one question that mattered. "There is only one purpose for which mortal souls are brought to Ginnungagap."

"Spelunking?" Snuffy asked weakly, his moment of confidence having officially evaporated in full.

Jaeger was pretty sure it wasn't spelunking, but whatever grim damnation the Asgardians had in mind, they didn't get a chance to voice it before an ungodly sound sucked the air from cave's collective lungs.

It was animal. Beastly. Everywhere. A low growl that set Jaeger's blood on edge. It seemed to be coming from every direction. Then the air changed. The faintest whisper of motion. A terrible whimper somewhere ahead. The *thunk* and *whoosh* of a body smacking stone hard enough to knock the wind out.

"Hey." Jaeger was a little surprised to find that the voice had been his own. Surprised to find he'd come to his feet, stepped foolishly forward into the unknown darkness. "Hello?" he croaked, throat suddenly dry.

Silence.

Infinite silence.

Another flutter of motion, then—

Terror.

It hit him like a physical wave, sending him reeling. He crashed to the ground, limbs frozen with the sheer magnitude of it. He tried to move, tried to cover himself, sharp edges of memories clawing their way back to the churning surface. The creature—this *thing*—finding him. Ripping the escape pod apart like cheap plastic. Hot breath and a low, rumbling growl. Someone was crying nearby. The terror built, swelling like a dark ocean, paring out all other sensation. The rumbling, gone. The smell, gone. Overwhelming darkness.

He was dying.

And then he was panting, alone on an island of silence, the crushing waters of his terror lapping almost gently at the edges as they receded, inch by inch.

"Boss?"

Ramirez, pawing at the nearby stone until his hand found Jaeger's head in the darkness.

"Hey, Boss, speak up. You good?"

"I'm good," Jaeger croaked. He sounded anything but. "I'm good," he repeated anyway, forcing himself to sit up, then reaching out to find Ramirez's shoulder with a reassuring touch for good measure.

"We have to get out of here," someone whispered.

The creature was gone. Jaeger could feel it in the air. For a few seconds, he allowed himself to revel in the comfort of that simple fact alone. Around them, no one seemed in any hurry to argue. There was nothing but the sound of their collective, terrified breathing.

"We have to get the *fuck* out of here," that someone repeated, at a low growl this time—Elmo, he was surprised to realize. The big man sounded angry. Shaken.

A delirious whimper broke the silence ahead. The same whimper of whatever—whoever—that *thing* had dragged in, Jaeger thought. He'd nearly forgotten.

"Carter," he called, not sure yet what the plan was, only that he needed to do something. The crushing weight of that thing's presence. The tone in Elmo's voice. He took a breath, not all that surprised to find his hands still shaking as Carter's reaching hands found him in the darkness. The medic was unsteady, too.

She was never unsteady.

"Something chemical," she murmured quietly, like she was reasoning it out with herself. "Pheromonal, maybe."

It wasn't hard to guess what she meant. He'd never felt a fear response like this in his life. It was well beyond anything he'd ever experienced in battle. Almost… weaponized.

He set the shaky nerves aside as best he could and oriented himself and Carter toward those pitiful whimpers.

"Please," whispered the darkness as his blindly reaching hands closed on a warm arm, slicked with what felt too much like blood. "Please."

"Amelia?" he whispered.

There was no verbal response, but the language of her tensing was answer enough. It was the tensing of a beaten dog, helplessly waiting to see whether the next blow would come, frozen in place but for the soft trembling.

He reached out, cupping the Atlantean's head with slow, careful movements. "It's okay, Amelia," he said gently, even as the voice in his head ruthlessly pointed out that it was anything *but* okay—that they had no freaking clue what the hell they were up against, or where that thing had even gone. At least Amelia's trembling eased a shade at the sound of her name. That was something. "It's okay," he repeated, gently stroking her hair. "We've got you now."

Whatever that was worth.

"Did it bite you?" Carter asked somewhere behind the Atlantean, probably conducting her limited in-the-dark examination. Her voice was steady.

It was kind of hard to distinguish from the trembles, weak as it was, but he was pretty sure that was a head shake.

"No bite," Jaeger translated aloud. Then, to Amelia: "So you were awake the whole way in here?"

A shaky nod this time. Jaw quivering.

"Okay." He took her face in his hands, wishing to Christ he could see her, uncomfortably aware that he was pretty sure he felt blood on her cheek, too. "You're okay, Amelia," he said anyway. "You're going to be okay. Are you with me?"

Jaw steadying. A dry swallow. A nod. Stronger this time.

"Okay. Good. First things first, then. I need you to tell me what you saw out there."

# CHAPTER 16
# ONE EYE OPEN

"For the record, Ex," Nate managed through panting breaths, "you suck at keeping watch."

*Nonsense,* Ex said, safely confined, at least for the moment, back to the inside of Nate's head. *Exhibit A: You. Not dead. You're welcome.*

Nate looked down at the three broken bodies scattered on the ground around him, feeling equal parts repulsed by the things that'd just attacked him and disgusted that, despite everything, he was still freaking hungry.

*Kind of ironic, considering,* Ex said.

*So, these ARE what I think they are?*

*Preliminary scans and gross anatomy do suggest so.*

"Ooperians," Nate whispered, testing the word in the silent night air. *What the hell are they doing here?* he added to Ex.

*It's cute, the way you always seem to think I know the answers to these questions.*

*Well, you ARE the most sophisticated intelligence ever known to mankind and all that, aren't you?*

Somewhere in the murky distance, he swore he could feel Ex narrowing his nonexistent eyes. *Would you like to know what I miss about Arthur Pendragon?*

*I'm guessing you're about to—*

*The fact that he wasn't such a sniveling piss pot.*

*—tell me,* Nate finished. *Even though you don't actually remember Arthur at all.*

*Oh, I would remember this. Not even the Merlin could make me forget this.*

Nate was pretty sure it was the first time he'd ever heard Ex even marginally question the Merlin, even jokingly. He was about to point as much out when a startling growl perforated the cloying jungle air, so low and monstrous it took him an extra second to recognize it as his own rumbling stomach.

*We could start a fire,* Ex said, pointedly highlighting the dead Ooperians on Nate's HUD. *Probably tastes like chicken.*

"Vampire chicken," Nate murmured.

*There would be a certain poetry to it, though, don't you think?*

Nate looked away from the bodies, stomach turning. *Jesus, Ex.*

*What? I'm just saying. The hunter becomes the hunted, and all that.*

Nate frowned off in the direction the fourth Ooperian had fled, wondering what that last "hunted" would do once it caught its breath and finished licking its wounds. Did it have friends? A nest, or whatever wild Ooperians had? And what about the rest of the jungle, with its alleged terrible beasts and haunted souls and so forth? He looked back to the dead Ooperians. Felt another wave of reluctant hunger and general disgust.

*Thank the Lady you don't have to see what I normally feed you from e-dim.*

Nate grimaced. *I thought it was mostly converted Light.*

*Mostly. Sometimes. In a pinch. 'Mostly' being perhaps a strong word, if we're being perfectly honest.*

*I don't think I wanna know.*

*Oh-ho-ho,* Ex chuckled. *You DEFINITELY don't want to know.*

Nate let out a half-hearted groan in solidarity with his aching stomach. *Do I actually need to eat an Ooperian right now, Ex? Where are we at with you, you know...*

*Transdimensionally spoon feeding you?* Ex offered. *Tirelessly tending your every sad, squishy need?*

*Doing your job,* Nate countered.

*Hmm. Well, assuming you continue on at your previous pace, for at least as far as Mount Doom up there...*

Nate turned his attention eastward—or at least what they were calling eastward on this magnetic clusterfuck of a planet—waiting for Ex to finish his thought, idly wondering when dawn would come on this haunted tri-solar jungle.

*Nathaniel.*

That tone. Nate froze mid-breath, eyes sweeping the foliage for threats. Following Ex's attention downward.

*About my skill at keeping watch...*

"What the fuck," he whispered before he could stop himself.

His right leg was already buried up to the shin in the fluidly reaching tendrils of—he didn't know what. It was like the soil itself had sprouted inky black hands and reached up to grab him by the ankle, like some kind of sentient quicksand. And it seemed to have heard him, he couldn't help but think, as it reached for his left foot almost tentatively, like it knew damned well he saw it and was simply waiting to see what he'd do about it.

*Let's think about this*, Ex started, no doubt sensing his intentions. But Nate was already yanking away. His leg ripped free from the grasping tendrils with a strange kind of squelching crack. Then all hell broke loose.

The entire jungle exploded with motion and sound around—more rushing incoming than he could process. He ran. Unthinking. Blindly stumbling in a sudden hailstorm of speeding particulates, smacking and tugging at every inch of him. No time to think. He ran. Heart thundering. A solid wall of swirling, thrumming darkness nipping at his heels, like the jungle itself was chasing him.

He vaulted a downed tree, tripped, and crashed straight through another. He kept running, the terrain sloping upward underfoot, vines and thick leaves smacking his shoulders and face. He kept running, shouting to Ex for answers.

*I think perhaps we've found what became of that nanoswarm*, was all Ex could think to say. *You're doing great, Nathaniel*, he added a moment later. *Just great. Oh, watch out for that—*

Nate growled a curse as his left shoulder clipped the jutting edge of a rocky overhang and punched through with the sound of pulverizing stone. He couldn't see shit through this jungle storm chaos. Kept running anyway.

*Doing great*, Ex repeated as he sped on. *Just great. Also, it appears we have a bit of a jump coming up.*

The words had barely finished touching Nate's mind when the thick wall of jungle foliage gave way with an almost violent suddenness—space exploding outward to open, dark night, and to fifty short meters of flat stone followed by yawning nothingness. Fast as he was running, he probably couldn't have stopped if he'd wanted to. Not without the gravitonic aid that Ex's tone made it abundantly clear they didn't have the power reserves to support.

So, he poured on the speed, the swarm clawing at him, trying to trip him up. Stone cracked under the force of his pounding boots. He plunged forward, trying not to think about how wide the canyon looked. Then he reached the edge and jumped.

It was a big canyon.

He might've cleared a hundred meters or more on the back of his jump. It wasn't going to be enough, he saw, as they reached the apex and began to fall. He triggered the gravitonics, feeding them whatever there was to feed.

It wasn't much.

He punched into the far side of the canyon several meters short of the top ridge, armored fingers boring into hard stone in a shallow death grip. He turned, gasping, Ex barking at him to keep moving. Some part of him was too busy praying the swarm simply wouldn't follow—that maybe, for whatever reason, like some supernatural force of evil, it wouldn't be able to cross the running water roaring through the canyon far below.

He caught a fluttering glance of the swirling mass back on the first canyon ridge. Felt a flicker of hope. Then something punched into his back, hard. *Through* his back. Screaming pain and a violent jerk, and suddenly he was hanging freely over the canyon drop, gaping at the dark, wicked spike that had just punched its way out of his right breastplate, skewering him like a meat hook.

He grabbed dumbly at the thing, reaching helplessly for energy barriers and weapons systems that weren't there to reach. Stared disbelievingly as the bloody tendril morphed and twisted, spinning him around, curling and tightening around him, the pale orange radiance of his cooling blood evaporating from the HUD's spectral scopes as the swarm absorbed it. *Drank* it.

"Give it… back," he heard himself growl, past the pain of a pierced lung, numb fingers clenching tighter, hot rage coursing through his veins. Rage at the pain. Rage at the sight of this thing—this vile darkness—drinking *his* blood. Feeding on an instrument of the Lady. Ravenous for her Light. Mindlessly consuming.

It was a perversion of nature.

He felt Ex there with him, bristling at the existence of the swarm. Their teeth clenching in animal defiance as the thrumming appendage retracted, lifting them back across the canyon, utterly unconcerned by their growing rage. Nate beat his armored fists against the main arm, ripping large chunks clear only to watch them disintegrate to particles and race back into shape like self-assembling sand. He swung harder, the edge of his palm glowing with energy he hadn't known they had.

A moment of freefall as he cut through. A moment of hope.

Then the swarm shot back out with half a dozen tendrils and caught him by the legs and arms, driving him deeper onto the rejoining meat hook. He screamed pain and defiance, fighting on. Flailing just like the useless boy they all thought he was. Greedy Synth particulates drawing him in, cracking him open like some scrumptious snack. Drawing him back to the ridge he'd jumped from.

And there, at the furious heart of the swarm—a dark body coming into shape, roughly humanoid. Reaching out. Reaching for him.

*Mordred*, some terrified voice whispered at the back of his mind.

The swarm, tightening in around him, clinging to his every inch. Struggles weakening. Failing. Failing to stop this blackened scourge, just like they'd failed to protect the Beacon out in the Tarkaminen sector. Failed to protect all the devoured Light that even now might be coursing through this freak storm, somewhere deep beneath its churning surface.

*Stolen* Light.

"Give it back," he growled.

Stolen just like his blood. The swarm hefting him higher, thrumming carelessly on. Hungry. Endlessly hungry. That blackened figure, reaching out for more. Squeezing him dry.

"Fuck you," he growled. "FUCK YOU!"

He'd asked for this. Whined about frontlines and fighting the good fight. Here it was, reaching out to him, drawing him the last few meters to its deadly embrace.

His feet caught on the edge of the ridge. A moment's unexpected leverage. He planted hard, tapping reserves of strength from somewhere well beyond reason.

"Give. It. BACK!"

Then he tore away with everything he had.

What happened next, he couldn't have said. All he knew was that an explosion of light and sound lit the jungle night between them, punching through him, sending him flying, half-blind and fully scrambled, until he crashed through what felt like a hundred meters of jungle thicket, and at least a few trees.

"Ex," he gasped, when the turbulence was done and he lay panting in the dirt, every breath a blossoming inferno. *What the fuck was that?*

*I... don't know.*

He tried to raise his head. *Is it still coming?*

He was almost too tired to care at that point.

*I don't think so.*

Good enough. He gave up and let his head thud back to the upturned jungle soil, blackness wrestling with his vision.

*Perhaps you should rest, Nathaniel,* Ex said, tone grim. *I'll keep watch.*

*I've heard that one before,* Nate tried to think, but he was already gone.

CHAPTER 17

# PODDED

Dawn light cracked through the jungle canopy in cruel, twinkling shards, welcoming Nate to a fresh world of weird, and an even deeper landscape of pains.

"Fuck," he groaned, not even trying to sit up

*Good morning to you as well, Nathaniel.*

"I take it repairs are still ongoing?" he asked aloud, painstakingly testing the integrity of his innards. Ex seemed to have re-inflated his punctured lung, at least. As for the rest of the damage...

*Ongoing indeed,* Ex admitted. *Believe it or not, you should be thankful. I wouldn't have had much to work with at all after that fight if you hadn't clawed some of the stolen Light out of that peculiar swarm.*

*Is that what happened?*

*As far as I can tell, upon retrospective analysis.* Ex paused a moment. *Perhaps you might give me a warning next time you're about to tap a veritable goldmine.*

Nate frowned at the swaying jungle canopy. *You mean next time we're trapped on a Lightless planet, hunted by a—a whatever the hell that was?*

*Precisely,* Ex agreed, neatly glossing over the troubling memory of that dark figure at the center of the storm. *I might've captured more, had I had more than a few milliseconds to prepare.*

*You've got it, Ex.* Bracing himself, Nate sat up. The pain was no picnic, but it wasn't quite as bad as he'd have expected after an episode of *manhandling via meat hook.*

*As I said.*

*Thank you, Ex,* he thought, mentally annunciating every syllable. Then, mostly looking to change the topic: *So, daylight, huh?*

*Ah, yes. The weather. Classic. On that note, you'll be pleased to know I've clocked this planet's current night-day cycle at approximately 103 hours, based on our position and travel relative to the dusk line at landing.*

*And I'll be pleased by that, because...?*

*Because you seem rather set on busying yourself with trivialities rather than confronting the topic of the dark figure who nearly killed us last night. Pardon my lack of clarity.*

"Killed us," Nate echoed, testing the words at a whisper. *I mean, we would've... You could've... Right?*

*They eat Beacons, Nathaniel. That was no casual assassin. The Synth do not play by mortal rules. You know this.*

Nate looked around the jungle, not knowing what he expected to find. Certainly not any reassuring answers. At least he wasn't disappointed on that front. Nothing but exotic plants, as far as the eye could see—which, given the density of the greenery, wasn't far at all.

In the daylight, he was almost surprised to finally spot a few signs of animal life—flittering bugs and skittering amphibian-looking critters. A few curious chitters and chatters here and there. He'd been beginning to wonder if this place had any fauna at all, save for at least four—now one— feral Ooperians. After the eerie silence of last night, the soft sounds of the jungle's daylight existence were practically deafening, even if they did seem a bit... he didn't know what. Off. Ill. Like maybe, on some level, he wasn't the only one missing the Light.

"Well," he said, as much to himself as to Ex, pulling himself gingerly to his feet. "Guess we'd better get a move on, then." He thought about saying more, but what was there to say? Whatever that thing had been, whatever it was doing here, they didn't really have any choice but to keep moving, at least until they found more answers. It wasn't like Ex didn't more or less know exactly what was going on in his head, anyway.

A thoroughly unimpressed *Hmmph* was all Ex had to say about that.

NATE TOOK the first couple hours at a leisurely run, watching the projected distance to the mountain ticking down on his HUD with a kind of deter- mined mindlessness, trying not to think of dark figures, or the image of

Tessa's blood-drained face, or anything at all but the piston-like pounding of his boots on the jungle soil. The going wasn't any easier than it had been the night before—every minor annoyance of the terrain compounded by the jagged pain in his chest and the deepening hunger in his stomach. But at least the jungle felt slightly less haunted in daylight, if still not quite inviting.

At one point, Nate deigned to break the silence and ask Ex about the mustachioed, fancy-butler-esque likeness Nate had seen him take on more than once now. It was almost like the jungle had been waiting for his attention to lapse.

Something smacked his armored shoulder before he'd even registered the motion—hard and brutally fast. A chitinous spike, he dumbly registered, right before another one smashed down on his head hard enough to ring his bell through the helmet. He blinked his eyes clear just in time for something to yank him clean off the ground. The tentacles those long, curved spikes were attached to. Slimy, awful tentacles, reeling him up, up, toward—

"Agh!" Nate choked out, as he followed those dangling tentacles back to the hairy, amorphous *thing* in the tree above. By way of reply, the creature hissed at him with a mouth like a radial meat grinder.

Nate moved more out of repulsion than anything else, wriggling and ripping at the tentacles until the slack came, and his feet hit the ground. Tentacles still in hand, he planted his feet and heaved, tearing the thing from its perch and swinging it around like a freaking Olympic hammer toss.

*I'd call that a bronze effort, at best,* Ex offered, as Nate released, and they watched the hissing thing go crashing off through the jungle canopy in whirling flight. *Not entirely shabby, though. And I don't HAVE a mustachio, to answer your question,* he added, as if nothing had happened. *You simply... Bah. It's not worth trying to explain it when you're in this state.*

*What state?*

Ex hesitated. Somewhere in the distance, the jungle silence was punctuated with the crackle and thud of the tentacle spike monster breaking back through the canopy for landfall.

*Suffice it to say, your brain has an incessant need to employ familiar anchors, Nathaniel—visual and otherwise—when confronted with the bits of reality it's simply not ready to grasp. In other words...*

*It's complicated?* Nate guessed, when his companion's silence had stretched too long.

*To fifty percent of us, yes,* Ex murmured half-heartedly, clearly distracted by something else.

*Your support, as always, is the stuff of legends, buddy,* Nate thought, inspecting the sites of impact to make sure the thing hadn't breached his armor. *I'm fine, by the way,* he added, picking with a frown at the sizable hole still rent through his chest armor from last night, and thanking the Lady that first spike hadn't come down a few decimeters to the left.

*That's... good,* Ex said. *I think...*

Nate waited for his companion to finish the thought, hand tracing down to his mended side, mind following it, with a vague sense of unease, back to the memory of that unexplained shrapnel that had torn through him aboard the *Camelot*'s bridge at the kickoff of this entire shit show. He felt Ex's attention on a patch of jungle ahead. Felt it sharpening to something more like intention.

He started off at a jog by some unspoken agreement, aiming for the nearby patch, the flicker of curiosity dampened by some inexplicably deepening dread in his gut.

*Ah,* Ex murmured, as Nate pushed through one last particularly thorny thicket, and came across their next discovery. *I thought I sensed something. Damned interference.*

Nate was too busy gaping at the lightly smoking wreck ahead.

It was a *Camelot* escape pod. There was no mistaking it. And it was streaked with blood.

Nate stood there staring at the charred semi-clearing for several seconds, his stomach lurching between hope and panic. On Ex's nudge, he started cautiously forward, eyes darting everywhere for some clue. He was no tracker, but the signs of struggle seemed evident enough. Gouged soil and broken branches. Seared trunks and—

There. A spatter of dark blood. Nearly black.

More Ooperians?

He didn't know. Couldn't help but think of the bizarre tentacle monster he'd just chucked out of the area. A faint whiff of burnt hair lingered in the air, under the more prevalent smells of heated metal and charred jungle.

*Let me see that blood,* Ex said, indicating the patchy red streaked on the side of the escape pod. That blood looked a lot more human. Nate complied, scratching some of the dried stuff from the pod's hull and watching with an uncomfortable callback to last night's blood-drinking nanoswarm as Ex absorbed the sample. He waited silently as Ex tapped their critically low energy reserves to begin his analysis.

*Well,* Ex said, with the tone of someone making laundromat chit chat, *at least we have some soft confirmation that that may have indeed been the Camelot we saw last night.*

*I feel better already,* Nate thought, more than a little sarcastically. He looked over the scene again, trying to picture likely scenarios. Maybe signs of fighting were a good thing. Better than an empty, clueless pod? He didn't know. Whatever had happened here, at least it looked like his people had taken a shot at defending themselves. That was something. Hell, maybe they'd scared off the same pack of Ooperians who'd eventually found him.

Assuming they hadn't been eaten by a hairy tentacle monster.

*Let's see,* Ex said, indicating the black blood spatter this time. Nate gathered the sample, resisting the urge to pester his companion for the results. He didn't have to wait long, anyway.

*Amelia Sundercaste,* Ex said, pinging a HUD indicator on the escape pod blood smear. *Albeit with a few trace contaminants. And as for Sample Number Two... Well, I don't know what to make of this.*

*Is it Ooperian?*

*There ARE several commonalities, yes. But I could say the same thing about the genetic material of at least 37 other known species, and that's not even to mention that, well... Hmm.*

*Hmm?*

*Erm, yes,* Ex finally said. *Hmm.*

Nate waited a few apprehensive seconds, then tried again.

*Hmm?* Ex asked, clearly still distracted.

*What are we looking at, Ex?*

*Oh. That. Well, I stand by my initial assessment.*

Nate splayed his hands incredulously at the quiet clearing. *Which was?*

*That I most certainly don't know what to make of this.*

Nate spread his hands wider, waiting for more.

*Not sure I'd like to meet this thing in a dark alley, though,* Ex finally concluded. *You know, metaphorically speaking.*

*This thing? What thing?*

*Well,* Ex said, somehow managing to sound both totally distracted and also like this was all perfectly obvious anyway, *either Amelia was witness to a rather diverse blood orgy upon exiting that pod, or we're looking at the genetic material of some manner of hybrid, umm...*

"Ex!" Nate snapped aloud in his frustration, startling a few winged somethings from the trees. "Focus. A hybrid *what?*"

*A super predator! I don't know. Blackened hands with the nagging, Nathaniel. I'm running on low power mode here. Give me a break.*

Nate stood there considering that until the therapeutic drumming of armored fingers on armored thighs threatened to backfire and push him over the edge. *How do you even know this blood was Amelia's, and not, I don't know...*

*Some other random Atlantean who just so happened to wonder by the desolate lost planet jungle and hemorrhage on your nice escape pod?*

*Well, it could've been... Tor. Right? She's Atlantean.*

*Which is why I checked the sample against the central crew genetic registry, Nathaniel. Obviously.*

Nate felt his face scrunching. *And you have the crew's genetic registry on file because...*

*Because it's bloody useful, Nathaniel. Obviously.*

It seemed bloody creepy, more like it, even if Amelia herself *had* once pointed out that individual genetics were little more than spec sheets to her people—useful guidelines that pointed out probable aptitudes, weaknesses, and theoretical limits of each individual body. He doubted the Terran crew would feel so nonchalant about the rather intimate invasion of cellular privacy, but Ex was already past it, ranting on about whether Nate was going to pipe down and let him focus, or if he had any more pointless questions to get off his chest first.

Nate suppressed the urge to point out that *the most sophisticated superintelligence known to mankind* should hardly have trouble multi-tasking a chat with a petty little human—even if said superintelligence *was* operating in low power mode. Instead, he ground his teeth and looked around the crash site for the hundredth time in some futile attempt to feel less useless.

*There, there, Nathaniel. If it weren't for you, how would I walk over there and grab more samples from those bloody ferns?*

Nate rolled his eyes and went to service Ex's multiple request pings, wondering if they might be wasting time or resources at this point, trying *not* to wonder what had happened to Amelia. It wasn't a small amount of blood among those trampled ferns.

*Right? I'm rethinking the blood orgy theory. Honestly.*

He wasn't quite sure whether Ex was trying to lift his spirits or if maybe "low power mode" was simply calibrated to a slightly higher "insensitive asshole" setting. Either way, the more he thought of Amelia, and this potential super predator dragging her off through the bloodied foliage, the less he appreciated Ex's candor.

*Duly noted,* Ex said. *To wit, I think we're set here. It seems Amelia was not alone. I have a perfect match for Lieutenant Pierce here among the ferns, and two discrepant, highly modified Atlantean strains that suggest your Round Table squires were here as well.*

Nate considered the trampled trail from empty pod to chittering jungle, mind's eye playing out a hectic nighttime clash with some indiscriminate force of darkness—part freakish chimera of flesh and blood, part blackened nanoswarm ghost of Mordred LeFaye. Some unsettling whisper of déjà vu tugging the air. It couldn't have been the latter. He'd barely escaped that swarm himself last night. Low power mode or no, there was no way his crew would've survived that thing groundside.

Hence the trail of blood and wrecked jungle?

*Your words, not mine,* Ex said. *But now that you've said it, we might as well see where it leads, yes?*

~

YOU'RE *sure you've tried everything?* Nate asked some short time later, for what Ex's custom HUD "Snivel Alert" counter informed him was precisely the fourth time since they'd left the pod crash site.

*Of course I've tried everything, Nathaniel.*

*No contact with anyone?*

*No one.*

*Q nodes?*

*Still inexplicably inaccessible.*

*And still no luck with those Asgardian ships?*

*Still no... Oh.*

Nate slowed his pace on leaden legs, a flutter of hope rippling through his aching chest. *Oh? Oh, what?*

*Oh, nothing. I just wanted to see the look on your face. Of course I've tried the bloody Asgardians, Nathaniel.*

*You know what?* Nate growled, slowing further, thoroughly tempted to stop completely. Tired. More tired than he'd been since...

*I'm sorry, was that a rhetorical question?*

Nate snapped back to the jungle, where his zombie legs were still dutifully pounding dirt. *Obviously,* he shot back. Had he just fallen asleep running? *Just wanted to see the look on your*—"Shit!"

He watched with a kind of disembodied stupor as his reflexes took over, tucking him neatly under the first incoming tentacle spike he absolutely hadn't seen coming and catching the second in one armored hand as he rolled back to his feet. Then his brain caught up, pegging a second tentacle monster, and he ripped the thing down from its perch by one slimy appendage. A few second's struggles and a hard boot stomp later, it was done.

*Not bad,* Ex admitted. *We'll make a jungle explorer out of you, yet.*

Nate just turned away from the mess, far from excited about another gory kill, and started back on the path he could only hope would lead to answers.

*I've tried everything, Nathaniel,* Ex said, a bit more soberly, *I still don't understand what's happening on this planet, but I promise, you'll be the first to know when I do. Until then...*

*Find the Light. Find the crew. Fix the leak.*

He still wasn't even quite sure what he meant by "the leak." It was just what he and Ex had taken to calling the mysterious confluence of *somethings* that had somehow dropped a protoswarm on the Yggdrasian sector and led them here to Ginnungagap—assuming that *was* where they were, and that any of this was actually connected at all.

*That,* Ex agreed, *or find the Camelot and get us the hell off this rock. You know, not that we NEED backup, or anything,* he added a second later. *You're doing great, Nathaniel. Just great. Obviously. And yet—*

*I'd take Iveera over me, too, buddy. It's okay.*

*Oh, stop.*

*No, I'm serious, Ex. I know I've kinda been asking for this all along, but maybe—*

*No. STOP.*

Bone tired as he was, it took Nate an extra second to register the command, and he nearly fell over himself when he did. He ground to a halt, stumbling momentarily to his knees, trying to look everywhere all at once as he staggered back to his feet, sure he was about to be struck by a swinging tentacle or some other pouncing beast. There was nothing.

*Blackened hands, maybe it's a good thing we can't reach Ser Katanaga. Imagine her seeing you like this.*

*Yeah,* Nate thought, doubled over panting, *because I've been such a shining beacon of Knightly awesomeness all the other times she's seen me.*

*Strong point,* Ex agreed.

*I'm sorry, was there a REASON you wanted me to stop?*

*Ah. Yes, that. Over there.* A ping appeared on the HUD to the north, a couple of kilometers off the HUD-enhanced trail Ex had been helping him follow. *The signal's scrambled to nine hells and back, but I'm fairly certain I just caught a whiff of another Camelot pod.*

Ex might as well have tossed a cheeseburger and fries at his feet. Nate was running again before he knew it. Running hungrily. Heavy legs all but forgotten. He ran, smacking aside leaves, vaulting low thickets and one snapping trap plant, clipping a few trees, and generally making entirely more of a racket than was probably wise. He couldn't have reined himself in if he tried. Not until he laid eyes on the empty pod.

He slowed then, remembering some semblance of caution.

The pod was dented where it'd struck and felled a small tree on landing, but otherwise looked to be in fine shape. Open and empty. No one in sight. But also no blood or mysterious ichor spatters. That was something, at least. Even so, he felt his burst of hope waning, the heaviness settling back through his limbs with accrued interest.

He pushed aside a dense layer of fronds and approached the pod, keeping his weary senses peeled for any kind of trap. Ex pinged the thermal body signature above his head right before she spoke.

"Ah. It *is* you."

He looked up, recognizing the voice but not quite believing it until he spotted her there: Princess Elsavataryllianna Priatus, sitting in a tree. Or lounging, more like it. She was sprawled out in the smooth valley between three of the enormous tree's main branches, golden head resting on her hands, one shiny boot swaying leisurely back and forth from her crossed ankles.

Even dirt-stained and scraped up in the middle of a hostile jungle, she still managed to look like royalty.

She gave him a lazily satisfied smile, like she knew exactly what he was thinking beneath the helmet. Then, without a lick of warning, she slid sideways and came tumbling out of the tree in what quickly flowed into a graceful, twisting backflip. She alighted on the jungle dirt a good fifteen meters below with the weightless grace of a cat.

"Remind me never to board your ship's escape pods again," she said, rising from her landing crouch and delicately dusting herself off before shooting him an expectant look.

"Well then, where to next?"

"Huh?" He was staring, dumbstruck, suddenly gripped by the insane fear that she was going to evaporate away like some jungle mirage. By way of reply, she strode languidly up to him and laid her royal hands—well scuffed and scratched from climbing, he dimly noted—on his shoulders, like she had something exceedingly important to say.

"*Save me*, Ser Knight."

Nate popped the seals and pulled off his helmet, breathing the muggy jungle air, catching her perfumed scent, searching for something to say to that.

"Merciful Lady," she murmured, only then seeming to notice the bloody hole in his chest plate and the general air of hammered-to-shit-ness that clung to him and his battered armor, "what happened to you?"

"I—" he started, just before his legs cried *viva la revolución* and unceremoniously dropped him butt-first to the dirt, declaring an official end to their four-hundred-plus kilometer jungle hoofing, whether he liked it or not. He was shaking. From what, he couldn't say. Not until he looked back up to Elsa and realized just how desperately relieved he was to *see* someone —anyone—and, at the same time, just how goddamn terrified he was for his crew, wherever they were, whatever had befallen them.

It all hit him then. Everything he'd been holding back since they'd crashed down on this strange planet. And Elsa saw it all, watching him with those discerning golden eyes, reading it plain as day on his face that he didn't have answers, or hope, or even any proper semblance of a plan. She managed to whittle her observations down to two words.

"Well, shit."

"Yeah," Nate said, numbly bobbing his head as she settled on the downed log beside him. "Guess that pretty much sums it up."

CHAPTER 18

# RUINOUS

For a trek that'd started with him casually plowing through trees, it was kind of amazing, how difficult it was becoming for Nate to even hack aside a few vines and loose leaves.

"Admittedly, it's not quite what I had in mind when I set off for this life of rugged adventure," said a seemingly indefatigable Princess Elsa, picking her way through the greenery behind him. "But it's not so bad."

Somehow, he was breathing harder than she was. Possibly on account of the extra work playing Princess' trailblazer. Possibly on account of the lack of sleep, and the still very much unhealed torso wounds, and the several hundred kilometers of jungle terrain he'd already put behind.

*You forgot listening to the HER for the past five klicks*, Ex added.

It really said something that Ex went there instead of simply telling Nate to suck it up as he normally would've.

"Granted," Elsa continued somewhere behind, "I *had* rather hoped my brave Knight would have something in the way of a plan, when he found me. Perhaps even a bit of food and water. Or a hot bath."

Nate found himself drawing to a halt. When he turned to face her, she looked perfectly and politely nonplussed, like she couldn't imagine what was the matter. "Maybe you'd like to take the lead for a while," he offered, holding out his hand and brushing aside the next wall of fronds in invitation. "I'll check the planetary registry for the public baths."

"Oh, don't be silly," she said, touching him playfully on the chest. "I wouldn't want to impugn your chivalry, big strong man like yourself." Her nose wrinkled. "And I *certainly* wouldn't acquiesce to *public* baths. That simply would not do for the crown princess of Aesirheim."

For a second, Nate could only stare, thoroughly floored that, even here in a hostile jungle with absolutely nil in the way of civilization, she could still be so unflinchingly entitled. But then the haughty air thinned around her, and she showed him a grin that told him, almost conspiratorially, that she was at least a little bit fucking with him.

"People would talk," she added, lips curling just a touch more, "don't you think?"

"Yeah," Nate grumbled, pushing ahead into the brush, glad she couldn't see through his helmet that, for some infuriating reason, he'd almost smiled back. "Don't know what I was thinking."

Whatever glib comment was hovering on her lips, she didn't make it. Just fell back in line behind him, the two of them picking their way through an alien jungle at a pace Nate was increasingly beginning to worry was entirely too slow.

The blood trail had disappeared not long into the tracking—hopefully a sign that Pierce and the Round Table Atlanteans had at least had the luxury to stop and tend whatever wounds they'd suffered. What was left to follow was inconsistent and at times rather hard to spot, but even in low power mode, Ex was more than equal to the task of spotting footprints, broken branches, and ruffled greenery. Nate was starting to get an eye for it himself. Enough so that he'd noticed the one tiny detail Ex had failed to explicitly point out while scanning a disturbed patch of soil a few kilometers back: fine strands of platinum blond hair, plastered right where something roughly body-sized had clearly been dragged through the muck.

It was the only trace they'd seen of Amelia since the escape pod. And it'd been surrounded by the long, deeply clawed imprints of whatever the hell it was they were following. Maybe the thing had been carrying her since the escape pod and had tossed her down for a break. He didn't know, and Ex didn't speculate—as if avoiding the topic would do any good. They both knew Nate was thinking of little else.

The beast's trail picked up from there, resuming its startlingly long gait, gouged footprints disappearing for long stretches only to be replaced by claw marks high in the trees here and there, like the thing could fairly fly through its jungle habitat. Frankly, he wasn't sure how the hell Pierce and the Atlanteans had managed to keep on the trail. Ex seemed to have the beast's patterns figured well enough, but Nate would've been lost if it weren't for the more obvious signs of his crew's passage. Apparently, the Round Table meant business.

That, or Pierce had been one hell of a boy scout in a past life.

Nate trekked on, trying to focus attention on something other than the endless cycle of worry, mostly just landing on the unsettling mystery of what it was they were tracking, and whether or not it was one and the same with the dark thing that'd attacked him and Ex from the heart of the swarm last night. A couple of hours later—a couple of relentless hours of worrying and of Elsa hinting more than once (and not so subtly) that she wouldn't terribly mind if her brave Knight were to happen by a nice fowl to roast, or something of the sort—Nate came across as good an excuse as any.

He wouldn't have quite called the critter that came shooting through the foliage a rabbit—no more than he would've called the roaring creature behind it a dog—but it was a decent enough place to start. A tufty, vaguely lupine rabbit-thing, chased after by a knee-high, pale green, hairless blob on legs that looked something like the forbidden lovechild of a Komodo dragon and a large bulldog. And both were headed straight toward them.

Nate moved without thinking, plucking a stone from the ground and whipping it with a flick of the wrist, then pivoting into a backhand strike as the wild dragon-dog-thing caught sight of new prey and lunged. He felt his fist connect. Felt the rake of claws and the solid weight of the thing crashing against the strength of his own arm, barely aided by the dwindling power of his armor. Then the creature hit the dirt some ten meters off with a disgruntled *whoomph.*

*What in good graces is a snargladorf doing out here?* Ex asked—presumably to himself, as Nate was entirely too busy putting himself between Elsa and the frothing beast as it rolled back to wobbly feet. It snapped its powerful jaws, shaking off the blow, huffing an angry challenge. Nate braced himself to meet its next charge. Then, with one last snort, the thing puffed its bulbous green chest and turned to trot off into the jungle.

Nate watched it go, eyes peeled until—

*Wait, THAT was a snargladorf?!* he asked, Ex's words finally clicking, along with the sudden understanding as to *why* they had yet to set eyes on one of the so-called pets that Ex swore had been all the rage back in Arthur Pendragon's day.

*I know, right?* Ex said, clearly not following the source of Nate's surprise. *Out here in the jungle like it thinks it's some kind of predator.*

*Which it clearly is.*

*Well... Potato, potahto.*

*You told me they were small and useless.*

*Relatively speaking.*

*You compared them to corgis, Ex.*

*In my defense, I hadn't seen one in over a thousand years. And you might recall my memory banks were a bit fuzzy at the time. And besides—*

"Nice shot," Elsa said quietly beside him, giving Nate a welcome thread by which to extricate himself from Ex's developing rant. He followed her gaze over to the where he'd chucked his stone and was a little surprised to see he'd struck the rabbit-thing dead. He felt a flutter of guilt, shortly followed by a hesitant streak of pride. He couldn't help but be impressed he'd actually hit the thing on the fly with a freaking stone.

*Yes, yes. You're a regular Davy Crockett. Now are you going to eat that thing, or not?*

Nate grimaced at the thought, insides squirming even though—or maybe because—he already knew the answer. He looked up at the jungle canopy anyway, gauging their daylight only to remember that it was hardly in short supply, wondering regardless whether the nourishment was worth the time it would take. He remembered with a glance at Elsa that he wasn't the only one in need of energy and rest.

Helmet cover or no, Elsa seemed to read his intention well enough—even before his stomach gave a mournful groan.

She made a decidedly un-princess-like noise, wrinkling her nose.

"Are you hungry, or not?" Nate asked.

She just pursed her lips, looking generally disapproving.

He shrugged and trudged over, bending down to collect their rabbit-thing lunch—

And froze. Icy tingles creeping down his spine. Cold, terrible fear clutching his insides. Heart racing. The jungle darkening around them.

"Ex?" he gasped.

*I don't know.* Ex's voice was distant. Muffled.

Suddenly, out of nowhere, it felt like he was drowning.

There was an irritated growl. Ex's voice cutting through, a little clearer.

*Just breathe, Nathaniel. Focus, and breathe.*

He tried, trained mind fighting to get ahold of its frenzied counterpart, jungle lightening bit by bit, senses clearing, darkness receding. Elsa's hands crushing his arm. Tunnel vision, some detached corner of his mind noted. A panic attack. He was having a panic attack, or something like it.

Why?

He looked warily around, trying to make sense of the inexplicable weight still pressing down on his reptile brain.

A low growl rumbled from everywhere and nowhere, all at once. Fear crashing back in like a physical wave, ripping at his lungs and his mind. Elsa's tightening death grip. Ragged breaths in his ears. Something snapped above. A streak of black on the jungle canopy, then—

They both jumped as something struck the ground right behind them. A tree branch, Nate registered, fist cocked, heart thundering. Then a roar. Already distant. Still moving, fast. Retreating? For a split second, some tiny part of Nate thought to chase after the thing. The fear sloshed right back, sending his reptile brain recoiling like he'd touched a hot stove. He stared into the jungle, trying to untangle what'd just happened.

The loosening of Elsa's atomic death grip brought him back to reality, where she was releasing his arm, straightening back up to her proud height as if that might hide the fact that she was shaking, golden skin pale and waxen, lips trembling. Nate realized his own hands were shaking. He felt his better senses resurfacing, like they'd smelled the whole episode coming and had ducked under a rock for cover—or had been shoved, rather.

Whatever that was, it had been unnatural.

*Chemosignaling*, Ex murmured. *Partial match from the escape pod landing site.*

Nate looked back in the direction that black blur had disappeared, waiting for Ex to explain, acutely aware of Elsa watching him, aghast, searching for some explanation.

*Induced fear response*, Ex added distractedly, in response to Nate's vague query. *Possibly. I'm working on it.*

Add that to the list of fun jungle critters, then. Mind-controlling Ooperian glamour, spiked tentacle monsters, hungry snargladorfs, and now fear-spitting black blurs?

*Don't forget the nanoswarms and ominous silhouettes*, Ex chimed in—maybe mocking him, maybe not.

"Lovely place," Nate muttered under his breath, looking up to what little he could see of the sky through the jungle canopy. Barely midmorning by this nightmare planet's reckoning. It felt like it should've been midnight already—or at least late evening. He looked down to the nearly forgotten rabbit-thing still hanging limply in his left hand, and finally back to Elsa.

There were tears in her eyes, he was surprised to realize. But at least her shakes were calming, some composure returning as she wiped them hurriedly aside and met his gaze with something like a challenge in her eyes.

"I'll start a fire," was all he could think to say.

He'd never been so hungry in his life.

~

"PERHAPS I *SHOULD HAVE MARRIED* that spiteful shell of a man."

Beside the crackling campfire, Elsa was frowning at the hunk of charred meat Nate had just handed her on a broad, ruffled leaf.

"Not to dismiss your valiant efforts out of hand," she added, with a conciliatory tilt of her golden head. "I merely struggle to identify the lesser of evils between sharing Phaldissus' bed and eating this, um…"

"Rabbit-thing," Nate provided, taking a hearty bite of his cut and nearly gagging as the hot, greasy juices gushed forth, trickling down his chin. "Tastes like chicken," he croaked.

It most certainly did not.

He chewed and swallowed anyway, determined to keep it down—both as a point of pride and also for whatever hypothetical nourishment he'd gain from the exercise, provided he actually managed to digest the foul meat. It really didn't taste like something that belonged in a human stomach. And it smelled worse—like rotten fruit soaked in gasoline.

*A harmless peptide deterrent,* Ex promised. *Useless, too, if that snargladorf's actions were any indication. But I assure you that you and our dear princess will live. Albeit possibly with some slight gastrointestinal distress.*

Nate took another disgusting bite, beyond caring at that point.

He was exhausted, his aching stomach crying for food far in excess of each bitter bolus of half-chewed rabbit-thing he forced laboriously down. It was hard to believe how much he'd taken the last year for granted, perpetually dosed up on a well-rounded platter of Ex's Super Sleep and Sundry Special Sauces.

*I'll ask that you kindly remember those words next time we have the Light to spare.*

They were both distracted from Nate's lack of a satisfactory comeback by the sight of Elsa lifting her cut of fillet de rabbit-thing to her royal mouth on the far side of the small fire. She nibbled delicately at one charred edge with a cautious expression. Then, to Nate and Ex's supreme surprise, she shrugged, gave a quiet, "I suppose I've had worse," and dug in like a proper jungle survivor.

*Just full of surprises, isn't she?* Ex mused.

Nate leaned his head back against the tree trunk, declining to comment. Too tired to comment. Mostly, he just found himself oscillating between daydreams of hot showers, clean sheets, and his nice, cool room aboard the *Camelot*. What he wouldn't have given for the trifecta...

If he hadn't been more than a little worried that the fearsome black blur or some other lurking beasties might well come dropping down on their heads at any moment, he might've been tempted to pry his armor off. Between their anemic energy stores and Ex's admittedly rational move to conserve everything he could, for the first time since Nate had ever called it from e-dim, the armor seemed to be weighing him down more than it was helping. And that was to say nothing of the increasingly grungy internal situation, given the shared reduction of climate control and waste management systems.

*I told you, Nathaniel. Everybody poops. There's no shame in being an excrement-laden meat bag. Besides, we need the energy.*

*Don't remind me,* Nate thought back, queasily eyeing his next bite of charred rabbit-thing.

*Whoever would've guessed it?* Ex prattled happily on anyway. *An Excalibur of the divine Lady—the epitome and crowning achievement of all known technology in the universe—reclaiming his own Knight's waste just to keep on—*

"So, uh..." Nate said aloud, searching for some serviceable course of conversation with Elsa—anything to drown out Ex's ongoing musings. "Why *not* marry Phaldissus?"

He wasn't quite sure why that was the first question to find its way out of his mouth, not leastwise because it was a patently *stupid* question from anyone who'd been on that Vanaheim docking platform—and probably from anyone who'd ever met Phaldissus. The look on Elsa's face seemed to convey as much, albeit politely.

"Is it not enough that I find the man repulsive?"

Nate inclined his head, conceding the point. From what he'd gathered of Eldari politics and the Supreme Chancellor's reactions, it actually probably *wasn't* enough—not by a long shot. But that all felt pretty far behind them now.

Silence settled back between them, filling the void of non-conversation over the crackling fire and the chitters of the surrounding jungle.

"There was someone else," she said after a while, almost to herself. She was staring into the dancing flames.

Nate found himself frozen, waiting for more, captivated by this unexpected hint of something more, something vulnerable—sure that he'd only spook her out of sharing, were he to open his mouth. In the background, Ex vibrated amusement at Nate's apt self-awareness. When the silence stretched on, though, Nate couldn't help himself.

"What happened?"

"They sent her to meet the stars," Elsa whispered, staring through the fire now. She seemed to have forgotten where she was. "A lesson in propriety. Mustn't squander royal blood. Mustn't."

"She was…" Nate didn't know what he was trying to ask.

"Asgardian." From light-years away, Elsa returned to consider him across the crackling fire. "She was the best person I've ever known."

"I'm… sorry, Elsa."

She straightened, face tensing like she'd only just remembered to whom she was speaking.

"That is not my name," she said, tossing the last bite of her meat aside and rising to her feet. Something in her voice left him feeling raw, scolded. Like maybe some part of this was his fault. But that was just empty guilt, talking. *Ruinous empathy,* he'd once heard it called—maybe jokingly—on some show.

"We should keep moving," she said, not meeting his eyes, "shouldn't we?"

Ruinous empathy or not, he felt bad. She was upset. Composed as she normally was, that much was evident enough in her restless shifting. She looked around the jungle, fingering her pendant.

Her pendant.

"I'll just find my own way then, shall I?" she said, turning irritably for the jungle.

"Wait," Nate murmured, too quietly for her to hear, still stuck on that pendant. He'd nearly forgotten about Ex's comments—the fine projectiles that'd inexplicably ripped their way through the *Camelot's* bridge. Through *Tessa.* He saw the look on her face in his mind's eye, the blood stemming from her wounds.

Louder. "Wait."

The princess slowed at the edge of their small campfire clearing, looking warily back.

"What happened on the *Camelot…*" he started. Something about her words, *to meet the stars.* Something in the way she insisted on calling her rocks celestial bodies, and in the defensive edges creeping into her posture now. "I saw the way you were clutching that pendant up there, when the shit hit."

Her face darkened. "I didn't…" She pursed her lips, slipping on some royal composure. "I don't know what happened up there any more than you do."

"But you know your *celestial bodies* were involved somehow."

"No. That's not… That's simply—"

"Weirder than getting yanked halfway across a star system by a glowing planet and hunted by a… whatever the hell that thing was?" Nate asked, gesturing vaguely in the direction their black blur had taken flight. "I've seen more," he added, tapping pointedly at the ugly puncture in his breast-plate. "That's just cracking the surface. So don't tell me that it's impossible."

For once, she seemed off-balance, working through multiple false starts before she finally heaved a resigned sigh and came closer. She looked around the campfire site like she was contemplating sitting back down for this, then settled for crossing her arms and staring down at him, holding the high ground.

He waited for her to start explaining.

She just stared.

"You wanna tell me what the real deal is with your rocks?" he finally asked.

A faint scowl flicked across her face at the mention of *rocks*, but it faded quickly enough. "It's personal."

Nate held her gaze, waiting. There was obviously more.

"It's silly," she said.

He kept waiting, her flawless Eldari brow wrinkling with growing irritation as he failed to relent.

"Fine," she sighed. "After…" Golden fingers drumming on crossed arms. "After I'd learned my *lesson*, I went looking for her. For her body. They'd… They'd left her out there, you see, and…" Soft lines of grief turned hard, her attention rousing back from memory to focus on him with renewed frustration. "And this really isn't any of your damned business, Knight. My celestial bodies have nothing to do with any of this."

Nate studied her, feeling uncharacteristically calm. He wasn't used to being the one in control in these conversations.

"You took something to remember her by," he guessed.

It wasn't much more than a thin intuition, but he saw it in her face that he was close enough.

"Everyone needs a hobby," she said, frowning at the fire. "Especially those of us doomed to lives consumed by empty sycophancy and the greedy touch of one who knows nothing of giving."

"So that's why you started collecting your… celestial bodies?"

Her face darkened. "Not exactly. It was…" She chewed on her next words, expression simultaneously begrudging and accusatory, like she resented being pumped like this but was also secretly kind of relieved for the chance to get it off her chest. "It was something we did, Annithia and I. Deep space trysts. Unscheduled detours. I'd make a show of gallivanting around the galaxy on daddy's yacht like a good, spoiled princess is supposed to do. No one was ever supposed to know, but, well…" She tilted her head expressionlessly, like he already knew the rest.

He waited patiently, still not quite sure where this was going.

"We'd walk together sometimes, afterward. Suit up and go exploring. She loved drifting in the expanse, just the two of us. Loved asteroids, too." She shook her head at some memory. "Nearly got herself killed more than once, trying to get in close. But she always snagged one for me to keep. A souvenir for each forbidden triumph of ours. She used to say it was… Well, it doesn't matter now."

"Sounds like maybe it does," Nate said quietly.

Her face hardened. "It. Doesn't. Matter," she repeated, pointedly annunciating each word. "I was a heartbroken girl, and I wanted a rock to remember my lover. It was sheer dumb luck that the asteroid I captured from her final resting place happened to be… different."

"Different?" Nate asked, Ex's words and flashes of *Camelot* shrapnel shifting with a dozen other disjointed pieces in his head, some ineffable intuition suddenly certain he knew exactly what she was talking about, even if he couldn't begin to understand how.

"I don't remember exactly *why* I got it in my head to look at her final souvenir under the advanced optics that day. I suppose I'd exhausted myself on the macroscopic features. I'd spent an inordinately unhealthy amount of time, staring at that rock, looking for something that wasn't there. At least not until I looked closer."

"Nanoparticles," Nate murmured, watching again in his mind's eye as that strange wave struck the *Camelot*, yanking it cross-system, yanking a thousand tiny *somethings* straight out through the viewport.

"It was nothing," she said, reading the look on his face well enough. "I had the particulate analyzed. It was all perfectly normal. Rare enough that it wasn't present on any of my other souvenirs, but such particulates are not at all unheard of throughout the galaxy, even if the so-called experts can't seem to agree on what exactly they're made of."

"I might have a theory."

"Then you find yourself in good company. Everyone I spoke with had a theory. Higher dimensional residues and partially annihilated exotic matter condensates and so forth. Some simply called it 'the dust' and left it at that. Probably the wise move. I've always wanted to believe it was something more than random star dust, but I've seen no evidence to support the notion."

"No evidence," Nate heard himself whisper, somewhere in the distance.

He felt dizzy. Tectonic plates shifting beneath his feet.

Unidentified particulates.

Inexplicable flechette.

*More* than random star dust.

Ripping its way toward Ginnungagap.

He felt sick. Worse, Ex did too. No derisive laughter. No *calm your squishy superstitions, Nathaniel.* No anything.

"You're telling me this stuff is everywhere?"

"No." Elsa was maddeningly calm. "I'm telling you it's *not*. Which is precisely why I became infatuated with this silly idea that maybe…"

She let out a heavy breath, shaking her head at the chittering canopy above as if to ward off that silly idea. Nate's mind churned on, spiraling down and out into the void, wondering why, in the name of the Lady, she hadn't told him all of this sooner. Except… tell him what, exactly? What *should* she have told him? He wasn't even rightly sure what she was telling him now—or what he was to make of it.

He realized he'd missed whatever she'd just said.

*Her lost lover,* Ex provided. *She wanted to believe some part of her was preserved in the dust.*

*And that maybe,* his mind filled in the blank, *if she could only find enough of it…*

The princess dropped his gaze the moment he focused back on her. But not before he saw the expression there, hovering just beneath the surface. Wistful longing. Hopeless hope. Like maybe, even though she knew damn well he wasn't going to have the answers… maybe. Just maybe.

"It doesn't matter now," she told the campfire.

Nate stared blankly through her, lost in the breadth of it. The distant ache of sympathy. The chances that Elsa would find that particular rock. That she'd then end up stuck here with Nate. That the two of them would even meet at all, in a galaxy of trillions.

*The Lady works in mysterious ways, Nathaniel. You know that more than most.*

He couldn't argue with that any more than he could make sense of this.

There was something there. Something his spinning head was too tired or simply too small to pull together. Something unmistakably, profoundly wrong about whatever was happening here. Someone needed to hear about this. Iveera. Zedavian. The Merlin. If he was right about this...

Christ, someone needed to hear about this.

But he couldn't reach any of them.

He considered the princess, the only one he could reach at the moment, reluctant to believe that this was the way it was meant to be. But here they were, either way.

"Thank you for telling me, Els... Elsavataryllianna."

She stirred from her revery and wrinkled her nose distastefully. "Oh, just call me Elsa, if you truly must. It's better than listening to you butcher it. Now, can we get moving?"

She didn't wait for a response. Just stalked off into the jungle at a decidedly stubborn pace.

"As you wish, Highness," he murmured to the empty clearing—only to realize it wasn't quite empty.

The snargladorf was watching him.

It lurked in a thicket between two great trees, bare green snout peering out from beneath a gnarled root, unmoving. It knew it'd been spotted. He was pretty sure of that by the way it seemed to freeze in place that much more intently, like a house cat spotted mid-sneak.

Unthinkingly, he chucked the last gristly bit of his charred rabbit-thing its way.

The thing did its best to maintain its stealthy freezing act and wary disposition, but even across the clearing he could practically feel its taut muscles quiver with excitement.

"Better you than me," he said.

He felt Ex watching the exchange curiously. Felt oddly self-conscious, all of a sudden. Then, remembering they had a black blur and Lady knew what else on the loose out there, and that Elsa didn't exactly know where she was going, he rocked to his tired feet and started after the princess, setting the snargladorf out of his mind.

A hungry scarfing noise followed him out of the clearing.

There was a moment of mild panic as he failed to spot Elsa through the dense, weaving jungle way. Then his better senses caught up—along with Ex's HUD indicators—and he set off after her physical trail. He caught a glimpse of her ahead a minute later, just in time to see her disappear through a dense wall of fronds and jungle greenery.

Her distant gasp sent his heart lurching, mind roaring to life with dark monsters and terrible certainty. He charged forward across the gap, cursing himself. Tore through the fronds, expecting the worst.

And ran straight into her royal highness.

"Merciful Lady," she hissed, as they stumbled together, and Nate got more of a handful than he meant to in his hasty effort to right their collective balance. "That story was *not* an invitation to lay your grimy hands on me, Knight."

"Sorry," Nate stammered, hands raised in innocent surrender as he backed off. "Sorry, I thought you were..." His gaze trailed out across the open stretch of peculiar gray landscape, to the structures beyond. "In... danger. Huh."

"That's what I said," she agreed, "moments before being groped by a presumptuous Terran."

"I said I was sorry," Nate pointed out.

She might've had more to say about it, but they were both too busy staring at the compound ahead—a long and low stretch of simple, boxy gray structures. Old prefabs, maybe, that looked to have become more permanent fixtures. Some standing as separate installations, most strung together into a single U-shaped structure. Extremely old and extremely abandoned, judging by the level of vegetation and general dilapidation.

*New Avalon*, came those troubling words of Ex's *last LeFaye*. That's what this reminded him of. The ruins of Avalon.

It looked like the better half of the main structure had burned down at some point. And something about the flat gray terrain that stretched out around the place, spreading toward that mountain...

"You don't suppose they have baths in there?"

Elsa's tentative voice brought him back to reality. He looked at her, processing, taking in her expression. Then her words landed, and he couldn't help it. He laughed. Amazingly enough, she did too. For a moment, they wrapped themselves in something startlingly close to friendly camaraderie. Then the moment passed, and the cheer dwindled, the silent weight of Ginnungagap settling back in.

He eyed the distant structures and the looming mountain several kilometers beyond.

"Guess there's only one way to find out."

## CHAPTER 19

# RESIDUE

"Well," Nate declared, kneeling at the edge where the damp jungle soil—and, coincidentally, any trace of Pierce and the Atlanteans—gave way to the strange grainy gray ground surrounding the compound, "this planet keeps getting weirder and weirder."

"Some of those burn marks look fresh," Elsa said. "Relatively speaking." She was squinting at the distant main structure from back where Nate had bidden her to wait.

"No, not that. I mean, this is…" He hesitated midway through gesturing at the non-dirt, thinking about everything she'd just told him about her lost Asgardian, Annithia, and her quest to scour the universe for the mysterious dust. "Elsa, I think this is…"

*It is,* Ex confirmed. *As far as I can tell, at least.*

Elsa was following Nate's attention to the dark ground, with its decidedly unnatural texture—like someone had splashed a lake-sized bucket of carbon fiber across black sands and forgotten to clean it all up. Her eyes widened as she understood.

"No," she breathed. "That's…"

*Not possible,* were the words he assumed she was looking for. She didn't clarify. Just joined him in gaping at the vast stretch of strange terrain that stood between them, the compound, and the mountain beyond.

*On a side note, she's not wrong about the burn marks,* Ex said. *That's forensically curious.*

"Weirder and weirder," Nate muttered to himself, frowning from the compound back down to the line where normal ground met the bizarre. *Is this even safe to cross?*

*Define 'safe.'*

*How about 'not gonna come alive and eat us,' for starters?*

*Or otherwise stab, maim, or molest at the malevolent behest of an as-of-yet-unidentified dark spirit?* Ex clarified.

*Exactly. You get it.*

*Excellent. Well, in that case... I have absolutely no idea.*

"What are you two talking about?" Elsa asked.

"Nothing. Just checking a few things." He hadn't told her about his run-in with the Dark Lord of the Swarm. Didn't see any reason to, really. At least not until he could put any kind of name or explanation to it. All he really knew was that all roads seemed to lead to that damned mountain, and as far as he could see, this sea of dark gray... *nanostuff* seemed to cover the entire multi-kilometer stretch between them and it.

"You know what?" he said, turning back to Elsa. "Maybe you should, uh—"

"Hang back here to be eaten by that black terror while you go on ahead to make sure it's safe?"

He closed his mouth, reassessing his half-formed plan.

"Maybe just stay here for a minute and make sure this stuff doesn't immediately try to eat me?"

She considered the terrain, then tilted her head in concession. "Fair enough."

"Good." He bobbed his head, turning back to the field. "Good."

The first step was a little too *Indiana Jones and the Last Crusade* to inspire confidence, his foot hanging over the dark sands by its own volition, reticent to touch down, mind diligently playing back the episode from the previous night. Nanostuff creeping up his boots. Angry swarm kicking up to chase him through the dark jungle.

"So glad you're here to protect me," Elsa called.

He shot a thumbs-up over his shoulder, then braced himself and stepped forward.

Nothing.

No movement. No rushing wave of fury bursting up to meet him.

Nothing but the faintest whisper of...

*Verrry curious*, Ex said.

*I'm not imagining it?* Nate asked. He took another step forward, senses peeled, and was pretty sure he felt the answer for himself: the faintest echo of Lady's Light.

*I can't quite seem to touch it*, Ex agreed. *But it's there. Somewhere.*

He took a few more steps, blind hope warring with caution, but there was nothing more. No blessed treasure trove of Light. No upward gradient to speak of. Just that pale, flat whisper, barely an echo. A reflection on translucent glass. He turned back to Elsa, discouraged, his inner pessimist quietly and assuredly deciding that he had fallen for the trap after all, and that this would surely be the moment the dormant nanostuff exploded up to swallow him whole.

Elsa was watching him with one arm crossed, the other propped up by the elbow, fingers delicately perched beneath her chin like she was studying some museum exhibit—or waiting for exactly the same thing.

"So," he called, splaying his hands like *guess that's that*. "What do you think? Take a peek inside the creepy ruins, then?"

She made a face and turned her chin hand up in a fractional shrug. He shrugged back.

They were met by a blissful lack of springing traps and dark apparitions as Elsa stepped carefully onto the gray stretch and started across its textured sands. He went to meet her on eggshells, and they continued toward the compound in the same manner, sticking closer together than they otherwise might've—though whether that was Elsa's doing or his own, Nate wasn't quite sure. He was too busy scanning for threats, waiting for the other foot to fall. After the constant chittering of the jungle, the quiet of this place was unsettling—the air thinner, more sterile. Dark nanostuff oddly solid yet silent beneath their boots.

They reached the compound unmolested, save for the angry shriek of some shrouded, beaked creature that cajoled them from within the shadows of the fire-exposed second floor. It took flight on membranous wings as they neared, angling off toward the jungle with a series of caws that might've been meant in taunt or reprimand. Maybe in warning.

*There's that squishy Terran superstition, rearing its ugly head*, Ex said.

Nate ignored the comment, too busy studying the way the dark cover of the nanostuff ended just shy of the compound structure walls, skirting the perimeter as if it were held at bay by some forcefield, afraid to touch whatever was inside.

"That's not ominous," Elsa said, under her breath. But even so, neither of them particularly lamented leaving the sea of nanostuff behind for the refuge of something clearly manmade. Especially not when Ex picked up signs of Pierce and the Atlanteans leading into the open wreckage of the first floor.

*By the way,* Ex added, as Nate scanned what he could make out of the dusty, dilapidated interior. *I believe you've made a new friend.*

Nate looked around, not sure what he was talking about until Ex pinged it on the HUD and dialed out the optics. There, from the cover of the jungle, Nate could just make out the snargladorf watching them, bulbous head resting on its oversized paws, like it was content to merely rest and see what happened next.

"Great," he murmured, turning back to the matter at hand.

"I don't imagine you're expecting *me* to go first?" asked Elsa, from over where she was still ogling the depths of the ruins.

He spread his hands to broadcast the dramatic scoff she couldn't see behind his helmet. "What kind of Knight do you take me for, your Highness?"

"Not the kind who comes equipped with a plan, apparently. Speaking of which—"

"I told you—"

"Find the Light, find the crew, fix the leak," she repeated diligently. "Which all sounds well and good, but for the fact that you cannot explain precisely what you mean by two-thirds of those objectives, not to mention that what remains is not rightly a plan at all, so much as a hopeful wish."

"Yeah, well"—he crouched over one of Pierce's light bootprints in the dust and ash, not really needing a closer look so much as wanting to point out that it was there—"potato potahto, right?"

"What?" she asked, and he was somewhat smugly pleased to see genuine confusion in the sidelong frown she shot him.

He tapped the bootprint and rose, thumbing his chest. "I'm gonna go find my crew," he said, stepping past her and not looking back. "You're welcome to stick to your own plan, Princess."

*Look at you, being all confident,* Ex said. *Look out, Ginnungagap! Big Man coming through!*

Behind them, Elsa was muttering something about arrogant boys and stupid plans. But she was also following, and Ex seemed to be in bright enough spirits, so Nate decided to roll with the punches and ignore them both as he entered the scorched remains of the compound.

Surprised as he still was to have found anything of manmade origins at all on this bottomless pit of a planet, there really wasn't all that much to see once they made it past the worst of the damage. Just a string of mostly empty rooms, haphazardly strewn with archaic bits of equipment that took even Ex a few moments to place, corroded and dusty as they were. Research equipment. All fairly standard by Ex's reckoning, minus the fact that it was all at least a millennium outdated.

They followed Pierce's tracks through the ash and dust, not speaking. Through the fire-damaged wall of a second-story corner, Nate glimpsed the snargladorf sniffing distrustfully at the border of the dark gray terrain outside, bulbous head cocked to the side. He focused back on the tracks and moved on. The place looked to have been ransacked more than once over the years, though by looters or wild animals, Nate couldn't have guessed. The rather creepy number of rusted cages—all of them open—not to mention the faded stains on the walls and floors, all seemed to suggest maybe the latter. Maybe this had been a place for animal experiments, he thought. Or some kind of black site prison or torture camp, he loosely amended, when they found the wing of reinforced cells that were very much sized for more sentient Alliance species.

Whatever had been going on here, he doubted someone had dragged all this equipment to this off-the-map hellhole because their work had been morally praiseworthy.

Ex kept his guesses to himself, other than to indicate that, if ever there had been any kind of records or a central control node for what few scraps remained of the structure's basic subsystems, they must've been consumed in the fire.

*Speaking of which,* he added, as they slowed at a convergence in the dust prints that seemed to suggest Pierce and the Atlanteans had paused here to pace and discuss, *judging by the pattern of spread, it would seem that the blaze did not die of natural causes, so to speak.*

Nate was staring at a thick smear of blood on the wall, where one of their people must've leaned for a break. It took Ex's words an extra second to land.

*Someone put it out?*

*Or something. And quite recently.*

Nate considered the smeared wall again. It was a lot of blood. A souvenir from their scrape at the escape pod? Or fresh wounds?

*How recently?* he wondered, looking around for any other sign.

*Weeks, maybe. But... Hmm.*

Maybe by some shared thread of his companion's focus, Nate noticed the prints a moment later, tracking through the far side of the room, where the shadows were thick enough that his HUD vision had to do the heavy lifting.

"Huh," he echoed. "That's strange."

Elsa stirred from her inspection of the bloodied wall. "What's strange?"

"These prints," Nate said, walking carefully over for a closer look. Human-shaped—Terran or Atlantean, probably—but smaller than Pierce's. "They're new. Different, I mean. Someone else was here."

*Right?* he added silently to Ex.

"Someone other than Pierce and the Atlanteans," he continued aloud for Elsa's benefit, a spark of hope fluttering through his chest as Ex confirmed his amateur deduction. "These prints are smaller than Pierce's. Could've been an Atlantean, maybe," he said, thinking of Amelia, somehow knowing that wasn't the answer. "Or maybe…"

*It wasn't Tessa,* Ex said.

"Or maybe it was a very tiny Asgardian who smelled of elder flowers and juggled teacups left-handed," Elsa suggested—probably sarcastically. He only half-heard her anyway.

*How do you know?* he thought back to Ex, still thinking of Tessa, not bothering to do Ex the injustice of trying to pretend otherwise.

*Too old,* Ex said. *Unless, of course, your girlfriend experienced some manner of spacetime hiccup on the way down, relative to us. Not impossible, I suppose. But the age of these prints appears to correspond more neatly with the likely age of the fire damage.*

Nate studied the room from the new lens of a potential arsonist. It didn't get him any closer to making sense of any of this. He realized Elsa was still watching him with a politely incredulous expression. "Yeah, sorry," he said, shaking his head as he wiped his hands off and stood from the crime scene. "I'm not getting 'Asgardian little person' from these prints."

"And why exactly do you care?" She pointed in the other direction. "Your people clearly went that way, and I don't see any other crew members hiding underneath that table there, so *maybe* we should—Wait, where are you going now?"

"I'm gonna see where these lead."

"What is this, a treasure hunt?"

"I thought you wanted adventure."

"I thought *you* wanted to find your crew, not some bloody"—she waved a frustrated hand—"mystery person. Interloper. Whatever."

"It's mystery solving 101."

"I don't know what that means."

"Everything's connected. It's always tied together in the end."

"That's…"

*Stupid*, Ex said, as she searched for the words.

"… Moronic," Elsa finished.

*Ah, no, she's right. Moronic. That's much better. You know, I really am starting to like her, Nathaniel.*

"Listen, you two can laugh it up all you want—"

"So, your Excalibur *does* agree with me."

"—But *I'm* gonna follow this trail, because I don't know if you noticed, but we're not exactly flush with options here. Worst case scenario—"

"We get eaten?"

Nate paused, mid-turn. "Well, I was gonna say 'we waste a little time and then loop back around to pick up Pierce's trail.' But yeah. I guess there's that, too."

She didn't say anything more. Just extended a prim hand in the universal sign for, *lead the way then, asshole,* and crossed her regal arms in a rather disconcerting haughty princess pose.

He bowed and set off to do just that, hoping to the Lady this wasn't a supreme waste of time.

~

"It's possible a gentleman should never say 'I told you so,'" Nate said ten minutes later, as they emerged into the dusty courtyard area running through the center of the U-shaped compound and Nate caught sight of encouraging signs. "But—"

"*But* you found a chance convergence of tracks," Elsa finished for him, "and are perfectly eager to assume it actually *means* something, even without the faintest bit of proof."

Nate closed his mouth, frowning at the filthy statue at the center of the otherwise barren courtyard, surprised she'd picked up the faint footprints with her naked eyes.

*Eldari eyes,* Ex reminded him.

"I'm not blind," she confirmed, striding glibly past him. "And you, Ser Arturi, are not so much of a gentleman."

"Ouch," Nate said, rubbing self-consciously at the back of his neck.

"Come now," she said, wrinkling her nose at the corroded, greenish mess of the statue, and giving it a wide berth. "We might as well see where your treasure trail leads."

"So, you *are* on board, then," Nate said, falling in beside her, seeing on second glance that the statue's greenish-white hue was thanks not to copper corrosion but to what looked like multiple layers of bird shit and other donations from the surrounding jungle critters. Through the foul veneer, he could just make out what looked like the weather-worn shape of a humanoid figure rising from the waves of stone, holding aloft something that must've been taken by time, gravity, and/or angry jungle birds, right along with the statue's hands.

"You'll recall I never explicitly said I wasn't," Elsa's voice cut in.

He turned from his inspection of the crumbled ground remnants—what looked like a spear and shield, along with a few other indecipherable wrecks—and shot Elsa an incredulous sideways glance. "Will I, though?"

*Lovely as this all is,* Ex said, *if you're quite done flirting, I should—*

*What?* Nate snapped.

*What?* Ex shot back, like he didn't understand. *I'm reading—*

*This is so not flirting, Ex. No way in hell.*

*Very well, then. My mistake. If you're quite finished NOT flirting, you might as well know I'm reading thruster residues throughout the courtyard, most concentrated right up—*Ex dropped a color-scaled gradient overlay on Nate's HUD, pinging a point around the corner up ahead—*there. I suspect our potential arsonist may have set down here, and... Oh. Oh?*

"Oh?" Nate asked, drawing a look from Elsa.

*That can't be right,* Ex muttered.

"Oh *what*, Ex?" Nate started to say. Only it came out as more of an, "Oh whaaat the hell?" as they rounded the corner, and he got a look at the gray stretch of flat terrain ahead. He blinked a few times just to make sure it wasn't some jungle hallucination—then glanced back to make sure that, one, Elsa was actually still there, and that, two, she was seeing the same thing he was. Check, and check.

He blinked again and looked back to the landing pad, gaping at the inexplicable sight of the *Kalnythian Wilds* sitting there on a bed of dormant nanostuff.

"See?" he heard himself murmur somewhere far away, head buzzing with a kind of dreamlike fuzziness. "Told you so."

Maybe that explained the weird pressure he'd been ninety percent sure he was imagining in this place. Mostly, it just opened the door to five billion new questions.

The rest of the details started catching up. The subtle pallor of the ship. The marked absence of the ineffable vitality he'd come to expect from a Knightship's presence. The way the ground—a continuation of the dark gray sea of nanostuff from the other side—had begun to subsume the vessel whole, covering its landing legs completely, creeping up to latch onto—*into*—the ship's underbelly.

He started forward, some part of him hoping, irrationally, that somehow, he'd find Iveera aboard. That somehow, since the last time he'd spoken to her barely a day ago, she'd managed to not only recover her stolen Knightship but also somehow follow the Synth trail to Ginnungagap and beat him here. One of Ex's spacetime hiccups, maybe.

He made it about two steps and two more futile hopes before someone —*not* Iveera—popped out of the main hatch, humming plasma rifle raised. Nate froze, hands held where the shooter could see them, mind racing.

At the top of the ramp, Pierce lowered his weapon, blinking bloodshot eyes.

He looked like hell as he croaked his first words.

"What took you so long?"

## CHAPTER 20
# A PIRATE'S LIFE

"What the fuck took you so long?" Pierce repeated, staring Nate down with the sunken eyes of a man who'd been through entirely too much in the past twenty-some hours. It was only after a few takes that he seemed to notice Nate's matching hammered-shit appearance. "The hell happened to you?"

"Same thing that happened to all of us," Nate said. "This planet."

"I told you," Tor said, appearing behind Pierce at the top of the *Kalnythian Wilds'* boarding ramp, "the Lady has forsaken this place. My Lord," she added, bowing her head Nate's way.

Pierce looked from her to Nate, and back again. "Well, I didn't know you were being literal about... Wait. Fuck." He glared back down at Nate. "You're telling me you're, what? Tapped out? Running low on juice, or what-the-fuck-ever?"

"No one's tapped out," Nate said, gesturing for Elsa to follow him aboard. He nearly forgot to be cautious as they left the relative safety of the courtyard dirt and stepped back out onto the sea of dark gray, but the nanostuff remained blessedly dormant.

Pierce watched Nate approach from the top of the ramp, mouth open, eyes a little wild. "Son of a bitch," he murmured, eyes roaming Nate's battered armor, understanding setting in. "You really are. You're really fucking—You're... FUCK!"

Nate jerked back, more surprised than anything, as Pierce slammed a fist against the hatch frame.

"Bullshit! This is—What are you gonna do about the others? They're all —That thing is—"

"What thing?"

"Are you fucking kidding me?! Where the fuck have you—"

In the blink of an eye, Tor had Pierce pinned face-first against the bulkhead in an almost casual arm bar.

"Get off me, you Atlantean fuck!" Pierce growled.

"Not until you calm yourself and apologize to our lord," Tor said, looking calmly to Nate for confirmation.

"Fuck you," Pierce growled. "He doesn't even know what the fuck he's doing."

"Let him go, Tor," Nate said.

She obliged, stepping back with a disapproving frown.

"Thank you," Nate said, stepping past them into the ship and trying to summon something like an air of calm.

"My lord."

Inside, the ship was just similar enough to the *Camelot* to stir an ache of longing in his chest. But it was hardly a warm welcoming, other than that. Pierce was still glaring daggers. Tristan was laid out across a bench, heavily bandaged, and pale enough that Nate was pretty sure it must've been the Atlantean's blood he'd seen smeared on the wall.

"Is he okay?" Nate asked.

"Just resting my eyes, my lord," Tristan croaked.

Nate was surprised the big Atlantean was even conscious. He touched Tristan lightly on the shoulder, looking around. The ship's plant life—an extensive network of floral vines and other exotic greenery Iveera had cultivated practically wall-to-wall throughout her ship—looked unmistakably ill. He looked back to Tristan, painfully aware there was nothing he could do for the Atlantean in his present state.

"Maybe you guys should catch me up on what happened out there."

Pierce extended a hand to Tor in a gesture that said, clearly enough, *after you, fuckface.* Tor didn't bat an eye.

Nate listened attentively, nodding along with the bits they'd already more or less figured out, as Tor filled him in on how that last planetary pulse had caught them mid-tether with the first Asgardian cruiser and yanked them closer. How another nanoswarm—or more of the same, maybe—had been there to meet them, pulling them down into atmos, bound for that mountain. How Jaeger had ordered them into the escape pods and remained behind himself, refusing to leave Tessa—not to mention the forward half of the bisected Asgardian cruiser they'd inexplicably yanked along with them. How they'd plummeted to a rough jungle landing in the pod, Tor, Tristan, Pierce, and Amelia.

And then the attack.

"Like someone bred a giant panther with a giant asshole and hopped it up on goddamn PCP," Pierce muttered.

"It appeared to employ a rather potent neurological agent," Tor said, frowning at the memory.

"Yeah," Nate said, thinking of the black blur. "Think we might've come close to a run-in ourselves." If these three had experienced anything like the onslaught of fear that'd struck him and Elsa, Tor's reaction was admirably self-controlled. "What about the rest of the crew?" he asked.

"Was hoping you'd be showing up to tell us that," Pierce said. "We touched down planetside figuring you'd come flying down to find us all, lickety-split." His expression darkened. "Then that thing showed up and took Amelia, and we were stuck trekking through the set of fucking Predator like a bunch of assholes."

"I was kinda busy," Nate said past a tight jaw, tapping pointedly at the hole in his chest armor.

Pierce's sneer told him exactly what the second-string pilot thought of that excuse. And much as that sneer irritated the shit out of Nate, it also hurt. Part of him—not a small part—was plainly aware of just how much he'd let them all down. If it was anyone else but Pierce, he probably would've apologized.

"Forgive me for asking, my lord," Tor said, stirring from her post by the hatch, shifting like she wasn't quite sure how to say whatever was on her mind. "We have been... unable to hear our Lady's song, since arriving planetside," she finally said, the words seeming to leave a bad taste in her mouth. "Am I correct in gathering that you, too, have had... difficulties?"

"Difficulties," Pierce muttered, shaking his head. "Look at him. Obviously, there are difficulties." He fixed his scowl back on Nate. "So, what the hell gives? You telling me this place is some kind of dead zone?"

"No Light," Nate admitted, not sure how else to say it. "No Light, and no pre-warning to roll out the more mundane energy systems before we touched down. We're practically running on empty in here."

"Shit," Pierce said, frowning around at the ship. "Might explain a few things, I guess."

"Any idea, by the way, how—"

"How Ivy's ship ended up on this shit hole planet?" Pierce finished for him. He held onto his scowl for a moment longer, then seemingly decided to stow the mood for the moment. He tilted his head toward the bridge looking, of all things, almost excited. "Come on. You're gonna love this shit."

"I will keep watch, my lord," Tor announced, bowing her head to Nate before turning back to the open hatchway.

Nate shot an uncertain look at Elsa—who merely shrugged like *what do you expect me to do?*—then set off after Pierce. Whatever Blackthorne had done to the ship in her year-long tenure—however the crafty pirate had convinced a Knightship to accept her unrightful command in the first place —cosmetically, the *Kalnythian Wilds* seemed to be perfectly intact on the inside. Yet Nate couldn't help but get the feeling he was walking through the inside of a dying tree as he stalked down the main corridor.

On the bridge, everything appeared pristine and spotless. Not a thing out of place, save for the item toward which Pierce jabbed an almost accusatory finger: a single yellowing sheet of old-fashioned parchment laid across the main console, sporting four words inked by an eccentric hand: "Apologies, Katanaga. Happy hunting."

There was no question who'd written those words.

Pierce plucked the page from the console and offered it out to Nate. Reluctantly, almost not wanting to know, Nate accepted the parchment and turned it over, sensing there was more.

"Chin up, Arturi," it read on the other side. "Sowaiy?"

And finally, scrawled at the bottom of the sheet, like a last-minute afterthought: "Beware the Promethean."

"Weirder and weirder," Nate murmured.

"Cheeky fucking pirate," Pierce agreed. "So, what's it mean? Who's the Promethean, and how the hell did she, you know... *know?*"

Nate just shook his head helplessly.

"No more freaky psychic visions, or whatever you people get?" Pierce asked.

More head shaking, mind spooling up the visions he'd once shared with Anastasiya Blackthorne, centered around their clash at Avalon with Mordred LeFaye. But that had been different, fueled by the galaxy-class spatiotemporal distortions of a collapsing Beacon. And he hadn't experienced anything like it since.

Pierce blew out a sigh. "Well, shit."

"So, the rumors were true, then?" Elsa asked. "The Seventh Knight's ship actually was stolen? And by *the* Pirate Blackthorne, no less?"

"The one and only."

Elsa considered that, then gave a delicate little *hmph*. "Of course I miss the good bits of the rag tag adventure."

"You're telling me you *don't* consider dying of jungle dysentery, the good bits?" Pierce asked.

"Eldari do not suffer that particular… distress."

Pierce gave a bitter huff. "Christ. Figures. Good to know."

"So Anastasiya… what?" Nate wondered aloud. "Just… Just brought Iveera's ship here and…"

Pierce just gave him one of those irritated *how the hell should I know* looks of his.

"Is there any particular reason it should matter?" Elsa asked. "We have a ship now, right? We should use it."

"I like the way you think, Princess," Pierce said, maybe a little lecherously, "but sadly, no dice on that front. Ship's dead, as far as I can tell."

Apparently, that came as a surprise to Elsa.

"Dead?" she asked.

"Yeah, you know. Dead. No juice. Drained. I didn't think that could happen to Knightships, but if our Wonder Boy here is tapped out—"

"Not tapped out," Nate repeated, earning himself a dubious *oh yeah?* pitch of the eyebrows. "We just need to figure out what's going on here, okay?"

"Find the crew, find the Light, fix the leak," Elsa dutifully recited.

Pierce turned his frown on her—albeit with a good deal less aggressive judgment than he'd reserved for Nate. "What leak?"

"Ask your Knight."

Pierce turned back to Nate, expectant.

"Look, it doesn't matter what we call it. Something is going on here." He glanced at Elsa, thinking of the nanostuff allegedly dispersed on some level throughout the galaxy. "Maybe something big. But none of that really matters until we can find our people and figure out how to get out of here or… or how to stop it."

He'd almost said *call for help*. Somehow, his blinding desire to curl up and hide in Iveera's skirts didn't seem like the most useful confession he could make right now.

"You notice that gray stuff growing up onto the ship?" he added, mostly to fill the uneasy silence.

Pierce nodded, watching him uncertainly. "Didn't love the look of it."

"I think it's a kind of dormant form of what attacked us up there."

Pierce tensed, then visibly forced himself to relax, probably more out of some macho point of personal pride than out of any comfort at Nate's dormancy hypothesis.

"I think it's the same stuff that attacked me in the jungle, too," Nate continued, tapping at his ruptured breastplate. "And I think this planet, or whatever's controlling it, is using it to, I don't know, to *feed* on the Light somehow."

Pierce watched him, considering that—maybe wondering, maybe rightly, if Nate hadn't just made that all up on the spot. Only it didn't *feel* made up, as the words left his mouth. It felt like synthesis. The logical summation of everything his mind had been chewing on since they'd dropped into the Asgard system and encountered that first arcane pulse. And Ex agreed.

Elsa, on the other hand, looked a shade surprised—or maybe dubious—that he hadn't thought to share these specifics before now, but she said nothing.

"Okay." Pierce nodded slowly, tentatively accepting. "Any idea how to stop it?"

Nate shook his head. "Not yet. But I think the answer might be somewhere in that mountain."

"Yeah. We kinda got that impression."

"Why?"

"That's the other thing," Pierce said. "Come on, I'll show you."

*WEIRDER AND WEIRDER.* The words, quickly on their way to becoming a mantra, were hanging on Nate's tongue when Elsa stirred beside him and said, quietly, "It just gets stranger and stranger, doesn't it?"

He glanced at her, then back out to the view afforded by their hilltop perch. Long, low grassland rolling gently down to the great river a few kilometers distant, roughly midway between them and the darkly looming mountain whose runoff must've fed its rushing waters.

And there, plastered across the natural landscape like some dark highway to hell, was the nanostuff. Not a dark, impassable sea of it, as Nate had half-expected from the wide coverage around the compound. The trail leading to the mountain was more of a surgical strike. A single, coherent tendril, stretched across the terrain. He eyed its path back down the gradual hill they'd just ascended, down to where the *Kalnythian Wilds* sat still as the grave at what was unmistakably the epicenter of the nanostuff's reach—like the mountain itself had cast out a line and splatted nanostuff across the entire region.

Unbidden, the childhood image struck of one of those gelatinous, jolly-rancher-colored sticky hands. The kind he'd gleefully cast out like a yo-yo trying to stick it to the windows. The absurdity of the mental image shook loose an uneasy chuff—half-laugh, half sheer disbelief.

He turned his attention back to the compound, the one place in the affected swath that was peculiarly devoid of any nanostuff. Whether the compound had somehow repelled the stuff or the other way around, whether the stuff had come in a mad rush or crept across the kilometers over months, he had no idea. *Something* had stopped the stuff short of the compound walls. He would've paid dearly to hear from Blackthorne about what that something might've been, or what in nine hells had moved her to abandon a priceless Knightship on the lost planet of Ginnungagap in the first place. But then again, he also couldn't have trusted a single damn word the back-stabbing pirate might've told him, so it probably would've been for naught anyway.

"So, on to the big creepy mountain, then?" Pierce asked, breaking the long silence that'd settled over their hilltop gathering.

"Seems that way," Nate replied absentmindedly, eyes following the dark trail back toward the mountain, and toward the steep canyon wall that rose on the far side of the river, likely hewn from that very river's flow over untold millennia. Pity he couldn't simply fly them all the rest of the way. Not without wasting what little stores Ex had been scrounging together for emergencies, at least.

He considered the narrow gulch opening on the far bank of the river. The one that looked to be their best bet for a likely footpath. Slowly, almost guiltily, his gaze drifted rightward, to the twisted stretch of nanostuff that bridged both the rushing river and the high canyon wall, lingering from its apparent mountain ejection like a thick jet of black silly string that'd frozen in place, mid-droop. He wondered if the stuff was sturdy enough to cross like that. Just as quickly, he dismissed the thought. Or tried to. Behind him, he was vaguely aware of the others turning to descend back to the *Kalnythian Wilds*—Pierce asking something about what they should do with Tristan, Tor making some remark that, even grievously wounded, a warrior of the Round Table was no helpless bystander to be fretted over.

Nate found himself tracing the trail of nanostuff from that foreboding bridge all the way back to where it crested the gentle hill a few paces to his right, bound for Iveera's ship. He stepped closer, wondering if he was crazy, drawn by an odd sense of purpose. The stuff had shown no sign of danger or activity. And if it was somehow hogging the Light, or sequestering it, or whatever... Maybe...

Carefully, feeling Ex watching attentively over his shoulder, so to speak, he touched the toe of one boot to the trail of nanostuff.

Something moved through him. Something spectral and ancient, bringing a sharp breath and a fresh wave of not-quite disorientation, not-quite inspiration.

"Wait."

*What is it?* Ex asked.

Nate stepped back from the nanostuff, double-checking there'd been no damage done, no sneaky spirits creeping through his mind.

*This... this mountain.* He turned back to the looming thing, dialing out the optics, following his gut more than anything else. Tracing the craggy slopes down to a point at the base. Something about that point. Something nearly forgotten, hauntingly familiar, as if from a dream. He could just make out the dark entrance to a cavern.

And there it was.

*I've seen this place before, Ex.*

*What?* It wasn't often he got to hear Ex sound so legitimately surprised. *When? Where?*

He dialed the optics further, trying to make sense of it, to be sure. No looming bipedal jungle cat monstrosity standing there in the distant cave mouth, as he was half-expecting. But still.

"Nate?" Pierce asked. "What's up? You got something to share with the class?"

He looked to Pierce and the others, head spinning a little. They were all watching him. "No," he heard himself say. "No, it's..." *Just a bit of deja vu*, he thought to say. "It's nothing," his mouth added instead. "I was just think-ing... I think you guys should stay with the ship."

"What?" Elsa said.

"Yeah, fuck that," Pierce agreed. "And you know what? Fuck you, too. I'm not sitting here babysitting a dead ship while you go look for my people."

"They're *my* people too." It came out more heated than intended. He took a steadying breath. "And if Ex and I can find a way to un-fuck whatev-er's going on in there and get the Light unstuck, my money's on us needing an able-handed crew ready to man the *Wilds* out here. We don't even know where Cammy's at for sure. This is the smart play."

"That's bullshit. This is the play where you run off thinking you're better than us just 'cuz you're a Knight. But in case you forgot—Which would be quite the damn feat, considering how much you've been milking it—that big ass hole in your chest plate's still there. And it's there because you don't have shit going for you on this planet, Nate."

"Tor."

The Atlantean straightened at the sound of her name, expression dark, like she knew what was coming.

"If I were to order you to return to the ship with Lt Pierce and Princess Elsavataryllianna."

"If that ogre lays one hand on me…" Elsa started, drawing to her full, regal height.

"I would prefer you didn't, my lord," Tor answered.

"But if I did."

"It is my sworn duty to see your will done, my lord. Just as it is my duty to protect you at any cost. Which is why I pray you might consider another course."

Nate turned at the possibility in her voice. The Atlantean's jaw was tight, but she was controlled.

"Leave these two with Tristan," she said.

"What?" Pierce growled.

"Allow me to accompany you," Tor continued, ignoring him. "Tristan is still more than capable of functioning in a defensive capacity."

"You Atlantean fuck!"

"But he's…" Nate followed Tor's attention down the slope and realized the maimed Atlantean was already standing guard at the open hatch of the *Wilds*.

"Allow Tristan to do his duty, my lord. And allow me to do mine."

Nate considered it.

"You're not seriously going to leave me with *them*?" Elsa said, turning her scornful look from Pierce to search Nate's expression.

Pierce was too pissed to notice, much less take offense. "Nate, I swear to god, if you try to leave me behind—"

"No." Nate cut him off with a swipe of the hand. "No. There's no leaving behind. You're all staying."

"That's exactly the fucking definition of leaving behind."

"Tor, take them back to the ship and stand watch."

"My… lord."

"Nathaniel." Elsa actually looked betrayed.

"I want you all taking stock of supplies—"

"Just in case we're somehow still alive to use 'em?" Pierce muttered.

"That's the idea," Nate agreed. "Get the supplies in order. See what you can do about getting the *Wilds* separated from that stuff, but just… be careful with it. Don't…"

"Provoke it?" There was an unmistakable double edge to Pierce's words, but Nate thought little of it. He would've been more concerned if the pilot *wasn't* generally outraged by whatever decision he came to.

He nodded. "I'd rather it didn't wake up and try to eat the ship, is all."

"And us without our brave Knight," Pierce muttered, waving his hands like *what could we possibly do?*

"And you, my lord?" Tor asked.

"I'll have a look ahead and report back when I can."

It didn't satisfy them—nor, he supposed, would it have satisfied *him*, had the tables been turned—but they said their bitter *farewells* and *be carefuls* ("You better not fuck us, Kid," in Pierce's case) and turned to go. Ex, having been waiting with deteriorating patience throughout the exchange, wasted no time as the three of them marched stiffly off.

*Why can't I see what's going on in your head, Nathaniel? What the bloody hell is this?*

*The Lady,* he replied, turning back to the towering mountain. *She showed me this place, Ex. Back on Atherton, when she took me… wherever the hell she took me. Just before she gave me you.*

He waited for Ex to tell him he must simply be imagining it, that he was letting his squishy human superstition get the best of him again, or that, at the very least, he was being ridiculous, sending away his only backup just because of a little divine coincidence.

*That is… curious,* was all Ex said instead.

*Well,* Nate thought, setting course for the rushing river and the narrow gulch, *you know what they say about curiosity and big angry cats.*

**CHAPTER 21**

# SPARKS

As far as totally blind, equipment-free excavation gigs went, Jaeger figured they weren't doing half bad. Which was mostly to say, he had no fucking clue.

It was a real pain in the dick, trying to operate in total darkness. Hard to escape a box when you couldn't even establish whether it *was* a box at all. They'd done their best anyway. Awkward, hand-linked sweeps of the space. Nothing but damp, unbroken cave walls all around. No outlets, or passages, or doors. Nothing but slimy stone—and more than a few clattering some-things that felt too much like dried, roughly Asgardian-sized bones.

"Girl goes through all the trouble of smuggling the goods…" murmured Hannah O'Sweeney somewhere nearby. She sounded thoughtful. Or like she was up to something.

He still wasn't sure what to make of the academic super-journalist/quite possible Lady James Bond operative the UN had gone and slipped into their midst aboard the *Camelot*. She never said much, but if at any moment he'd been asked to guess who in the room had their shit together in the thick of it, Jaeger was quickly coming to the conclusion that O'Sweeney was always a safe bet.

He still wasn't sure how or why that Myrr thing had known to so methodically scour them each for any useful gadgets upon capture. Still wasn't sure where their "journalist" had been keeping her multitool that the creature *hadn't* found it, either. He'd been told he didn't *want* to know, on the latter point—quite to the opposite effect. But it hardly mattered anyway.

Their multitool was for shit in here.

As far as they could tell from their blind sweeps, they were stuck at the bottom of a pit of indeterminate depth. And even if the cave walls hadn't been too smooth and grime-slicked to climb, none of them were dying to go for a pitch-black free solo for god only knew how far.

One of the Asgardians had tried anyway, after they'd all gotten tired of waving their dicks at one another. Him and his broken leg had informed them, one sickening crunch and thud later, that they were fucked by at least a good fifteen meters, or so. Probably more.

How they'd all gotten down here to start with was still anyone's guess. The few who hadn't been venomed unconscious for the ride—seemingly those who'd been too terrified to put up any fight in the first place, he'd gathered—hadn't been in any state of mind to recount precise details, other than that there'd been a lot of movement in the dark. Fast movement. Like the thing wasn't remotely troubled by navigating in total darkness. Amelia was sure the thing had simply jumped down here with her and jumped right back up. No one had heard a thing to corroborate the story. They'd all been too busy tripping fear balls together.

Grunts and scraping sounds drew his attention back to the present. Indiscriminate. That was the word of the day. Everything was indiscriminate down here. *Someone* was busy at work with *something*.

A spark. Brief and paltry. Practically brilliant in the absolute darkness.

"The hell?" someone whispered.

Another spark. The flash of a face. Impact echoes ringing up the pit walls.

"O'Sweeney," Jaeger hissed.

She kept going. Spark, spark, spark, and—

Flame.

The smallest, most fickle flame he'd ever seen, wiggling feebly to life. It was goddamn beautiful. And in that moment, so was Hannah O'Sweeney, rising to her feet in the flickering tendrils of light, holding aloft a makeshift torch. A length of Asgardian femur, by the look of it, bearing the precious fire of multitool sparks on one of the torn shirt rags Carter had ordered Elmo and Ramirez to stockpile while she'd been busy triaging their various cuts and bruises.

"Holy shit," said the Ramirez-shaped shadow.

"Yeah, but seriously," added it's Snuffy-shaped counterpart, fanning the air. "Smells like—"

"Burnt shit," O'Sweeney chimed, looking almost lovingly at the flames reflecting in her dark eyes. "Charmin', eh?"

Jaeger's nose wrinkled at the smell even as his lips pulled into a grin. That must've explained why she'd been rifling around so much in the bone-yard earlier. Looking for more than just a femur. Dried excrement.

Their multitool was literally for shit. Jesus.

He almost could've laughed.

Then a gasp and a rattling hiss yanked them all back to claustrophobic reality, where Snuffy had just hit the deck and was furiously crab crawling away from—

"Merciful mother of fuck, what is that?!"

Jaeger followed the mechanic's frantic attention upward, to where two iridescent *somethings* were gleaming in the shadows. O'Sweeney took a step closer, and the pit sounded with a round of tense curses as the thing came into proper view.

It clung to the sheer rock wall a mere meter above where Snuffy had been sitting, headfirst toward the floor, long, spindly limbs clamped to the slick stone in a grip that should've been impossible. It hissed as the light struck it, turning its oversized eyes away, casting bared fangs in profile. Then the thing skittered off for the deeper shadows, practically slithering across the slimy stone wall with a flagrant disregard for gravity.

"That's a fucking Ooperian," Ramirez growled, his voice thick with anger. Jaeger didn't blame him. It was creepy as shit, and the airman was probably far from forgetting about the days he'd spent entombed in a crit-ical care medpod after their first run-in with Ooperian assassins back on the Forge. As for this particular specimen, though...

Jaeger wasn't quite sure what to make of it. It looked wild. Or *more* wild than the ones they'd crossed paths with in civilized space, at least. Feral, even. But maybe that was in part to do with its state of undress and the withered skin-and-bones glimpse he caught before the thing made it back to the cover of shadows.

Mostly, he was just glad the thing didn't attack. It merely scuttled off and reorientated itself to watch, twin orbs gleaming out at them from the darkness.

"Ghhhirrrithhhaaa," came an airy hiss, followed by a few guttural hacking sounds. "Shhhiiiethhhyah."

Another hack.

"Anybody get that?" Jaeger asked, accepting the medium-sized bone Elmo quietly handed him. A few of the others were already brandishing similar clubs.

"I'm about to," Ramirez growled, plucking a large skull up in the flickering torchlight like he fully intended to hurl it at their Ooperian pit-mate.

"Hold it," Jaeger said, raising an arm in front of Ramirez and looking around for a better solution, or maybe just a sliver of context. The crew poised all around him, ready to fight. Their genius doctors still clinging to each other from the initial shock. Gendra and Amelia only slightly more composed. All of them tensed to the gills.

The Asgardians, on the other hand, were just sneering at the creature from the other side of the torchlight. Spitting at it like it was beneath them.

"You guys don't seem too surprised," Jaeger observed. "You used to finding Ooperians in the dark?"

"You are slow to listen, Terran. We have come to Ginnungagap. This frail wretch is but a shadow of the evil that lies in wait here."

"Hiiirithhhar," breathed that shadow.

"What's it doing down *here*, though?" Jaeger asked. "And what the hell language is it speaking?" he added, mostly to himself. He wasn't really expecting answers, and the Asgardians' derisive snorts didn't disappoint.

The creature just stared on from the shadows.

"Creepy fella, isn't he?" Snuffy asked.

"Yeah, Snuffs, the fucking *Ooperian* IS a bit creepy. Who'd have thought?" Ramirez was rattled, trying to force some bravado.

Snuffy didn't seem to notice. "You think maybe we shouldn't talk about him like he's not here?" he asked. Then, louder, "You got a name, Mr. Ooperian?"

That began a fresh episode of *Snuffy Says What?* among the crew, Hannah O'Sweeney standing idly by, frowning around the circle of torchlight, up to the unbroken darkness above. Jaeger studied the shadow wreathed Ooperian, wondering.

A fellow prisoner?

It seemed unlikely, given that the thing could clearly put the finest wall-hopping mountain goat to shame. But why stay down here, then? Unless...

"It's afraid," someone whispered beside him. Gendra. She'd barely spoken since whatever that Myrr thing had done to her. She didn't need to speak more now to explain what she meant. Why stay down here... unless it was afraid of whatever was lurking outside of this pit. Afraid of whatever had put them here.

Afraid of Myrr. Whatever the hell it was.

Jaeger set his bone club down and took a few steps closer to the tensed Ooperian, hands raised in peace. "We're not your enemies," he called. "Not so long as you leave us be."

Snickers from the Asgardians. Jaeger ignored them.

"Do you know how to get out of here?"

No response. Those gleaming orbs swaying ever-so-slightly back and forth in the darkness. Watching. Creepy as all fuck.

"A way out?" he tried again, pointing upward. "Escape. How do we escape? Why do you stay?"

The creepy-ass thing just hissed at him and shrank further into the shadows.

"Perfect," O'Sweeney said, looking around at the group with some renewed purpose. She settled on the biggest Asgardian and offered out her torch. "How about a toss then, big boy?" she asked, tipping her chin skyward. "Unless anyone has a better idea? Let's see where we stand."

If anyone had any objections, O'Sweeney's Big Boy didn't give a shit. The Asgardian strode forward and plucked the torch from her with a marked, almost violent lack of respect for her personal space. Then he turned and hurled the torch upward like some young bull eager to prove just how strong he really was.

The Ooperian lost its shit. Hissing like a wild cat, tensed on the wall like it was about to spring after the flying torch to swat it down. Jaeger was dimly aware he'd snapped his hand up for quiet—as if the frothing wild vampire would give a fuck. Didn't matter. The torch spun upward, whipping flames clinging for dear life in the wake of the brute's throw, dancing weakly across the smooth rock. An uneven rim some twenty meters above. Another edge closing the empty space in three or four meters above that. The torch slowed and began to fall.

Movement and boot thuds in the dark below. O'Sweeney and the Asgardian both rushing to snag the falling torch from the air. Colliding with a breathless grunt. He glimpsed O'Sweeney hitting the ground, the torch speeding down to join her. From the sound of it, the torch shattered on impact. Hard to tell for sure as the abused flame died out for good.

"A+ effort on the teamwork, you bloody dolt," came O'Sweeney's voice from the ground in the resultant darkness.

Jaeger closed his eyes—not that it made any visual difference whatsoever —and did his best to burn the glimpsed details into his mind before they could fade. A tunnel, of some sort. That's what he'd seen, passing by the lip of the pit twenty meters above. The pit's sheer wall continuing upward on the opposite side, for who knew how far. They'd found themselves in a laundry chute situation, minus the opening at the bottom. A big, stone laundry chute.

"It is you who are the dolt, Terran. I would have—"

"Guys?" Ramirez's voice was tense. "Anybody got eyes on the—" He faltered, like he'd just realized no one had eyes on jack shit. "Just, Jesus, just —Where's the damn vamp?"

A tense moment of silence. Then, Snuffy's voice.

"Mr. Ooperian?"

Nothing. A whole fat lot of nothing.

"Bob?" Snuffy called.

"Bob?!" Ramirez hissed. "Seriously, Snuffy?"

"What?" Snuffy hissed back. "People with names don't eat other people with—"

"Hiiirithhhar."

Jaeger paused at the icy whisper, mouth caught open, having been about to tell them both to shut the hell up.

"Bob?" Snuffy whispered back.

A pair of those hacking coughs from the darkness.

No movement. No screams.

"Hannibal Lecter," Ramirez said flatly. "Jeffrey Dahmer."

"Fine, fine," Snuffy said. "I get it."

"The Donner Party," Ramirez murmured, like he hadn't heard. "People with names."

"Right, then," O'Sweeney said. "On that ray of sunshine, someone fetch us another bone and cloth, will ya?"

Jaeger had already been feeling his way back toward the boneyard where he'd laid down his club.

"Yep, yep," came Snuffy's voice from a few scuffling paces ahead. "Ten steps ahead of you. Maybe. I don't know, I can't see shit over here."

"Oh, it's right by the innominates."

"No, not *the* shit. I meant… Wait, what? Innomi…"

"Hipbones," a small voice provided. Dr. Ramachandra.

"Yeah. Right. Guess that… makes sense?"

Jaeger paused at the clattering of dry bones being picked through, Snuffy rambling on as he worked, pointing out to no one in particular that it wouldn't be the worst thing if See-In-the-Dark Bob wanted to lend him a hand.

Something else. Something... wrong.

A hopeless weight sinking through the darkness, leeching at his insides like the soggy misery of a cold, wet day.

"—but then again—"

Jaeger moved without thinking, reaching in the dark. Snuffy tensed as Jaeger's hand closed over his yapping mouth. The mechanic's hand found Jaeger's wrist with a kind of experimental quality, like he genuinely didn't feel what all the fuss was. Then it hit him. Jaeger felt the soft gasp against his palm. He let Snuffy go but kept him close.

All of them, silent as the dead. Even the Asgardians.

In his gut, Jaeger felt that thing watching them from above. He waited, expecting that low rumble of a growl, fearing another sudden thrust of that weaponized terror.

Silence.

Terrible silence.

Something rustling above. A disgruntled voice.

Then two firm thuds on the pit floor. A moment of trickling fear. Enough to tell Jaeger that that *thing* was there among them. Then a whoosh of musky air, and a roar above, seeming to echo back to them from a distance. From down the tunnel, Jaeger thought, mind grasping to make sense. Multiple creatures? Or was this Myrr thing really that fast?

"Brothers," one of the Asgardians said, from over where the thuds had sounded.

More prisoners, Jaeger registered, as he listened to the Asgardians drop their harsh edges long enough to check on their battered brethren. More of Myrr's Asgardian catches. Jaeger felt for Carter in the dark. He found her in silence, still wondering at the speed and power of a creature that could handle a twenty meter fall under the weight of two Asgardian soldiers, then spring back out of the pit and away in the blink of an eye. He took Carter's hand. Neither of them said a thing. For a while, no one said a thing—the pit silent, save for the groans of their new fellow inmates being picked over by their Asgardian brethren.

*What the hell is it doing this for?*

He felt the question permeating the damp cavern air between them. Everyone wondering. The pit coming slowly back to muted life as the minutes ticked by, and no sign of Myrr returned. Still, no one spoke the words.

Spark. Spark. Spark.

Hannah O'Sweeney, Bringer of Light, striking another torch.

The Ooperian hissed in protest as the fledgling light spilled through the pit, but no terrible death rained down from above.

"All right," Jaeger said quietly, sliding his hand discreetly free from Carter's and waving them to gather round. "All right, people. We've got a shit torch, a multitool, and a twenty-meter wall to clear. Any thoughts?"

They all looked around at one another.

"Don't suppose any of you Yanks has a black belt in professional cheerleader tossin'?" O'Sweeney asked, tipping her head back like she was gauging the distance.

A movement in the shadows drew their attention before anyone could answer—the Ooperian creeping forward just enough so they could see as it waved down the torch with a series of agitated swipes. It looked up meaningfully, swiped a few more times in the direction of the torch like an old man telling the kids to get off its damn lawn, then scuttled back into the shadows, like it had said its piece and wasn't going to be caught dead with these idiots when its fears came to fruition.

"I don't think Bob approves of our torch," Snuffy said, as if that might've been unclear.

"Well," O'Sweeney said thoughtfully. "Sounds like all the more reason for him to give us a hand out of here, then."

Jaeger, who'd been eyeing the Asgardians' tunics and considering the synthetic polyweave pants, belts, and other garments most of his crew wore, met O'Sweeney's eyes in the torchlight and felt his lips tugging into a grin, the beginnings of a half-assed plan starting to take shape in the darkness.

## CHAPTER 22

# THE CAVE

*S*omething is definitely amiss with this mountain, Ex declared, for the third time since they'd cleared the gulch with a hop, skip, and a slight thruster-powered jump and set off hoofing it the rest of the way across the rocky terrain stretching between the river and the mountain. Nate had to admit, the total absence of life in the area didn't inspire any great ease about what they were likely to find inside, but it was still unusual to hear Ex fret like this.

*It doesn't count as 'fretting' when I don't have clear data to work with, Nathaniel,* Ex grumbled.

Nate smiled at the sheer informational privilege of the sentiment. *Yeah. Welcome to life as a squishy meat bag, buddy.*

*Ugh. It's every bit as dreadful as I imagined.*

*Well—*Nate slowed beside a rusty orange outcropping, that sense of deja vu swelling—*we'll just have to figure out what the hell's going on here, then.*

This was the place. Or close enough that it might as well have been, he thought, glancing over to the unerring trail of dark nanostuff they'd been following in toward the base of the mountain.

This was the spot where the Lady had brought him, back on the day she'd taken him on galactic walkabout. He could see the crumbling cave entrance ahead. He looked back at the distant green blur of the jungle, remembering how he'd assumed, based on what he'd seen at the time, that this was some desert wasteland of a planet. All a matter of perspective. He closed his eyes, trying to remember exactly what it was she'd told him.

The memory was oddly fuzzy.

*Probably because I can't see it,* Ex said. *This is all you. Squishy meat bag memory. No recall enhancement.*

It was a sobering reminder of what he'd been before Ex had come into his life—and, in a very real sense, into *him.* Nate set the thought aside, focusing on the matter at hand.

He remembered asking pointless questions. *Why are you showing me this? I don't understand what's happening.*

He remembered the way she'd smiled at him—that indescribably radiant smile. *And thus, I believe you have answered your own question.*

He remembered seeing this mountain, this crumbling cave entrance it'd never even occurred to him he might actually see in person. Remembered the lone figure that'd stood there—that great, black-furred biped with the head of a fierce jungle cat. Remembered the way its roar had shook the air, as the Lady told him how Earth's days of peace were coming to an end.

What was it she'd said of the creature, just before they flashed on?

Something about people meddling with forces they didn't understand. He hadn't thought twice about it at the time, given how batshit crazy the rest of the ordeal had been—not to mention the fact that she hadn't given him the *chance* to think twice before she'd warped them on to meet the frothing edges of a massive Synth swarm. But now...

He looked back in the direction of the old, half-incinerated compound, hidden behind the twin ridges of the canyon, but still palpable there in the distance. Legends of Ginnungagap. The lost planet of demons and abominations. A pre-fabbed ghost town full of cages and cells, meddling with mysterious forces right next to a mountain full of unidentified Synth presence.

"What the hell happened here?" he murmured, mostly to himself. Ex, understanding the question to be rhetorical, merely let the silence do the talking.

It was high time they figured that out.

INSIDE, the cavern was dark, cold, and slimy—and pretty much every other adjective Nate figured one might use when imagining the sort of place a creature like Gollum might go slinking around. Only it wasn't a shriveled little geriatric hobbit he was worried he might run into in here. It was a goddamned Asgardian-sized supercat with superspeed and mind-melting fear beams.

*Find the crew. Find the Light. Fix the leak.*

Over and over, the words ran through his head, despite his best efforts to rein them in. What he needed was a clear head. Mind like water, and so forth. He needed his Iveera Face. But with every persistent round of his mantra—find the crew, find the Light, fix the leak—all he felt was the dwindling strength of his suit and his own body, the utter lack of the Lady's power in this place.

He'd almost forgotten what it felt like to be this afraid. To be this vulnerable.

*I will not fear*, he shifted his manta, channeling the wisdom of the famous words he'd only, in the crucible of the past year, truly began to appreciate. *Fear is the mind killer.*

He felt Ex stir with some pithy remark, then think twice about it. Somehow, his companion's reticence to tear him a new one only made it all worse.

The Light was there. That much, he was almost certain of. There, somewhere. Somewhere near, maybe. Tantalizing him like the smell of some heavenly dish cooking in the next apartment over. So close, and yet…

A low growl, rumbling through the uneven tunnel.

And yet that. Shit.

*Need I remind you that you ARE an Excalibur Knight?*

*Sans batteries, Ex*, Nate mentally snapped back, scanning the grainy gray darkness on his HUD. *I'm a sturdy Terran in dead armor. I'm practically an Asgardian.*

*You take that back, Nathaniel. That's a low blow. I'll have you know you're—*

Another rumbling growl. Closer, he thought. It was hard to tell up from down in this unruly network of tunnels and offshoots. He thought fleetingly of Shelob's cave, chest tightening. Then the real fear washed over him, setting to shame the petty apprehension he'd felt creeping into this place. This fear was unnatural. Pharmaceutical. Targeted with surgical precision. He forced a breath and let it seep through him, accepting it, holding his faith in Ex like a talisman against the darkness.

*That's sweet, Nathaniel.*

*Shut up.*

The fear didn't lessen. Not really. But it did begin to shift from the foreground of his mind, just like they'd talked about.

*Really, I'm touched.*

*Ex.*

The rake of scraping stone from somewhere ahead, or maybe from the outcropping off to the side. Sharpening its claws, he thought—the echoing crumble and patter of fine debris eerily loud in the dark tunnel.

*Almooost there.*

*You're a dick.*

Silence. The faintest ghost of a heat signature flickering across the HUD.

*Showtime.*

Nate felt the movement in his bones more than he actually saw it coming. One second, he was staring at darkness. The next, that darkness was crashing into him with a wild animal roar.

He tumbled with it, punching blindly at the center of mass, growling like an animal himself as unexpectedly strong claws ripped at his armor. They hit hard rock and rolled, tied together by claw and two indiscriminate handfuls of dark fur—muscles like banded steel beneath. A wall of roaring sound hit his face, blunted almost instantaneously by Ex's audio filtering. Then the damn thing tried to bite his head off, hard enough to crack the faceplate.

Nate fed a few blaster bolts into the thing's ribs and took advantage of its howling recoil to haul back and punch the beast across the tunnel. It struck the opposite stone wall with a heavy *thud* and *whoomph*. Nate rolled to his feet, ready for the next rush, but the thing had vanished.

It was fast. And damn near impossible to spot in the dark.

*Working on it,* Ex said, the ethereal lines of sonar readings weaving their way onto the blended spectrum of Nate's HUD vision. *Blackened thing is as hard to read as the rest of this planet.*

It was only then Nate realized he was wounded—bleeding from at least three or four fiery spots where the claws had gouged through his dying armor. At least he'd done the thing one better with his blaster bolt, he thought, as Ex's sensors picked up the faint echoes of labored breathing and pinged them to an imperfect sonar silhouette in the shadows behind a tall outcropping.

He stalked forward, fists and wrist blasters at the ready, reminding himself that, mindless predator or not, this thing had taken Amelia, maimed his people. He stepped forward, ready to finish it.

The sonar specter dropped off his HUD.

He tensed, fists raised, trying to look every which way at once. Something hit the back of his head, damn hard. A rock, he realized, right as another hit him from the other side. He lurched for the cover of the outcropping, resisting the urge to waste precious energy on return fire until he actually had a target. Another rock struck his side.

He staggered into cover. Or started to, before something whipped across the ground, sweeping his legs out from under him.

*Traps*, he realized, as he hit the damp cave floor in a rush. This thing had laid *traps*. And more than just trip lines, he realized, as he rolled over and felt the sluggish numbness creeping through his limbs from the very spots that'd only a moment ago been on fire.

Some kind of neurotoxin in the claws?

He was aware of Ex snapping that he was on it, on it. Aware of his own hands snapping reflexively out to catch the beast by the wrists as it charged again. They slammed into the cave wall like thunder, the impact rattling his teeth, the rest of his body disconcertingly numb.

He squeezed off a barrage of blaster fire into the thing's chest. Broke its hold with a numb elbow and took another wild swing that the beast easily sidestepped. The blaster fire hadn't even slowed it.

*A trick*, some corner of his mind registered, as he planted to turn after the beast and felt his numbing leg buckle beneath him.

The damn thing had feinted injury on the first shot just to draw him in.

He'd underestimated this thing, he realized, as the creature circled him in the shadows, seemingly content to wait for its toxin to take effect. He'd overestimated himself in his Lightless state. Left his only backup sitting safely back on a dead ship. And now...

Now, he pushed himself back to unsteady feet, just to watch his other leg buckle out from under him.

"Dammit, Ex," he growled, clutching the damp cave floor with numb hands, heart thundering.

*That would be the stimulants*, Ex said, with forced calm. *Now, if your squishy body would just—Ahhh.*

Nate felt the first itchy pins and needles of his body responding to whatever Ex had just done. Ahead, the dark beast sniffed the air like it could smell it, too.

*Oh, blackened hands*, Ex growled.

Then the beast sawed out an angry roar and charged.

Nate tried to move, tingling limbs flopping like fish out of water, the creature lunging in for the kill. A dark blur caught it mid-flight, driving the thing just wide of Nate—a roaring tangle of dark body parts thrashing into the wall and back again, jockeying for position. In the chaos, Nate couldn't even tell what he was looking at until one smacked the other across the tunnel, and Nate watched a whimpering, big-headed quadruped hit the cave wall with an unsettling smack.

The *snargladorf*.

Before he could so much as blink, bright light flooded through the tunnel, and a trio of crackling blue blaster bolts ripped by, casting the beast's snarling features in sharp relief as they punched into its dark-furred chest. It sped forward, unaffected, racing for the broad-shouldered shooter.

Tor was already in motion, spinning her lance about as she braced behind her thrumming shield, planting the lance to the ground behind her. The creature crashed into her shield with a rushing detonation of sound that sent it flying back the way it'd come, the ground behind Tor erupting with ballistic stone debris.

*Gravitonic shield*, Ex said, while Nate's brain was still struggling to catch up. *Lance outlet for the blowback. Nice.*

Nice was one way of putting it. But it didn't explain—

"What are you doing here?" he asked, before he could stop himself. He was surprised to find he'd regained his feet, Ex's counter-toxin concoction apparently working its magic.

Tor was scanning the shadows like she hadn't heard him. Nate, remembering himself, joined her in checking their surroundings. Nothing but the soft pitter patter of rock debris and dripping moisture. The creature was nowhere to be seen or heard. Not that that convinced him it was gone for good.

"My lord," Tor finally answered, concluding her scan and straightening to attention. "I identified an unexpected hostile on your trail."

Nate frowned, confused, until his eyes landed on the groaning quadruped laid out under Tor's bright lights on the cave rock nearby.

"The *snargladorf*?"

Tor remained at attention, eyes sweeping the area, avoiding him. "I spotted it following you as we returned to the *Kalnythian Wilds*, my lord. Thus, I was forced to unilaterally amend the plan, in light of my privileged information and our lack of communications." She looked some combination of repentant and defiant. "It was protocol, my lord."

For a long moment, all Nate could do was stare, thinking that this *protocol* of hers sounded an awful lot like nothing but a convenient excuse to buck his orders. And he had no idea how to respond.

What kind of asshole did he want to be here? The ungrateful, domineering sort who demanded obedience to a fault, or the kind who admitted he'd foolishly snubbed his allies and walked into the Cave of Doom without a proper plan?

A faint buzz of sound in the distance interrupted the decision.

"Well," he said, trying to focus in on the distant sounds. Voices? Maybe. "Thanks for your concern."

Her rigid at-attention stance softened long enough for her to shoot what might've been a surprised glance at him, then she nodded tersely, gave a quiet, "Of course, my lord," and returned to watching their surroundings.

*Those were voices*, Ex confirmed, as the distant buzz faded from Nate's straining ears. *Though before I say more, I'd be remiss not to point out—*

*That it could be a trap*, Nate finished for him. *Was it our people, or not?*

*It SOUNDED like our crew*, Ex said, rather pointedly.

Nate tamped down on the urge to charge straight ahead.

"Blaster fire didn't seem to bother it," he said quietly, thinking of the way their shots had been gobbled right up in the beast's fur—the same fur that was apparently rather adept at masking its body heat.

"If it had," Tor replied, "we would've slain the beast back in the jungle."

Nate looked at his selectively attentive warrior servant, still thinking. The uncanny strength and speed. The way it'd actually *feinted* injury to lure him into a rudimentary trap. Sentient intelligence. There was no mistaking it. And it had taken Amelia. And maybe the rest of the crew, too. Why?

"Come on," he said to Tor, starting forward—only to falter a moment later as something stirred in the shadows of Tor's shield light. The snargladorf, trying to rise.

He'd nearly forgotten the thing was there.

"And the snargladorf, my lord?" Tor asked, following his gaze. "Would you like me to end its suffering?"

"What?" Nate glanced at Tor and her lance, taken aback. Across from them, the snargladorf sank back to the cave floor, big head plopping heavily to its forepaws, breathing ragged. "No. No, it..."

It what? Had tried to help him? Was on their side?

*Give me a break*, he thought to himself, glancing deeper into the cave, painfully aware of his waiting crew and the heavy press of each passing second. Back to the snargladorf watching him with panting breath and big, oblong eyes.

"Dammit," he whispered, starting toward the wounded animal.

*You DID steal its dinner and punch it across the jungle*, Ex pointed out. *Fair is fair.*

*So NOW you grow a conscience*, Nate thought back, the bitter tang of guilt eating at him just as he and Elsa had reluctantly eaten at their "stolen" dinner of charred rabbit-thing. This thing tracking him all the way here, probably in hopes of another handout, only to come charging in at Nate's moment of need—and against what must've been this planet's undisputed heavyweight champion, no less.

He needn't have approached the wounded creature as cautiously as he did. The snargladorf plainly had no fight left in it. Its head dipped as he approached, in what could've been deference. Maybe just fear, or submission. Except…

Something in him shifted as the poor creature weakly sniffed at his boot, then looked hesitantly up at him, head cocked, panting nervously.

For a flitting second, all he could think of was little Copernicus sitting back home, waiting, and he was filled with an ache of longing, quickly chased by another wash of guilt. He hadn't thought of home once since they'd crashed down to Ginnungagap.

"My lord?"

"Hmm?"

"Should we not be on the move?"

He looked to Tor. Back down to the frozen snargladorf.

"Come on," he said, gesturing with a hand. "Can you stand, boy?"

*Girl*, Ex corrected. *Roughly speaking. If you're going to adopt the pitiful thing, you might as well be anatomically correct about it.*

*No one said anything about adopting it*, Nate shot back, even as he bent down to help the struggling snargladorf stand. A mistake, it turned out, as he reached to loop his hands beneath her ribs. The snargladorf snapped around like a viper, catching his wrist in a multilayered mouthful of fangs. But she didn't bite down.

Something in Nate—the same part that'd refrained from jerking away, he imagined—felt oddly calm with the development, like it knew exactly what to do, as she held him there, eyeing him uncertainly. He reached out and patted her gently on the head.

It was only as she released him that he realized Tor was standing there, lance at the ready. He waved the Atlantean down. "No stabbing anything unless we're damn sure it's an enemy, okay?"

She frowned from him to the snargladorf. "Very well, my lord."

"Great." The snargladorf was already trotting away—or limping, more accurately, moving with one of her hind legs held gingerly off the ground. "Well then. Let's go find our crew."

CHAPTER 23

# PLAN A

Nate wasn't really sure what he'd been expecting in the depths of the mountain. A creepy supercat lair, he supposed. A mysterious well of Light in the depths of the mountain. Unstoppable nanoswarms, and the ghost of Mordred LeFaye.

What he *hadn't* pictured was a couple of dozen figures hanging out at the bottom of a pitch-black stone pit with bone clubs, like freaking Children of the Flies. But that was exactly what he found.

It checked the creepy box, at least. All of them standing dead still down there, having heard but not seen him in the darkness. A terrible smell of burnt *something* clung to the air. He signaled back to stop Tor, then peeked back over the edge.

A sigh of relief left him as Ex's HUD readings began tagging heat signatures based on size, shape, and probably a few dozen other metrics. Jaeger's name appeared. Snuffy and Carter. Ramirez. Elmo. Hannah O'Sweeney. The Drs. Lundquist and Ramachandra. Amelia, and Gendra, and a whole handful of unknown Asgardians. Most of them staring in Nate's general direction, blind in the dark, holding... not *clubs*, he realized. Torches. Creepy bone torches. Recently doused, judging by the awful smell in the air.

"Nate?" Jaeger's voice. Cautious in the pitch black. "Nate, is that you?"

"It's me," he called down in a pitched whisper. Not the most inspired words for a would-be rescuer. But Snuffy, at least, sounded plenty relieved anyway.

"Oh, thank Jesus!"

Nate leaned further over the edge, scanning again through the thermal signatures down below, hyperalert for any hint of a speeding supercat coming to knock him down into the creepy pit. Sore as he still was about his own lack of foresight, he had to admit he was glad to have Tor here, watching his back.

He didn't consciously register what he'd been looking for until he realized she wasn't there.

"Where's Tessa?"

"Cammy had her." There was bitterness in Jaeger's tone. Guilt. "I tried to stay with her. Your ship had other ideas."

"We're fine too, though," Ramirez added. "Thanks for asking. Any chance we can get a proper light down here, by the way?"

Nate was too busy taking aim with his wrist blaster at the last signature Ex had just flagged on the HUD.

"You know there's an Ooperian down there, right?"

"Oh, yeah, that's Bob," chimed Snuffy's heat signature. "I mean, we don't know his *actual* name, but..."

"But you landed on *Bob*?" Nate asked, as Tor tapped on his shoulder, offering a compact hand torch.

"Bob the Space Vampire," Snuffy said with a shrug. "It's got a ring to it."

"It doesn't," said Ramirez, squinting up past a raised hand as Nate clicked the torch on and flooded the pit with sterile white-blue light.

"And is Bob...?"

What? Hungry? Friendly? The answer to either question seemed self-evident enough in the way the emaciated creature was clinging to the wall in a freakily unnatural position, watching the figures below.

"Bob's frustratingly reluctant to give us a ride out of this hellhole, is what he is," Jaeger said, squinting in the light of the hand torch. "Any chance you could be a dear and step in? I don't know if you met Myrr—"

"Big angry cat, smells like weaponized fear?"

"Thought we heard a scuffle out there. That's the one. I'm thinking we blow this popsicle stand before it gets back. Unless...?"

"It's still alive," Nate said, in answer to the unspoken question. "I'll get you out, I just need to..."

"Just need to what?"

"You don't... happen to have a rope down there, do you?"

A moment of uneasy silence, the crew no doubt parsing that *something* was up, even if they weren't sure what.

"There any particular reason you can't jet down and grav lift us out of here?" Jaeger asked.

"It's kind of a long story. Just—Just let me think for a second."

"Sounds personal," he heard Snuffy murmur below, followed by a sharper, "What?!" as Ramirez swatted him to be quiet.

Another tap on the back. Nate turned to find Tor brandishing the poly-weave filament pack she'd just drawn from her utility belt.

*Mayhap we should've taken more than two of these Round Table acolytes,* Ex observed.

*You can say that again,* Nate thought, as he accepted the pack with a grateful nod, clipped the hand torch to the side of his helmet, and turned back to start reeling the line down into the pit.

"I'm casting a line down," he called. "How about we get you out of there and save the twenty questions for later?"

"Sounds fair to me," Jaeger said.

"I was just sayin'," Snuffy murmured. "I'm here to talk. That's all."

BY THE TIME Nate and Tor got enough Asgardians and crew members hauled out of the pit that they could effectively take over, Nate's arms and back were on fire, and Ex was officially running out of the go-go juice to deal with it. He did his best to avoid directly thinking the thought that now he really *was* practically an Asgardian, in terms of rough physical capability, but Ex seemed to read the sentiment anyway, and went a few shades moody.

"What's going on?" Jaeger asked quietly, appearing beside him. "Don't tell me that swarm busted Ex."

*As if,* Ex growled. *Busted. Bah.*

"Something's hogging all the Light on this planet," Nate answered quietly, less than eager to broadcast the fact to the entire party here in the belly of the beast. "I'm pretty much—" He thought of Pierce. Rejected the words, *tapped out.* "Pretty much running on empty, at this point."

He heard Jaeger's intake of breath, saw the tight line of his lips. He waited for the colonel to curse this turn of events, or throw blame, or at least grimace. But Jaeger just let that breath out, calm and somber. "All right. We'll just have to regroup outside, then. See if we can't get the *Wilds* up and running."

As usual, the man's ability to roll with the punches and adapt to outlandish circumstances left Nate feeling like he'd underestimated Jaeger at every turn. But even so.

"The Light is in here somewhere."

*Somehow*, he didn't add. *Maybe. Possibly.*

They'd caught up on the pertinent highlights as best they could while Nate and Tor had hauled them out, but Nate had yet to get to the more bizarre details of the thing.

"I don't quite know what's happening on this planet," he admitted, "but I'm pretty sure finding the Light is our best bet of stopping it."

Jaeger was watching him with that assessing look.

Something—maybe just plain old weariness, or the longing to have someone else calling the shots again—convinced Nate to keep talking. "I saw this place once. A long time ago. The Lady showed me, back when we first met. I'm not sure why. But whatever's going on here, I think maybe she wanted me to stop it."

Jaeger considered that, watching the crew organize themselves, bickering with the Asgardians, distributing crude weapons, Snuffy and Amelia cautiously attempting to befriend the dubious snargladorf.

"Whatever yanked us down here did pull Cammy straight toward this mountain," he finally said. It sounded like a concession. He turned watchful eyes on Nate. "You got enough juice left to take on that Myrr thing if it finds us in here?"

Nate held his gaze. "I'm running on empty. Not dead. I can handle it."

He felt the silent weight of Ex's knowing presence. Felt the creeping guilt that he might've just lied to Jaeger compounded by the fact that the man actually seemed to believe him.

"Good. In that case, I say we—"

"Hey, uh, Boss?"

They both turned at the tone in Ramirez's voice. Both followed without question at the airman's silent tilt of the head, gesturing toward the exit tunnel like *you should probably see this*. They didn't have to go far before Nate cursed at what he saw.

"Coulda swore this wasn't here five minutes ago," Ramirez said.

"That's because it wasn't," Nate confirmed, approaching the fresh grown wall with a sinking certainty that culminated with an experimental brush of his armored fingers. Not rock at all. Nanostuff.

Something was caging them in.

He thought of the dark figure at the heart of that swarm on the canyon gorge and looked back to Jaeger in the dim runoff light.

The colonel's face was too stony to be anything other than a mask. "Guess we all go on ahead, then."

"I'll take point," Nate said.

COWS TO THE SLAUGHTER.

That's what Nate couldn't help but think of as they moved deeper into the mountain: the disturbing movie clip one questionable, frizzle-haired substitute teacher had decided to show his class back in the seventh grade— Bessy and all her mooing friends, packed in like, well, *cattle* and forced down the chute, up the slaughterhouse ramp. *Pop, pop, pop*, went the bolt gun.

He'd never in his life empathized so much with those cows as he did now.

To say the going was tense would've been putting it lightly. Nate could feel the group's unease curling the air, thickening with every passing meter, every faintly off-gray plaster of "cave wall" that looked like it should've been a branching path, or an offshoot. There was no missing it.

They were being herded.

"What the hell is this stuff?" someone whispered, somewhere down the line.

"Magic Fairy dust," rumbled a low Asgardian voice. "Perhaps you should try some, Terran."

Nate tried to keep his focus front and center as Jaeger spoke up to cut the chatter back there. He still wasn't sure what to make of the Asgardian people other than that, even amongst ostensible allies, they seemed pathologically driven to compare dick sizes at the drop of a hat.

*Hard to imagine how a people who literally engineered themselves in the image of another species could be harboring some deep-seated insecurities,* Ex commented dryly. He'd seemed markedly less fond of the Asgardian people in general ever since Nate's comparison comments.

Nate forged ahead, senses peeled, what few of Ex's sensors they could currently afford dialed up to eleven. Not that there was much to look out for. There'd been no trace of the monster the others called Myrr. Nothing at all but an irregular tunnel, devoid of forks or choices, leading their winding way into the heart of the mountain—the smell of fresh-baked Light tantalizing the peripheries of his senses without any clear sense of direction.

They'd been at it for about half an hour—the party growing increasingly restless behind him—when the snargladorf he'd nearly forgotten was prowling the tunnel beside him drew up short with a low, rumbling growl.

"That's always a good sign," someone whispered behind them.

Nate was more focused on the snargladorf's unmistakable postural equivalent of *hackles raised,* and on checking the HUD for anything amiss.

*There appears to be an opening ahead,* Ex provided, adding a vague, open-ended overlay to the HUD. *It's muddled like nothing I've ever seen, but... definitely an opening. A very large opening, from the feel of it.*

A sense of terrible foreboding filled the air. Unbidden, Nate thought of Bob, back in the pit. Thought of the way the Ooperian had watched them depart with that soft, rasping hiss, still clinging to the wall like *yeah, you guys have fun with that.* Maybe Bob knew something they didn't.

A look back to Tor at the group's rear confirmed it didn't matter now anyway. The tunnel had closed in behind them. The chute was primed.

Pop, pop, pop.

Nate took a deep breath, thought briefly of asking Tor for that handy dandy gravitonic shield of hers, then let the breath out and moved forward, sure and steady. There were clear signs of light ahead now, trickling in where the craggy tunnel ended in a tall wedge of an opening that looked more like a natural crack than any kind of doorway. Nate wanted to take some iota of reassurance from that small fact—like maybe, if the passage had been formed of natural causes, that somehow precluded the possibility that they'd been made to come to this place. Yet the sense of some greater intervening will was unmistakable as he approached the opening and stepped into the chamber. The giant—freaking *enormous*—chamber, his mind started to register. Right before his boot and hand cleared the threshold and caught fire.

Glorious, *electrifying* fire, he realized with a gasp, caught midway through jerking back. He plunged forward instead, barely able to believe it.

The Light hit him like a supernova. A raw mountain of power crashing into him the second he crossed the threshold, roaring in on a beam of azure radiance that flared from everywhere at once, setting his every atom to blissful, crackling song.

*Ahhh,* Ex sighed, shifting in Nate's mind like a supple cat luxuriating in an exquisite post-nap stretch in the sun. *My sweetest Lady.*

Nate was gasping in relief, caught in something between sobs and incredulous laughter, utterly taken with the beauty as the dancing Light receded, dimming from pure inferno to shimmering motes of blue. He felt the remnants of injured flesh knitting themselves together. Realized there were tears in his eyes. The hunger was gone.

"Nate?"

Jaeger was tensed at the threshold, arm thrown out to keep the others from stepping over the line—all of them looking at Nate like they half-expected he might just explode at any moment. Nate straightened, breaths ragged from the intensity of it, thinking to tell them that everything was okay—*better* than okay. They all recoiled a half-step, eyes gleaming reflected Light, and as he registered that it was *him* casting that wild, glowing aura, he understood why.

"I'm good," he breathed, willing the influx down to something less visually alarming. "I'm... good."

It was only then that the rest of the details began to fall into place. The sheer, breathtaking expanse of this mountain hall—well beyond anything he'd expected. Beyond what even seemed physically possible. It was practically an underground city, minus all the buildings and people, and with the addition of a vast network of erratic scaffolding and tubules that reminded him vaguely of a beehive, or—

The thought died as his gaze drifted down to the familiar shape tucked there between a few building-sized stalagmites.

The *Camelot*.

She was sitting right there—barely a stone's throw away, he thought for a moment, until his adjusting HUD optics and reluctantly-sputtering brain factored in the true size of the cavern, and he realized it was a lot farther than it looked. His stomach sank as the dialing optics revealed more of that damned nanostuff glommed onto her hull, running up from the underbelly to join that hectic network of whatever the hell was being built—or building itself—throughout the enormous cavern.

"Jesus," Jaeger said at Nate's left shoulder, gaping up at the gargantuan structure stretching into the distance. There was something aberrant about the thing. Something unnatural.

"Lady's grace, be with us," Tor agreed, appearing on his right.

In front of Nate, the snargladorf began to snarl, fangs bared in the direction of the *Camelot*, like he smelled an intruder.

*I believe WE are the intruders here, technically speaking*, Ex pointed out— just as a distant dark figure came gliding out from behind the *Camelot*, born smoothly toward them on a swirling mist of nanoswarm. *Not that I'm saying we SHOULDN'T smite that thing straight to hell and take back our girl.*

Nate stared at the approaching figure, just trying to process what the thing was. It looked like some kind of mystical golem—dark, armored appendages of what might've been concentrated nanostuff held together at the joints by a nebulous, ruby red haze of energies that pulsed through the thing's core, rippling out through the swarm. Its face, a disconcerting blur of crackling red energy and shifting stone features.

"Whaaat the fuck is that?" came Ramirez's dumbstruck question from behind, as the thing came to a resting hover some fifty meters ahead.

"I have no idea," Nate said, calling his sword down from e-dim, reassured by the shudder of raw power the weapon sent rippling up his arm. "But it's about to give us our ship back."

# CHAPTER 24

# METTLE

It felt good to cut loose.

Air rushing. Gravitonics thrumming. Sword arm strong.

The Light enveloped Nate in a glowing nimbus of power as he sped in to obliterate the dark figure at the heart of the swarm. No use trying to talk. He felt it in his bones just as surely as Ex did. This was the Enemy. Not the ghost of Mordred LeFaye like he'd been privately fearing. Not the Synth in any shape or form he'd ever seen before. But the Enemy, nonetheless. He could feel it in the cloying darkness at the edge of his senses, and in the thirsty song of the Light coursing through his blade as he thrust it in for the kill.

It just felt good.

Right up until the thing moved like lightning, catching his blow on a raised forearm, and the cavern lit with a hellish thunderclap of light and sound, the impact ripping through Nate's sword arm like the physical manifestation of the old *unstoppable force v. immovable object* paradox.

*Interesting,* Ex said, ever so casually, as the blast wave dissipated to the soft pitter-patter of loosened debris falling around them, and the helmet filters dialed back to confirm that the golem thing *hadn't* had the good decency to rip apart at its crackling red energy joints—or to disintegrate into a million tiny pieces, as he'd half-hoped. It was a little concerning.

Then the thing hit back.

A blinding crash of impact later, Nate blinked his half-conscious way to the realization that he was embedded in a shattered patch of cavern wall, some hundred meters distant from the spot he'd just stood. He'd nearly forgotten what it was like, to take a hit like that—the force of a speeding destroyer packed behind a fist. It was the kind of hit he would've expected from the likes of Zedavian Kelkarin, or the Black Knight himself.

*Very interesting*, Ex confirmed, with all the concern of a commentator watching a golf match. Nate was too busy trying to shake his senses clear to give him shit about it. His head was spinning. Ruptured organs mending themselves back together on a tingling pull of Light and newly re-available e-dim stores. Down at the mouth of the tunnel, Jaeger and the others were all watching him like the exchange had not at all gone as they'd expected. Ahead, the pulsing red golem thing was just hovering there.

Nate waited a few breathless seconds, sure the thing would come at him with a flash of ruby fire and fury, or send its orbiting nanites speeding for the crew. But the thing didn't budge. Just hung there, perfectly still, waiting to see what he'd do. Or maybe not. Frankly, it was hard to tell where its attention was focused.

*What the hell is this thing, Ex?* Nate demanded, pushing out of the impact crater on gravitonics, and reaching to call a few pulse rifles from e-dim—as if they'd do any good—as he floated down to rejoin Jaeger.

"Think he won that round," Jaeger murmured to Nate as he accepted a rifle and tossed the others to Elmo and Ramirez. "Any idea what we call this one?"

"Not a clue," Nate said, when a thrice-prodded Ex finally admitted as much.

*I have guesses*, Ex grumbled indignantly. *Just none that seem especially possible, technically speaking.*

Ahead, the golem thing raised one long arm, its hand thrumming to life with ruby red energy. Curses sounded behind Nate and Jaeger. Nate held his ground, defenses at the ready, as threads of nanoswarm came flowing forth from that glowing hand like sands on the desert wind, twisting their way almost lazily down to the cavern floor, where they began piling up. Nate reached for Cammy, thinking to call her over, but he could barely even feel her there, much less communicate.

"Just get to the ship," he said to Jaeger, eyes never leaving the dark figure. "I'll keep our friend here off your back."

He felt Jaeger's sideways glance. Felt the unspoken *and if you can't?* lingering in the stark silence of the cavern. Ahead, the nanite sands were growing faster now, rising from the rock like a dark obelisk before the shape deepened, loose nanites falling away to reveal a dark structure some-where between a jagged throne and a tall, narrow prison cell.

"You heard the Knight," Jaeger called over his shoulder. "Let's get to that ship, people."

Nate adjusted his grip on his sword, flexing stiff fingers and noticing the wide-eyed looks of Amelia and Dr. Lundquist. A few of the Asgardians—who'd offered muttered slights and nothing in the way of thanks since he'd pulled them from the pit—were making some gesture he didn't recognize but that seemed to carry the same reverent weight as a Terran drawing the cross in hopes of divine protection.

*Those impossible guesses of yours,* he thought at Ex, focusing back on their eerily patient enemy. *Any of 'em happen to include how we might kill this thing?*

*Kill it?* Ex seemed confused by the question. *I'm not sure it's alive, Nathaniel.*

*Destroy it, then. Annihilate it. What-the-hell-ever.*

*Well...* Ex thought about it. *The same way you annihilate anything, I suppose.*

"Helpful," Nate muttered, drifting up on gravitonics to keep the thing's attention centered on him as the others set off to the left to give it wide berth on route toward the *Camelot.*

*I'd refrain from having a seat in the Throne of Thorns over there, for starters,* Ex shot back. *How's that?*

*Not bad,* Nate had to admit, if for no other reason than that it was just about the last seat in the universe he would've willingly taken. But that was exactly what the golem thing seemed to be waiting for, hovering there with its dimming ruby hand extended in invitation, as if it expected Nate to simply float over and surrender. Or so he gathered, right up until he sensed the nanotendrils drifting in from the sides like the slow-closing jaws of a flytrap.

He threw himself forward, pelting the dark leader of the swarm with a column of plasma that would've given fully powered dreadnaught shields a run for their money. The golem turned the brilliant blue blast aside with a wave of its arm that sent Nate's HUD wild with electromagnetic noise. In the resultant spattering of slagged, red-hot particulate rain, Nate was suddenly and painfully aware of the proximity of Jaeger's party off to the left, rubbernecking to see who and what had just cranked up the heat. He stowed a curse and darted in close, thinking to force the fighting to a range that hopefully wouldn't cook his team alive.

The golem reached for him almost dreamily. He dipped easily beneath the thing's reaching arm, moving into a familiar fleury of slashes. Or starting to, until the golem's entire body flickered in space and his blade went ripping through thin air on the first strike, displacing a swirling streak of the golem's form like smoke.

The curling wisps of matter snapped back into place the next instant as the golem caught him by the throat, perfectly solid, and started driving him dispassionately toward that obsidian fixture. Nate clamped an arm around its neck, grappling in for leverage, and shoved his sword straight through the thing's glowing chest. It pierced the golem's dark plating with a flash of ruby red light and a sound like rusty iron. He thrust through to the cross-guard, feeding enough energy through the blade to atomize nova steel. And atomize, it did—acrid smoke and superheated plasma washing over Nate's crackling shields in great, dripping globs as the golem pushed diligently on, taking no notice of its melting chest cavity.

Nate flipped them around mid-flight, gravitonics straining against the force of the golem's propellant swarm, and kicked off of the thing's torso, hard. He ripped free with a sound of scraping metal and caught himself in a hover, darting a glance to check the crew's distance. Clear enough.

Below, the golem touched absentmindedly at the molten core of its chest, turning its flickering red non-face slowly up to him, like it was trying to compute. Nate pointed his sword and let it have the solution, loud and clear. He kept up the onslaught this time, determined to slag the thing *and* its creepy obsidian chair right back to whatever hell they'd come from, some part of him simply reveling in the power. He didn't back off until he heard Jaeger's voice some couple hundred meters distant, barking his name.

He killed the death ray—distantly noting that it was a damn good thing the golem didn't seem remotely concerned with the crew, hard as it would be to cover their asses if it changed its mind and set that swarm on them. Mostly, he just tried to convince himself that it didn't matter anyway, because in a moment, the smoke was going to clear from that sinister orange glow below, and he was going to see that he'd finished the thing, through and through.

With a word to Ex, they hit the wall of smoke with a harmless grav pulse, ventilating the area enough to clear line of sight on the glowing pool of lava he'd made of the cave floor below. The obsidian shrine, at least, had gone down with the rest of its surroundings. The golem thing, on the other hand, hovered on, perfectly unharmed.

And it looked pissed.

It turned its crackling red non-face up to him, one hand flaring bright with more of that ruby energy, the nanoswarm dancing around it, searing into place where it met the light, merging to form a long, dark sword in crude imitation of his own. Then the thing flashed up to meet him like a runaway train.

The clash shook Nate to the bone, the shockwave of sword on sword ripping through the enormous space, knocking loose a rain of dust and debris from the cavern walls and the sprawling girders and lines of whatever this thing had been building. The golem struck again, faster. Nate parried, moving solely on reflexes Iveera Katanaga had painstakingly drilled into the core of his being. Crash. Crash. Crash. Flashing across the cavern. Each blow an explosion. The golem barely seeming to care as they blasted through entire sections of its insane, cavern-spanning superstructure. Nate glimpsed debris raining down on his people. Too close.

Half-frozen by the sight, he caught the golem's next blow on a hasty mix of sword and half-cocked gravitonic feedback, some corner of his subconscious apparently inspired by Tor's grav shield act—and sadly lacking the time to make it an effective reality.

*A little warning, next time,* Ex grumbled, on the far side of the resultant flight and teeth-jarring *smack* of a very large, very hard obstacle shattering around him. One of those building-sized stalagmites, Nate realized, as he pulled himself up from the rubble on the other side and realized he'd come down not far from the ship.

*Outclassed by an Atlantean,* Ex added. *Honestly.*

Nate ignored him, bent instead on reaching the *Camelot.* He covered the distance in a long leap that landed him just above the bridge and knelt smoothly down, planting his hands to her ventral hull, calling to Cammy. Willing the Light to flow freely through them both. He felt her there, trying to stir. Felt Ex coaxing her up right alongside him, sassy comments be damned.

The golem had paused above, hazy red non-face studying this new interaction like it didn't know what to make of it. At least not until Nate and Ex tugged Cammy far enough out of the darkness to convince her groggy systems to help them fry the nanostuff off of her underbelly.

The sound that escaped the golem then was like nothing Nate had ever heard. Not a bellow. Not even a voice. It was like the discordant cacophony of an untuned cathedral organ caught in a rockslide, and it shook the entire cavern, rushing back in on its creator in a thrumming build of power.

"Get down!" Nate screamed at Jaeger and the others, caught in the last leg of their mad rush for the *Camelot* just below.

The golem erupted before they could do anything more than hit the open dirt. The attack ripped out in a ruby red ocean of destruction, blasting everything in its path to dust and shrapnel. It crashed to a furious halt just shy of the crew, washing over the shields Nate hadn't even registered he'd called. Cammy's shields, he realized, with a flutter of relief—hissing and thrumming as they shirked off more physical tonnage of falling debris and speeding nanites than Nate could shake a stick at. The ship was groaning to life beneath him, disoriented and furious, and ready to lash out at whatever had dared to attack her crew.

In the deluge of falling rock and superheated debris, Nate pointed their girl at the culprit, and set her loose.

He wasn't sure what he'd been expecting. That something in Cammy's expanded arsenal—pulse turrets, magnetic acceleration cannons, broad-spectrum laser barrage, and a few dozen varieties of torpedoes, just to name a few—might actually find a way where his uninspired plasma attacks had failed, even if they were somewhat limited in what they could safely throw at the thing in the atmosphere.

None of it left a mark on the golem thing.

It did, however, succeed at blowing the entire gods-damned side off of the mountain.

Nate gaped at the swath of open Ginnungagap sky staring back at them from outside, watching in awe as ship-sized hunks of rock shook loose from the crumbling cavern walls, ripping through the giant rat's nest maze of the unfathomable superstructure on the way down. The entire damn thing was starting to rattle, the cavern floor shaking with the low-grade earthquake of steady impacts.

Jaeger got his shit together before Nate did, pulling Amelia and Dr. Lundquist up from the ground, shoving them forward, and shouting at all of them to move their asses for the *Camelot*, on the double. Nate watched the golem thing taking in the extensive damage they'd just done to its habitat, stuttering non-face turning from one crumbling section to the next, and finally back to the *Camelot*.

*You know what to do*, Nate thought to the ship, patting her affectionately on the hull as Snuffy and Ramirez charged aboard with the Drs. Lundquist and Ramachandra in tow, closely flanked by Carter and the others—Jaeger and the Asgardians bringing up the rear. He felt Cammy's flicker of reluctance, her fear for him tugging momentarily against her even fiercer loyalty, both to him and to the crew.

*Take care of our people*, he told her, easing on the gravitonics and drifting gently up from her hull to go meet the golem. The thing watched him rise, still poking and prodding at Cammy's shields with the thick tendrils of nanoswarm that extended from the writhing darkness at its back like a pair of overstretched angel's wings.

Nate's HUD pinged with Jaeger's comm line as the *Camelot* closed shop and lifted up, banking around for the jagged gash it'd blown through to the outside world.

"Get to the *Wilds* and see if Cammy can't jumpstart it," Nate said, before the colonel could utter so much as a *what the piss*. "I'm right behind you."

He heard the scramble of the crew strapping in. Could practically smell the tension on Jaeger's end—the clamp-jawed, hard-eyed fury at being so summarily dismissed, shipped off without a choice in the matter. He waited for the colonel to tell him to go to hell, or to at least point out that this was a total shithead move and that they'd be having words about it just as soon as this was all over.

"Be careful with this thing, Nate," was all he said instead, as Cammy punched it for the exit. "Don't get—"

The cavern flared with that strange ruby energy, flooding Nate's HUD with sputtering noise and wiping away everything but the terrible sight of the vast swarm suddenly racing toward the *Camelot*. It came from every-where at once. The golem. The cavern walls. The superstructure itself, dismantling to throw itself on the fleeing ship, enveloping it from every side.

Nate was already racing forward, firing, atomizing the broad tail of the reaching swarm here, there, everywhere—Cammy fighting against the tide like a wild animal caught in a snare—but it just kept coming, crushing in from all directions. It battered at Nate, straining his shields, obscuring his view. He blasted one thick body away only to watch in horror as the rest of the swarm wrestled the *Camelot* down to a sputtering crash just outside the blasted edge of the mountain wall.

He fought on through the harrying swarm, cutting a smoldering trail, determined to rip his ship free and carry it away by his own hands, if he had to. Ex's warning was sharp and sudden—too fast for words, too slow for Nate to react as the swarm parted and the golem came crashing into him from the side. They hit a painfully solid section of superstructure some couple hundred speeding meters later, the golem pinning him roughly to the surface. Nate was too focused on the *Camelot* to hardly care.

"Get out of there," he heard himself hiss, eyes locked on the swarm-ridden ship. She was drowning. His people trapped aboard. He almost forgot to worry about himself, right up until his shields gave their own sputtering hiss and he found his hands helpless to do anything about the furiously scalding something that'd just pierced his chest.

*Payback*, he realized with a nauseous twist, gaping down at the red-hot sword the golem had just plunged through his torso. One searing chest stab for another. He hadn't even noticed the superstructure morphing behind him, nanite surface rippling to engulf his arms. Shackling him. He'd been too desperate to notice.

"That's twice," he heard himself grunt past the pain, thinking of the canyon river run-in the previous night, thinking of how he'd broken free then.

A flash of azure brilliance outside interrupted Ex's pending comment. Cammy, he realized with a rush of pride, pulsing her way clear of the swarm. Or not quite, it turned out, as the boarding ramp sprang open and the first of the crew came racing out—the swarm obstinately refusing to release the *Camelot*'s tail.

They were going to hoof it, he realized. Fleeing down the ramp, limping across the rocks in twos and threes. Cammy bitterly holding the heart of the swarm at bay on her hissing, sputtering shields, incinerating any bits that slipped by with her point defense lasers before the darting tendrils could reach the crew.

The golem thing was watching too, Nate realized. Both of them staring off to the conflict outside like they'd forgotten Nate had the thing's sword buried through his chest. He tried his hands, found the nanite shackles firm. Outside, the swarm gnashed hungrily at the *Camelot*'s tail end, ripping and tugging, reeling her back toward the cavern. The golem watched, crackling red non-face pulsing almost in time with the erratic surges and flares of rushing swarm and crackling shields. Nate watched too, counting heads, spotting Carter, Elmo, and Ramirez firing back into the swarm to cover their hectic retreat. And there. Jaeger, hurrying down the ramp with an unconscious Tessa slung over his shoulder, Tor on their heels, looking like she had half a mind to pluck the weight from the colonel's shoulder and pick up the pace properly. Nate felt something like relief at the sight. Something like anger as Jaeger paused, looking back to the mountain with a flash of the *leave no man behind* bullshit in his eyes.

"Get out of here!" Nate cried, his amplified voice booming with an intensity that left his head ringing. The golem's attention snapped back to him, its entire body emitting a strange buzzing noise, thrumming red hand-thing tightening on its blade.

"GO!" Nate bellowed, distantly startled to find his hands broke free with the word—nanite shackles shattering like cheap ceramics, something wild and furious screaming to escape. He threw himself into the golem, ignoring the pain, hammering at thing's dark torso until his hand swept through smoky nothingness, and the thing phased back into shape halfway across the vast cavern, amid the regathering heart of the swarm.

It didn't matter. Jaeger was gone. Disappeared past the edge of the opening along with the rest of the crew. Cammy's struggles weakening as the swarm dragged the *Camelot* back into the cavern—the gaping mountain-side weaving itself shut like a plague of locusts nestling in. The fiery wound in his chest following suit.

The golem thing was watching him across the wrecked cavern, dark sword clasped in its hands in a manner reminiscent of a nun brandishing a ruler—like Nate knew damn well what it was he'd done, and now it was time for the spanking.

*To nine hells with it,* Ex growled, as the last patch of Ginnungagap sky disappeared behind the growing wall of nanoswarm. *Off with the kiddy gloves, then.*

Nate was too revved to even mentally formulate any of the pithy lines that stirred. Ex knew. Ex felt the ache of his burning muscles and the divine kiss of the Light flooding in to replenish them. Felt the rage bubbling through him, begging for release. The guilty relief at being alone. No more vulnerable teammates to worry about. No one to accidentally flash fry. Just his ship, and the crackling red golem asshole who'd hurt her for the last time.

It hardly even mattered what this thing was.

This was what he'd been waiting for.

This was what he'd *wanted*. A chance to take on the Synth. To prove that he could—that the Lady hadn't been wrong about him like the Knights and half of the galaxy so clearly thought.

His people were clear. His Enemy was here.

Zedavian Kelkarin could suck it.

Nate gathered his will, steeling himself for what was about to happen.

Then he let loose with everything he had.

# CHAPTER 25
# FALLOUT

The mountain collapsed behind them barely a klick out.

That was the only thing Jaeger knew for sure—the last coherent glimpse he caught of anything before the world became a wild, whipping storm of dust and rock. A long, unsettling string of thunderous booms, like the gods themselves were duking it out back there. Then total collapse.

He barked at the others to take cover, plainly aware there was no way in hell they actually heard him over the rolling thunderclaps of overwhelming sound. He barely even heard himself. Just clasped Kalders' limp weight tight to his shoulder, grabbed the closest body he could find in the mess—the arm of one gaping Dr. Lundquist—and dove behind the outcropping that was their nearest hope of cover.

The sky vanished, choked out by the instant rust-red sandstorm. Gale force winds ripping at their clothes, their exposed skin. Jaeger clamped the crook of one elbow over his mouth and nose, scanning the chaos for his people. Watched the dusty outline of a staggering Asgardian brained by a flying hunk of rock. Felt the old, terrible realization of helplessness as another boulder came speeding down on Carter, only to be inexplicably batted aside by Tor's shield as the huge Asgardian darted in at the last moment with amazing speed.

It all happened in the familiar rush of combat—that agonizing place where the senses slowed time to an almost supernatural degree, even as they infuriatingly refused to do a single damn thing to let his brain react accordingly. Carter and Tor hit the dirt together, crawling toward him. The others lost in the blinding rush of dust.

Then the fury receded, albeit only slightly—violent winds slowing, world-shaking sound dying down just enough to make room for the steady crumble and patter of falling-rock rain and settling landslide in the background. Jaeger heard his own rough breath against the crook of his elbow, felt his heart pounding in his ears, the air still packed well beyond easy sight with a displaced mountain's worth of dust, and ash, and something that smelled a bit like—

"Ozone," whispered Dr. Lundquist, lowering the arm that'd been shielding his face just enough to hazard an unimpeded *sniff-sniff*, his eyes still wide and dazed. "Ozone and sulfur. Must've been..."

The doctor's trailing thought was cut short by a deep, booming crack, the ground beneath them coming alive with a rumbling earthquake like Jaeger had never felt before—every bit as intense as the preceding collapse, but somehow... deeper?

It felt like the planet itself was waking from some ancient slumber to shake off the collapse of its favorite mountain. Jaeger clung to Kalders' unconscious form, waiting for the aftershock to pass, as the voice of reason insisted it had to. But the rumbling went on, thickening, deepening—something shifting in the planet's core. He laid Kalders carefully with Lundquist. Peered over the outcropping they'd taken cover behind. Flinched as the huge stone cracked right up the center, peppering him with bits of debris.

There was nowhere to run. He scanned what little he could make out of the surrounding area, feeling like the ground was about to open up and swallow them whole. Watched with a kind of detached fascination as a sudden chasm ruptured across the arid landscape, following the dark trail that must've been the same one Nate had followed in.

"Okay," someone was saying, as the voices—and, probably, the shock— began to emerge and multiply throughout the group. "Okay. Okay."

"—got eyes on Nate?"

"—was in there. He was—Fuck! He was still in there!"

Jaeger found his hands fashioning a makeshift mask in the thick cloud of hanging dust, old training taking hold in place of good senses. "Roll call," he called out, his voice surprisingly steady, albeit rather thick and buzzy in his ringing ears. "Everyone gather up here."

"Boss," Snuffy said, appearing through the veil of red dust with a dazed look in his eyes. "Nate was still—"

"Still the only one who might've survived that shit, last I checked," Jaeger cut him off. "So, we need to take stock, get our shit together, and assess the situation, hooah?"

"Yeah." Snuffy blinked, clearly trying to pull it together. "Hooah."

"Effin' A," O'Sweeney agreed somewhere nearby.

Jaeger was busy tracing that chasm line again, remembering what Nate had said about having followed it in from where he'd left Pierce and the others aboard Iveera's apparently Lightless ship. More than a few too many questions, there. Most of them thoroughly irrelevant for the moment, with an unstable mountain of debris next door, and the ground still rumbling underfoot like a living thing—not to mention the potential threat of any surviving hostiles. Hopefully, they hadn't all just been lethally irradiated by whatever brought the mountain down. Beyond that, though…

"We're gonna follow that line and regroup with Pierce," he called, waving for the crew to round up on him. "See if we can't get the *Wilds* up and running. We'll find Nate once we have eyes in the sky and—"

A particularly violent crack from the widening chasm seemed to convey the rest just fine: Eyes in the sky, and shelter that wasn't liable to crush them in a landslide or swallow them whole at any moment. He heard himself divvying out orders from there, tallying their non-ambulatory wounded, pairing escorts. In the hangover of the initial adrenaline rush, he could no longer ignore the hot, growing balloon of pain that told him something had gone critically wrong in his ankle during their mad dash. His knee, too. And whether there'd been some new injury or just a re-flaring of the recent, his ribs were on fire. Left shoulder too. And he seemed to be bleeding from somewhere he didn't have time to pinpoint. None of them had eaten in Christ knew how long. He couldn't imagine anyone else was in much better shape than him—of those who were even standing to start with.

"I will begin the search now," Tor announced quietly at Jaeger's side, when he'd finished speaking, and the rest of the crew were busy at work preparing to transport the most heavily wounded.

"No," Jaeger said automatically, following the Atlantean's gaze toward the cored ruins of the mountain, crunching the grim facts as best as he saw them—the size and extent of the rubble to be searched, the amount of rock still shifting throughout the mess, the clear misbalance of wounded to non-wounded here on their end, and the fact that the towering Atlantean before him could no doubt handle at least two on her own. "Help us get the wounded to stable cover first. It's better chances for all of us that way."

He wasn't sure what he was expecting. Aside from the briefest of assertions from Nate as he'd leapt out of the *Camelot* to go racing the swarm back in orbit, there'd been no clear chain of command established here. And clearly, the Atlantean was devoutly set on protecting her Knight above all else.

To his surprise, though, she only deliberated a few seconds before setting her shoulders, nodding without any discernible bitterness, and marching off to go help. For one moment, watching how easily the Atlantean hauled Kalders up over one shoulder and turned to take the weight of a bloody-, maybe broken-legged Elmo from an only marginally less battered Ramirez, Jaeger almost allowed himself to hope that, somehow, this still all might actually turn out all right.

~

EXCEPT THAT THE *Kalnythian Wilds* was missing.

Or so Jaeger was forced to assume, some hours later, as they crested the hilltop on the far side of the Battered March from Hell and spotted nothing at the end of their mysterious chasm line but a gigantic sinkhole where he could only assume their errant Knightship was supposed to have been. Tor confirmed the bad news a moment later, by somber look alone.

"Son of a bitch," Jaeger whispered under his breath.

The trek had been bad enough, beaten and bloodied as they all were. Shifting grounds and persistent tremors—full-on earthquakes, really—threatening their every step. And even without a full cadre of wounded, crossing that hellacious swell of a river wouldn't have been a picnic. The waters were still running wild in the aftermath of the mountain's collapse. Probably would be for weeks. Between the fury of the currents and the muddy shit show they'd made of the flooded grasslands beyond, it seemed a minor miracle no one had drowned in the crossing. Luckily, Tor had been there with her gear and her freakish bioengineered Atlantean strength. But now...

Now, they needed a lick of rest, and far more resources than they had. Food and shelter. Weapons. A plan. They needed a goddamned plan.

Jaeger eyed the distant line of the jungle, not quite praying that it hadn't just come to an extended wilderness survival situation—but not *not* praying, either. Because without ships... without *Nate*...

He scanned the surrounding area from their height, noting the distant, decaying buildings Nate had mentioned, trying not to think too much of Nate himself. The compound was little more than the bare bones leftovers from some hush-hush resource expedition, from the sounds of it. Or maybe the shady old remnants of a mad scientist's lair, if Nate's gut had pegged it right. Decent enough shelter, maybe. But also about as obvious as a baboon's asshole.

His attention drifted on, dismissing the obvious, donning the cynical eyes with which he imagined Pierce might've scanned the options here, assuming he *hadn't* still been aboard the *Wilds* if and when the ship had gone for an involuntary spelunking trip into the abyss, as seemed a reasonable enough conclusion, all freaky things considered. He supposed it was also possible his moody pilot might've gotten the Knightship airborne with the help of Tristan and Princess Elsa, or that something else entirely had happened to all of them. But even if Pierce and the others *were* up there flying recon, the best Jaeger could do for the crew right now was to find adequate shelter until they could safely signal.

His eyes settled on an embankment in the hill, another klick or so down the line. Maybe slightly obvious in its own right. But probably the best place to hide, short of hoofing it all the way to the potentially deadly jungle.

It'd do for now.

No one was especially excited at the prospect of marching any farther, but nor did they have any energy left to complain. Jaeger, for his part, might've been too busy to notice if they had, engrossed as he was in scanning the terrain for signs. For threats or for Pierce, he didn't quite allow himself to say. At first, there was nothing more than dirt, tufts of bone-dry grass and assorted bushes, and the odd animal droppings here and there. As they moved downslope and into the lusher grasses, though, and came in line with the likely route one might've taken from that gaping sinkhole, had one been forced to flee a sinking Knightship, Jaeger couldn't help but think he saw signs of passage here and there. Bent blades of grass. The faintest indentations of what could've been boots. The soft outline, seemingly scuffed by a deliberate hand, but still just barely visible, of something heavy having been set there in the thickening grass.

He traded a look with O'Sweeney, who'd taken to scouting the way with him, then back at Tor, who was bringing up the rear. At his look, the Atlantean touched one finger to an eye, then pointed ahead, as if telling him to pay attention. Jaeger turned just as the deceptively shallow embankment gave way to a deeper, more sheltered hillside inset than he'd expected. He spotted Pierce and Princess Elsa therein—right about the same moment a humming lance tip appeared in his face.

"Well met, Colonel," Tristan said, lowering the weapon respectfully if not quite apologetically as he recognized Jaeger and spotted the others behind him. The Atlantean's hands were impressively steady on the lance, considering how much he looked like hammered shit.

"Sister," he added, over Jaeger's shoulder.

"Brother," Tor responded, having appeared beside Jaeger entirely more quickly and quietly than someone her size had any business moving.

Jaeger was caught somewhere between straight up surprise, irritation at Tor's less-than-ample heads up, and a flitting curiosity as to whether these two, and maybe all of the Round Table acolytes, actually shared some literal family bond, unlike most of their vat-birthed Atlantean kin. Probably, the words were merely meant in the parlance of brethren in arms. Probably, it didn't matter one bit right then, as Pierce sauntered—or maybe limped—up beside his beefy sentinel, meeting Jaeger's eyes with a kind of weary assessment before glancing almost guiltily back at the extremely basic camp they'd only barely begun setting up.

"Took nice orderly stock of the *Wild's* supplies, just like the kid said."

Pierce's voice was almost wistful. Jaeger turned from the pilot to consider the sad bundle of supplies Elsa was sitting on, waiting for the rest of the story.

Pierce shrugged beside him. "Kid didn't mention the planet might go and eat the goddamn ship. We grabbed what we could on the way out."

Jaeger killed the building sigh. Let out a long, slow breath instead, accepting this new obstacle, looking for the next step forward.

"Was he in there?" Pierce asked quietly, eyes flicking toward the collapsed mountain, back to Jaeger, waiting for the obvious.

Jaeger nodded, mildly surprised the pilot looked so distraught by the fact. He chastised the internal snipe as soon as it occurred. Pierce had never been a fan of Nate's, that much was true. But the crew meant more than such personal squabbles to each and every one of them. Even to Pierce.

And that was to mention nothing of their slim prospects of survival and escape, sans a living Excalibur Knight.

"You think he made it?" Pierce asked, even more quietly.

Jaeger didn't know what to say. Meant to say *yes*, he supposed. Hell yes. No doubt. Pierce seemed to glean enough from his silent stare. The pilot nodded, looking back to their camp with forced confidence and a murmured, "Right."

The small relief of their reunion was short-lived, and ultimately about as satisfying as the rest of the chatter as they set about taking stock of their extremely limited supplies—a few choice bits of survival gear and barely enough rations for two square meals, given the size of their group. The temperature of morale around camp, in light of the fact, was about as comfortable as the hot, humid heat of the prolonged Ginnungagap midday. The lingering pressure of incomplete decompression. Lots of *did you see* this and *what the holy hell* that, with no answers to be had. Eventually, Jaeger couldn't help but pitch in and ask anyway.

"Anyone have any ideas what that thing was, or what it was up to back there?"

His question directed itself toward Dr. Lundquist—maybe by default, or maybe because Jaeger had the distinct impression the doctor had been chewing on whatever he'd smelled in the wake of the collapse. He wasn't really sure what he'd been hoping for. Lundquist hardly looked like a man with answers at that moment. Especially not as he realized how many more stares were following Jaeger's to fix themselves on him.

"It was definitely Synth," Snuffy spoke up. "Right?"

"That's impossible," said Gendra the Gorgon, though the doubt in her swishing jin was evident even to Jaeger. "The Synth are mindless swarms. They do not build and plot. They certainly do not take physical form like... like that."

"Well, that thing definitely seemed to be in control of that swarm back there," Snuffy pointed out. "And it was hardly mindless. It could've killed us a dozen times over. It just wanted Nate and the ship. I'm not the only one who saw that, right?"

Jaeger let the group stew on that a minute, watching Lundquist.

"I smelled ozone and sulfur," the doctor finally said, quietly. "Coupled with what felt like severe tectonic activity."

"No shit," Pierce murmured in the background.

"I'm not sure what that... that creature might've been up to in that cavern," Lundquist continued, like he hadn't heard, "but its apparatus was extensive, and it seems its roots might well have run quite deep. Perhaps... Perhaps, if we could aggregate what small details each of us remembers, we might begin to tease out some general function."

"Your best guess, Doctor," Jaeger said. "Humor us."

Lundquist thought about it. Shrugged. "It's either doing something to this planet or using the planet to power something else. Perhaps whatever it was building in there. Given how little we have to work with, it'd be irresponsible for me to speculate any more than that." He looked to Dr. Ramachandra for support.

"I agree," she said distractedly, clearly still dazed from the entire episode.

Jaeger didn't love the answer, but his gut told him now wasn't the time to push.

"So," Pierce said, stepping into the open silence with decidedly less tact. "We've got an unknown something doing an unknown something to another unknown something. That's fucking golden."

"You forgot the part where all of those somethings wanna kill us," Ramirez pointed out.

"*Maybe* wanna kill us," Snuffy amended, like the distinction was actually important.

"You see the way that thing hit Nate?" Ramirez asked.

"It was strong," Elmo grunted, from over where Carter was at work splinting his leg.

"Freaky strong," Ramirez agreed.

"I didn't think anything could smack him around like that anymore," Snuffy admitted, shaking his head. "I thought he was, you know, stronger now. Or whatever."

"Perhaps he was merely distracted by..." Elsa started, only to trail off with a curious expression, like she was surprised to realize she'd spoken aloud.

"By what?" Snuffy asked.

Elsa just gave him one of those *look at the talking Yggdrasian slum monkey* looks.

"No, Snuff's right," Ramirez said, keying in on the uneasy feeling suddenly clogging the camp air. "What are you trying to say, Princess?"

The tension was palpable.

"I'm only saying that, if a few well-armed Asgardians managed to land a few shots—"

"Well, maybe if you hadn't gone flying straight into their arms," Ramirez shot back.

"Pretty sure that's exactly what her highness is trying to say," came Kalders' voice from behind. Jaeger hadn't even noticed the pilot stirring over in the medic's corner. She was sitting up, still wrapped in the thin, reflective survival blanket that'd come from their small stash of *Wilds* gear. The sight should've been a happy one, but the entire camp was too busy glaring daggers at their outspoken princess-envoy.

Elsa, for her part, didn't flinch under the stares. Just said, calmly and without apology: "You can't expect a Knight to be unbeatable when they're too busy trying to avoid stepping on the little people."

"The hell are you trying to—"

"Princess, you can bring your little—"

"Enough," Jaeger called, rising to stiff legs and immediately regretting it as his throbbing ankle and knee came alive in a fresh world of pain.

There was something else there, beneath her words. Something off about all of it, despite the ring of truth. He was more certain of that than about pretty much anything else on this planet right now. But now wasn't the time—and not just because it was about all he could do to not fall back on his ass right then.

At some point, and maybe some point soon, it seemed likely they were going to need to vent their excess steam before the fists started flying. But he'd prefer it wait until they had the food and the time to spare.

"What's the plan then, Boss?" Carter asked, apparently sensing as much. She made a show of walking over to offer him an improvised crutch, dissipating the sharpest edge of the tension as she passed through the center of camp, bisecting the verbal combatants and neatly inviting him to close the door on this little drama.

"The plan, is…"

He eyed Carter's offered crutch, trying to formulate, ankle pulsing in hot, sickly waves. She'd already told him, in multiple quiet asides during the trek, that he was being an idiot, walking any farther on the thing. The plan, though. Food and water. Better shelter. Scouting. He was opening his mouth to use his words when a gentle motion caught his attention— Hannah O'Sweeney, picking her way up the last of the hillside at the edge of camp. No one seemed to have noticed her leaving amid the brewing drama.

"The plan is… hold that thought a minute," he said, taking the crutch absentmindedly from Carter. He felt their focus shifting, Ramirez and a few of the others glancing up to the hilltop, no doubt wondering what'd caught his attention, but O'Sweeney had already passed out of sight.

More importantly, so too had the snargladorf Jaeger swore he'd just seen perched up there, waiting. The very same snargladorf that'd followed Nate through the mountain tunnels like a loyal lapdog, lest he missed his guess. It seemed a bit preposterous—they'd lost track of the thing in the mad dash from the mountain, and he didn't really see how the hell the thing could've survived—but he knew what he'd seen. More or less. Nate's snargladorf, sniffing and waiting. Sniffing its way back toward the muddy mess of the river and the flooded grasslands beyond, like it had something to show them.

"Better yet," he said, focusing back on Pierce and the others, "why don't you all put your heads together and start figuring out our best bet for finding food. You too," he added in the direction of the brooding Asgardians. "Play nice. I'll be right back."

He didn't wait for an answer, just turned and started crutching his way toward the shallowest stretch of the nearby hillside. Probably, he was being crazy, but something in his gut—that same well-tuned but frustratingly vague flutter of instinct he'd come to trust over the decades—told him it was worth a quick look, even if O'Sweeney *had* taken it upon herself to go ahead without asking. He was actually kind of taken aback by the anger stirring as he took his first few steps up the hill. Anger he hadn't even realized he was holding back in the rush of all their bigger problems. Anger that hadn't yet found its proper target but was suddenly rearing for a mark, like it sensed one was close. He didn't argue when Tor fell silently in beside him. Didn't look back as Snuffy called after him.

"But... Where are you going?"

"Just need to see a man about a dog."

MANY FAR LEAPS AWAY, huddled deep in a dark stretch of mountain passage, Myrr was something it had never been before. Something that set its banded muscles to twitching. Something that reminded it of the early times, back when the Meyerwitz had dominated all of creation. The time of birthing. The time of first recall. Of hard cages and soft observers poking, and prodding, and bringing pain after pain. Before the bloodsuckers and all the Cursed's creations had run free by Myrr's own doing. Before Myrr had reigned supreme in this land.

Those times were hazy now. Uncertain. Distant. So very distant that Myrr had all but forgotten the thrill of escape—the hot, bloody pride it had tasted, the first time it'd taken one of those soft observers in its powerful jaws. The burning rage when the Meyerwitz had fled the Cursed Place, escaping vengeance, bound for the sky on jets of fire and lightning.

Myrr hadn't sighted those times for many seasons. Not until *She* had returned, just four suns past. She of the soft flesh that belied the hard will beneath. She, the Mother of Myrr's creation. Of all creation. She who'd once been Prisoner of the Meyerwitz herself. It was the only reason Myrr had spared her life back then. And then again, four suns ago. Pity and curiosity. A mistake. A terrible mistake.

What had happened in the wake of Her recent departure, Myrr still struggled to sight clearly. All Myrr knew for certain was that something had awoken in the depths of its old mountain home. Something that shook the foundations. Churned the rock. Closed long-trusted tunnels. Something that poisoned the air with dark sands. Drained it of the lifesong. Something that'd lashed out from this very mountain with a great black arm, racing to capture the strange vessel She had left behind, mere moments after She had taken back to the sky aboard another.

It all smelled of deceit and traps. And yet, also peculiarly of lifesong. A sick perversion of it. But lifesong, nonetheless.

Myrr bared its fangs and hissed at the useless mind sights. The mysteries of the dwindling lifesong. The soft-bodied creatures that'd fled the safety of the pit, right into the Dark Invader's waiting arms. Only the wise old blood-sucker had remained behind. He who was born of darkness and paid homage to Myrr. Myrr kneaded its claws, wondering why it had bothered at all with those fools—the golden ones and their smaller, paler friends. All of them so similar to Myrr's memories of the Cursed Meyerwitz and its soft observers.

Curiosity. Pity.

Hunger.

Movement in the dark stilled Myrr's twitching muscles. Black on black. A wisp of that strange blight, drifting by the mouth of the passage. Myrr slowed its breathing, allowing its body to cool past the threshold of even a bloodsucker's detection. The wisp passed on by, ignorant of Myrr's silently bared fangs in the dark.

It wasn't the first such wisp Myrr had observed in the passages since the Disturbance. Myrr had fled instinctively deeper as thunder crashed and the mountain shook all around it. Perhaps a mistake. Many of the old ways had closed in the rumbling chaos, plugged with falling stone. Many more teeming with those unnatural sands, flitting about on unseen threads of lifesong or dark magic. Perhaps both. Myrr cared not.

It heard more nearby, felt more still boring into the mountain depths, burrowing deeper, deeper. Deeper than even Myrr had ever gone. Myrr felt the vibrations even now.

Invaders all around. Thrashing Myrr's caverns. Destroying its home.

Something had to be done.

The jungle.

Return to the jungle.

There, Myrr could hunt. Assess. Breathe clean air. The tunnel air had been stifling since the Disturbance, thick with dust and the deep burn of the planet's insides. The mixture clawed at Myrr's eyes and lungs like a hive of agitated firecrawlers. Infernal, irritating things. But Myrr would survive. Could survive many suns on very little. Had done so before. Had done many things before. Defeated many rivals.

None like this.

Return to the jungle.

The jungle, where Myrr reigned supreme. Where no foe had ever bested Myrr. Where Myrr could move freely, unencumbered by the narrow confines of twisting rock.

Two more paths to try before Myrr resorted to tearing its way through untold suns' worth of dust and rock. Myrr picked the closer of the two and began to move, silent and easy as a shadow.

The tunnel exploded above Myrr—blasted rock and molten droplets raining down without warning, cast in a ruby red glow. Myrr moved faster than any other child of the jungle could. Faster than the Strong Armored One or its crafty shield-friend. Faster than this Dark Invader. Myrr vaulted debris, darted beneath the descending figure, easily ducking its grabbing hands, repaying the effort with a violent slash at one glowing red joint. Ripped the Invader's arm clean off. Kept moving. Sprang wall-to-wall as the Invader's dark sands came rushing in like a vine spike's tail. Barely noticed the Invader's dismembered limb disintegrating like sand in its hands, right up until those sands solidified to catch Myrr by the hindpaw.

Myrr staggered to regain its gait, more sands rushing in all around. It went to all fours, running harder than it had in many suns. But the dark sands kept piling in, cutting off movement, thicker and thicker around it, until Myrr found itself completely trapped from the neck down, arms and legs pulled to untenable angles. It gnashed its teeth and shook the twisting passage with a roar. The sands only piled in faster, forcing their way down its throat. Choking it.

Myrr coughed and spasmed, redoubling its struggles, fighting with all its fury. Fighting until there was nothing but darkness—the true, impenetrable darkness of total confinement. Myrr stilled, survival instincts cutting its futile struggles, conserving the energy.

Something there in the darkness. Something unlike anything Myrr had ever known. A presence. A dark stirring in the lifesong. Pain, and fire, and alien faces. Great bodies of metal and thunder clashing in black skies. Destruction. Total destruction.

And there, blazing through the center of all of it. The Strong Armored One. A *Knight*, Myrr sensed, somewhere in the gaps between the sounds and the mind sights. An *Excalibur Knight*. One, the source of all the suffering that'd befallen Myrr's home. The other, naught but an innocent source of pure power and strength, caught in the clutches of one who abused its gift, wielded it as a blunt weapon in harsh perversion of its true nature.

The Excalibur.

*Myrr's* Excalibur, it sensed, should Myrr find it, should Myrr bring the Strong Armored One's bones back to this... this... the sensation swelled, momentarily dislodging Myrr from the spell of sights and sounds, then crashing back over it with renewed force. A name. A mess of clashing sounds, like a screaming nest of hoopwings. A sense rising above the mess, soaring high.

*Azmodeus.*

The sensation crashed over Myrr like a peel of dark thunder, washing through it like a flood. Washing out everything else until Myrr tipped its head back and howled, too frenzied in the moment to notice that it could once again move, or that, as it did, it felt somehow stronger, faster, than ever before.

Then, deep in the changed stretch of mountain passage, Myrr awoke to itself, searing power crawling through its flesh, searing violence stamped across its singular mind sight. No longer encumbered. No longer uncertain. Deep in that changed mountain passage, Myrr roared its mightiest roar, and charged into the darkness, seeking its prey.

# CHAPTER 26
# WASHED UP

Consciousness came in flickering stages. Roaring water and twinkling light. Dreamy weightlessness. Mucky darkness. The first thing Nate noticed with any real certainty, some indeterminable length of jostles and jolts later—it could've been seconds or eons—was the gaping maw of frighteningly sharp fangs in his face. Not biting, he faintly noticed. Panting. Happily? Vision waned, consciousness slipping away to the backtrack of Ex's exasperated grumbling, and then—

"Tess," he whispered, reaching for the face that was suddenly there, hovering above him, wreathed in a blinding halo of sunlight. Freaking angelic. His fingers brushed a cheek. Soft, he imagined. Couldn't tell. The fine sensors of his gauntlet seemingly busted right along with what felt like his entire body. Her hand found his, returned it to his chest with an awkward pat. He blinked. Not comprehending. Time passing again, maybe.

Voices.

Sunlight.

*Arguing* voices.

He cracked his eyes open, squinting through the harsh sun.

A panting snargladorf laid by his side, panting happily in the bright day. It sat up at attention as Nate tried to move, lolling tongue reeling itself in like break time was over. Nate tried to sit up, hands clawing through waterlogged sand and… No. Not sand. Not a river embankment, as he'd started to imagine from the sounds of rushing water.

He pulled himself up to a sitting position, taking in the mess of flooded plain, taking in how thoroughly caked he was in mud and tangled wild grass, searching dumbly for some clue as to where the fuck he was. He'd just begun to trace from the stagnant floodwaters to the cruising river ahead, just begun to place the fallen wreckage of the mountain in the distance, and to remember the preceding clash, when someone grabbed him by the shoulder. He turned, head spinning with the motion.

Jaeger looked some uneasy combination of concerned and moody. "You with us, kid?"

*Kid.*

Nate nodded absentmindedly, dimly noting that Tessa wasn't there anymore. Just Jaeger and Tor. And Hannah O'Sweeney lingering nearby, arms crossed, watching him with a thoughtful expression. And—

*Kid.* That was… something.

"Maybe you should get up, then." Something in Jaeger's tone. "If you can."

*If I didn't know any better, I'd say he's cross with you,* Ex observed.

Nate couldn't help but agree as he looked back at the colonel. "It's been a bit of a day."

"I saw," Jaeger said, not softening. Assessing. Brows edged with tension. It was only then that Nate registered the colonel was propped on a makeshift crutch, clearly keeping the weight off of one foot.

"The mountain," he murmured, trying to gather his thoughts and remember, looking back to Jaeger with renewed worry. "Is everyone okay?"

Definitely getting warmer.

"No thanks to the mountain," Jaeger said. Definitely a bit pissed. He was reining it in, though, dragging his stare from Nate to consider the distant wreckage. "You at least get the bastard?"

Nate tested the air and was relieved to feel the Light there, singing around him, through him. He thought better of releasing his helmet back to e-dim anyway. He pulled the seals and removed it the old-fashioned way instead, taking a welcome breath of fresh air, trying to remember what he'd seen in those last moments—the fury of his attacks washing over the golem, bleaching it from sight. An entire mountain's worth of rock crashing down on top of them as he'd thrown himself at the creature, the construct, with all of his might.

"I don't know," he admitted.

Jaeger considered that, then nodded slowly, like he wasn't all that surprised by the answer. That unspoken prickliness still clung to the colonel, poking Nate's aching body in all the wrong places.

"I'm sorry, did I do something wrong, pulling you all out of the creepy murder pit back there?"

"That's not what anyone's saying, Kid."

*Kid.* That word poking at him like a hot needle to the brain.

He pulled himself to his feet, momentarily regretted it, then gathered himself and turned to face Jaeger anyway. Good as Jaeger's cool-as-a-cucumber act was, Nate knew it got under the man's skin on some level, the way he towered head and shoulders over Jaeger at full height now.

"Maybe you should tell me what they *are* saying, then, John."

Jaeger opened his mouth to fire back, Cool Cucumber Mode fully engaged, then paused and shot a sideways glance at the onlookers Nate had forgotten were even there.

"Maybe we should leave you boys to it," said Hannah O'Sweeney, making no move whatsoever to leave.

"That's okay," Nate said, right at the same time Jaeger gave a curt, "Please."

They traded a look—one of the ones that always made Nate feel a little bit like he was staring down a dick-tied bull.

"Maybe a moment, then," he conceded to Hannah O'Sweeney, who looked them both over one more time, shrugged, and strode off up the hill. Nate turned his gaze to Tor, who hadn't budged an inch, and gave her an appreciative nod. She touched fist to chest, bowing her head, and strode off after O'Sweeney.

Nate looked back to Jaeger, feeling drained and a bit more like a scolded schoolboy than he would've liked, but also like this was as good a place and time as any to get a handle on whatever this was. "Maybe you should tell me what's on your mind."

"Maybe," Jaeger agreed. "But first, maybe *you* should tell *me* why you've been letting us think the princess' snatch and grab was all smooth sailing back there, when really—"

"She told you?"

Nate saw the words were a mistake the moment they left his mouth.

"No," Jaeger said, grim frown darkening a shade. "She didn't. Didn't have to. Truth be told, I think she actually—" Jaeger shook his head, as if to clear it of some annoying thought. "Doesn't matter anyway. What *does* matter is that you're running around like Don Quixote out here, trying to pretend like you're some storybook hero when really—"

"I never—"

"No." Jaeger cut him off with a sharp gesture. "Listen. It may be your ship we've all been riding in, Kid, but that's my team licking their wounds back there. My team that's damn near died three times over since this shit show kicked off."

Nate caught hold of the emotion swelling in his chest, forced himself to relax, to remember whose side they were both on. "I never read Don Quixote, is all I was trying to say."

Jaeger blew out a neutral huff. For a moment, it almost looked like he'd smile. Mostly, though, he just looked damned tired. "Look, Nate. Our people need us. They need *you*. At your best, preferably." He raised a finger, like *here's the kicker*. "But they *also* need to know what's real, when your best isn't enough. You get that?"

Some small part of him wanted to point out that his *best* had just taken a goddamned mountain to the head covering their escape—and that he'd never technically lied to them, besides the fact. The rest of him, though, did get it. At least on some level. More importantly, he didn't miss the change. *Our* people. Jaeger was trying, here.

"I get it," he said. "I'm sorry. I'll do better."

The words tasted a bit sour on the way out, but he knew Jaeger wasn't wrong. No point getting twisted up over what was and wasn't fair to ask of the team's superpowered punching bag, here. It would've made about as much sense as Cammy bickering over having to shuttle their sad asses around all the time. They all had their parts to play, and so forth.

At that moment, Nate accepted it, and it actually felt pretty damned good, despite everything. He even felt Ex's approval lightly radiating from the place where his companion had been silently observing the exchange. But ahead, Jaeger was still shaking his head like Nate had missed the point entirely.

"What? What else do you want me to say?"

"It's not about what you say, Nate. It's not even about what you do. It's..." Jaeger grimaced and shifted on his makeshift crutch, searching for the right words. "It's about what happens when the people around you *trust* you know what you're doing. And it's about everything it's gonna cost them on the day you don't."

Nate swallowed, uncomfortably aware of just how thoroughly that day might already be upon them. "And what do we do on that day, if it does come?"

Jaeger eyed the distant mountain wreckage with an unmistakable aura of *when, not if,* like that was indeed the question. "The right thing, I hope," he finally said, focusing back on Nate. "You remember the moral of the story?"

It took Nate a moment—and a soft nudge from Ex—to pinpoint what story he was talking about. That shiny little chestnut of advice the colonel had once given Nate, right after the clash on Avalon.

"War is fucked?"

"War is fucked," Jaeger agreed. "And then you die." He tilted his head. "Or not. But either way, there's no escaping the decisions you've made." He hesitated, like he wasn't sure he should say whatever else was on his mind. Nate was thinking about the slight discrepancies between Jaeger's present words and those contained in his Ex-powered memories, recalling how the man had cocked three fingers the last time, like he'd only been getting started.

"Two of the Asgardians died in the collapse," Jaeger said. "More than half the group was wounded. Some pretty bad. Carter'd be dead right now if it weren't for your Round Table buddy back there. Maybe Elmo, too."

The words settled over him like a landslide, crashing down like the very same deluge that must've hit his people in the wake of his mountain clash, despite his best efforts to buy them time to get clear. His fault. His decision. Not the wrong one, maybe. But clearly not the right one, either.

"You never did tell me the rest of that story," he said quietly.

"Guess I'm saving it for a rainy day," Jaeger said slowly, gaze distant. Nate didn't know what to say to that. Didn't particularly want to point out that they'd left rainy-day status in the distant rearview a while ago. Finally, though, the colonel stirred, and the rest settled to the murky sidelines for the moment being. "Come on," he said, thumping Nate on the shoulder despite the uneasy airs lingering between them. "Team's waiting."

# CHAPTER 27
# PLAN F

"So just one question, Ser Nate," said Ramirez, some short time later, once Nate had returned to the crew's rudimentary camp with Jaeger and gotten through the initial rush of the *greetings* and the *glad you're not deads*. "Am I, or am I not going to need to be worrying about three-eyed children if and when my seed happens to be sowed?"

"What, you and the big guy breaking up?" Pierce cracked.

"I didn't use nukes, if that's what you're asking," Nate answered Ramirez, ignoring Pierce. But the pilot only perked up more.

"No nukes? The hell'd you do in there that toppled a goddamn mountain, then?"

"I…" He wasn't even rightly sure how to quantify it with words. "I hit it. Really hard."

Somehow, that drew a round of laughs.

*Well said*, Ex chimed in. *Honestly. The stuff of legends.*

Nate was too busy looking around the bare frills camp, realizing in mild disbelief that, despite everything Jaeger had said, none of them seemed to blame him for the mountain. For any of it. Their smiles and good cheer at having him back felt so genuine that he couldn't help but wonder if Jaeger hadn't twisted the knife harder than was actually warranted, whether intentionally or otherwise. But all it took was a second glance to see how beaten and bloodied the team really was, beneath their surface level grins and jibes. They'd been through hell and back.

198

And that was to say nothing of the two Asgardians who'd been caught in the collapse.

The rest of their golden-skinned kin watched him from the other side of camp with guarded expressions, decidedly not laughing. He moved on to the mutely shell-shocked expressions of Amelia and Gendra, Lundquist and Ramachandra. A trio of odd looks from Tessa, Carter, and O'Sweeney across the camp, where Carter was checking on the pilot's wounds in her makeshift medic's corner. He met Tessa's eyes and hung there for a moment, thinking of that delirious moment of confusion back on the flooded shore—wondering in a flush if Hannah O'Sweeney had told her that it'd been Tessa's name on his delirious lips as he'd awoken.

He moved quickly on, stowing the thought as best he could, reminding himself that his most pressing concern was that he probably owed the group at large some kind of... what? An apology? The facts played themselves through his head. The decisions he'd made.

Maybe an apology. He didn't know.

Luckily, the conversation picked itself back up without him, Pierce asking the others what this so-called Myrr thing had done to them, where it'd been keeping them, how they'd been planning to escape before the Boy Wonder had dropped in on them.

"Hey, ask the Bringer of Light, here," Ramirez said, hooking a thumb at Hannah O'Sweeney as she settled down on the other end of his narrow log bench. "She's the man with the plan when all you've got is jack shit to work with."

"Literally," Snuffy murmured, face wrinkling.

"I missed something here," Pierce observed.

"But hey," Snuffy continued like he hadn't heard, "isn't that, like, what they called Lucifer, though? Bringer of Light?"

"What about Prometheus, then?" Ramirez asked. "He was a fire guy, right?" He turned the question to a surly-looking Elmo and got a firm *how the hell should I know?* shrug in response.

"Still better than Bob," Ramirez muttered, with a defensive shrug of his own.

"Aww." Snuffy turned an almost wistful look toward the ruined mountain. "Say, you guys don't think—

"We're not worried about Bob, Snuffs."

"I know, but—"

"Bob was a dick."

"I definitely missed something," Pierce decided.

Nate was still just stuck on the name, Prometheus, and on the sudden memory of the inscrutable warning Anastasiya Blackthorne had left scrawled on that yellowing scrap of parchment. *Beware the Promethean.*

There was no way, he thought, as he eyed Hannah O'Sweeney, almost one-hundred percent positive it had to be nothing more than some cosmic coincidence. But only almost.

"Anyway," Ramirez was saying, gesturing at O'Sweeney, "our girl Prometheus, here—"

"Snuck in a toy, lit some shit on fire, and cast light on a hairy situation," Jaeger cut in, with a *back to business* air.

"Again, literally," Snuffed added.

"Personally, I'd lean more Loki on the whole thing," Jaeger continued, shooting a mild sideways frown O'Sweeney's way, "but I'd just as soon we all set the mythology grab-ass aside and get back to—What?" he added, scowling at the looks of plain surprise from Dr. Ramachandra and a few of the others. "I read. Sometimes."

"Girl could do worse than Loki," O'Sweeney reflected.

Somehow, the implied parallel didn't ease Nate's funny feeling.

*There's that squishy meatbag superstition.*

"Splendid," Jaeger said. "In that case, maybe we should get back to where we were before Loki and her alien dog ska-doodled off. Chiefly—"

"Snargladorf," Snuffy corrected, waving at the bald green beast that'd been happily shadowing Nate's every move since she'd apparently fished him out of the floodwaters. "Snargles the—"

"C'mon, man," Ramirez groaned. "You lost naming privileges after Bob. You can do better."

"My ass can do better," Pierce said.

"*Chiefly,*" Jaeger repeated, scowling the lot of them into obedient silence, "what the piss that thing was back there, and what it was doing in that cavern."

*About that,* Ex said, with that half-excited, mostly superior, *you'll never guess what I just read* tone he always got. *After reviewing what few records I could find in existence—and, admittedly, a rather piecemeal existence at that, courtesy of our Greatest of Purges—I am beginning to believe we might've found ourselves an Archon.*

Nate frowned, rousing himself from the mental haze that'd been creeping in. *A what?*

*An Archon,* Ex repeated, as if that explained anything. *But that's obviously impossible,* he added a second later.

*Right. Sure. But impossible because…?*

*Because the Synth are barely a year back from galaxy's edge, Nathaniel. And because, assuming the Alliance's oh-so-patchy records and esoteric doctrines are at all to be trusted in the matter, the Archons of the Great War couldn't have even begun to manifest until well into the third century of—*

*Can we just…* Nate forced taut muscles to relax. *Maybe we should start over here, Ex. Why don't you just tell me what the hell an Archon IS, and then maybe we can move on to how I kill it. You know, assuming I didn't already.*

*Kill it?* Ex seemed confused by the proposition. *I already told you: I'm not rightly sure it was alive to begin with. Pay attention, Nathaniel.*

*That's—fine. Whatever. Just the first question then.*

*What IS an Archon?* Ex thought about that as if it were a philosophical question more than a factual one. *I'm not sure anyone knows, to be honest, save for possibly the Merlin. The records of that era were—*

*Shot to shit by paranoid Luddites,* Nate finished. *I get it.*

*Well, that's putting it rather simply—*

*Imagine my shock.*

*—But what I was GOING to say is that the records of that era were particularly vague on a few choice branches of Synth lore—the Archons being one of them. More to the point, the very existence of the Archons seems itself rather hard to describe in any precise, deterministic way.*

*And if you had to summarize for a noodle-brained monkey anyway?*

*Hmm.* Ex sounded pleased by the admission. *I suppose you could do worse than to think of them as the Synth's answer to the Knights. Synth-powered Anti-Knights, if you will.*

Nate thought of the pulsing red golem thing, and the casual nonchalance with which it'd shrugged off his attacks. *I'd rather not, if it's all the same to you. Any idea what it was doing in there?*

*Possibly. I'm running a few simulations. In the meantime, your meatsacks are speaking to you.*

"—ny input, Ser Knight?"

Nate broke from their shared mental space and brought his focus back to the campsite discussion, where the group was turning expectant looks his way. He made use of Ex's enhanced recall to catch up on the last few seconds of conversation he'd missed—all of them unanimously agreeing that the golem had been one freaky operator, Ramachandra and Lundquist riffing a few ideas about its apparent control of the nanoswarm, Jaeger agreeing that Snuffy hereby lost all naming privileges after the mechanic had referred to the thing as Ruby Stonestockings. All of them dancing uncomfortably around the burning question: was it still kicking?

Nate scanned the group, returning to the present, and noticed Princess Elsa had joined them, sulking on the outside edge of the gathering. She looked subdued, and there was something almost like a flicker of guilt as she met his eyes, but it passed quickly enough, her usual demeanor reasserting itself.

"Not much," he said, looking back to Jaeger. "We think it could've been something called an Archon."

"Well, that sounds fun," Pierce muttered.

"The hell's an Archon?" Jaeger added.

"Still trying to sort that part out. Ex says it shouldn't be possible this early on, but details are apparently hard to come by, thanks to—"

"Ye old Great Purge?" Ramirez offered sagely.

Nate nodded.

"I thought that was more folklore than definite historical fact," Lundquist said.

"There are several conflicting theories," Amelia admitted.

"Yeah, *because* of the Great Purge," Pierce said, as if he'd been there to witness the act himself. Even Ex didn't have adequate records to confirm what'd actually happened back then—whether the Alliance 1.0 had deliberately wiped their own systems for the fear that some kind of Synth infection had taken place, or if it'd merely been a string of more straightforward casualties of war. Either way, the records had been lost, and Pierce didn't seem even a touch uncertain as he declared, "Morons set up a self-fulfilling prophecy."

"A self-sucking data void," Ramirez added thoughtfully.

Snuffy cracked a wry grin. "Hey, I think they sell something like *that* back on…" He frowned as he realized what he was saying. "Uh, never mind."

"And I love that we're still talking in *shoulds* and *coulds* right now, by the way," Pierce continued, to no one in particular. "Really gets the old confidence juices flowing, you know?"

Nate refrained from pointing out how delighted the grumpy bastard would be, then, to hear that they *could* be dealing with a bona fide Knight Killer, here. He also made a point of not asking Ex whether that description would technically be appropriate. He had a feeling his companion would fill him in, if and when it behooved them.

*That's me*, Ex murmured distractedly. *Here to serve.*

"So how do we kill an Archon?" Jaeger asked.

Nate almost could've chuckled. "Inconclusive." He frowned toward the mountain. "Assuming I didn't do the job already."

*I think we both know you didn't,* Ex chimed. The look on Jaeger's face seemed to say much the same, and honestly, Nate couldn't really bring himself to even try to disagree with them.

"Wait." Pierce was looking back and forth between them. "You're telling me you think this thing's still alive? *After* the punch that knocked down a mountain?"

"Inconclusive," Jaeger said, eyes on Nate.

"Christ," Pierce said. "And if death by mountain didn't do the trick? We got a Plan B?"

"That kinda *was* Plan B," Nate admitted.

"Well, shit."

Dr. Ramachandra looked disheartened. "I'm sure between all of us we can conceive of a viable Plan C?"

"Sit on our hands and hope Zedavian Kelkarin comes riding in to kill that thing?" Ramirez suggested.

"Or that Iveera finds us," Snuffy offered. "She was headed this way, right? And also not halfway across the galaxy like the Z-Man?"

"I can kill it," Nate said. "*If* it's still alive," he added, scowling at the lack of conviction in his own voice at those words. "Look, it caught me off guard, okay? It won't happen again. If it's still around, I'll deal with it."

They all traded looks. Too many looks. Too much uncertainty. Nate felt the weight of the Asgardians' stares, watching him from across camp, where they'd stationed themselves close enough to hear, but decidedly apart from the team.

"And for what it's worth," Nate pushed on, "I... I'm sorry I almost dropped a mountain on you guys."

"You were engaged in just combat, my lord," Tor said, eyeing the Asgardians warily. "Lamentable as the collateral may be, such is the cost of war at times."

"We serve, my lord," boomed Tristan, from over where Carter was now tending to the sitting Atlantean's midsection with concerningly bloody hands. Tessa, having shed off the survival blanket to help Carter with Tristan, gave Nate a look and a succinct nod that stirred something inside, even if he couldn't quite parse in the moment what it was.

"Yeah," Snuffy added weakly, in the pregnant silence. "Don't sweat it, big guy. Happens to..." He trailed off with a thoughtful look, like he had no idea what his mouth had been intending to say. "Well, you know. Happens."

An incoming ping from Nate's comms array thankfully saved him from having to decide how to feel or what to say to any of that. It took him a full second to even place the cue, unexpected as it was. His breath caught when he saw the name on Ex's retinal HUD.

"What is it?" Jaeger asked, picking up on Nate's expression. But Nate was furiously jamming on his helmet, opening the channel.

"Iveera," he gasped, the second the comms connected. He barely cared that he sounded desperate. The helmet acoustics were sealed. The crew wouldn't hear. And he *was* desperate, he was just then realizing. Christ, he was desperate. "Iveera, there's something down here. An Archon—At least, Ex thinks it's an Archon—And it's-it's..." He slowed as her still image flickered, frowning in stutter-step, like they were caught on a bad connection.

*Ex, what the hell?*

"—thaniel," came the Gorgon Knight's voice in a burst before Ex could answer, her image sputtering back to crisp life. "Did you just say there's—"

"An Archon. Down here. I don't know what it's..."

The words died in his throat at the way her eyes widened.

He'd never seen her eyes widen. Not like that.

"You're certain?"

"No," he admitted, reading her flattened jin, not liking what he saw. "Not entirely, but..."

The connection sputtered again, Malfar the blight-spotted Troglodan Knight appearing over Iveera's shoulder, beady eyes scanning them both in patchy stutter step.

"—e're outbound from Asgard," Iveera was saying. "Hold o—"

The signal died completely.

"Shit," Nate hissed at the empty comm line. *Ex?*

*Something's happening under the mountain,* Ex reported, laying some incoherent energy tracings across Nate's HUD. *Something rather large.*

Which seemed like a fair enough assessment, right up until a mountain-sized sound split the air, like the firing of some massive world cannon—or the splitting of the planet's crust, Nate decided, as the sound deepened and stretched, the ground shaking in full-scale earthquake.

"Down!" Jaeger snapped, as half the camp reflexively came to their feet, looking around for incoming threats. The SAS crew listened. Nate and the rest just stood there, staring dumbly off at the mountain, where sky-high jets of dust and debris had started spewing up from the wreckage. The dry, grating rumble of colossal bodies scraping against one another, shifting beneath the surface. Nate watched with a kind of blank, helpless wonder as something came plowing up from the planet's crust.

Something rather freaking enormous.

A dark, winding spire growing straight up from the planet, thinner and even taller than the mountain from whose ruins it sprung, all cruel angles and jagged edges.

"You know, something tells me maybe you didn't kill this thing after all," came Pierce's voice from down in the dirt.

Nate spared a sideways glance at the pilot, who, despite his blasé tone, was watching with eyes set just as wide as the rest of the camp's. All of them staring speechlessly at the giant tower of doom still ripping its way out of the planet, ruby red energy crackling up its black surface in stark contrast to the faint azure haze that began siphoning down its length in great, soft waves.

No one even seemed to notice the ground was still shaking.

Nate gaped at the looming spire light show, waiting for Ex to rouse from his analyses long enough to tell him something, trying fruitlessly to piece it together himself in the meantime. The otherworldly interference. The Archon's superstructure. Abandoned labs, and supercats, and sinking Knightships. The Last LeFaye. And now this tower—nearly ten damned kilometers high, and still growing.

It was only when Jaeger crutched up beside him that he registered the earthquake had lessened, if not quite ended. Ahead, the dark spire's ascent to the heavens was slowing, its upper reaches blossoming outward in a haphazard maze of jagged tendrils, stretching far and wide across the sky. The air was thick and sulfuric. The steady churning rumble of impossible masses in motion giving way to the clattering rain of rock and displaced earth still tumbling down from the structure's many sharp edges.

"It was Iveera," Nate offered to Jaeger, after a length of silence—both of them coming to some unspoken agreement to set aside their mutual flabbergasted-ness and focus on something more tangible, even if neither one of them could pry their eyes away from the thrumming spire.

"You tell her about the Light?"

"Didn't really have time."

"About Myrr, then? About her ship?"

A length of silence later, Jaeger finally pried his gaze away from the spire long enough to take in Nate's blank look. "Christ, did you even set rendezvous coordinates in case we lost comms again?"

Nate blinked at him, mutely wondering which part of this Jaeger was missing. They hadn't had *time*. End of story. Nate wasn't sure what more the grumpy bastard wanted. All he knew was that his mouth probably didn't do him any favors, spontaneously deciding to make like a flopping fish out of the water instead of pointing any of this out.

"Maybe next time we're all marooned on a derelict planet, we take the lifeline call together, hooah?"

The fog of stunned silence finally broke.

For one hot-headed second, Nate was actually tempted to grab the colonel and shake him. To scream in his face. What the hell did he think Nate was doing, here? Who the hell did he think he was? His hands, he realized had already traveled the first few inches toward the colonel, fingers curled like talons. Jaeger didn't miss it.

"Yeah," Nate said, turning himself forcefully back to the spire. "Maybe you're right, Jaeger."

He felt the colonel's lingering stare. Felt the man's Commander Brain ticking back and forth like a game of retro Pong between two options: push the kid, or let it go and pray for the best. Somehow, Nate didn't imagine the third option—freaking *trust* him, for once—even entered the colonel's calculus.

He didn't even fully register what he was doing until Jaeger's sharp, "Where are you going?" cut in.

"Going to get Iveera back on the line," Nate replied, already drifting upward on gravitonics. "Please hold."

He didn't wait for an answer. Just shot off like a rocket, bound for space. Bound, he hoped, for some damn answers. It felt good to fly uninhibited, kilometers dropping away like nothing.

*Nathaniel.* Ex sounded nervous, of all things, as they broke the sound barrier. *We should talk about this.*

*Not now, Ex.* They were already approaching the upper atmosphere. *If he's gonna act like—*

*Not that,* Ex growled. *There's something seriously wrong with the—Nathaniel! STOP!*

It was like he'd fallen upside down, straight into vacuumed crusher space without a suit. One second, Nate was reaching for the brakes, stirred by the edge in Ex's voice. The next, the breath had left his lungs. The heat left his body. For a moment that stretched confusingly between a blink and an eternity, it was like he'd fallen halfway out of existence—senses fading, compressing. The Ginnungagap horizon warping oddly. A hazy miasma of pale red nothingness crowding in around him, glomming on like some arcane, soul-sucking specter. It waxed stronger, coalescing around him.

Nate ripped free from the hazy void with a scream of effort, open sky exploding out around him, decompressing, senses reeling. He toppled end over end. Rushing air and a blinding flash of light. Searing ozone and booming thunder. He was falling. Plummeting. The heavens above coming alive with an angry storm of ruby red energies. There was just enough sense left in his brain to adjust toward Ex's nav point, throw on the gravitonics.

He reached the ground faster than seemed to make any sense. He hit the dirt with a dull thud on all fours, head spinning, dimly aware of distant voices shouting something. His name. Pounding footsteps in the dirt. He heard and felt them in some paradoxical combination—muddled by whatever had just happened to him, yet somehow also sharper, like the first plunge of a cold hand into hot water.

He looked up as the first runner reached him.

Tor, shortly followed by Tessa—*actually* Tessa this time.

"Nate?" Tessa asked, kneeling down beside him, reaching out only to jerk back as she felt the heat pouring off his suit. Beside her, Tor was ready with shield and lance, like she half-expected the sky itself to come falling down on them at any second.

"What the hell was that?" Jaeger called, limping his way over in a bounding hobble of crutch steps, trailed by Ramirez and Snuffy, who both hovered like they wanted to help the colonel but didn't want to incur the wrath.

Nate blinked at the question, higher faculties still coming online, the daylight flickering oddly in his eyes. He wasn't especially sure whether Jaeger was referring to his impromptu space race, or to the burgeoning hellstorm he seemed to have awoken above. Didn't have answers, either way.

"'Sure looked like the Dark Tower there just tried to zap him like a fly, Boss," Ramirez replied, when Nate didn't.

That might've explained a few things. But only a few.

A ruffle of movement and sound beside him. Tessa, fanning him off with the thermal blanket Tor had just tossed her from her pack. He gathered his wits enough to tap into his systems and help vent the excess heat from his outer shell. His head was pounding. His insides, like a half-cooked frozen dinner.

He tried to focus up as Jaeger and the others neared, Snuffy talking a mile a minute about the size of the lightning bolt the spire had apparently just pegged him with, Ramirez adding something about how he looked to have already been in free fall when it struck.

"Nate," Jaeger grunted, crutching right up to him and Tessa, his breathing labored as he dropped to a knee beside them and fixed Nate with a serious look. "What happened up there?"

"I… Some kind of energy barrier," Nate said, trying to play the scene back in his head and reconcile it with their words. He dimly noted that Jaeger didn't even look that pissed—or not *just* pissed, at least. There was worry there, too. And the quality of the light on his face…

He hadn't been imagining it. Not just a trick of the light in his scrambled eyes. Above them, through the disconcertingly silent haze of dissipating energies, the daylight was actually shifting. Waxing and waning. Wavering in and out with a kind of surreal, almost nebulous quality. The effect might've actually been beautiful, had he witnessed it in a dream. Still *was* beautiful, he supposed, in a way. Mostly, though—crashed there on a hostile planet, knowing the likely source of the disturbance—it was just unsettling.

He looked back to Jaeger. "I think we might be stuck here."

Faces fell. Jaeger chewed on the words.

"Well," he finally said, looking down from the eerie sky and back over to the Dark Tower, "guess it's a damn good thing you got your Light back, then, because it sure is looking like you might have to make good on all that *I'll deal with it* talk."

But Nate was already testing the words as Jaeger spoke them. Already eyeing the hazy blue waves descending that dark spire with a sinking feeling. He knew, even before Ex emerged to confirm as much, that it was *exactly* what it looked like.

The Light wasn't gone. Not exactly. But it wasn't exactly where it should've been, either—the sweet, ethereal touch of the Lady's song waxing and waning in strange waves, just like the daylight. Strange *planes*, he thought, for some intuitive reason he couldn't have put to words. Something about the feel of those crests. Like it wasn't oscillating in intensity so much as actually shifting in and out of… what? Existence? Reality?

"Kid. Tell me you still got your Light."

He felt Ex searching for answers. Felt the clear lack of any good ones, and the eerie gravity of colossal bodies at work in the planet's depths. "It's… complicated."

Faces fell further.

"So, uh… What was after Plan C, then?" Snuffy asked.

"Plan F," Ramirez muttered.

"Sounds about right," Jaeger said, standing back to his crutch with a heavy sigh and looking around for some inspiration he clearly didn't expect to find. Begrudgingly, he offered Nate a hand. "Maybe we should go figure out what the hell that looks like, hooah?"

# CHAPTER 28
# SYSTEMS

"Right, then," Lundquist said, looking around the somber gathering with what Nate imagined must've been his standard Professor Face back on Earth. "Let's start with what we know."

In a strange way, the man looked more at ease at this moment than he had at any other point since he and Dr. Ramachandra joined the *Camelot*. Like he was simply in his element with a class in session and a good problem to solve—even if that problem did seem rather liable to get them all killed at the first misstep.

Nonetheless, at an affirmative nod from Dr. Ramachandra, the two scholars began listing off the observed facts in meticulous detail, taking additional notes here and there from the peanut gallery—including but not limited to freakazoid terror cats, huge fucking towers growing out of the ground, and a distinct lack of adequate campfire snacks.

Nate sat back and tried not to interrupt the proceedings, conferring instead with his own internal roster of hard facts and intestinal intuitions as they went. Even after Jaeger's call to order upon their return to camp, it'd taken the group a while to collectively unclench and shake off the looming certainty that some horrible attack would come raining down from the eerily shifting sky at any moment, or that the looming Dark Tower would simply smite them with a choice bolt of lightning. Slowly, though, something like a sense of moderate stability had reasserted itself over the camp—

even if they *did* all know deep down that it was totally superficial—and they'd moved on.

They'd elected two of their three multi-doctorates to lead the discussion, not because Lundquist and Ramachandra had the answers, but because they were feasibly the most qualified in the party to think about how they should attempt to get them—provided, of course, that the Asgardians weren't hiding any world-class academics in their ranks. If so, none of the gold-skinned titans had stepped up to bat. They sat apart from the crew, pitching in with a scathing remark here or there, but mostly just sitting in surly silence, casting glares at Nate and occasionally eyeing up Princess Elsa in a way that made him worry they might have problems if they didn't find something productive to focus on soon.

"I think that leads us right up to what we might begin to deduce from these collective data," Dr. Lundquist was saying. "Would anyone care to offer their hypotheses to the group?"

Nate almost chuckled at the resultant crickets. Looming Doom Spire or no, for a second there, it almost felt like he was back at Penn State, sitting through yet another one of those painful lecture moments where pretty much everyone in the room *probably* had an answer to the teacher's question, and exactly zero of them were willing to be the one to step forward and prove themselves the idiot who'd gotten it wrong. He caught Tessa's eye, saw his grim amusement mirrored there, and couldn't help but smile a little. Beside her, Carter frowned at the both of them.

"I think you'd better tell us what you're thinking, Friedrich," said Dr. Ramachandra.

"Very well. I'll begin with the supposition that there's something special about this Archon's swarm."

"No shit, Doc," Pierce said, earning himself a stern look from Jaeger. "You know, with all due respect," he added, with an unapologetic shrug.

"Special how?" Jaeger asked, turning back to Lundquist.

"Well, there *is* the obvious," Lundquist admitted, with a permissive gesture toward Pierce. "It clearly moves and functions like nothing we've seen since the first Synth protoswarm attack on Demeter-12. But I was referring more to the curious feature that there doesn't seem to be all that much of it."

More than a few gazes shifted uncertainly to the rather mind-bogglingly expansive spire jutting out of the planet's crust a scant handful of kilometers away.

"Relatively speaking," Lundquist clarified, in response to their collective confusion. "As compared to the total mass available here on this planet."

"Yeah, that part is kinda weird, right?" Snuffy said, looking around for some support. "I mean, chewing up planets and assimilating them into Team Synth is like, kinda their thing, right? So why not just gobble this whole place up and crap out more nanoswarm?"

"Precisely my question."

"Yeah, but the fact that it hasn't doesn't really *prove* anything, does it?" Pierce asked.

"No," Lundquist agreed. "Not in and of itself."

"But," Ramachandra picked up, smoothly as if she were finishing his sentence, "if this Archon could simply, as Airman Killian says, 'gobble this whole place up and crap out more nanoswarm,' it's prohibitively hard to explain why it hasn't found us yet. Because *were* that the case, it could literally tear the planet apart, simultaneously increasing its search power *and* effectively decreasing the searchable area as it went—and both of those at an exponential rate. Provided, of course…"

"Provided that it *is* looking for us at all," Lundquist finished for her. "And that we haven't missed some other crucial aspect of the situation."

"And provided I didn't already kill it," Nate pointed out, albeit not even half-heartedly. "The Dark Tower over there could be running on autopilot, for all we know," he finished anyway, mostly just wishing he'd kept his mouth shut. Since the moment he'd washed up on that muddy flood plain, he couldn't seem to do anything but kill the team's faith in him a little more every time he opened his mouth.

"Yeeeah," Pierce said, clearly not buying Nate's alternative. "Look, I don't wanna burst anyone's bubble here—"

The group erupted in a chorus of snorts and assorted *mmhmms* and *oookays*.

Pierce spread his hands. "Fine. So, sue me for being the voice of reason. But don't we all think the fact that that thing tried to peg our boy here with a lightning bolt kinda suggests it probably already knows exactly where we're at?"

That shut up a lot of the chatter right quick.

Nate had an alternate explanation—or liked to think he *would* have, had Ex not pointed it out faster than he could blink or say *wait a second*. Either way, he was still grateful he didn't have to be the one to speak up in defense of his own idea.

"I won't claim to know who's controlling what here," Lundquist said, a little hesitantly, "but I will agree with Nate on at least one point: it's entirely plausible that tower was merely responding in an automated fashion. Nate's flight could have triggered some kind of proximity alert, coupled with any manner of atmospheric perimeter sensors. Indeed, for my money, that seems the best guess here, given the speed and pinpoint accuracy with which Nate was targeted upon contacting this, ah, mysterious barrier."

Pierce didn't look all that convinced, but it seemed good enough for the rest. Or most of the rest, at least.

"We are in the demon's domain," one of the Asgardians rumbled, raising his bowed head long enough to cast them a haughty glare. "It matters not. You weigh ember to ember whilst we sit in the depths of the ninth hell."

"Thanks for the reminder," Tessa said. "Think we got that the first hundred times, though."

"Just be thankful you weren't there for the pit," Ramirez told her with a pointed look, flapping his hand like *talk, talk, talk*.

Nate tensed as the affronted Asgardian rose smoothly to his feet, muscles tight and golden chin held high, but after a few moments, the tall warrior satisfied himself with spitting on the ground and stomping off into the unyielding daylight. His kin watched him go with an air like they were considering joining him, possibly for good. It was a pointless waste, this dickish culture clash of theirs, but Nate didn't have the energy to begin to try sorting it out. Maybe a word with Elsa was in order. Or Jaeger. They both knew how to win friends and manipulate peons far better than he did.

"At any rate," Lundquist was saying, glancing around like he expected someone might have more to say, "it seems to me that the most likely, and indeed, possibly the most *desirable* explanation for this lack of proliferating *nanoswarms*"—he made air quotes like he still wasn't wild about that terminology—"is that we are witnessing some kind of finite limitation to this so-called Archon's influence. Perhaps it's something unique to these nanoswarms, or to the Archon, or perhaps we're merely looking at evidence of some more universal constant governing the, ah..." He rolled a hand, searching for the words. "Whatever you'd like to call it. The maximum effective 'control units' of a particular Synth hivemind entity. The total possible bandwidth of a single swarm's intrapolymeric cohesion. Something to that effect."

"Provided the Synth are composed of discretely functioning entities to begin with," Ramachandra added, earning herself a concessionary tilt of the head from Lundquist. "That much seems rather unclear, based on the available data."

"Indeed. Regardless, whatever this Archon creature—or construct—is aiming to do here on this planet, it seems likely there's some reason, some rate-limiting step, that explains why he—it—hasn't simply proliferated its swarms to the degree necessary to, ah, as you Americans might say: 'just do it.'"

"Maybe it's waiting for something," Pierce suggested. "A signal from the motherland. The fucking Age of Aquarius. Who knows?"

"The signal hypothesis does seem possible," Lundquist admitted. "Though it does raise several questions about the nature of the mechanisms the spire seems to have employed to disrupt communications with the outside world. Not to mention"—He gestured demonstratively to the skies unnatural roil of mismatched daylights—"to modulate the environmental lighting situation." He glanced thoughtfully at the sky. "Potentially worth noting, as an aside, that there appears to be a low frequency phasic component to this… let's call it interference. Somewhere on the order of decihertz, I believe." He looked back to the group, scanning the class. "Anyone have any idea what to make of that?"

Crickets.

"So just to be clear," Snuffy said slowly, gauging faces around the camp, "we're *not* sold on the tower-as-fly-zapper theory, then?"

"Insomuch as we can't technically rule out anything, I suppose we're not *not* sold," said Dr. Ramachandra. "I personally find it unlikely the structure is purely defensive in nature, but all we can really say at this point is that the data are inconclusive."

"This is why no one likes scientists," Pierce said. "Can one of you just tell us what you actually think, for Christ's sake?"

"What I *think*," Ramachandra said, "is that it is a capital mistake to theorize before one has data. Insensibly one begins to twist facts to suit theories, instead of theories to suit facts."

"Arthur Conan Doyle," Jaeger observed.

"*Sir* Arthur Conan Doyle, thank you very much," amended Hannah O'Sweeney.

"Huh," Snuffy said, looking back and forth between them. "Coulda swore that was Sherlock Holmes. No?"

Ramachandra and O'Sweeney turned incredulous looks from Snuffy to Jaeger, as if imploring for some explanation.

"We'll teach Snuffy about books later," Jaeger said, pinching his nose over crossed arms. "For now, Dr. Lundquist, as the most qualified expert here…" He glanced at Ramachandra like he realized how that sounded, but she only gave a curt nod, like he was undoubtedly right in this particular instance. Jaeger focused back on an uneasily shifting Lundquist. "I'd like your professional best guess as to what the hell's going on here, please."

The physicist worked his jaw, clearly not wild about being backed into a corner like this. "May we see the imagery again?" he finally asked Nate.

Nate obliged, casting the holo imagery Ex had reconstructed of the superstructure they'd dropped a mountain on. Lundquist walked around the three-dimensional image, as he'd already done half a dozen times, frowning and tut-tutting to himself all the while.

"Knowing virtually nothing about this structure as it stood, not to mention this new development," he finally said, indicating first the holo, then the dark spire towering in the background, "if you *insist* I start casting wild speculations... I think this Archon may be attempting to construct its own version of a Beacon relay here on this planet."

The words settled through Nate's brain like deceptively warm honey, clogging out his racing thoughts until they all turned, all at once, and struck like anvil and hammer on hot steel, ringing their terrifying conclusion.

*I believe the good doctor is correct,* Ex confirmed, as soon as Nate began to ask.

Nate gaped. *And you're just saying this now because...?*

*Well. Not that I place much stock in the jabberings of superstitious meatbags, as you well know...*

*You don't freaking say,* Nate mustered, when it became apparent Ex was waiting for some response.

*But,* Ex rolled on, *I suppose it's POSSIBLE I wished to hear a second opinion. One unaffected by any, shall we say, higher influences.*

*Well now you're just being modest.*

*Be that as it may...*

"We need to go have a closer look at that spire," Nate said aloud to the group. "Get to the bottom of this. Figure out how to stop it."

It was the first thing he'd said that didn't seem to cause an uncomfortable silence, if only for the simple fact that the uncomfortable silence had already arrived by the time he said it. Because if Lundquist was right—if the Synth actually did manage to open a backdoor straight into Alliance space... It was hard to even begin to quantify what kind of catastrophe they might be sitting on, here.

Maybe that was why no one seemed all that displeased to hear Nate stepping up and putting on his Big Boy Knight Pants.

"I agree," was all Lundquist said.

"Yep," Jaeger added.

"Hear, hear," O'Sweeney agreed.

"Thought you'd never ask," Tessa said.

"Okay," Nate said, before the momentum could falter. "I can get two in, fast and easy."

"Without Light?" Jaeger asked.

"Just trust me, okay? I can take two."

There was that uncomfortable silence.

"Or I can go alone."

"I would accompany you, my lord," Tor said, rising with her lance.

"As would I," Tristan added, drawing a rare look of admiration but also consternation from Carter as he stood, torso plastered in bandages, and moved to gather his gear.

Across the camp, one of the Asgardians gave a great *hrrrmph* and shoved forcefully to his feet. "If it's warriors you need, you need look no further."

"*Is* it warriors we need?" asked Dr. Ramachandra, seemingly to herself. It still turned pretty much every eye in the camp first to her, then more pointedly to Lundquist, who, after a moment, did a double take like he'd just found himself naked in a dream.

"Me?" he asked weakly.

Just as quickly as the wild thoughts began passing into the gathering, though, Tessa dispersed them with an air of gentle practicality.

"No offense, Doc, but how's your mental clarity in a life-or-death situation?"

Lundquist made a dry swallowing sound. "Suboptimal, to date."

"So, seeing as we've *also* got a ship in there in need of flying—"

"And seeing as she's the *only* worthy pilot in all the land," Pierce added, though he was clearly in no rush to volunteer himself.

"—I say we check to see the coast is clear," Tessa continued, gesturing to herself and Nate, "bring our girl back if we can, and then, if everything's clear, *then* we take our Doc in for a closer look—With a ship and a backup plan. Everyone wins, right?"

The look on Jaeger's face—not to mention the uneasy tug in Nate's gut— said that plainly not *everyone* won, sending Tessa right back into the lion's den after they'd just gotten her back. Tessa, though, was unimpressed by their unspoken concerns.

"Look, you're all hammered to shit, Pierce is a cock—

"I resent that," Pierce said, though he sounded unconvinced.

"—and no one knows Cammy like I do," Tessa finished, ignoring him, eyes still fixed on Jaeger as she stepped up beside Nate. "Let me get her out of there, Boss."

Tor appeared to Nate's left, wordlessly claiming the other ticket, Nate's insides churning with some mixture of warm-and-fuzzy gratitude to the both of them, and a sudden wriggling certainty that he should've kept his mouth shut, kept things simple, and gone alone to start with, with or without the old man's blessing.

"Fine." Jaeger considered the three of them, clearly not thrilled. "Fine. You poke your heads in, you have a look, and you get the hell back here." He focused on Nate like he wasn't quite sure whether it was even worth trying. "No going rogue and pissing off the Dark Tower, hooah?"

Nate touched his middle and index finger to his forehead in a casual salute, narrowly resisting the temptation to fold down the index finger for full effect.

"Good luck, then," Jaeger said as they gathered up to go, the mood in the camp somber and tense. Nate eyed a pair of Asgardians as they rose, seemingly in disgust, and set off after the comrade who'd stormed out after Ramirez's comments. It wasn't the most heartening sendoff. Everyone looking for something useful to say. No one finding it. No one but Snuffy, as Nate took hold of Tessa and Tor and began to lift off.

"Take lots of pictures!" the mechanic called after them, as they flew off to see what they could see.

A FEW SHORT KILOMETERS DISTANT, on the far side of the hill, Celdór stomped across the dusty yet softening soils at the edge of the flooded grasslands, scanning the muddy waters below for any signs of catchable food, and generally cursing the Terrans for their undying arrogance.

"Excalibur Knight," he growled under his breath, and spat into the shallow edge of the dark waters for good measure.

He'd considered returning to their paltry camp. Had considered it doubly at the sight of that cursed Terran Knight flying off across the strange skies, bearing two of his compatriots. Celdór couldn't help but think about what proper respects he'd have drawn from the brown skinned Terran for his earlier insolent words, without his so-called Knight there to protect him.

As if the Terran could protect any of them, here in this hellish place.

The boy was no warrior, and this was no tale of the fay. Perhaps, had the

Lady seen fit to bestow her gift upon one more worthy... It hardly bore thinking, what a good Asgardian soldier could have done with that amount of power. Yet think on it, Celdór did, resting down to his haunches, staring through the brackish waters, thoughts of nourishment momentarily forgotten.

It was hardly the first time the Asgardian people had witnessed such an utter lack of appreciation for martial might. Such were the times. Just as their soft Atlantean ancestors had forsaken the rule of the lance and the shield for that of their skewed words and political maneuverings some many generations ago, so too now went the way of the Alliance's oldest and most sacred of orders. The Knights. The Alliance. All of them cheerfully building their house of fancies on a wobbling foundation of polite smiles and lies. All of them pretending they could somehow escape the unerring edge of nature, as it swung back to consume them for their generations of trite decadence and soft-bellied weakness.

On some level, Celdór couldn't help but delight in the knowledge that the entire Alliance seemed nothing if not well poised to reap exactly what it had sown these past millennia. He wasn't alone in that thinking. But nor was it an especially useful line of thinking in the interest of Asgard's survival—or otherwise—were the tales of the Great War to be trusted, as Celdór believed they were.

Centering himself back on that most banal of concerns, Celdór palmed a rock from the dirt and stood to calmly face whatever was coming, unstartled by the shadow that'd just flitted over him and his worthless ruminations. Unafraid of whatever that shadow brought.

He did not jump or startle as the slender figure punched into the dark waters some hundred meters ahead, seemingly from the sky, or perhaps having launched from the distant precipice on the far side of the overrun river. He did not recoil as a grotesque form emerged from the disturbed waters, hissing and tearing straight toward him like a wild, drowning beast.

An Ooperian, he realized, at a splashing glimpse. Mayhap the very same half-starved wretch from the pit, he thought, as the thing neared, its movements wild and flailing.

Celdór hefted the rock, suitable enough for a crude missile, or to the purpose of braining the half-starved savage, and waded into the stagnant waters, going to meet it. It was only at his first good glimpse of the thing's face—and more specifically, its cloudy eyes—that he felt his first hint of surprise.

A blind Ooperian.

Perhaps this was more a tale of the fay than he'd imagined.

Celdór nearly could have laughed.

"Be still, demon," he growled, plucking the pathetic wretch from the churning waters, holding his stone at the ready. "Be still, or I will teach you the meaning of—"

The sound was wet and startlingly sudden. It came on a blinding thud of impact. Came from his own stunned throat. So fast that Celdór's mind failed to keep pace as he looked down, dimly aware that he'd dropped the Ooperian wretch into the shallows, and that the creature was scrambling clear with a frantic terror of speed and churning water. Fleeing. Something innately unbelievable, nonsensical, about the black, clawed fist sticking out of Celdór's own chest. His bloody, screaming chest.

Celdór tried to scream too, then, as his flailing senses realigned. Tried to spin and fight, to look his cowardly assassin in the eyes. But all that left his throat was a weak, wet gasp, his powerful legs buckling beneath him without permission.

Shame.

Voices in the distance, crying his name. Crying challenge to his cowardly attacker. Stabbed in the back. The Ooperian, gone. Gone. Scrambled off up the hill with its frantic hisses. Fleeing. Not him. Paying no mind to the charging Asgardians it passed. Charging for Celdór. Charging to his aid.

Stabbed in the back.

Shame.

The last he saw was a curious sight, as that clawed fist tore free and spun him around. A great, upright jungle cat, awash in bloody waters and a black flood of whirling particulates. The swarm dancing around it like living armor. Utterly silent. Senses failing. Shame and fury.

And the black jaws of Ginnungagap, coming to swallow him whole.

## CHAPTER 29

# JUST THE TIP

"**Y**ou're sure you're—"

"Ask me one more time," Tessa cut him off, "and I swear I'll break my foot on that rock solid ass of yours."

"Okay?" Nate finished. Or maybe acknowledged. He wasn't sure. He showed his hands in surrender anyway, then glanced back to the ridge where Tor was keeping watch. It was hard to fight off the feeling that they didn't have the faintest clue what they were looking for here. Maybe in large part because it wasn't really a feeling at all. More an unfortunate fact. But that was kind of the point of this recon, wasn't it? Best case scenario, they found the *Camelot* right off the bat—and maybe discovered a nice big "Detonate" button for the Dark Tower, to boot. Worst case…

He frowned after Tessa as she puffed her chest at him and started off down the treacherous slope.

"Just be—" he started, then darted forward as some loose stones skittered out from under her boots.

Tessa caught her balance just fine on her own, then regarded the armored hand on her forearm with a wry grin. "Wouldn't wanna slip and hurt myself *before* we get inside the big evil Synth tower, right?"

Nate looked up at the enormous dark spire—it was kind of hard to look at anything else this close up—and released her arm with a sigh. "Point taken."

The flight over had been uneventful, albeit uneventful *with* bated breath, the spire looming so large and sinister he swore the thing had its own gravity—a fact which, as Ex had helpfully pointed out, was indeed true of almost any and all matter in the known universe and not *at all* unique to spooky towers. They'd spent the rest of the short flight bickering semantics and *you know what I mean*, the spire not so much coming nearer as simply blotting out more and more of the sky, until Tor had interrupted to point out a prime lookout perch and request landing. For a minute, Nate had almost forgotten he was carrying Tor and Tessa.

Nothing like a know-it-all Ass Bot riding shotgun to keep things interesting inside one's own head.

*You fly on gravitational manipulators,* Ex grumbled. *Forgive me for assuming you should understand the most basic fundamentals of your toys.*

*I'd rather someone explain to me the most basic fundamentals of THIS thing, if you don't mind,* Nate countered, peering down into the oddly hazy depths of one of the many fissures that'd opened between the crumbling mountain roots and the pulsing spire that'd plowed its way up from what may or may not have been the ninth hell these Asgardians were so fond of. *What is it doing with the Light?*

*Conducting it, obviously,* Ex replied. *I thought you already understood that much,* he added, before Nate could manage an indignant remark. *I watched that very thought chitter across the spaghetti soup you call a brain not thirty minutes past, whilst you ogled the descending waves. Is it my fault I assumed that implied some level of comprehension?*

*Yes. That's exactly your fault.*

*Hmph.*

Nate considered those faint blue waves of Light disappearing down the length of the spire, each one adding a subtle thrum to the ongoing showers of crumbling rock and shifting earth raining down into the open cracks of Ginnungagap—down to Lady knew where. *Any idea where it might be conducting that Light to?* he wondered hesitantly.

*Presumably to something that has some use for Light,* Ex replied, oh-so-helpfully. *Something thataway,* he added, pinging toward the planet's core on Nate's HUD. *Alas, that's hardly the strange part.*

Nate considered Tessa as she turned to him from the chasm she'd been surveying. *What's the strange part?*

*The strange part is that it's conducting Light at all—obviously. I don't know of anything else in the universe that can do that, aside from the Excaliburs, their Knightships, and the Beacons. Unless we count the Merlin, or the Lady herself.*

*So maybe...* Nate trailed off, trying the pieces on for size. The way the swarm had hunted him through the jungle at his most vulnerable. The way it seemed desperate to glom onto the *Camelot* and the *Kalnythian Wilds*. The way it had yanked them here across the Asgard system to begin with—possibly by the threads of Elsa's damned rocks. *Maybe that's Lundquist's rate-limiting step, then. Maybe this Archon just didn't have enough Light to power its relay. Maybe that's why...*

Ahead, Tessa was hooking a thumb deeper into the gorge, like *we gonna have a look or not?* Atop her ridge lookout, Tor's dark form was still and vigilant against the murky ripples of shifting daylight.

*It could explain a few things,* Ex confirmed. *Including how and why that protoswarm ended up strewn across the sector at the beginning of this mess. An underpowered relay would likely be quite erratic. It might even provide some clues as to when and how the Archon awoke on this planet. Which is why I already thought of all this well before Dr. Lundquist hatched his bold relay hypothesis back there.*

Nate raised a *wait a minute* finger at Tessa's splayed *what gives* hands, processing that last sentence, weighing it against yet another flutter of indignation. But something about the way Ex said it. Something about the way he invoked Lundquist's name.

For a second, Nate couldn't help but wonder if maybe his companion wasn't stretching the truth—maybe even straight up fabricating it—out of plain, old jealousy that he hadn't been the one to think of it all first.

*Oh, please. You can't comprehend the number of diverging probabilities that cycle through my processors every nanosecond, Nathaniel. If I inundated you with every tiny little maybe that passed through my mind—*

*You're really gonna tell me my brain would've turned to jelly if you mentioned you'd solved the entire damned mystery?*

*No. I'm telling you that what you're proposing right now is predicated on more maybes, remote possibilities, and outright unknowns than you're consciously capable of perceiving at once, much less processing. I could provide you with over seventy-million alternate macropossibilities of virtually identical probability, not to mention compelling mathematical proofs that strongly suggest neither one of us truly even possesses free will, thus rendering this entire exercise rather pointless, but suffice it to say, Nathaniel, that I'd simply rather have a look around before I go wagering the fate of the galaxy on your singular intuition.*

*That's... Yeah, okay. Fair enough. I'm just saying, in the future—*

*You'd prefer I turn your brain to mush and spell out everything in nauseating detail. Understood. I shall henceforth make no assumptions of probabilistic competence, especially—*

*Especially where my sad noodle-brained intelligence is concerned*, Nate finished for him, guessing the gist of it. *Or, for that matter, where—*

*Where the safety of the crew is in doubt*, Ex fired back, just to show two could play that game. *See?* he added. *We're getting so good at this, Nathaniel.*

*Two peas in a freaking pod*, Nate thought. *Just—*

*If you see something, say something?* Ex offered.

*Something like that.*

*Never trust the obvious to land*, Ex confirmed. *Got it. No assumptions here. Radical transparency, all the way. Lady be praised.*

"I feel better already," Nate muttered, turning to go meet Tessa, and drawing up short as his HUD overlay came alive with a positively overwhelming stream of ghostly virtualities—hundreds, thousands, of Alternate Reality Nates stepping forward only to trip and fall down the chasm on the left. More still falling at Tessa's feet on the right. Several others falling and knocking her into the pit with him. Alternate Reality Nates attacked by the spire in a sudden rush of dismantling swarm. Zapped by spire lightning. Unleashing hell on the spire only to watch the planet sundered through at the core. A few poor Alternate Reality Nates spontaneously combusting on the spot.

"Everything okay?" came Tessa's voice somewhere through the chaos of a thousand Nates, adding a whole new universe of diverging possibilities to the mess.

*I get it*, he snapped at Ex.

The HUD cleared instantly, like magic, leaving one mildly concerned looking Tessa watching him a few meters away.

"Trouble in paradise?" she asked, as he went to join her.

"Who, us? Never."

But some part of him kept chewing at the edge of the irritation he wanted to feel for his partner as he and Tessa resumed their sweep of the area.

*You really see all that, all the time?* he finally asked.

*In grossly oversimplified terms, yes. That, and much, much more.*

Something in the way Ex said it struck at Nate's heart. He'd felt hopelessness before—genuine Up-the-Creek-Without-a-Paddle Blues. But the thought of being unable to rally his mind and body back around the definite —to be stuck drifting among a mess of diverging madnesses without a lever to collapse the world back down into one predictable reality... That seemed... Not just horrifying. Lonely, too. Like some desolate traveler cursed to wander the spaces between countless lush realities without ever having one to call his own. And to think he'd gone this long without understanding such a basic fact of his friend's existence…

*Oh, spare me your pity,* Ex grumbled, sounding properly disgusted. *I could make a similarly pathetic assessment of your single-minded perceptions. And besides, I do have methods for modulating the convergence of my so-called 'experiences' when the need arises. In particular, I find it… enhances my deterministic focus, shall we say, being forced to interact with—*

*With my sad noodle brain?* Nate offered, unable to hold back a smile.

*Just so. Though it's possible 'enhance' is entirely too positive a word.*

"Ass Bot," Nate muttered beneath his smile, as if Ex couldn't hear.

They spent some time picking their way across the wreckage from there, hovering from one vantage point to the next on Nate's gravitonics, Ex running scans all the while. As many precautions as Ex had prepared for the contingency of losing the Light again, their energy stores held just fine throughout. The only thing that was missing was the *Camelot.* And the Archon. Ex's sweeps showed no hint of either nearby. Interesting readings from the tower, they had in spades. But not enough to draw any hard conclusions from the outside. Nate didn't push Ex to speculate.

Finally, they reached the point where there was nothing left to physically inspect on the surface level but the tower itself. It stood massive and silent as they approached, its surface oddly smooth close up, compared with how violently sharp and prickly its higher extremities looked from afar.

"Sooo…" Tessa said, eyeing the jet-black wall from what felt only nominally like a safe distance. "You reckon we just knock, or what?"

Nate tipped his head back, tracing the gargantuan obelisk into the sky. The spire's surface seemed to eat the warbled daylight. He wasn't sure he could even see the top of the thing this close up.

"Guess that depends on whether or not we think it's a good idea to *touch* the giant lightning rod."

They both looked at each other. Back to the tower, considering. Back to each other.

"Just the tip, then?" Tessa asked.

"Something tells me you're not taking this as seriously as Old Man Jaeger would prefer."

"Defense mechanism. I'm actually shaking in my boots, beneath all the bravado." She followed his pointed look down to her planted boots and shrugged. "You know, metaphorically speaking."

Nate considered the tower, trying to weigh the options like a responsible Knight type would, knowing even as he did that he didn't have any better alternative. Jaeger and the others would be waiting, probably beginning to worry. But Cammy was waiting somewhere too. Quite possibly somewhere in there. And they needed answers, regardless.

Ex, for his part, was at least marginally convinced that the thing probably wouldn't be able to possibly, mayhap suck them dry of Light and life at first touch. Perchance. Maybe.

*I believe in you, Nathaniel. I swear.*

*But which me?* Nate wondered, picturing a fleet of Alternate Reality Nates stepping forward to try their luck.

*That IS the question, isn't it?*

He blew out a long breath. "Fine." He glanced at Tessa. "Fine. We'll do it. Just the—Just take cover, will you?"

"I shall duck behind this rock," she chimed, practically beaming, definitely far too chipper for any sane mortal in this particular situation as she sidled over to a long, flat boulder.

He wanted to argue with her choice of cover—wanted, in truth, to pick her up and fly her at least as far back as Tor's lookout. Farther, if they were being even remotely realistic about the kind of power the structure might be ready to unleash. But then again, if they were really being realistic, even the camp might not be safe. Probably wasn't.

"Nate." The playfulness had gone from Tessa's tone. From her face too. She saw his hesitance. Wanted him to know it. "Let's find our girl," she said, in a way that made it clear she decidedly wasn't screwing around beneath that chipper surface. "Hooah?"

He nodded, waited for her to take cover, then turned and stepped up to the monolithic monstrosity. It screwed with his ears, standing so close to something so gigantic yet so eerily silent. It was only as he drew up the last few meters that he was able to fully appreciate the extent of that silence— like, in addition to daylight, the jet-black surface ate sound waves as well. Like it consumed everything that touched it, refusing to reflect anything back to the outside world. Nothing but those crackling arcs of red energy racing across its surface here and there, and the soft waves of azure Light descending. He felt each passing thrum more as a tingling in the hairs of his forearms than as actual sound.

None of it seemed to bode well.

He thought of Iveera. Tried not to think of the way her eyes had widened at that word, Archon. Let out another long breath, sinking into focus, pulling up every shield and barrier he had at max power. Then he reached out to touch the thing.

The wall rippled and parted before his hand like fluid magic.

The effect was so unexpected, so smooth yet unsettling, that he jerked his hand back before he could think about it. The tower wall fell back into place like a waterfall resuming its shape after some perturbation, but other than that... Nothing. No furious alarm or flaring defense cannons. No bolt of ruby red lightning.

*Well, that was unexpected,* Ex said.

*Even for you?* Nate asked, too stunned to be sassy about it.

*Exceedingly improbable, then, if you'd like to split hairs about it,* Ex amended. *Roughly equal in likelihood to the scenario in which the wall spontaneously became ham.*

Nate just gaped at the black wall, unsure what to make of any of it.

*Okay, that was a teensy-weensy exaggeration,* Ex admitted, as if a wall of ham was surely the bit that Nate was hung up on, here. *Regardless...*

Nate glanced back at Tessa's rock. Saw a pair of peeping eyes caught up in a stupefied look to rival his own. He gestured for her to get back behind cover, then turned and tried again.

Again, the black wall parted several centimeters ahead of his reaching hand, like flowing water preemptively fleeing a coming glob of oil. He reached a little farther in, tracing his fingers back and forth, surprised to see the outer wall didn't appear to be more than a few centimeters thick—at least in this spot. That seemed rather improbable too, for a structure of this size. But he was more captivated for the moment with the way the wall continued to react to his tracing fingers, parting wherever he moved his hand whilst closing back at the places he left behind, like the material was electrostatically repelled from his armor.

"Huh," Tessa said behind him, so close he almost jumped. He glanced back at her with a flicker of anger that she hadn't stayed behind cover.

"Well, that was easy," she said, too busy gaping at the flowing gap around his hand to notice.

"A little too easy," he thought out loud, withdrawing his hand and watching the wall close back up with a disconcerting lack of sound.

"Mmhmm," she said, nodding thoughtfully, looking between him and the once-again flawless black tower wall, wheels turning.

"I think maybe I should get you and Tor out of here."

"That wasn't the plan, Mr. Knight," she said, stepping closer to the spire with a strange, almost dreamy expression. He was barely aware of her moving till he caught her hand in mid-reach for the black surface. She looked at him, trance broken.

"How much of this has been 'the plan,' Tess?" He felt her tense at the heat in his voice. It surprised him too. "I..." The words caught in his throat. Now wasn't the time for this. *Anytime* wasn't the time for the thoughts going through his head. He undid the seals and pulled off his helmet, willing her to heed his words. "Look, you weren't awake to see what happened here before, but you saw the state everyone's in back at camp because of it. I need space to work without having to worry about you or anyone else."

She looked up at him, searching his face in a way that made him suddenly and overtly aware of how close they were. "I hear what you're saying," she finally said. "I really do. But you need to get it through your head that we're with you in this, Nate. In all of it. What do you think happens to us if you go die in there because you didn't have a third hand to take the stick?"

He searched her face. She didn't back down.

He broke first, and they both knew it.

"Pretty sure Ex could grow a third hand, technically speaking," he muttered, scowling at nothing in particular.

"A quick peek. That's all I'm asking."

Nate blew out a sigh. "Just the tip?"

"Just to see how it feels," she confirmed, with the most solemn of nods.

"Tess..."

She pitched an eyebrow, like *didn't we literally just do this?*

"If I tell you to run..."

"Ah." She threw him a loose salute and made a *clack-clack* sound with her tongue. "Then you'll already be talking to an empty room. Promise. C'mon, Mr. Knight," she added, brushing past to take cover behind him, like she already knew he was going to ask. "What could possibly go wrong?"

# CHAPTER 30

# SHAFTED

There were no floors to stand on inside the spire.

In hindsight, Nate wasn't sure what he'd been expecting. A black onyx welcome lobby, maybe—inlaid with a nice, inverted pentagram, he supposed. Arcane elevators, and orc guards, and goblin receptionists sitting behind deceptively tidy desks, manning the ol' nine-to-five. Aside from a lifetime spent around Terran buildings, he supposed there really hadn't been any reason to expect the structure's innards would reflect its outward tower-ish appearance at all.

And they most certainly didn't.

He looked down at Tess, hovering there in his arms. She sensed his gaze in the eerie red light and met it with a clear *are you seeing this shit?* look. Neither of them spoke for some silent fear that the structure would hear them and respond. Which *part* of the the structure, he wasn't exactly sure. But there were more than enough potential options to choose from.

Everywhere they looked, dark whirring pieces of all shapes and sizes drifted about their business, some relatively fixed in position and apparent function, others more amorphous and flighty. The entire dance had an almost organic sort of feel to it, coupled with the long, rhythmic waves of Light that seemed to go pulsing down the length of the spire every ten seconds or so. In another light, something about the whole production might've felt mesmerizing, even satisfying. Cast in the ominous red glow of the crackling storm high above, though, it just kind of felt like they'd gone and wandered onto the busy streets of hell.

He glanced up at that angry ruby electrical storm—seemingly raging at the spire's distant peak, though it was hard to actually gauge distances in here. A rush of azure Light descended from the chaos, searing dark red shadows to violet and sending glitchy jitters through the machinery as it passed, on and on, down into the heart of Ginnungagap.

Watching the Light descend into the depths, watching all of it, Nate wasn't sure what to think. There were a lot of moving pieces to take in, and the structure *did* invoke the feeling of some dark wizard's tower, in more ways than one. But... He wasn't quite sure. For some reason, watching it all, he had the vague intuition that they weren't really in a "tower" at all, so much as they were floating inside one impossibly long, synthetic nerve, just doing its thing—whatever the hell that thing might be.

And that, he figured, was probably that for the moment.

They'd come. They'd seen. There was no *Camelot* waiting to be snatched, and as far as interior details went, Ex could replay the whole thing in holo schematic for Lundquist and the others. Not that Nate really expected they'd have any more idea what to make of all this than he did. But still. For now, getting out while they still could seemed the smart move. At least until he could come back unencumbered to scout deeper.

Tessa must've felt him starting to drift them backward for the spire wall. She turned palms upward in silent question, jerking her head back toward the heart of the dim shaft like *we already came this far, right?*

*Not to side with Ms. What Could Go Wrong, here,* Ex added, *but in keeping with the Great Noodle Brain Accords of Ten Minutes Past, I'd be remiss were I not to tell you that I'm fairly certain I feel our Camelot down there somewhere.*

*Somewhere?* Nate wondered, eyeing the drop. The blue rings of descending Light seemed to go on forever in that darkness. Far enough to blur together in what little snippets Nate could see before they were obfuscated completely by layer after overlapping layer of swirling spire machinery.

*At least a few hundred, um... Hmm.*

*Hmm?*

*It's difficult to tell with all this interference. It could be a few hundred kilometers down. Could be... thousands? The Light pingback is quite finicky in here. Can't imagine why.*

Nate stared unseeingly at the unfathomable pit, trying and failing to grasp the magnitude of the depths Ex was proposing.

*My most convergent guess is that the Archon is moving shop,* Ex added. *Either closer to the core, or perhaps to the pole on the far side of the planet. Either way begs the question—*

*Wait—This thing goes... all the way?*

But even as he asked, the image was already taking shape in his mind—a central shaft, some nine or ten thousand kilometers in length, connecting the vast array of dendritic tendrils blooming out by the tens of thousands from those jagged spire peaks high above. Tendrils he might well have unknowingly contacted, it seemed, on his hasty flight up into the soul-sucking void. Tendrils that stretched untold kilometers through the atmosphere, too fine to notice but for the accumulated red haze. All of them funneling, funneling. Funneling an entire planet's Light back to this bipolar, planetary backbone. And not just funneling. There was something else there, too. Some function he couldn't quite grasp. Teleportation. Spatial folding. *Un*folding.

Unreality.

*Are you...? Are we...?* Nate tried to parse the murky schematics in his head, distantly aware of the thought, if not quite the sensation, that he smelled something burning. *Are these my thoughts, or yours?*

*Yes,* Ex replied, in a mildly self-satisfied tone. *Though the latter is still clearly somewhat lost in translation to the former. With a bit of practice, though— and a good bit of dumb luck, I wager—Lady willing, perhaps I won't have to continue spelling out my every cycle for you with clunky words for all the centuries to come.*

Nate considered that.

*Be careful what you wish for, I think, is the pertinent phrase here,* Ex concluded, when he'd been silent too long.

*Maybe I'm just touched you still think we have centuries right now,* Nate countered, coming back to the dim red world of the shaft and all its fastidious worker bees with the realization that Tessa had just said something. For a moment, he'd nearly forgotten he was holding her. For the next, he could only look around in mild alarm, waiting to see if the busy streets of Spire Hell would spring to red alert at the intrusion of her Terran voice. Tessa looked around too, clearly cognizant of the same possibility.

Nothing changed.

Not as far as he could tell, at least.

Finally, Tessa looked back to him like she was still awaiting some answer. "You didn't, did you?"

"Didn't what?"

"Stroke out on me."

"Oh. Technically, no."

"Reassuring," she said, hyphenating the syllables out as she gazed around the apparently largely mindless business of the tower. "So then… onward?"

"Just a quick look," he agreed, hovering them gently forward into the open. "Ex thinks he has a read on Cammy somewhere below."

Tessa gave a sober nod. It still didn't feel right—or particularly intelligent—speaking aloud in this place. Or lingering a second longer than necessary. He pointed them toward the nearest curiosity and eased them downward.

While such pedestrian modalities as floors were wholly absent from the spire shaft layout, there were multiple series of geometric nodes interspersed down the length of the shaft—most of them spaced every few kilometers or so, from the looks of it, with the nearest being a quick hundred-meter descent away. He approached cautiously, steering clear of the quivering nanite tendril linkage and taking care to make sure Tessa was enveloped inside his energy shields, just in case.

The darkness thickened noticeably with every passing meter they drew away from the already distant spire apex—Ex's Light-sucking dendrite, with its raging red electrical storm. There was no sign of the *Camelot* below, or of anything else patently non spire related, really. But that probably wasn't surprising if Ex was anywhere close on his estimated distances. Nate wasn't really sure what he was expecting to glean at all as they drew closer to the node, aside from maybe a slightly less obstructed line of sight down the length of the shaft.

What he definitely *wasn't* expecting was for the thing to lash out at them with angry nanite tentacles.

The first rushing arm glanced off his energy shields with a sharp sputter and hiss, the breath catching in his lungs. Freezing. Freezing right along with everything else.

It was like a switch had been thrown.

One instant, he was recoiling, reaching to conjure his sword, Tessa sucking a sharp, "What the—" in his arms. The next, it was like his mind had gone and fallen right off the edge of chartered time and space, leaving his body behind. Space constricted. The depths of the spire rushing up to meet him. His limbs heavy, leaden. Time coiling in on itself. The whirring worker bees suddenly still. In his arms, Tessa was frozen. And below…

Below.

Two thousand kilometers and a hair's breadth away, the Archon turned from its work to look at him, the only thing moving in this frozen world of theirs—just him and it, the space between them bizarrely telescoping in on itself. Collapsing. He noted the megatons of collapsed superstructure cargo it seemed to have shuttled along from the surface. Felt Cammy's presence buried somewhere therein. Felt the Archon's will bending, sharpening, frozen space quivering as it set its sights on him.

In that moment, Nate knew beyond a shadow of a doubt that it would be suicide, challenging the Archon here, at the seat of its power.

He pulled back against its hold, willing the world to unfreeze.

Below, the Archon flared brighter.

Nate strained harder. Felt Ex straining with him. Felt searing heat and pressure, the Archon thrusting a glowing hand forward across the impossible distance.

They fought, its will crushing in around them. Absolute.

Fought harder. Screaming. Straining. Straining until—

Time shattered.

Disbanded. Uncoiled. Snapped back into place, ripped across the vast space by Nate's ragged gasp.

"—piss?!" Tessa concluded.

Nate was already moving. Moving on pure instinct. Grasping her tighter. Punching the gravitonics.

"Nate?"

The walls closing in on them. Coming alive.

"Nate!"

He leveled his wrist cannon and blasted through the spire wall where they'd entered, positive that whatever magical visitor's pass had let him in had been revoked the moment the Archon laid eyes on them. He fed more power to the gravitonics, nanites hammering their shields from behind.

They broke through the gaping spire hole into murky orange daylight, hounded by more nanoswarm than Nate could process. It came from everywhere at once, plunging after them through the opening, tearing itself from the dark spire walls, clogging the air. The entire damn tower rippling to life. Enough to swallow twenty *Camelots* whole. More.

He didn't think. Just moved. Tearing out of the ruins on the gravitonics. Barely slowing to snatch up Tor from her lookout perch on the way. It was only as he did so that he registered how molasses-slow she was moving, and the strange stillness gripping the land. The daylight frozen. The swarm slowing behind them. Tor and Tessa practically stuck to his sides like magnets as they flew, their faces twisting in slow motion expressions of pain and alarm.

It was so disconcerting Nate almost lost track of their flight and brought them down at full speed.

*Well, that's one way to break into the wonderful world of flash-stepping,* Ex chimed, rather cheerfully, as they thudded down to the camp site in a sudden rush of air. The *empty* camp site, he registered dumbly, save for two surprised looking Asgardians and an openly gaping Pierce and Snuffy. And had Ex just said—

"Ughh," Tessa groaned, doubling over to clutch at her knees like she might be sick.

*Typically inadvisable with sensitive cargo,* Ex added, as Nate hurried to stabilize her, feeling a bit inside out. Beside them, Tor looked a little green at the gills too. *You'd best be careful next time, Nathaniel. A little more spacetime warpage and you could have killed them. And speaking of which—*

"The hell'd you come from?" Pierce asked, before Nate's spinning head could properly begin to process Ex's words, or even think about asking where everyone was.

Beside them, Tor dropped to one knee and vomited.

"Yup," Tessa said, grimacing at the sight. "That feels about right."

"Nate?" Pierce tried again. "What's the deal? What happened over there? You all look like you—"

They all whipped around at an awful, airy hiss from the direction of the flooded river valley, Nate preparing to fight, fully expecting to see a tsunami of nanoswarm blocking out the sky. Instead, he took in one emaciated Ooperian cresting the hill, running like the devil himself was on his tail.

*—I believe we have company,* Ex concluded.

"Bob?" Snuffy asked, like he couldn't quite believe his eyes.

The Ooperian hissed and hacked as it ran, waving its arms like a survivor flagging down a passing plane.

*And not just this one,* Ex added.

Then the sky *did* go black, and the thing chasing Bob came flying out of the flooded river valley on a rushing wave of darkness.

# CHAPTER 31

# SUPERSONIC

I t happened faster than Nate could process. He threw his hands wide and pushed the others aside on twin bursts of gravitonic force, clearing the way. Then the darkness crashed into him like a force of nature.

Myrr, he registered, as his heart leapt on a surge of bioengineered terror. Stronger than before. No doubt about it. And coated in flowing swaths of jet-black plating that looked too much like nanite armor. Even gassed up on Light as Nate was, the impact sent them skidding across the soil, tearing a deep furrow, and damn near knocked him on his ass.

Something—three guesses what—had supercharged the homicidal supercat.

He didn't have time to wonder how before Myrr quite literally tried to bite his head off. He moved without thinking, jamming a defensive forearm into the beast's jaws, trying to conjure up some of that newfound super-speed, focus breaking like a brittle twig as Myrr chomped down with crushing force. Nate gritted his teeth and shoved back, adding a gravitonic blast that sent Myrr cratering into the hillside.

The swarm was already descending on his people, ripping into the fleeing Ooperian, Pierce and Snuffy firing hopelessly into the mass as the Asgardians dragged them back. Tor and Tessa hurried their way, Tor's shield disintegrating from her arm as the Atlantean tried to defend them, Tessa waving and shouting at the others, "Go! Go!"

Nate lifted off, catching the thickest swath of nanites with a column of plasma that probably singed his friends' hair off. He might as well have been trying to punch back an ocean, as fast as the swarm kept coming. He charged forward on his gravitonics, hoping against hope that the nanites would focus on him and let his people escape.

Snuffy went down, Pierce crouched protectively in front of him, firing all the while as one of the Asgardians snagged the mechanic's weapon and the other plucked him up, threw him over one broad shoulder, and started running.

Nate felt Ex offering something. A weapon. A distraction. He didn't ask questions, just took it and swung for the hills. The air ruptured with a frenetic burst of sound waves and electromagnetic chaos. For a moment, it almost seemed to work—the nanites reeling in an unfocused mess, like a colony without a queen. Then the swarm coalesced back around some central will, and Myrr came flying in for Round Two.

Nate was ready this time, smacking the beast down with a hammering blow. He conjured his sword from e-dim, preparing to follow for the kill, but the swarm enveloped him, pressing in from all sides, obscuring his view of anything else. He cooked the surrounding area with a flare of his energy shields, resisting the urge to start swinging wildly. In the moment the blast bought him, he caught sight of that crazy snargladorf charging onto the scene from...

The facility. The abandoned buildings.

Shelter.

"Get to the buildings!" he shouted. Unnecessarily, it seemed, as he glimpsed Vampire Bob dragging a bloodied Asgardian and a struggling Pierce that way, hissing at the snargladorf, which darted over to grab Snuffy by one tear-resistant pant leg and start dragging.

The swarm was back on him before he could spot Tessa or the others.

He did start swinging, then, hacking through the mess with sword and plasma. It wasn't as futile as it should've been. Something about this swarm. Weaker than the one he'd clashed with before. More erratic. He pushed on through the thick of it, bolstered by these observations, determined to find Myrr and end this.

He didn't have far to go.

Myrr was waiting for him when he broke through the swarm. Waiting with Tessa held high in one black clawed hand—a kicking, cursing human shield. Or a trophy. Either way, designed to give Nate pause. It just lit a fury instead. Some internal dam breaking. This thing. This planet.

He exploded forward with a wild bellow, pushing the gravitonics. Pushing till the swarm slowed around him, the world caught in molasses. Tessa's face frozen mid-snarl. Myrr's yellow irises tracking him from behind her shoulder, moving faster than the rest of the world. Not fast enough.

He took the beast's arm off with one clean cut at the elbow—glowing sword edge hewing through armor and flesh and bone like nothing. Time snapped back into shape with a keening animal scream as he took Myrr by the throat and ripped the creature away from Tessa. They crashed through a dead tree, Myrr snapping its powerful jaws at him, flailing. The chemical fear wilting. Spoiling. Shifting to something else completely.

They slammed into the dirt, Myrr first, hard enough to kick up a shock-wave of soil and dust, Nate plunging his sword into Myrr's abdomen to end it. The blade was halfway buried when the beast caught hold of his wrist with both enormous hands, and something alien and half-crazed washed over him—*through* him.

Pain.

Terrible, gnawing pain.

Ripping at his flesh. Crawling under his skin like fire ants. The world flashing before his eyes, desperate and out of control. Filthy cages and probing stunners. Leering eyes. Blood on the walls. Wild gray curls. Tang of burnt herb. The Children. The Meyerwitz. The Cursed—

Nate jerked back from Myrr, breaking away from whatever spell it was exuding, gripping his sword to try again. But not before he saw her. Black-thorne, standing there in his mind's eye. Alone and shaking in a wrecked room. Here. The facility. Dangling wires and blood on the walls. Blood on her. Turning to him. Turning to it. *Seeing.*

Myrr's kick took him in the stomach like a runaway train. He was too stunned to see it coming, too slow to react. He hit the dirt rolling some twenty meters later, gasping for air. He kicked up on gravitonic wings, fully expecting waves of nanites to come crashing down on him with a vengeance, but the heart of the swarm was there—a rather small swarm, he registered, as he finally got his first clear look—gathering in a swirling mass around the dark predator that somehow seemed to have become its master.

He locked eyes with Myrr across the battlefield. Read the thing's intent clearly as if they were still caught in some kind of psychic link. The beast was clever. Too clever to press on with a fight it knew it wouldn't win. So, it was off to go lick its wounds, find another way. Cunning predator's eyes scanning the field for an out. Spotting it.

"No," Nate choked past a paralyzed diaphragm, eyes falling on Tessa right at the same time Myrr loosed its swarm like a thousand-thousand archers letting fly at once.

Nate exploded forward, pouring on the speed, uselessly blasting holes in the swarm's leading edge, Tessa pulling herself up from the ground in slow motion. He was so focused on reaching her—so caught up on Ex's warning about flash-stepping precious cargo—that he never saw the second prong coming.

The nanites punched into his side out of nowhere. Not enough to overload his shields outright, but more than enough to rip him off course. They rode him to the ground, driving, constricting, seeking some flaw in his defenses. He clawed at dirt, smoking energy shields burning off his attackers. Tore up from the ground, throwing himself toward Tessa. Too late.

Slow motion terror as the swarm fell over her, reaching tendrils slashing at her back, her legs. Rushing forward to consume her completely. Her mouth and eyes wide with horrible realization.

An animal scream tore from his throat, fists thrown wide. A thrumming blue shockwave punching out in all directions, washing over Tessa and the swarm. He didn't understand. Not as he crashed to his knees in front of Tessa. Not as the buzzing masses around her sputtered and died, nanites dropping to the soil like someone had killed the network signal, the fringes at the edge of the shockwave recoiling as if burnt, then speeding away for the river valley.

Myrr was gone.

The camp site air muffled, silent but for the sounds of their breathing.

*Well,* Ex said, stirring warily from combat silence, *that was—*

"Exceedingly improbable," Nate whispered, watching nanites fall like a fine ash rain.

*Just so.*

Tessa pushed up to her knees in front of him, looking around in disbelief, black nanite dust falling from her hair, clinging to her bloodied cheek. Nate hurried to wipe it clear, some part of him paranoid the things might somehow reawaken in her blood, crawl right in for a swim. The touch drew her shocked attention back to him, her hand reflexively shooting up to stop his. For a moment, they were caught in something like a struggle, wrestling more with what had just happened than with each other. Then he pulled her to him, and she didn't fight it.

"Jesus," she breathed against his shoulder, arms clutching at his sides. "Jesus Christ, that was—"

"Too close."

They sounded like someone else's words. Someone else's voice. Almost by surprise, he found himself pulling them to their feet, chest tightening with more anger than he knew what to do with. He let her go, turning toward the facility, thinking to look for their people but mostly just trying to calm himself. He wanted to hit something. Was being childish. Wanted to hit something anyway.

"Nate..."

He yanked his helmet off, rounding on her, finger raised. He wanted to scream at her. To grab her. Crush her. Crush her lips to his. For one dizzying moment he was sure his body would, whether he liked it or not. It was only as she stood there, jaw set, daring him to do his worst, that he remembered she'd taken at least a few slashes before he'd gotten there. A crash of thunder and ruby red lightning won out over their impromptu staring contest before he could ask, drawing their attention to the spire, and to the sizable swarm stirring up around its base.

"Fantastic," Tessa sighed.

Nate spun at the sound of something approaching. That hissing Ooperian, hurrying their way, moving at an inhuman clip despite the pronounced limp he seemed to have developed from whatever wounds he'd sustained.

Vampire Bob looked like he'd gone for a run through a nice field of razor wire.

*Lady's Grace, he's blind*, Ex pitched in, as the Ooperian drew up several meters short of them, gangly hands raised in peace. Nate was too washed out from everything else to feel surprised, or to even wonder whose side the creature was on. He just took dim note of the cloudy gray haze in Bob's eyes as the Ooperian began gasping some wild, hissing gibberish that even Ex couldn't understand. Bob seemed to be functioning well enough on his remaining senses, if his frothing concern and wild gesticulations for the growing swarm on the spire horizon were any indication.

"Shit," Nate muttered, eyeing Tessa, then turning to consider their options, exceedingly slim as they were. Pierce and Tor were hoofing it back their way, bloodied but still on their feet. Further down the way, Tristan and Ramirez had appeared along with some of the Asgardians, all of them pitching in to bear Snuffy, the snargladorf, and the injured Asgardians down the sloping plain for the abandoned facilities where Jaeger must've decided to move camp.

Nate eyed the flat stretch of ancient prefabs, knowing there was no way those walls—or any others—could hold against the swarm. Ex agreed emphatically. But shelter was shelter, said his primal caveman brain.

And the swarm was coming.

"Shit," Nate repeated, as the black clouds began peeling off from the distant spire in earnest, headed their way. Fast.

There was no time to deliberate. No time to fret over the sudden realization that his Light stores weren't nearly as recovered as they should've been in the wake of his clash with Myrr. He grabbed Tessa, ignoring her indignation, gesturing furiously down the slope and barking orders that roughly rhymed with *get the duck back to those gildings*. Then, saved at least one decision as Vampire Bob recoiled from his offered hand and turned to bolt, Nate took flight.

Moments later, Tessa delivered, he turned back to relieve the others of Snuffy and the half-frantic snargladorf. Then again. Back and forth like some ping-ponging ferryman, plucking wide-eyed crew and indignant Asgardians to safety with borderline violent speed, painfully aware at every leap that he was losing the race to the closing swarm.

He sped in with the last cursing Asgardian, nanites nipping at his shields, just in time to witness Vampire Bob arriving on foot—only to skid to a hissing halt, dancing awkwardly right at the perimeter of the facility. Nate adjusted course, not even remotely sure if or when the Ooperian had become an ally, but intending to yank him into the courtyard with them all the same. At the last second, though, Bob gave a strange, high-pitched yowl, and threw himself forward.

They all touched down more or less together at the corner of the forwardmost building, Nate and his cursing Asgardian passenger whirling to face the coming swarm, Bob merely cocking his head like he was listening. But there wasn't anything to hear.

Just an utterly silent, ocean-sized swarm crashing down on their heads.

For an instant, Nate was back in Atlantis—a helpless boy standing frozen as the dark, icy waters came plunging down on him. The swarm blotting out the discolored Ginnungagap sky.

Then his better senses took hold, and he tensed to throw himself at the swarm, to tear into the enemy with everything he had.

He was already mid-leap when the entire swarm jerked to an abrupt halt, just clear of the facility walls. It happened so suddenly, so unexpectedly, that he touched down on the rooftop and almost pitched over the edge. He stayed there, perched and frozen, as the swarm did much the same

—an ocean of blackness, staring him down like some cocked serpent, waiting to strike.

The silent standoff stretched. Nate a hair's breadth from saying to hell with it and taking his best shot. Terrified what might happen if he didn't. Equally worried what might if he did. His finger was stroking the metaphorical trigger when the perfectly repelled swarm gave a sudden, network-wide shudder and began to recede from the facility. Slowly, at first. Then in greater swaths.

*You know, I'm getting kind of tired of saying this,* Ex started slowly, *but—*

"What the actual fuck is going on with this planet?" someone murmured from somewhere in the courtyard below.

*Just so,* Ex agreed.

Nate was too razor focused watching the nanites slink away, racing heart still pounding in his ears. He held steady, waiting for the other foot to fall, for the Archon to come screaming in. The greater swarm looping almost lazily around in the distance, headed back for the spire.

It was only when the last of the nanites had turned tail, with no sign of coming back—and when someone down in the courtyard had sounded the cry, "We're not dead, yet!"—that Nate finally allowed himself to unfreeze and look down at the ancient prefab rooftop beneath his boots. Only then that he allowed himself to wonder what in the hell had happened within these walls all those many years ago, and what they were hiding now.

"I think maybe we'd better have a closer look at this place," he said, watching the inky black clouds reunite with their mother spire in the distance.

*Just so,* Ex agreed.

 

~

 

It happened in less than a blink.

One instant, Myrr was perched safely in the arms of the jungle canopy, devouring the last of its latest catch. Willing the aching stump of its arm to regrow faster. Dark-sand armor tingling weirdly against its chest as it watched the Dark One's swarms turned back by the lingering taint of the Meyerwitz's cursed ruins, and by the Strong Armored One who seemed wholly unaffected by the place.

One instant, Myrr was watching the Dark One's forces retreat to its Dark Tower, beginning to question the strength of its new ally.

The next, the jungle was gone, and Myrr's flesh was screaming.

Myrr reacted with jungle-honed reflexes, springing into motion, senses leaping to full alertness in the dark. But there was nowhere to spring. An unnatural lack of things to sense. Something other. In between. As if the sleeping mind sights had come to join the waking. Pain and alarm. Dark-sand armor ripping free from its flesh. Betraying Myrr's control just as it had during Myrr's retreat, when the Strong Armored One had conjured his scalding sorcery.

But the Strong Armored One was not here, now.

Only the Dark One.

They were deep. Far deeper than Myrr had ever been. Its chest burned. Flesh failing to mend. The Dark One hovered there, considering Myrr with its glowing face-spot of red light and tainted brimstone. Myrr should have known, it realized. Knew now. The smells were wrong. Had been all along. Myrr should've listened. Had tried to listen. Senses fooled. The smells never lied.

There was no anger as the Dark One took Myrr into its sharp embrace. Rent flesh and deep pain. The touch of darkness, leeching the lifesong from Myrr's bones. No sense of failure or regret. Only pain. Pain, and betrayal, and an overwhelming sense of otherness. Failing senses. Foiled senses. Tricked by this force of un-nature. This Azmodeus. This Dark Invader. Its touch a portal. An entrance to a place Myrr dared not venture.

The Dark Invader took Myrr by the scruff of the neck, unrelenting, and pushed it through.

# CHAPTER 32

# FROM BEYOND

*N*athaniel.

The voice was like a drop of water breaking against the perfectly flat plane of his world. Which, at the current moment, was nothing more than darkness. Long, sprawling darkness. Unbroken. Alone. Alone, but for—

"Nate."

He opened his eyes to find Iveera watching him. Only… not Iveera. Not in the simple flesh. Something more.

Her jin swished back and forth in a familiar gesture of casual disapproval. "You haven't been practicing your mental defenses."

"I…" He stood and looked around, some dim corner of his mind noting that it was a tad strange, the way Iveera remained right in front of him, unchanged in his frame of reference, as he did so. Nothing else to see but hazy light and wispy nothingness. "Where are we?"

"I would very much like to know the answer to that question myself."

"Dreaming," Nate figured out loud, connecting the dots as the details came trickling back.

"Uncoupling," Iveera countered. For some reason, she'd never liked that word, *dreaming*. One of those cultural things he'd never gotten around to clarifying.

Someone snorted at that thought from over behind a traipse of ruby red curtains.

"Oh, never mind me," Ex said, poking his mustachioed face out from behind the curtains. "We have more important matters to tend to."

"The Archon," Nate said, looking back to Iveera.

She was studying the place where Ex had just appeared, like she knew exactly what was there but couldn't quite see it.

"It's building a relay," he added. "I think." He glanced at Ex. "We think."

"I surmised as much, from what few readings we've been able to gather."

He blinked. He should've known better than to expect to be a step ahead of the Gorgon. But still. She hadn't even been here. There. Wherever the hell. Hadn't seen what this Archon thing could do.

"So how do I stop it?"

She turned away, jin flitting in thought. Somehow, he still saw her face, brow wrinkled in consternation. "Destroy its apparatus," she finally said. "Break this shroud it's cast upon the planet. I will take it from there."

She considered the posture he hadn't meant to let tense. Even in a dream —an *uncoupling*—his body defied him on some level.

"The Troglodan and I will help you finish it from there," she amended.

Somehow, the appeal to his ego only made the slight feel that much worse. He decided to move on.

"What do you mean, the shroud it's cast?"

"Whatever you're facing down there, it's phased the entire planet out of reach."

"I... don't think I understand."

"Ginnungagap is there, and yet not."

Nate thought uneasily of the soul-sucking annihilation he'd felt when he'd tried to clear the atmosphere, just before the spire had zapped him from the sky. "How is that possible?"

"I suspect in much the same way that siphoning an entire planet's Light is apparently possible."

"So, you didn't..."

He tried to parse what he was even trying to ask.

There was a lot to unpack here, even without that most basic question of what the hell was going on. Like why she didn't already *know* that siphoning an entire planet's Light was possible, for instance. Or how the hell they could possibly be so short on all the details surrounding nanoswarms, Archons, and everything else when their predecessors had ostensibly dealt with much the same in the last war.

The Great Purge this, he imagined.

The mystery of history, that.

"What *is* this thing, Iveera?" he finally asked. "How is it here?"

"I wager you learned as much in your clash with the entity as I could tell you from our purged records."

A flicker of suspicion. He couldn't help it here in this strange dreamscape, knowing his body was stuck back on a planet that was very much cut off from all comms.

"How'd you know I fought it?"

He hadn't had time to tell her that before, had he?

"Because, unlike your mental defenses, your physical strength appears to be developing on course," she said, paying no mind to his reaction. "I felt the perturbation in the Light, Nathaniel," she added, when he failed to take her meaning. "In much the same way our uncoupled minds are currently sharing this lovely congress."

She gave the jin-flicking equivalent of an eye roll when she saw some piece of his tension lingered. "Something was clearly responsible for the momentary interruption of the construct's communication jamming. A conflict, complete with concomitant property damage, seemed a likely enough explanation."

"Right. Makes sense."

"All I truly know is that this level of construct synthience should not have been feasible for another several centuries, were the Synth invasion to proceed in similar fashion to what we know of the Great War, as everyone expected it would."

"Even the Merlin?"

She gave him a look like he should know better by now than to ask about what went on inside the Merlin's head. No one knew the answer to that. Not even Zedavian Kelkarin, probably.

"Yeah, well, Ex said as much. That we're too early in the… whatever, the progression, for this to be happening."

She bobbed her jin in benign acknowledgment. "As for *how* the construct arrived on Ginnungagap, then, I cannot offer any more than baseless conjecture."

"Plenty of that going around these days," Nate said, thinking that Lundquist and Ramachandra, at least, would probably appreciate the Gorgon's intellectual honesty. He tried to think of anything else he could tell her about the Archon. "I think it's made a friend down here. Some kind of… I don't know. A mutant predator. Feline. Has some kind of chemical fear trick. I think it's been here for a long time."

He was debating how to broach the topic of Blackthorne when Iveera spoke up.

"There were legends about this planet, long ago."

"So our Asgardian friends have informed us."

"It's more than superstition, Nathaniel. There was an Atlantean. A disgruntled Castor. One of the earlier generations, from back when vat births were only beginning to overtake natural reproduction among the rapidly expanding Atlantean Empire. It's said he went rogue, began conducting all manner of profane experiments, shaping life in unnatural ways."

Nate was thinking uneasily of the time-withered cages back in the facility. Myrr and the fire damage. The perfect perimeter the nanostuff had left around the place. The protective bubble that seemed to linger around the facility even now. Something else teasing at the edge of his memory. He felt Iveera's watchful eyes on him.

"It's said he was determined to bend the Light itself to his will," she continued.

Nate met her eyes, the word surfacing.

Meyerwitz. *The* Meyerwitz.

That got a reaction. Iveera's brow crinkling in a rare frown.

"Where did you hear that name?" she asked.

He hadn't realized he'd been thinking out loud. Quirks of dreamspace, apparently.

"The Archon's pet predator, Myrr," he explained. "And where were *you* on all this stuff, by the way?" he called over at Ex's ruby red curtains, only to find they'd vanished. When he turned back to Iveera, though, there was Ex, hanging out behind a rich mahogany bar in an even richer silk vest, polishing a rocks glass with a tidy white bar cloth. He just shrugged and tipped his head at Iveera like *pay attention.*

"None of this is common knowledge," Iveera said, paying little mind to his side conversation. "I learned of it in person, from a source close to the matter, quite some time ago."

"Blackthorne," Nate guessed, grasping at the proximal dots, and at something in the way those last words seemed to irk her.

"The Pirate," she agreed, like she didn't want to say the name. "She made many curious claims of Ginnungagap."

"What kind of claims?"

"I suspect you've already experienced much of it firsthand. Bizarre creatures, born of something well outside nature's course. Mythical beasts. The

Asgardians' so-called demons. The Pirate stubbornly held, despite something of a lack of ecological evidence, that the place was in fact the birthplace of the Ooperians."

"And you didn't think to…"

"I assume, based on your waning accusation, that you are perhaps beginning to appreciate just how many strange tales I have encountered across this galaxy over the centuries."

He was. He just didn't want to admit it.

"This Meyerwitz was hardly the first to attempt to bridge the understanding between the Light and known science," Iveera continued. "Nor was he the last. Admittedly, the manmade creation of an entirely new sentient species—Even one now approaching extinction—is something of an oddity, provided that bit happens to be true."

"No kidding," Nate muttered.

"Alas, the Pirate's fickle relationship with the truth has become something of a legend itself throughout her long history, and the legends of Ginnungagap, while plenty curious, hardly struck me as requisite learning for a fledgling Knight who'd yet to learn the difference between jin and jinra."

Behind his bar, Ex helpfully set down his polished glass to make a crude and repetitive finger-in-the-hole gesture, just in case he'd forgotten that particular lesson in Gorgon culture. Nate scowled at the both of them.

"Nevertheless," Iveera relented, "given current circumstances, perhaps it was in error that I failed to bring my full attention to Ginnungagap before now. It occurs to me, based on this planet's history, that this construct might well have been buried here since the Great War. Driven to the planet in defeat, perhaps. Dormant for millennia."

"Hibernating," Nate murmured, mostly to himself.

"Perhaps," Iveera agreed.

He sat back, dimly noting he didn't remember having sat down at all—much less having done so on the snargladorf he suddenly found himself riding like a loyal steed, trotting along through the cascading landscape of random memories and colliding factoids. He watched the pieces of dreamscape pass by, sensing the existence of some great underlying connection even as its precise nature eluded him. This facility. This planet. Dark figures in the night. The Archon. Meyerwitz and Myrr, and Blackthorne and the *Wilds*, and Avalon, and the last LeFaye, and… and everything. All of it flitting by, faster and faster, until the scenery became little more than a messy blur, kaleidoscoping out to the infinity of an endless Synth swarm waiting patiently by to consume it all.

The more he learned, the more every damn thread of this galaxy seemed to be tied together in some mystically complex knot—a single thread weaving its incestuous way through every single piece of existence.

"Lady be praised," Ex agreed as Nate rode by, his mahogany bar having morphed to a well-worn workbench, where he was diligently cleaning what appeared to be several dismantled modules of Nate's armor and armaments.

For once, Nate considered the words beyond their face value, testing them against the odds. The Terran Beacon arriving at Atlantis—or to Terra at all. The Merlin, too. Following it. Finding him. *Him*, of all people. Blackthorne too, out there in the ruins of Demeter-12. Waiting. Collapsing Beacon. Lady's visions. This planet. Some darkness rising to the surface.

He eyed that vague shadow closer, captivated, clarifying.

It was on the verge of taking shape when Iveera drew him back to her orbit with an abrupt hiss—the kind he'd more or less come to understand as the Gorgon equivalent of a deliberate throat clearing. The teeming trail of memories faded, color and detail draining, bleeding out, until he found himself back in their pleasantly featureless dreamscape, Iveera watching him with crossed arms. Slight tension in her jin, he recognized past the flicker of annoyance. Tension at odds with the casual timbre of her interruption.

He realized that darkness was still there, then, passing beneath their amorphous gossamer dreamscape like the gargantuan shadow of some deep-sea monster. Not some internal revelation, he was suddenly certain, but an external presence. An interloper.

"Three guesses who," Ex muttered, from over where he was now trimming his mustachio in the mirror with a pair of preposterously delicate scissors.

Iveera kept her eyes trained on that murky darkness until it passed from sight, sinking back into the depths—or into some other subspace completely. She turned back to him. "Perhaps we should keep our time here short. Is there anything else you need to tell me?"

Nate stared dumbly for a moment, trying to collect himself, gather his thoughts. He perked up. "There is one thing. Good news, if you can believe it."

The look on her Gorgon face—or the lack thereof, really—conveyed a complete lack of curiosity or intrigue. "We'll worry about my ship once the Archon is dealt with."

Nate was floored. "How the hell'd you know?"

She gestured behind him with a flick of her jin. He glanced over his shoulder, to where the *Kalnythian Wilds* had appeared in the mists—apparently on plain display to Iveera's eyes, unlike Ex's persona. The ship stood in clear detail and to believable scale, save for the comically large tag that hung off the prow, signed, "Love, Blackthorne."

"Have I been doing that the whole time?" he wondered aloud. He nearly jumped when Iveera spoke right next to him, having appeared without a sound.

"You still have much work to do in learning to guard your mind, Nathaniel. Uncoupled and otherwise. Give the pilot my regards, by the way," she added, looking a touch amused as Tessa appeared in the haze, watching them with a smoldering *come hither* look. "And don't even think about it."

The soft touch of Elsa's smooth golden fingers on his cheek, the sweet warmth of her leaning closer. He shook his head to clear it, the phantasms dispersing with the motion like smoke in the wind.

"I *wasn't* thinking about it, for the record."

In the corner, Ex cleared his throat loudly enough that Iveera almost seemed to hear.

"I wasn't, dammit," Nate insisted. "People—*Terran* people—have these thoughts, you know? It doesn't mean anything. I'm just…"

"Lonely."

The word struck him silent. He didn't know what to say.

Iveera watched him, jin swirling, gently thoughtful. "That, too, will pass with age," she finally said. "Eventually. In a manner of speaking."

He didn't love the way that sounded, coming from a six-hundred-some-year-old immortal. He glanced at the empty space where Tessa's likeness had appeared a moment ago. Was surprised to feel Iveera's hand settling on his shoulder. She looked like she'd come to some decision.

"There's one last thing you should know before we go, Nathaniel."

Something about her tone set his stomach sinking in advance.

"We've had word from Zedavian and the others on the frontlines. Multiple reports now that the protoswarms have ceased their inward drive across most of the rim, with a few notable exceptions. They appear to be amassing, as if—"

"They're waiting for something."

Her jin bobbed a soft affirmative. "There's more. Some central fixture drawing them out there. Zedavian believes it to be the missing Tarkaminen Beacon."

"Holy shit," he whispered, the tectonic plates shifting in his mind even as some detached observer noted that this was merely the obvious culmination, the inevitable end of the chain they'd been tugging at all along. "He's... It's..." The pieces played through his mind anyway. Vanaheim. A test drive? A misfire? It hardly mattered. "That ruby red bastard's trying to warp an entire armada in from the outer rim."

"Perhaps."

"Iveera."

"Breathe, Nathaniel."

"But it's—We need to—You need to tell everyone. Call for backup. This is—"

"This is but a hunch," Iveera said, taking his other shoulder in hand, holding him steady. Or maybe preparing to shake him. "One simple hunch amidst a galaxy that already stands far closer to the brink on more fronts than anyone wishes to acknowledge. We've made the pertinent calls. We're attempting to contact the Merlin directly. Even as we speak, there are numerous fires bidding for Alliance attention."

"But—"

"We will have reinforcements, Nathaniel. The Asgardians at the very least, whether they like it or not."

"What about the Eldari? Phaldissus—"

"Phaldissus, like many power-hungry tyrants at the moment, appears to be using the chaos of the attacks to his own ends. He stirs Vanaheim to anger, turning their gaze inward and stoking anti-Alliance contempt even as he seeks to elevate himself within that very same power structure."

"The High King, then," Nate said, but he could already read it in Iveera's jin that it was a moot point.

He opened his mouth, looking for the next option anyway. They could invoke the emergency authority of the Order Excalibur. Have Princess Elsa make an appeal to Vanaheim, get Phaldissus and the others to understand. Except, as things stood, they had no way of letting her communicate with anyone, and he was pretty sure they'd already blown that particular bridge anyway, the moment they'd blasted off from Vanaheim with their shiny new Envoy Princess. And as for invoking the wartime authority afforded the Knights in the Accords...

It'd only be fuel to the fire, he knew deep down, for the very same reasons he knew that an appeal from Elsa could never change Phaldissus' mind at this point. Yet another unavoidable culmination of all the shit they'd been seeing and hearing throughout the Alliance this past year, playing Council Errand Boy. The conspiracy theories. The outright denialism. The preposterous agitation that flared up at even the slightest brush with the undesirable truth, from the lowest commoners up through entire bodies of ruling class elites.

No one wanted to deal with the existential threat in the room.

So, no one did.

"This stuff is happening galaxy-wide? Just like Vanaheim?"

He read it in the weariness of her motions as she released his shoulders. For all of his power—and all of hers too—he couldn't remember the last time he'd felt so small and alone as he did right then.

"Strong the Alliance may be, Nathaniel. But brittle, too. More brittle, I think, than even the Supreme Chancellor fully appreciates. And often in the very places upon which the Council is least likely to cast their well-meaning gaze. Something is clearly afoot here. The Synth appear to be demonstrating a level of coordination previously thought impossible, redoubling their efforts at the few key points where fighting continues even as the heart of their forces amass behind the lines. But even were that not the case..."

She hesitated, like she wasn't sure the rest bore saying, then continued on.

"It was all fine and good, so long as the conflict was contained out there, on the rim. But now... I fear the Alliance has grown too accustomed to peace and prosperity. Too addicted to its identity as the Victor of the Great War, even as our people have sought to cleanse the unpleasant details of that victory from sight and mind. I'd hoped that the resurgence of our enemy would one day be sufficient to galvanize the people of the Alliance back under one cause. And perhaps it yet shall. But for the time being, it seems the galaxy must first confront a universal panic to which everyone subscribes but to which none are willing to confess."

Nate stood there, steeping in the bleak weight of it all, thinking, of all things, of the time he'd lost his parents in the grocery store. The rushing panic of finding himself alone in a strange land. Five years old. The certainty he'd never see his parents, or home, again. The all-consuming relief when they'd finally found him and restored order to the universe. The adults were there. The adults, with all their answers. All their infallible power.

It had never occurred to him—at least not back then—that they hadn't had a goddamn clue what they were doing. That his infallible adults had been, in that situation, little more than panicked children in their own right. Panicked children in aging bodies, with just enough practice and worldly experience to think to try the front desk and its mighty PA system.

There were supposed to be adults running the show.

Iveera was watching him, waiting for something.

It occurred to him that she'd been considering not telling him any of this and merely letting him carry on without the weight of massing Synth hordes and crumbling Alliance civility riding on his mind.

Concern over his ability to handle the pressure, no doubt.

Concern over what might happen if he *didn't*.

Concern for all of it.

He didn't blame her.

"So, what do we do?"

"We do whatever we can," she answered, without hesitation. "Destroy the apparatus, Nathaniel. The rest can wait. Must wait. Pierce the veil of Ginnungagap. The Troglodan and I won't be far behind."

"Tell me how," he said, clearing his mind to listen.

# CHAPTER 33
# THE DISTANCE

Sometime later, in the dim ruins of what must've once been the pristine—or at least functional—labs of the Mad Castor Meyerwitz, Nate opened his eyes. His mind briefly stutter-stepped between realities before continuing to churn like an idler-wheel with everything he and Iveera had been discussing in their uncoupled dreamscape.

For a second, he couldn't help but wonder if it hadn't all been in his head —little more than a standard dream. Some amalgamation of his and Ex's thoughts and memories of Iveera, combined with their lengthy list of factoids, worldly assumptions, and general doomsday pessimism. But he dismissed the thought as soon as it arose. He knew it'd been real, despite— or maybe *because* of—the fact that their meeting of minds had ultimately culminated in nothing but the hard reality of a problem without any convenient solution.

Versed as she was in saving the day and kicking asses of all shapes and sizes, Iveera had never fought an Archon. Never even seen one. There were no secret weapons lying in wait. No instruction manual on how to disarm a potential planet-sized Light bomb.

Outside, the strange, spire-touched daylight of Ginnungagap was slowly dying. The beginning of the long night, Nate thought, until Ex pointed out that it was more like early afternoon, sunwise, and that the dimming must've been something to do with whatever spell the spire had wrought on Ginnungagap. The veil, as Iveera had called it.

Nate scanned the sleeping crew, idly counting, consulting with Ex to make sure none of the Asgardians had gone missing from the next room over. A few of the golden grumps sat awake, brooding in view of the open doorway. Nate considered Tessa's sleeping face nearby, thinking about everything and nothing. Wondering, not for the first time, what it was he'd unleashed on that swarm, and how the hell to reconcile it with the fact that Tessa's wounds, exposed to the same mysterious pulse, had somehow closed themselves by the time Carter had had a chance to look at her.

A hair-raising scratching sound drew his attention to one dark corner of the room where Bob the Creepy-Ass Space Vampire was carving something into the wall with one grimy claw, hissing quietly to himself under his breath. Nate didn't spend long wondering over it. It was possible the Ooperian might know a thing or two that could help them unravel some of the mysteries of this planet. Hell, old and ragged as Bob looked, Ex thought it was possible the Ooperian might've actually been here since Meyerwitz's time. But none of that did them much good, considering they hadn't been able to communicate a damned word with Bob. Even Ex couldn't yet understand the creature's bestial language—if that's even what the airy sounds were. Too old. Too wild. Too potentially irrelevant to worry about, with everything else going on.

Moving quietly, Nate rose and padded out of the room, seeking fresh air, or space, or maybe just some reprieve from Bob's damned scratch-scratch-scratching. The snargladorf rose from nearby and came with him. The thing had practically been glued to his side since he'd returned. Outside, though, it roamed the arid courtyard, sniffing every square inch like the place told a story, pausing only occasionally to glance back at Nate, like *you gettin' all this?*

In the distance, the spire still loomed at angry attention, spouting brilliant red fury into the hazy skies, a great band of nanoswarm circling at the ready, a few hundred meters up its length. Some kind of defensive pattern, they'd assumed, ever since the swarm had returned from its pants-crapping probe run on the facility and taken up this new holding formation. Like the Archon was overall less interested in hunting them down than it was in merely making sure they kept out of its business.

Nate still wasn't sure what to make of that, but it didn't seem to bode well for the Archon's timeline. No more than did the dwindling Light in Ex's coffers, and in the Ginnungagap air all around them.

Whatever they were going to do, it needed to happen fast if he didn't want to end up running on fumes again.

He felt someone appear in the doorway behind him. Felt a flutter of disappointment at the first crunch of boot on pebbles, quickly chased by annoyance that he should be disappointed at all, as his mind's eye shifted from the image of Tessa to reassess the data. The footsteps too heavy. The presence too stiff. Not to mention the abundantly clear creak-and-shuffle of a makeshift crutch under load. He didn't look as Jaeger drew up, spared a brief scratching for the snargladorf's head, and took a seat next to him. For a while, they sat in something like an easy silence, the colonel waiting for something.

Grumpy bastard was always waiting for something.

"Spoke with Tess," he finally ventured aloud, probably fishing for a reaction.

Nate kept his face neutral. Probably, Jaeger just wanted answers. Answers Nate didn't have. But the casual sound of her first name still irked him coming from Jaeger's mouth. The man never called her Tess. Always Kalders, or Lieutenant. Maybe it was just some unconscious mirroring thing. Or maybe he really did want to get under Nate's skin—make it clear he knew damned well how Nate thought of her, how he felt about her. It was kind of uncanny, the way the colonel could always get in his head and put him on the defensive with the tiniest, seemingly inconsequential details. Nate wasn't sure the man even meant to. But he had a feeling.

He looked at Jaeger. For a brief moment, the colonel met his gaze, positively earnest.

"Thank you, by the way, for getting her out of there."

The somber weight in Jaeger's eyes left Nate averting his gaze, stuck for words, defenses forgotten. He knew Jaeger cared for their people. They all knew. But sometimes it was easy to forget just how deeply those roots ran.

"So..." Jaeger pushed on, like that was enough of that. "You wanna tell me how long you two've been knocking boots, then?"

"I—What?"

So maybe *not* enough of that.

Nate was still trying to recover from the unexpected accusation when Jaeger laughed a good, full laugh and clapped him one on the back. The contact slapped the words right out.

"Look, just because half our crew's getting it on doesn't mean—"

"Christ, I'm just pulling your leg, Kid," Jaeger chuckled. He sobered at whatever he saw on Nate's face then, sliding back behind his Resting Commander Face.

For a second, Nate almost felt bad. Laughter wasn't exactly something he heard often from Jaeger. It wasn't an entirely unpleasant sound. Hell, maybe the man was even trying to reach out in his own way. But still.

He opened his mouth, unsure as he did whether he meant to apologize or tell Jaeger to screw himself.

Jaeger raised his hands in peace, nipping it in the bud before he could speak. "Bad joke. Forget it." Then, with a wry twist of the lips: "Failing your willingness to take the bull by the horns, though, so to speak—"

"Jesus."

"You at least wanna tell me how you stopped that swarm out there?"

Nate glanced up at the ghostly ripples of the darkening "afternoon" sky, thinking again how it might've been beautiful, if it hadn't been so tinged with all the ruby red dread of what they were up against. "I'll keep you posted if I ever figure that out."

"Aw, come on now. I said I was sorry."

"You didn't, for the record," Nate pointed out.

"Hmm," Jaeger agreed thoughtfully, awaiting an explanation anyway.

Nate wasn't being coy. He really didn't know how to answer Jaeger's question. Ex didn't even have a satisfactory explanation for what had happened back there, beyond some hand-wavy mumbo jumbo about Light pulses and transdimensional resonance.

Ex roused with an indignant air. *It's not 'hand waving' when a slightly more accurate explanation would literally require weeks to jam through your obstinate noodles.*

Nate gave him an exaggerated mental eye roll. They both knew he was glad for the jab of camaraderie. Just like they both knew that, exquisitely complicated explanations aside, even Ex was still a touch confused by what had happened. And maybe a little unsettled too. Nate wished he'd remembered to bring the incident up to Iveera, but given how little they knew about nanoswarms in general, he doubted she would've known more than Ex.

Ex practically purred at the concession.

"You know, I popped off for a pretty girl myself, once upon a time," Jaeger said out of nowhere, clearly still stuck on this little pet theory of his. "Susie Bedingfield. Mmm-mmm. Pushed her truck straight out of a ditch with my own two hands like you wouldn't believe. Swear to god I tapped a higher power that day."

"Well, I'll be sure to call up Mr. Springstein's Glory Days Hotline for you, old man, but that's not what this was."

Jaeger just shrugged, unconvinced, and let the uncomfortable silence do the talking for him. Nate eyed the dusty courtyard, looking in vain for some distraction.

At the center of the space, the snargladorf had worked its sniffing way over to that battered, vaguely statue-of-liberty-esque monument—drawn, no doubt, by the veritable buffet of assorted animal droppings, just as Nate imagined each other contributor had been drawn by the one before it, like some sick, never-ending version of the chicken and the egg. The shit and the shitter. He frowned at the shit-stained, weather-worn shapes of the spear and the shield at the monument's base, noting how they looked at place there, unlike the crumbled remnants of what might've once been—

*A pentascope*, Ex provided, rousing to overlay a simulated reconstruction of the pieces into a thin, cylindrical device on Nate's retinal HUD. *Once an iconic tool of the Castors' guild*, he added, as the virtual reconstruction continued, the reassembled pentascope hovering up along with some of the other rubble to complete the image of a humanoid figure holding his iconic instrument aloft.

*A less than subtle statement of the triumph of science over the barbarism of war, perhaps*, Ex concluded, clearly unimpressed. It seemed to fit the mold well enough, from what little they'd gathered of this rogue Castor turned would-be god. The thought brought a faint grin to Nate's mouth as the snargladorf shimmied in to add its scent to the pile of droppings.

How the mighty inevitably fell.

Nate turned to find Jaeger watching him with a kind of expectant air, like he was still stuck on this whole pretty girl thing.

"So, how'd it work out for you, then?" Nate asked, somewhat hesitantly, and mostly because he didn't know what else to say.

"What, the truck thing?" By the look on his face, Nate had read it wrong, and Jaeger had already moved on. Now, though, he returned to the memory with a wistful look. "Blew out both hamstrings and my back. But Christ if it wasn't worth it. Met my first wife that day."

"Wow." Nate couldn't help but smile a bit. "I take it Susie was grateful, then?"

"Hmm?"

"Your, uh… Your wife?"

"Oh." Jaeger roused from his recollection, eyed Nate with a soft frown. "What, Susie? Oh, hell no. I mean, about the truck, yeah, I suppose. But… Well, it's a long story."

They traded a searching look, like they were mutually trying to suss out via some intangible interpersonal telepathy whether the two of them, as a unit, were quite "there" yet.

"Suffice it to say," Jaeger continued, breaking eye contact, "you never know which one's the one you really needed until you've busted your ass—Literally, metaphorically, any other way—for the one you thought you wanted."

He looked at Nate then, like he'd only just realized what he'd said, and to whom.

"You know. Sometimes," he added. Almost apologetically.

But Nate was already drifting down the spirals that seemed to be becoming more familiar these days than the subjects themselves. How long since he'd last spoken with Gwen? Seen her face? How long since he'd thought about his friends back home? Since he'd even thought of it as *home* at all?

"Long distance," Jaeger grunted toward the passive horizon, in the kind of tone he might've normally reserved for such anachronistic dudebro aphorisms as, *women, right?* "Not that there's anything wrong with it," he added, almost looking uncomfortable himself for the first time since ever. "Just, you know. Never was for me."

"I spoke with Iveera," Nate said. Partly because Jaeger needed to know. Mostly because Nate just needed the man to shut up.

But Jaeger didn't seem to hear him. "I know it's not really any of my damned business, Nate, but—"

"Nope, you were right the first time. None of your damned business."

Jaeger raised his hands in peace, lips pursed like *too hot to touch, got it.* "Sorry."

Jaeger shrugged. "Hey, as long as it doesn't get in the way."

And there was the crux of the matter, hiding beneath the rest of Jaeger's words like an angry little ember. He was worried Nate's head wasn't in the right place. They all were, probably. But Jaeger was already moving on.

"How'd you two break the comms blockade?"

So, he *had* heard that bit, then. Nate pushed the rest aside for the moment, thinking about how to explain it to Jaeger, and kind of wishing he'd done something more heroic and impressive than the tame, half-bored tone of Jaeger's question seemed to give him credit for. Sadly, all he had was the truth.

"I... had a dream with her. Sort of. It's—"

"Light stuff?"

"Complicated."

"Sounds about par for the course," Jaeger said, unshakable as always. "You sure it was, you know… real?"

"Maybe. Probably. I'm not really sure it matters."

"Well, there's the broody old Nate we all know and love. So, what did this dreamy Gorgon specter of yours have to say?"

"Nothing good." Nate considered how to sum it up in as few words as possible. "I don't think the Alliance is taking kindly to the news that Y-Sec is finding bits of Synth protoswarm in their porridge out here."

Jaeger gave an amused chuff, like that much went without saying. "Welcome to Polite Society 101. Anyone declare civil war yet?"

Nate stared at him, taken aback, as always, at just how naturally the man always seemed to grasp the emotions and power dynamics of an entire smorgasbord of alien civilizations. Jaeger stared back.

"What are we doing here, Nate?"

"Aside from being stranded?"

The colonel just held his gaze with an even and wise *no shit* expression. Nate was grateful for the distraction of the snargladorf, returning from its olfactory voyage—or *hers*, he remembered—to come lay down at their feet. Briefly, she rose to sniff the ground once more, then settled back down for good, panting contentedly.

"We need to bring it down," Nate finally decided aloud.

"The Archon? The spire?"

"All of it," Nate said, eyeing the black tower in the strange half-darkness. "Destroy the apparatus. Pierce the veil."

"Pierce the veil?"

He met Jaeger's curious look, waiting for the colonel to ask him what, how, and why. Knowing the man wouldn't be sold on any of it until Nate played the big guns: Iveera and Malfar, waiting in orbit, ready to come to their aid. But it wasn't what he wanted to say.

"I know I haven't been…" He searched for the words, uncertain what he was really trying to say. Somehow, he couldn't come up with anything other than *Knightly*. "I know I could've handled things better, down here," he finally said instead. "Before here, too. The pirates. Elsa. Vanaheim. I'm…"

He frowned at the *sorry* lurking in his throat, frustrated that it wouldn't come out. Frustrated it was there at all. Ex hovered at the edge of his mind, watching as he often did at moments like these. Waiting to see what kind of Knight he was becoming—what kind they were both becoming, together. Down in the dirt, the snargladorf paused in her panting and looked up at him, like she was wondering too.

"I'm doing my best," he told Jaeger. "I swear, I'm doing my best."

Jaeger licked his lips and frowned at that, then settled into a thoughtful silence. Nate waited, feeling suddenly and uncomfortably on the spot. Finally, Jaeger sighed and tipped his head back.

"Christ," he muttered at the darkly nebulous sky, before begrudingly fixing his gaze back on Nate. "Look, Kid. Nate. I was"—his jaw muscles twitched—"I was wrong to come down on you earlier. I know you did everything you could."

Nate stared, taken aback.

"Any other situation," Jaeger pushed on, frowning thoughtfully at some indiscriminate point in the dirt. "Any other engagement…" His frown took on a pained edge. "Your pal Tor is right about the cost of doing business. I just…" He shook his head, like the rest didn't bear saying, and focused back on Nate. "You care about the team?"

"What?"

"The team. Our people. You care? You care enough to do anything?"

Nate blinked at the sudden change in direction. "I… Of course, I…" He measured the somber weight in Jaeger's eyes and straightened a tad. "God-damn right, I do."

Jaeger watched him, impassive. "And the mission?"

"What about it?"

"Do you care?"

Nate opened his mouth to give a resounding *no shit*, and drew up short, realizing that wasn't actually the precise truth—or not the whole truth, at least. "It needs doing," he finally said. "And I don't see anyone else who's in a position to stop this thing."

"Right," Jaeger agreed, nodding. "I get that." Something in his face tight-ened. "So, what about you, then?"

"What are you—"

Nate cut himself off, not entirely sure what Jaeger was playing at here, but also not in any rush to ask *what* for a third time. He met Jaeger's scruti-nizing stare, recalling again how the colonel had cocked those three fingers on that day back on the *Camelot*, in follow-up to the *war is fucked* scriptures he'd never finished handing down. He wanted to ask what the colonel was after—what it was he was really asking Nate, here. He waited in stubborn silence instead.

"Well," Jaeger finally said, dropping Nate's stare to shoot a furtive frown at the eerie horizon, "I'm not so sure we're going to be getting that rainy day, after all, so I guess I'll just say I've made my share of fuck ups too, Kid.

Some have cost lives. Some have saved 'em, too. The worst one, the one that landed me in a cubicle under some god forsaken mountain for insubordination, monitoring for space aggressors back when that was still a complete fucking joke, did both. And now here we are."

Nate looked to Jaeger in the following silence, waiting for more, *sure* there must be more. There had to be. But, after a thoughtful pause, Jaeger just nodded to himself, like that was probably that, and sat back to gaze at the distant spire in peace.

It all seemed rather anti-climactic.

"So, pierce the veil, huh?" Jaeger asked out of nowhere, glancing back to Nate like no part of the last few minutes had happened at all.

"Pierce the veil," Nate echoed, his throat dry and thick, uncertain as to what actually *had* happened. Only that Jaeger seemed to have been looking for something—not to mention that the man had nearly apologized, for the first time since ever. It occurred to Nate that that almost-apology was what Jaeger had truly come out here for in the first place—that that might've in fact been exactly why the colonel had been hesitant to speak at first, and quick to beat around the bush with all the talk of Tessa and old pickup trucks.

Jaeger, for his part, just chewed on this new thought another minute, then shrugged, like *why the hell not?*

"All right," he said, dusting off his field pants and rising to his feet. "Pierce the veil." The snargladorf rose with him, excitement in her quivering body language, as Jaeger turned back to offer Nate a hand. "Let's get to it, then."

# CHAPTER 34
# THE NUCLEAR OPTION

When all was said and done, Nate hardly should've been surprised that Pierce would be the first one to take qualm with… well, pretty much everything.

"Someone wanna tell me again why we can't just blow the whole damn planet and be done with it?" the churlish pilot asked, looking around the arid compound courtyard where they'd gathered around the campfire in the not-quite-darkness of the not-quite-night.

"You mean aside from the part where we're currently stranded on said planet?" Tessa asked.

"Trapped in atmos," Pierce countered, jabbing a finger at the line of banged up *Camelot* escape pods Nate had risked the time and energy to fly out and haul back from the jungle in the past couple hours. "Not stranded. There's a difference. And that first one goes away as soon as *that* thing"—he hooked his thumb in the direction of the spire—"comes tumbling down."

"Emphasis on the sorely lacking *maybe*, there," Ramirez added, from over where he, Snuffy, and Tor were busy retrofitting one of the pods to carry a small away team to the far side of Ginnungagap, along with the arsenal of warheads Nate had pulled down from e-dim.

"Ad infinitum," Ramachandra agreed under her breath.

Somehow, Nate was almost comforted by how few shits Pierce obviously gave about their little stipulation. The pilot's moody dissent was an annoying drag of a constant, maybe. But it was a constant, nonetheless. Safe and familiar, in a way. Which was exactly why Nate assumed everyone—even their lurking Asgardian shadows and Space Vampire Bob—probably knew better by now than to bother trying to convince Pierce of pretty much anything other than his own scathing wisdom and rugged good looks. Lundquist, though, apparently hadn't given up hope.

"You're stuck in a room with an atomic bomb," Lundquist said, idly tracing the lines of one pod with his fingertips in the firelight. It wasn't the first time he'd started a thought experiment with the *you're stuck in a room* assertion. "The bomb is guarded by an extremely vicious dog, and you've naught but your bare hands and a single proximity detonator. One which you're told has a 1-in-10 shot, maybe less, of actually working."

"Stupid metaphor," Pierce said.

"More or less stupid than simply assuming that bombing the very machinery currently holding us in a quasi-alternate reality will somehow result in our perfect, non-catastrophic return to normal space?"

That got a nice *oh no he didn't* silence from the courtyard, complete with several snickers and grins. Ramirez clapped Lundquist on the back.

"Well gee whiz, Doc," Pierce said. "Why don't you tell me how you really feel?"

Lundquist, maybe bolstered by the show of support from the camp, just held his gaze like *answer the question, or don't.*

Pierce shrugged. "Fine. With the fate of the damn galaxy allegedly on the line? Blow the room. Hope for the best."

"How do you get past the dog?"

"Gee, I don't know. I think I might send my superhuman friend here to go *punch* the dog—"

"Dude," Snuffy protested, cringing at those last three words.

"—to punch it," Pierce pushed on, "and I quote, 'really hard.'" He raised a hand to mimic thumbing a detonator. "And then on with the clicky-clicky." He frowned Nate's way. "Though, now that you mention it, I'm not sure why we don't all just make like escape pod sardines and send Sir Mountain Dropper here to go do his thing again. We get airborne, he punches ol' Red where it counts, we ride the wave out, bada-bing-bada-what-the-fuck-ever."

"Or we all die," Tessa pointed out.

"Or we all die," Pierce agreed. "But it's still better than sitting around like a bunch of assholes trying to plan a tower heist or whatever the hell it is we're talking about here."

For some reason, all eyes turned to Nate and Jaeger at that point, expecting something.

The two of them traded a look.

"I'm still just trying to process the part where you think we're friends," Nate said back to Pierce.

"Don't get too excited, Wonder Boy."

"And provided any of that works as you imagine it should," Lundquist continued, still focused on Pierce like there'd been no interruption at all. "What happens to the civilization carrying on just outside the room?"

"What, you're saying…?" Pierce started, brow furrowed. "Look, I'm no astronomer, but last I checked, space is pretty damn big. You don't seriously think…?"

Lundquist patiently waited, inviting Pierce to fill in his own blank.

"The Merlin *did* use a collapsing Beacon to shoot an entire planet across the galaxy, right?" Snuffy chimed in. "I mean, what do you think might've happened if he hadn't channeled all that energy somewhere?"

Pierce spread his hands like *how the hell should I know?* "But this isn't even a real Beacon, right?" he added, directing the question at Nate. "We're talking about nukes here, but this thing might not be anything more than, like, a cheap knockoff. A pipe bomb, sitting off in a quiet corner of Alliance space."

"Quite close to a sun that appears well poised to go supernova via any number of even relatively minor perturbations," Lundquist added. "Not that I see any reason at all to lend credence to your pipe bomb analogy."

"And so what if it isn't?" Pierce said. He waved a hand at Ramirez's and Snuffy's fully loaded bomber pod. "I thought that was the entire point of sending a team across the world to blow off the other end of the cannon, right? And even if that all turns out to be for shit, and we *are* looking at another full-blown Beacon collapse, we're talking, what? A few thousand people? Hell, a few planets? That's still better than the entire damned galaxy, right?"

They all traded grim looks, most of them clearly less than satisfied with Pierce's utilitarian logic, but not so much as to speak up then and there.

"Perhaps if Nate could act as the Merlin did on Avalon, and contain the fallout…" Amelia started to offer.

Nate loosed a delirious huff before he could find out what was supposed to come next. He didn't mean to. It just slipped out. He'd had nightmares for months after witnessing that Beacon collapse firsthand. Still did. Strange dreams. The Merlin, everywhere at once, a blur in an explosion of frenetic activity. Visions of Mordred le Faye's withered corpse burned to a husk, black armor and all, by the fury of the escaping

Light. And that had been a man who'd known how to tap a Beacon's power.

The thought that *he* could contain a collapsing Beacon… Cheap knockoff or not, that was one hell of a tall flight of fancy.

"I think we'll put this train of thought up on the 'break in case of emergency' shelf for now," Jaeger said.

"Filed neatly under 'maybe blow up half the goddamn galaxy,'" Tessa chimed, with acid cheeriness.

"Not to mention ourselves," Ramirez added, poking out from behind one of the pods. "Just in case anyone's forgetting that bit."

"I, personally, would prefer not to die," Snuffy said. "If we're putting it to a vote."

"We're not," Jaeger said.

"We would stand with the one who punches dogs," announced one of the Asgardians, literally standing from the fire in support of the declaration.

"Worst. PR. Headline. Ever," Snuffy whispered to Ramirez, loud enough that everyone probably heard anyway.

The Asgardian paid him no mind. "If we are to choose a righteous end to our time here in this cursed land—"

"We're *not*," Jaeger repeated, with a stony weight that seemed to give even the Asgardian pause. "Not yet," he added, turning his stern gaze on Pierce. "And definitely not until we have something more on the table than half-baked dick swinging parading as a plan."

Nate was a little surprised by even that slight concession of potential future authority, but he had no doubt Jaeger knew what he was doing. Desperate times and whatnot. Pierce, for his part, nodded to Jaeger and backed off. He didn't even look all that pissy about it.

Somber silence settled over the gathering. The weight of everything they didn't know pressing down on them.

"There is one potential opportunity I believe we may have overlooked in all of this," Lundquist finally said. "One that's predicated upon entirely more 'maybes' than I'd prefer. But if what Nate says is true, and this planet has indeed fallen, for lack of more clear language, out of phase with our standard physical reality, then it seems to me that whatever might come through this putative relay might well be stuck here with us until the so-called veil is dropped. Indeed, I can't help but wonder if relay travel will be possible at all until Ginnungagap returns to, ah, standard phase, as it were."

Traded looks around the fire, checking for some mutual understanding.

"You're saying the Death Star has to drop its shields before it fires?" Snuffy ventured.

"I'm saying there seems to be a possibility, however remote."

"Makes sense though, right?" said Ramirez. "If we can't get in and out, neither can they?"

"I hesitate to agree with you on the matter of what does and doesn't make sense, standing here on a planet currently at work defying every bit of worldly sense I thought I knew how to apply. Even so..."

*Ex?* Nate asked, while the others traded uncertain looks.

*The doctor's caution is wise.*

*That's it? No transdimensional hiccups this or spacetime tangles that?*

*Allow me to answer your question with another question: Do you know where your excrement ends up when you flush the toilet, Nathaniel?*

*Um... Kind of?*

*Then we would be roughly on the same page were you to ask me whether relay travel is possible in this state.*

*Charming.*

"But we might have a shot," Snuffy was saying, back in the hellish firelight of the courtyard. "We just need to, like, find the thermal exhaust port, or whatever. Right?"

"Not to mention our proton torpedo," Nate pointed out.

"Oh." Snuffy shot him a look. "You were, uh, actually kind of the torpedo I had in mind in this scenario. Sorry, buddy."

"Don't mention it. But this is probably a good time to mention that that spire might not be coming down as easily as we all seem to be thinking."

"I don't get it," Pierce said. "You already knocked down this thing's house once."

"He brought a mountain down on top of its house," Tessa corrected, apparently having already connected the dots. "There's a difference. We all saw the way that swarm juked Cammy's direct firepower, out there in the black. Conventional weapons barely touched it."

"But that was..." Pierce glanced from the smoky void of the sky to the auspiciously absent nanostuff that had previously coated the adjacent landscape, prior to the Archon's great relocation act. Finally, he looked to the black tower, clearly connecting some dots of his own. "Well, shit." He looked back to them. "At the risk of sounding like a broken record, then—"

"I might've accidentally managed a mountain," Nate said, already guessing his drift, "but I'm pretty sure I'm not ready to blow apart an entire planet, even if I—"

"I was actually gonna ask why we can't use the Knightships to do it," Pierce cut in.

"—wanted to," Nate finished at a murmur, brow furrowing, unthinkable possibilities flitting in.

"We think Red took 'em down to his evil lair, right?" Pierce pressed on. "The lair that seems to be conveniently tucked down deep in the planet's crust?" He looked around the campfire. "You guys ever seen a lumberjack split a log with black powder?"

There was no way in hell. Not Cammy. He wouldn't. Probably couldn't. Except…

"Just a thought," Pierce said, almost apologetically. "You know, in case of emergency."

Tense looks darted around the fire, everyone waiting for someone else to pipe up. Lundquist looked like he'd just witnessed a monkey learning to talk.

"What do you think, Doctor?" Jaeger asked.

Lundquist roused, about to admit, Nate was pretty sure, that their girl might well be, or at least *had* been, carrying enough potential yield between all of her systems—probably even in her arsenal alone—to see the job done. The last job she'd ever see done.

They were mercifully interrupted before he could. A hacking hiss from their temporary shelter back in the ruins. It sounded like the throat clearing of a chain-smoking python. Bob the Space Vampire stood in the open doorway, milky, oversized blind eyes gleaming weirdly in the dancing firelight. He hacked a guttural scratch of consonant and vowel that easily could've been a cough but had the feel of deliberate speech.

"Bob?" Snuffy asked, perking up. "Did you just, uh…?"

"C-c-come," Bob repeated, slightly more annunciated on the vowel this time, waving one slender, clawed hand toward the room where they'd all caught a few winks earlier. "Cccome."

With that, the blind Ooperian turned and shambled back into the building.

"It's… learning to talk," Ramirez said. "That's just… that's super."

Nate could practically see the airman's skin crawling.

"I think he wants to show us something," Snuffy said, dusting off his hands and stepping away from the pod to follow the Ooperian. "What's up, Bob?" he called again, thumbing on one of the hand torches they'd pulled from the salvaged pod interiors.

"Cccome," came the airy whisper from inside.

Snuffy made it as far as the shadowy threshold before it seemed to hit him that he was willingly following a wild Ooperian into a dark room, alone. He looked back to them for support, eyes seeking out Nate. Nate traded a look with Jaeger, who shrugged, then went to go check with Ramirez and Tor on their final bomber pod prep.

"Okay, then," Nate said, as he turned and started across the courtyard to go see what Bob the Space Vampire had to share with the rest of the class.

# CHAPTER 35

# SIGN LANGUAGE

Inside, the Ooperian was waiting over by his creepy scratch marked wall, beckoning for them to come have a look. It was pretty obvious at a glance that he'd drawn out the facility they were currently standing in. To Bob's credit, the detail of his final work was actually damn impressive for something scratched out by claw in short order—and by blind vampire senses, no less. What was less obvious, though, was *why* the Ooperian had gone through the trouble. The answer though, Nate was pretty sure, had something to do with the cloud of nanoswarm Bob had peppered in around his masterpiece, seemingly scattering away from the facility based on the comparatively crude arrow marks he'd etched.

"I think he's saying the swarm's scared of this place," Snuffy said beside Nate. "But we already kinda knew that, right?"

"Something *in* this place," Hannah O'Sweeney corrected. Nate hadn't even noticed her and Tessa following them in, Lundquist and a few of the others on their tails. O'Sweeney stepped closer, reaching between Nate and Snuffy to tap at the squiggly markings Bob had embedded in his illustrated walls, right around the base of each arrow. Beside them, Bob gave an odd little shoulder bounce, sniffing the air like he could tell she was on the right track. He tapped emphatically at the base of another arrow near O'Sweeney's finger, blind eyes glinting weirdly in the torch light, then he shambled over to a fresh patch of wall to start tracing a big, wild circle, over and over.

"I, uh... I don't think we're getting it, Bob," Snuffy said after several frantic seconds of this.

Nate considered the squiggles, like some kind of electromagnetic field, or something of the sort, but...

*I still haven't sensed anything of particular interest,* Ex answered, before Nate could ask. *Perhaps the Archon and this flighty Ooperian merely share a mutual distaste for the smell of decaying—*

It occurred to them both at once, their joint attention snapping back outside, back to—

Nate paused midway through turning for the door, something catching the corner of his eye.

"What's this?" O'Sweeney was saying, leaning in to inspect the same point in Bob's handiwork. "The Gorgon's ship, maybe? He's saying it arrived... three suns past? A few weeks ago, then?"

"Ohhh," Snuffy said. "I thought that was, like, because there *are* three suns, you know?"

Nate hadn't even noticed the suns. Was too focused on the small, humanoid figure etched there beside the landed ship.

"Looks like maybe the swarm was after it," O'Sweeney continued, thinking aloud. "Chasing it. Or maybe chasing this... this woman? Would that happen to be your...?"

"Blackthorne," Nate murmured.

"What?" Tessa said, looking from face to face for some explanation.

"Oh, yeah," Snuffy chimed. "Guess you missed that episode of cave catchup. She brought Iveera's ship here, we think. Remember how she—"

"Yes, Snuffs, I remember. Why the hell would she bring the *Wilds* here?"

"For, you know, like... mysterious pirate reasons? She left you a note, right?" he added, turning to Nate for help, but Nate was already turning to Bob, possibilities awakening.

"You saw her?" he asked the lurking Ooperian, pointing at the small figure on the wall. "You saw Blackthorne? The... the pirate lady?"

O'Sweeney seemed to be biting her tongue to keep from pointing out that the additional words were probably not going to clarify the matter for Bob the Space Vampire. Tessa's lips were pinched, probably just impatient for more answers.

"What about Myrr?" he asked, more to the group than to the Ooperian.

The Ooperian, though, was the one who answered.

A guttural hack and a violent swipe later, Bob had taken a meaty gouge out of the wall, and Nate had yanked the others behind him without thinking about it. They all regarded the Ooperian in tense silence. It was only then that Nate noticed Tristan had appeared like a wraith out of the shadows at Bob's flank, dagger at the ready. But Bob was done. The Ooperian deflated, shoulders and head drooping almost like he was ashamed. Nate hadn't the faintest clue what to make of any of it.

For some reason, everyone looked to Snuffy to translate.

"Umm... Okay," the mechanic said, taking a tentative step toward Bob, wiggling his fingers like he was preparing for something. "So this, uh, Myrr—"

A ragged grunt from the Ooperian.

"Right, so you obviously... know him, or something. But uh... Hey, c'mon!" Snuffy fumbled as Bob turned, took hold of the wall, and ascended the first meter or so with a clear lack of concern for such petty obstacles as planetary gravity. "C'mon, Bob," Snuffy called after him. "Don't be like that. We're trying to help."

The Ooperian slowed his climb, peering back over his pale shoulder with blind eyes. Then, with disconcerting speed and an eerie lack of noise, Bob sprang from the wall and alighted back in front of them. Nate tensed as the Ooperian bared ancient, dirty fangs, but Bob's agitation wasn't with them. The Ooperian turned, slapping at the illustrated swarm. "Myrr," he huffed, clapping his hands together as if catching a firefly. "Myrr." Before they could ask, he abandoned the hand cage gesture, violently slapping at his own protracted forehead with both hands, then brandished claws and teeth in a dramatically intimidating fashion.

"The swarm... took him?" Snuffy hazarded. "Turned him, uh... evil?"

"Because he seemed like such a lovey bear before," O'Sweeney muttered.

Bob hissed at her like he didn't appreciate the tone, even if he didn't understand a word she'd said. She didn't flinch. Cool as a damned cucumber, that one. Bob, though, seemed to have had enough. He scanned them, ignoring Snuffy's awkward attempts to convey she hadn't meant it like that, then sprang back up to go crawling away across the goddamn ceiling at an impossible angle.

"So that's not *not* weird, right?" Tessa asked, as they watched him disappear into the darkness with one last foreboding hiss.

"Just when we were getting somewhere," Snuffy sighed, hands draped over his head in defeat. "Thanks a lot, Loki," he added, shooting a frown at Hannah O'Sweeney. O'Sweeney just shrugged and turned back to Bob's etchings.

"Blackthorne by the way?" Tessa said, turning to Nate for answers.

"Yeah. Like a bad penny," he confirmed, glancing to the door, eager to go test this other hare-brained theory of theirs.

"I don't get it," she said. "How could she have possibly known to... I mean, she left you a note? Left you a random note on some random lost planet in the middle of freaking nowhere, like—"

"Like she knew we'd be here," he agreed.

"A *very* tricksy pirate," Snuffy murmured to himself, studying Bob's wall art next to O'Sweeney.

Tessa just spread her hands at Nate in a clear *what the hell, man?*

"I don't know. Something to do with..." The gears of his brain turned round and round on collapsing Beacons and shared dreams. Ground to a noisy halt on lost planets and sprawling tendrils of Lady's Light. He shook his head. "You know what? I can't even try to guess anymore. I just need to go find that snargladorf real quick."

He started to turn. Registered the strangeness of what he'd just said.

"I'll, uh... I'll explain in a minute."

Confused looks followed him all the way out of the room.

"What the hell's going on on this planet?" Tessa asked the others, just as he reached the door.

No one seemed to have an answer for her.

"Anything important?" Jaeger asked as he emerged back out into the courtyard.

"I don't know," Nate said, scanning the dusty space in the dancing firelight. "Maybe. Think he's trying to tell us there's something about this place the Archon's swarms might be allergic to." He glanced at Jaeger, a manic flicker lapping at his brain. "Something that really rankles its nose, you know?"

Maybe he *was* losing his mind. Grasping at preposterous straws. Jaeger's frown was a palpable weight, suggesting so. But he couldn't stop thinking of the way Bob had drawn up at the perimeter of the facility, like his hyperacute vampire senses smelled something rotten in Denmark. And there. There was the snargladorf, still sniffing around the courtyard. Sniffing at everyone's legs. Sniffing the ground beneath their feet. Circling around that crumbling, shit-stained monument.

He met Jaeger's eyes.

"This is gonna sound a little bat shit, but I think maybe we should do some digging."

Jaeger looked from him to the snargladorf and back, understanding setting in on his furrowing brow. "You're right. That is bat shit." He considered the monument and the sniffing snargladorf again. Glanced off to the tower in the distance, and to the angry red lightning storm raging on at its peak. "I'm not sure we have time to be chasing geese right now, Nate. You really think this is worth it?"

Nate tried to think of a valid answer to explain, visions of the Lady's infinite threads dancing in his head. He blew out a helpless breath, eyes glued unseeingly on some distant point beyond the monument. "You're stuck in a room," he said quietly. "A room you were chased into by an unstoppable swarm. And you still don't have the faintest clue why they didn't just come inside and finish the job, once and for all."

"So, you decide to follow your space dog's nose on the inkling of some crazy old vampire?"

Nate shrugged.

"Longshot and a half, and then some," Jaeger muttered, frowning stubbornly at the monument. Finally, though, he sighed and shot a sideways glance at Nate. "'Least we don't have to worry about property damage though, huh? What'd you have in mind?"

"I was thinking maybe we could ask the Asgardians for a hand," Nate said, pretty much as the thought occurred to him. Partly because he was just damned tired of doing all the heavy lifting. Partly because it was about time the pale golden warriors did something other than piss and moan. Mostly, though, because blasting the courtyard open with Ex's artillery, on top of being dangerous and energy intensive, seemed fairly liable to result in the obliteration of whatever they might find below. Provided there *was* anything to find, of course. Which, admittedly, was feeling less and less like some fateful guarantee, the longer his rational mind chewed at the idea.

All he really knew was that the Lightsong was growing noticeably more muted by the hour. His energy reserves showing their edges here and there. The storm at the spire's peak was growing, raging brighter in the deepening night sky. He watched Ramirez and Tor cramming into their bomber pod, preparing to speed off for the far side of the planet with enough firepower to end a continent, and wondered if it was a mistake, sending them.

Jaeger was watching him with a scrutinizing look, waiting for some explanation.

Nate shrugged and tilted his head back toward the Asgardian huddle. "They look like they could use a good excuse to put their backs into it, don't you think?"

Jaeger just kept up that damned look of his. "You got more important places to be?"

"I need to have a word with the princess."

Not a lie. Just somewhat parallel to the inconvenient truth that he wasn't sure how many more casual feats of strength he'd be wise to toss around before potentially needing to crawl back into the ring with the Archon.

"Maybe save a little Light while you're at it?" Jaeger asked, as usual buying precisely zero of his bullshit. The colonel didn't wait for Nate to fumble into a coherent answer. Just nodded to himself like he'd already confirmed what he needed to know. Time to move on, just like that. Nate appreciated the general pragmatism of the sentiment, if nothing else.

"All right, then," Jaeger said, eyeing the hulking Asgardians and their surly scowls before turning back to Nate. "You wanna go tell the gods of thunder to stop moping around and get off their lazy asses, or should I?"

"You have a minute?" Nate asked Princess Elsa a short while later, once they'd gotten Ramirez and Tor safely off on their cross-planet flight, and Jaeger had succeeded in at least getting the Asgardians rounded up into a dubious huddle.

"My, my," the princess said, glancing up at him from the open pod lip where she sat beside a grim, bare-chested Asgardian. "Why do I feel as if I should be the one asking that question?"

"Gotta be the dehydration," Nate said, settling carefully down next to Elsa in the limited space, not missing the faint crack in that usual holier-than-thou calm of hers. "Jungle delirium and all that."

He kept his eyes on the Asgardian, his smile brittle and edged. Something about the Asgardian's body language, and the fact that he'd clearly decided himself above the meeting into which Jaeger had gathered the rest of his kinsmen across the courtyard. Judging by the tension in Elsa's posture, this one hadn't been asking her for directions to the corner store when Nate had interrupted.

Fortunately, the Asgardian got the message and left peacefully enough, going to lick his wounded pride on the pretext of rejoining his kinsmen. It occurred to Nate, in the unexpectedly benign exchange, that he'd just pulled a total Todd.

"I do admit I'm beginning to wonder whether I shouldn't have merely stayed in that tree," Elsa was saying beside him. "It was a good tree. And the manners of this planet do leave something to be desired."

"You did look comfortable up there."

They both watched the retreating Asgardian for a beat.

"So, how bad is it?" she finally asked.

"How bad is what?"

She gave him an unimpressed look. "Whatever it is you wish to speak to me about."

"Maybe I just wanted to save you from the big beefy Asgardian dude."

Her brow took on a delicate wrinkle, like she was having trouble parsing some part of that. "That's not a 'dude,' Nathaniel. Hetzfelda is one of the Unbridled."

She took in his blank look.

"I shouldn't need to tell my brave Knight that there are those among the Asgardian people who believe sex to be an unacceptable diversion from the path of the true warrior. Unfortunate for them, if you ask me," she added, even as Ex pitched in with an abbreviated explanation. The Unbridled. Vat born Asgardians engineered sexless, tweaked for the most desirable combat traits of both hormonal sexes, but beholden to neither.

"I haven't spent much time around Asgardians," Nate admitted. "Guess maybe I have a bit to learn."

"You and the rest of the galaxy," she said quietly, seemingly lost in some memory. She roused. "Not that I'd especially recommend prolonged exposure."

"So, these Unbridled consider sex a… what, an obstacle? A constraint?"

"Physiologically, yes. Behaviorally, it's merely a pointless engagement. A distraction from the true way."

"So, what did this, uh, Hetzfelda want with you, then?"

The unspoken implication of his words didn't really register until it was too late: like what could she possibly have to offer to an Asgardian who presumably wasn't interested in sex?

The look she gave him was a golden scalpel, coming right for the giblets. It was kind of scary, how intense her air of royal indignation could be. As soon as it came, though, it was gone—evaporating so quickly he was left wondering whether she'd actually taken offense at all or had merely wanted to give him a moment to think about what he'd said.

"I think it's safe to say that's personal business between myself and Hetzfelda," she told him.

He nodded, studying Hetzfelda across the courtyard, all the more curious now. He really had pulled a Todd.

"Now, you wouldn't be talking to me if there wasn't something uniquely urgent you require of me," she said, matter-of-factly. "An unexpected Synth attack shaking Alliance wills. My brave Knight shaking Vanir politics." She showed him a faint smile at the memory. "Scorning highly excitable Vanir princes. Coming to speak with his loyal Envoy shortly after presumably receiving some news of the outside world from his Gorgon colleague. So… How bad is it?"

Nate stared for a second, taken aback by her pristine read of the situation. Between her and Jaeger, it was starting to feel like it'd be a wonder if his every thought and twitch wasn't anticipated ten moves ahead from here on out.

"Iveera—Ser Katanaga—thinks Phaldissus is making moves," he said. "Attempting some kind of power grab."

"I expect he is."

"I'm not sure we'll be able to establish any kind of comms contact in time for it to matter…" he continued, fishing for the right words.

"But if we *were* to do so, you're wondering whether I would be willing or able to talk my disgraced betrothed—a man whose social station has no doubt been indelibly stained by none other than my own hand and intrepid pluckiness, by the way—into playing nice with others and rushing to our aid."

He couldn't help but smile a little. "See, when you put it that way…" He met her eyes, sobering. "If anyone can do it, it's gotta be you."

"Flattery will get you everywhere, Ser Arturi. But I'm afraid my good charm won't. Phaldissus' better nature will not be appealed to by the likes of me. Not in any way that could matter at this stage."

"We need the Vanir fleets out here. And we need them now."

She scrutinized his expression, and he imagined he could see the questions playing out in her agile mind: What would this favor cost her—in pride, in personal sacrifice? What might Phaldissus demand of her in kind? And would it be worth it? Would the Vanir fleets even make a difference, if the worst came to pass?

He didn't know. But there was only one thing to do about it.

"We need them, Elsa. We need someone."

She held his gaze a few seconds longer, probably sensing the uncertainty his tone sought to hide. Some part of him perched at the ready, waiting to remind her that, political ploy or not, she *had* bound herself to him as Envoy —that this was her duty. But something told him that would've been a mistake.

"Then I will of course do my utmost, my brave Knight," she finally said, tipping her head in a shallow bow. "Provided any such contact can be established."

"Thank you," he said, touching her gently on the shoulder. Meaning it.

She eyed the hand curiously until he withdrew the touch and stood.

Whatever Jaeger had told the troops seemed to have worked. The Asgardians were already marshaling around the crumbling monument with what hand tools they'd found in the pods, plus a few they'd improvised from parts around camp. Hetzfelda's compact shovel was the first to break ground. Nate felt a pang of guilt.

"I'd still be talking to you, by the way," he added, turning back to the princess. "At least once our asses were out of the fire. Even if I didn't need something."

Her lips quirked in a wry smile. "Do tell me should you ever find yourself in a state of needing for nothing, won't you? I'd quite like to know how that feels."

He smiled back. "I'll be sure to let you know if the day ever comes."

"Splendid. And speaking of which…" Her smile turned a shade wolfish. "I note your skill with damsels in distress has increased markedly since our misadventures in the belt."

He followed her pointed gaze to where Tessa had just emerged from the facility.

"I surmise you merely required the correct damsel for motivation."

"I don't suppose it's worth reminding you I was fresh out of crusher space when that happened," he said, frowning at her. "Literally suffering brain damage."

"Hmm."

"And that I'm sorry," he added.

She held him on the end of her stare, chin tipped up ever-so-slightly, as if balancing the weight of his apology against the veracity of his unspoken denial. Then her face broke into a warm smile—maybe the most genuine he'd ever seen from her—and she breathed a languid sigh, tilting her golden face to the sky as if basking in the sunlight that was only barely there, thanks to the Archon's otherworldly shroud. Even after everything they'd been through, there was a trace of floral sweetness around her. Like the universe simply refused to allow royalty of her caliber to stink outright.

"To tell you the truth," she said quietly, opening her eyes to focus back on him, "crazy as it might sound, I do believe there's no place in this galaxy I'd rather be."

Nate considered the camp, chewing on those words. His people, busy at work. Lundquist and Snuffy arguing over a pod thruster modification while Ramachandra and Carter shook their heads at them. Tessa, catching his eye across the courtyard. The dark tower crackling malevolently on in the distance. Everything riding on them. And through it all, a stillness in his heart—sure, and certain.

"It's not crazy," he said quietly.

Then the spire roared to life with a blinding brilliance, and all hell broke loose.

**CHAPTER 36**

# SURGE PROTECTOR

The spire lit the sky, and the world moved in a paradox of motion. The crew's movements, fast and slow. Desperate and disciplined. The courtyard suddenly alive with the presence of impending death. For one infinite second, Nate was locked to Tessa's eyes across the brilliant, ruby-stained yard, shocked that this should be happening now, even if there was no other way. Then the spell broke, and the world came crashing back in at full speed.

"Readings are spiking in the core," Ramachandra called from one of the escape pods, eyes riveted to the whining holo display inside. Nate felt the tremors waking in the depths underfoot, subtle now, but unmistakably growing.

*Ex?* he asked, pulling on his helmet to an overwhelming spill of flashing alerts and data streams.

*I can't tell for certain,* Ex said, quickly silencing all but the most pertinent metrics on the HUD, *but if we're going to do anything more than sit by and watch the Synth relay parade roll in, now is probably the time to do it.*

The rising tingles in Nate's bones seemed to agree with his companion's assessment. The air alive with a building charge. Jaeger jogging over to them looking, for the first time Nate could recall, like he was hoping to Christ someone else knew what to do next.

Nothing for it, then.

Nate hurried over to the monument, spurred more by buzzing adrenaline than actual thought. He slipped into the gap between Hetzfelda and another shovel-wielding Asgardian, took hold of the exposed foundation with both hands and a clumsy gravitonic construct, and heaved. Harder than he meant to, apparently, in the rush of nerves. He felt the crushing strain of overworked muscles, along with a disconcerting pop and a slackening as something gave way in his left arm. Then the entire monument ripped free from the earth with a dry *thunk* of sundered roots and showering rubble, separating into pieces as it flew, and struck the far wing of the facility some twenty meters away with a string of crumbling cracks that seemed entirely too brittle for that much stone.

A few of the Asgardians cursed. The rest just stared.

And there, at their feet, in the mess of upturned soil and settling dust... Nothing.

Freaking nothing.

Nate stared at the spot, feeling empty as Ex dutifully began to knit his torn biceps back together.

"You have the warheads," he said quietly, eyes still glued to the useless dirt as Jaeger drew up beside him. "Just in case."

Betrayed. He'd been betrayed by the errant clues of Bob the freaking Space Vampire. Betrayed by his own stupid graspings for hope. Delusions of fate and Lady's guiding Light. And what the hell else had he really been expecting, here? He couldn't believe he'd actually been expecting anything at all.

"That's it?"

Jaeger's voice stirred him back to reality. Nate pulled his eyes from the unmarked grave of their last fanciful hope and considered the colonel. In reference to the warheads, the question might've felt downright indignant. Nate had left them with the same payload they'd sent Tor and Ramirez. Two atomic warheads and one antimatter, plus one additional last resort kill switch on Jaeger's end, just in case. But that wasn't what Jaeger was asking.

The colonel's dark eyes flicked from the rumbling ground and remorselessly empty patch of dirt at their feet up to that damned spire. Back down to the most lethal escape pod on the hemisphere, and finally back to Nate. "You're sure?"

It was an indirect admission of the unspoken secret about which none of them had truly harbored any illusions. They'd all been hoping for something more. More time. A better plan. Any plan at all, really. Some miraculous outside intervention from Iveera and Malfar. Anything but this.

"Tor and Ramirez won't be making the far side for—"

"At least five hours," Jaeger finished for him, tipping his gaze up to the unnaturally reddening sky. "Which is starting to look like it might be a little late to the party."

"So, I'll take first crack here. Hope for the best."

He expected Jaeger to argue, or at least tell him to wait a second while they got the away team on the horn—provided that horn hadn't already succumbed to a fresh burst of Ginnungagap interference—and figured this thing out properly. But the colonel just stared on at the unholy storm above, mouth slightly agape. The Unshakeable Man, shaken at last. And when Nate followed Jaeger's gaze upward, it wasn't hard to see why.

The storm was propagating, bizarre ruby lightning creeping across the sky in slow motion even as it raged on at frenetic speeds back at the spire's peak. He'd never seen anything like it. And there, in the hazy red spaces between the brilliant arcs of oozing light, the faintest lines overlaying the muted sprawl of stars above. Lines that looked too much like the stirrings of some vast, ghostly ocean of protoswarm, drifting in the nether. An entire armada, waiting in the wings of some distant corner of the rim, tens of thousands of light-years distant, and yet right there.

It was happening.

"You should get everyone to the pods," Nate said, his voice oddly steady in his ears. The winds were picking up now. Flying was going to be a bitch. "Be ready to get airborne, just in case."

Jaeger caught his arm as he turned to go. Nate met his eyes. *I'll be fine.* The words didn't want to come out. Jaeger looked like he was struggling with words himself. Finally, he settled on a simple nod. Go get 'em, Tiger. Class dismissed.

"Hooah, Boss," Nate murmured, clapping the man's shoulder.

The impact seemed to slap Jaeger back to his usual self. He huffed a grim chuckle and accepted the tiny q-node earpiece Nate offered him. "Hooah, Kid," he said, slipping in the earpiece. "Give 'em hell."

Nate took flight before his brain could indulge in any more second-guessing. No sweeping gaze around the courtyard. No last look for Tessa. No reminding Jaeger of what needed to be done, should Nate fail.

Nate had never before thought to deploy a singularity bomb. He had only barely ever seen one in action, back when the Trogs had thrown the middle finger to Alliance laws and deployed one over the ruins of Old Avalon. But that had been enough. There was little question that unleashing one here would effectively damn Asgard, Yggdrasil, and the rest of the entire damned sector to a slow, crushing end in the years to come. And that wasn't even to mention the fact that it would undoubtedly kill everyone on Ginnungagap, with no guarantee of even stopping the Archon. He didn't particularly intend to find out what lay down that path.

Not when he might still end things with his own two hands.

Flying, though, was more than a bitch.

The air was alive with strange energies, wild thermals and spats of radiation bombarding him as he ascended, jerking him this way and that, energy shields hissing to bright life on the more violent flares.

*Any recommendations here?* he asked, as they drew roughly level with the spire's distant peak, preparing to do their worst.

*I'd suggest the kitchen sink approach*, Ex replied. *But as the pilot has deftly pointed out—*

*Conventional weapons might not do shit*, Nate finished. *Might at least throw a wrench in the cogs, though.*

*Or merely attract the Archon's full attention and earn us a nice fat lightning bolt in the crotch.*

*Graphic.*

*Let it never be said you taught me nothing, Nathaniel.*

*Well shucks, buddy.* Nate spared a look for Jaeger and the others several kilometers below, but he could barely even make out the facility ruins through the deepening shitstorm. *Guess it's the front door for us, then.*

*Knock, knock*, Ex chimed, generally radiating approval as Nate set his sights through the howling winds and gunned the gravitonics. He could practically see his companion's mustachioed likeness flying along beside him like some madly grinning sidecar phantasm. They cut through the turbulent Ginnungagap sky together, gathering their energy, preparing to lay waste to anything that tried to stop them. Straight in. Straight to the heart. To Cammy, and to all their combined strength brought to bear on the Archon's apparatus, right where it counted. To Nate's blazing sword straight through that bastard's ruby red heart, even if killing an Archon wasn't so simple. As long as he moved fast enough…

The Ginnungagap sky stilled. The slowing of the hellish storm atop the spire breathing life into the thought as he pushed them faster, spacetime warping beneath supercharged gravitonics, the angry nanoswarm peeling off from the spire to meet them slowing to an infinitesimal crawl.

Faster. They pushed faster, a nimbus of azure fury building around them. A lance of pure Light roaring in to pierce the veil, unperturbed by the shimmering wave of ruby charge coalescing down the black spire wall as if to stop them. Faster. The descending ruby arcs slowing, slowing, until they stood still, like a glowing ocean wave caught in freeze-frame.

They sped forward, a lance of Light wielded by the Lady herself.

Then the Light flickered like a sputtering light bulb, and time snapped taut.

The blast was blinding. It came before he knew it, the world lurching in a drunken burst of light and sound, bathing him in an all-consuming rush of searing heat. His every nerve screaming. Eyes bleached half-blind through Ex's filters. He hit the ground like a molten missile, only nominally conscious, smoke pouring off his superheated armor and everything he touched, so thick as to choke off his vision completely. An image leapt, unbidden, of Iveera's blackened husk after she'd been scorched half to death by the *Avalon Eternal*. Then some corner of his mind registered Ex's barked warning, and he gritted his teeth and threw himself into painful motion. The swarm punched into the scorched mountain rock behind him, angling to follow with a single-minded hunger.

He ripped his sword free and spun to meet them with a wild sweep that lit the twilight darkness and left a hundred meters of stony landscape in smoldering ruins. He rounded back for the spire, conscious of the nanoswarm reconvening at his back, and plunged forward, sword raised. He felt the resistance before his blade even met the spire. Felt it like an airborne pressure wave, the jet-black wall condensing to something impenetrable, rousing with angry red streaks of defensive energy.

He plunged his blade forward all the same. It struck with a solid *thunk* and *hiss*, gushing black smoke and atomized nanostuff as the swarm fell upon him. Blade sinking inch by agonizing inch. The swarm ripping at his back. The tower's angry energies spitting at his front, cooking him alive. He screamed and fought on like a wild animal, pounding at the wall, driving the blade deeper, clawing the rift wider with burning hands. He ripped the spire open, screaming into its depths as it scrambled to mend itself, tearing his sword free to plunge deeper.

He brought the blade down with everything he had, the Light flaring all around him. All *through* him. The power incomprehensible. At that moment, there was no stopping him. The blade passed through without resistance, the spire walls giving way completely, warping around him, condensing, expanding, and—

And suddenly he was spinning ass over teakettle through the dark, nearly weightless. He caught himself on gravitonic brakes, trying to process the combination of sudden pressure and too-weak gravity. Hazy purplish light crackling here and there throughout the stiflingly hot, cavernous space.

The answer hit him right along with the smell of rotten eggs, and Ex's sharp cry of warning.

Something closed in on him from behind, then from everywhere. Before he could so much as blink, he was smothered in it, drowning in a flood of constricting nanoswarm. He growled a curse as the swarm pried the sword from his hand. Kicked the energy barriers into overdrive, burning his way free, but the swarm just pressed in, and in, driving him down, down, until he hit something painfully hot and unyielding, the swarm crushing down on top of him.

It was like trying to hold off the ocean. Panic at the overwhelming weight of it, at the sudden certainty of where he was.

Somehow, the Archon had reached up through the backbone of its spire and instantaneously yanked him straight across a couple thousand klicks. Straight to the beating heart he'd thought he'd wanted to reach. Now, there the gargantuan relay superstructure thrummed on above, miraculously reassembled in this impossibly enormous space, mocking him for his conceited notion of coming here to stop its maker.

There was no stopping it. Not here, at the very seat of the thing's power.

Crushing oblivion, folding in on him, squeezing away sight and sound, thrusting him inward, down to the reality of what was about to happen. To the grim face of Iveera, waiting in orbit above, so close and yet so utterly unreachable. To the faces of everyone else he was about to let down. Tessa. Snuffy. Home. His knees buckled under the weight of the swarm, damming untold worlds. The entire cavern flaring brilliant violet with anticipation.

"Jaeger," he gasped into the comms, knowing even as he did that it was a fool's bet that anyone would hear him down here, where the Archon determined the rules of reality. He grated the words out anyway. "Jaeger. The warheads. Now."

But it was already too late, some part of him knew. The strength ebbing from his limbs with each dwindling struggle. The swarm pulsating around him like a living thing. Drinking him in. The cavernous sprawl of violet light and thrumming relay superstructure disappearing as the swarm enveloped him completely. He felt the Light draining from his armor, from his blood. Felt the ineffable rift opening at his center, threatening to tear him in two. Consciousness waning.

Then Ex was there beside him, his face pinched and grave, one arm raised against the crushing weight of the swarm, the other reaching down to offer his hand.

*On your feet, Nathaniel.*

Nate gaped dumbly at the phantom hand, dimly aware it wasn't really there at all. Dimly aware that he didn't care. He met Ex's eyes, holding to his companion's presence like a life raft in a raging ocean storm. He strained, teetering on the edges of his physical limits, barely a hair's breadth from what felt like certain implosion. Then something did burst, and he was through, reaching for Ex's hand. Reaching for his sword, calling for it, the Light flaring bright as it blazed free from the swarm, speeding for his hand. He caught it and launched upward with a furious bellow and a boom of speed, the swarm receding, recoiling from his burning aura like a scalded hand.

Nate tore forward, shaking with power, the world condensing to a single point in his mind. He threw his sword back for the blow, ready to crack the planet open from the inside. Believing, for the first time, that it was actually possible, with the volume of power screaming through him. Then a solid wall of nanoswarm blindsided him with the force of a vengeful god, and there was nothing but breathless flight and blinding impact.

By the time the world resolved into anything beyond pain and stars, he was already buried, the swarm coating his every inch, binding him to whatever surface he'd struck. Binding him so completely he couldn't so much as twitch a finger. He struggled, but it was pointless. He was too pinned down, the last of his strength flash-fried on that last wasted effort.

The ruby fire of the Archon's shifting non-face emerged from the swirling cocoon of darkness, the nanoswarm not parting so much as oozing forth, detaching from the larger cocoon to form its master a discrete body. The construct floated over to him with a kind of deadened, mechanical calm. No trace of smug victor's pride. No nothing.

Nate hated the thing in that moment—was surprised and even a little sickened to realize just how deeply he hated it. The construct ghosted silently forward, unperturbed by his hatred, reaching for him with one glowing red hand. Mindless. This mindless goddamn machine—this *construct*—ticking on like a dumb animal even as it pulled feats not even Ex could understand.

He bared his teeth as it closed its glowing hand over his faceplate, sending his HUD into jittering spasms. He couldn't move. Could only just make out past the Archon's hand the way that burning non-face began to shudder with strange shapes and afterimages, almost like it was flirting with the idea of trying to grow a new one. There was a sound like the fluttering of a thousand moth wings in a small room—otherworldly whispers creeping into his awareness in a place somewhere between mind and senses.

The first hint of real fear bubbled up through the surface of his rage. Fear at what this mindless automaton was truly capable of. At what it truly wanted. Because in that moment, Nate was certain of it: whatever eagerness he'd imagined in the swarm before now, whatever banal animal drives he'd chalked up to the simple motivations of an enemy at war, it had all been just that. Figments of his imagination. Clumsy attempts to anthropomorphize something that was simply beyond his sentient comprehension. Beyond all of theirs.

He felt it in his bones, as the Archon plucked his helmet free and crushed it like a tin can in one glowing red hand. Felt it in a place well beyond conscious understanding. This mindless machine. This ancient, infinitely complex construct.

He'd never stood a chance.

*Let go.*

Nate gasped at the breath of phantom winds in his mind, inaudible and yet unmissable—not a voice so much as a tangible force of nature. A static charge in his mind. Icy cold seeping through his insides. The rift at his center flexing. Stretching. Tearing.

"No," he whispered, sudden, horrible realization dawning as those phantom winds shifted—striking between him and Ex like an Ooperian dagger between the ribs.

*Nathaniel?* Ex asked, his voice small and afraid. Nate had never heard him so afraid.

"No!" he cried, bucking uselessly against the Archon's strength. "You get the fuck away from him!"

But it was already happening. Those strange whispers creeping into the cracks even as fine tendrils of nanostuff blossom from the Archon's glowing hands and slithered in for Nate's eyes and mouth. Nate fought helplessly, Ex's presence clinging to him like a frightened child. The rift widening, ruthless fingers of ice and apathy prying deeper.

Then the Archon paused. Full stop for no apparent reason, like someone had flipped a switch.

A flicker of hope in the dark. Nate's focus leapt upward, to the surface, clinging to some instinctive prayer—the only one he could think of right then.

Jaeger had heard. Somehow, he'd heard.

No sooner had the thought occurred to Nate than the Archon's glowing visage snapped around to follow his gaze up through the vast, cavernous darkness. Not a cavern at all, Nate realized, as the space awoke to the Archon's attention, but an unbelievably enormous, roughly spherical pocket of the spire itself. Nate watched breathlessly as the mouth at the top of the enormous dome expanded, dilating as if to consume the entire planet above —zooming their view telescopically, he realized. Up, through thousands of kilometers of spire innards and planetary mass, the arcane optics condensing the spire's endless length all the way to the angry red lightning at its peak, then expanding out to the surrounding area with crystal clarity.

Expanding right out to the escape pod that was currently speeding straight for the spire's peak like a kamikaze bomber.

Nate tensed alongside Ex, both of them knowing what came next, both preparing to fight.

Then the spire lashed out with a dark tendril and caught the speeding pod like a pond frog snagging a bug. Somehow, Nate felt the Archon's attention there, an invisible thread of will stretching up through the spire's length. He watched, breathless, praying for the blast to come anyway, sure there'd be redundancies. A remote trigger. A timed detonator, at the very least. But his heart fell as the Archon reached out from the spire with more tendrils, reeling the pod in like some giant arachnid webbing up its latest victim, ripping into its innards with ruthless, surgical efficiency, like it knew exactly what was aboard, and what to do about it.

*No*, the winds seemed to whisper, somewhere far away.

Nate could only watch as the tower danced to the Archon's will, dispassionately deconstructing his last hope down to its constituent elements. It swallowed the devastating warheads like it was picking apart a deli sandwich. Nate slackened in his relentless nanoswarm coffin, drained beyond resistance as that burning red non-face swiveled back to him two thousand kilometers below, bringing the full weight of those icy whispers back on his mind.

*Let go*, the winds sighed.

Then the Archon reached into him, razor sharp tendrils piercing armor and flesh like they were nothing, and Nate screamed.

## CHAPTER 37
# LIFE AND DEATH

Back at the campsite, in the absence of what *should've* been quite the booming ride, even with interstellar-grade shock absorbers and radiation shielding, the inside of the escape pod was deadly quiet. Which, frankly, was fine by Jaeger, right up until Pierce had to heave a sigh at the external display and growl an exasperated, "Mother of fuck."

That did it.

The pod's cramped inhabitants began to stir from their mesmerized spells of waiting, trading uncertain looks. O'Sweeney had eyes only for Jaeger.

"You're quite certain you—"

"Yes."

"And that you—"

"Yes, for fuck's sake," Jaeger growled, eyes still glued to the display, waiting to be sure. Doubly sure. Triply. Fumbling over thoughts of gravitational disturbances. Time dilation. He should've pulled Lundquist into this pod. Probably in place of O'Sweeney. Answers over accusations. It was only when he noticed Carter's pointed look that he registered it was time to reel it back, bring it down a notch, for everyone's sake.

"I armed the bomb," he added, notably more calmly. "And the detonators. And *both* backup timers. He must've disarmed them all."

"It," Amelia pointed out halfheartedly, frowning at the supportive hand

Pierce had rested on her leg like that was somehow the most confusing part in all of this. "*It* must've disarmed them all."

Right. Because Christ forbid they forget that the thing that'd just effortlessly swatted aside tandem weapons of mass destruction was *supposed* to be naught but some mindless, inorganic Pac-Man. Sucking down the galaxy chomp by goddamn chomp.

Jaeger stowed the smartass retort, looked around the too-tight cabin once more, then decided he'd rather risk painful death by atomic incineration or downstream ass cancer than sit around there another minute. He palmed the hatch panel, pulled the manual safeguard release, and slumped back out into the insufferably thick Ginnungagap air, feeling more like an achy old man than he ever would've thought possible even a few short years ago.

"Goddammit," he muttered at the distant hellscape of the spire and its deepening storm.

Impotent. That was the word he was looking for. Powerless. Both words notably clearer than the one he thought he'd heard from Nate through the static. He still wasn't sure he'd heard right. But then again, not all that much rhymed with *warhead*, and if he was being honest, he knew damned well what he'd heard:

Nate, desperate and afraid.

Beyond that, the exact details hardly seemed to matter. The kid's ingress into the spire hadn't been a cakewalk, if the fireworks had been any indication. Clearly, things hadn't improved on the other side. And now... Now, he tried the q-noded earpiece again, for what felt like the hundredth time. He'd lost count. He wasn't surprised to find dead silence on the line. No more than he was surprised by the sound of another pod hatch releasing, or the familiar presence of Kalders sliding up beside him a few moments later.

"We have to help him," she said quietly, eyes on the spire.

He didn't disagree one bit, but for the simple fact that he didn't have a single goddamn clue how they were supposed to go about actually doing it. It wasn't like they could grab their rifles and charge into battle. Not to any meaningful effect other than instant death, at least. Much as it stuck in his stubborn old craw to admit it, they were mere mortals here, pecking on the outskirts of a genuine clash of titans. Pirates and smugglers were one thing. But the last time they'd faced anything like this... Mordred LeFaye and the battle at Avalon... At least then, they'd had the *Camelot* to move the needle.

Now, he could only look around the reddening stretch of the courtyard, acutely aware of their distinct lack of options, and of the weight of the singularity bomb initiator burning a doomsday hole in his pocket. Acutely aware that, if Nate was truly in trouble in there, it might already be too late. He scanned the courtyard again anyway. He wasn't sure what he was hoping to find. A spare Knightship lurking about. A magic fucking wizard who'd decided to get off his drunk ass and actually come do something useful for once.

The other pods were hissing open now. A line of curious heads poking out, wondering what came next.

Jaeger noticed the snargladorf had resumed her ceaseless inspection of the courtyard, sniffing through the pieces of the monument Nate had shattered through the prefab wall with his fifty-ton caber toss. He was about to move on when he spotted Vampire Bob lurking nearby. The jittery bastard had refused to be ushered into a pod for the coming blast. Now, the Ooperian was watching the hairless space dog at work—or sniff-seeing, or what-the-hell-ever the blind Ooperian did—his pale nostril slits working overtime, spindly fingers plucking at one another in some kind of creepy anticipation.

"Hey, Snuffs?" Jaeger called.

The mechanic appeared at the open hatchway of Kalders' pod with a wary look, like he had a feeling he was about to be blamed in some capacity for Snuffing everything up, even if he pointedly *hadn't* touched the bomb pod for exactly that reason. Jaeger waved him over impatiently, gesturing at Bob. "Try to figure out what the hell has Mr. Burns all riled up over there, will you?"

He didn't wait for an answer, nor did he pay particular attention to whatever Snuffy murmured glumly under his breath as the mechanic dropped out of the pod and marched over to the gesticulating Ooperian. Instead, Jaeger turned for the shattered monument, ignoring the growing weight of questions spreading through the courtyard, vaguely aware Kalders was following him. He'd almost certainly lost his damned mind, he decided. That seemed the safe bet, as he knelt down and began picking through the rubble next to their stray space dog tagalong.

Judging from Kalders' tone of voice, he wasn't the only one who thought so.

"Boss?" she asked, entirely more cautious than normal.

He just kept looking. He couldn't have said why.

He could practically hear Carter's no-bullshit tone in his head, telling him he'd just gone ahead and finally cracked—no mystery whatsoever, and who could blame him? He kept looking anyway, clinging to something.

Nate himself hadn't even looked all that surprised when this pile of ancient stone had turned out to be hiding nothing beneath its shattered roots but equally shattered hopes. And yet...

A sharp hiss drew his attention over to where Bob was gesturing furiously at Snuffy, looking rather—

"Fuck me!" Jaeger growled, snapping his hand back so abruptly he pitched over backward, clutching at the spot where something had just... burned him? But that wasn't quite right, he realized, staring dumbly at his exposed palm. No angry red burns. Nothing but a bizarre sensation like nothing he'd ever felt before—skin crawling with effervescent, almost numbing tingles and warmth. It faded quickly.

Ahead, the snargladorf took a careful sniff at the spot he'd been foraging through, then backed away slowly, head lowered almost deferentially. A few meters back, it lay down on its belly and looked back and forth between him and the spot, panting.

"Boss?" Kalders was beside him, frowning at the unburned hand he was still holding up like he'd never seen it before.

He lowered his hand, only then remembering to breathe, and rocked back up to his knees, scooting forward for a closer look. Slowly, delicately, he reached for the last two chunks of rubble he'd touched, feeling the same tense anticipation he still remembered from childhood, when he and his thickskulled friends had gotten their kicks playing with the electric fences around the pastures.

Nothing leapt out from the parting stones. Nothing out of the ordinary among the rubble. Carefully, he turned over the piece in his tingling hand... And there. A shard of something embedded in the otherwise perfectly homogeneous stone. Embedded almost like the entire monument had been carved or cast around it on purpose.

He stared at that elaborately patterned sliver, knowing it without a doubt even as the voice of reason in his head—the one that sounded a whole lot like Carter—pointed out that he actually had no idea. He looked back at Kalders. Saw his own stark realization mirrored in her eyes.

"Is... that what I think it is?" Snuffy asked nearby, craning for a better look, Bob peering out from behind him to sniff the air.

"Doc!" Jaeger called, eyes returning to the object of their joint attention, mind sifting through options. Amelia. Gendra. The Asgardians. He wasn't sure anyone on this planet but Nate was actually equipped to properly identify a genuine Beacon shard.

"But... I mean, Nate would've sensed it, right?" Snuffy asked, apparently on a similar train of thought. "Or maybe… I dunno… you know, with the"—he waved his hand helplessly at the aberrant sky—"with the interference, or whatever. Unless…" He trailed off, scratching thoughtfully at his cheek stubble.

"Get Lundquist," Jaeger told Kalders. She nodded and sprang to it without questions, hurrying past Snuffy and Bob the Space Vampire, who was watching Snuffy curiously with those allegedly blind eyes, and mimicking his thoughtful cheek scratching like he suspected maybe it was somehow important. It might've been a funnier sight if Jaeger hadn't felt so equally clueless, turning back to their mystery shard, wondering what the hell it was there for, and how it'd gotten there at all. He checked the spire on the horizon more out of growing habit than for any actual gleaning of information. The sky was red. That creepy ass mega swarm mass still hanging high above like a phantom planet. The world, as far as he could tell, was still ending.

And they had a shard.

"You're saying we fed it," came one of the voices Jaeger was looking for. He turned to find Ramachandra and Lundquist caught in conversation as they rounded the nearest pod, hurriedly corralled by Kalders.

Lundquist looked agitated. "I'm saying the readings seem to suggest that…" He trailed off as he registered the look on Jaeger's face. "What's…" He turned his curious frown to the artifact in Jaeger's hand, eyes squinting, then widening. "Is that what I think it is?"

"Hey, that's what I said!" Snuffy chimed, patting Bob on the shoulder like *you see that?* The Ooperian jerked at the touch, startled.

"But… What in the blazes is it doing there?" Lundquist asked.

"Was hoping you two might be able to figure that out," Jaeger replied, knowing it was probably an impossible ask, even for two of the brightest minds Earth had to offer. The looks on their faces seemed to confirm as much. "On the double, if it's all the same to you," he added anyway.

"On the… double," Ramachandra echoed numbly, staring at the rock in Jaeger's hand.

Lundquist just looked openly confused. "Then, Nate isn't…?"

"Still no contact," Jaeger said.

"Well, there must be some manner of…" Lundquist trailed off, mouth drawn tight. He scanned the monument rubble and the surrounding area, looking for something hopeful to latch onto. Finding nothing.

"Look, it could be simple interference," Jaeger said. "Could be something else. Could be he's busy ripping that red-faced bastard a new one as we speak. All I know is that we've got a whole heap of shit preparing to rain down on our heads, a missing Knight, and—as far as I can see it—just two real options here. And seeing as one of those options ends with our collective and untimely demise by fledgling black hole," he added, drawing the singularity initiator carefully from his gear vest with his free hand, feeling like he was handling Death incarnate, "I'll ask again." He hefted the shard-bearing rubble up for the growing crowd, careful to avoid direct skin contact. "Does *anyone* have the faintest fucking clue what we're looking at here?"

Everyone stared. Jaeger did too.

Death in one hand. Light in the other.

It felt almost poetic, in some way that was almost certainly above his pay grade. Judging from the blank-faced head shakes and furtively traded looks, it was above everyone else's, too. Most of the camp had gathered around by that point, crew and Asgardians alike all staring like they half-expected the Lady herself might arise from the previously inconspicuous pile of rubble.

"Perhaps if we had the means to conduct a proper analysis," Lundquist finally said, apologetically.

"Or the time," Ramachandra added.

She didn't elaborate, but her wary skyward glance said more than enough. Whatever was happening, it was happening faster and faster by the minute—the entire sky alive with shimmering red light now, the charged air palpable, like the whole planet was about to go warp speed.

"All right, then," Jaeger said, the first—and frankly, maybe the *only*—scraps of a plan coalescing into a decision. *The* decision. "Load it in the last pod," he said, carefully handing the embedded shard to Kalders. "All of it," he added, to Snuffy and the others, nodding at the pile of rubble. "As much as you can fit."

"Uh, what?"

"You heard me. Get it in. We're wheels up in five."

Silence hung on the gathering. Everyone staring like he'd lost his mind.

Snuffy spoke with care. "You're… gonna launch a broken statue at—"

"I said move!" Jaeger snapped.

For a second, they all stood in stunned silence. It had been a long time since he'd gone straight disciplinarian on them. But quickly enough, the shock broke, and the camp proceeded to whip itself into shape, on the double. Even the Asgardians hopped to after a round of uncertain looks. In a past life, the whole scene probably would've buttered his ego real nice and good. Standing there at that moment, though, at what felt like the edge at the end of the map, he only felt tired. Tired, and maybe a smidge proud, watching his people work. It occurred to him that these people—and their away team on the far side—were the finest damn crew he ever could've hoped for. Finer, even.

Not bad for a band of misfit screwups just like him.

He huffed a derisive chuckle at himself, shaking his head. He really *was* getting old. God help him if he went and started going all sentimental, too. Now hardly seemed the time, as his gaze ticked back and forth between Carter and Pierce, weighing steady hands and burdens of conscience, and just how damn many entire planetary populations would be riding on all of this. He was kind of surprised where his eyes landed in the end.

"Lieutenant," he called, hoping to Christ he hadn't lost his gut instincts along with the rest of his marbles. "A word."

# CHAPTER 38
# WARRANTY VOID

On the margin of thought, if what was left to his awareness could even be called *thought*, he—whoever he was—was mostly just surprised he didn't seem to be dead yet. It was pretty much all he could think, even if he couldn't quite remember why. The thought circling back over and over again, like a simple binary loop, checking. Waiting.

Dead yet? False.

Dead yet? False.

Dead yet? Maybe. (So trinary, then. But...)

Something happening. Something from nothing. Miraculously novel in the blank drudgery of this infinite loop. Shapes in the murky gray nothingness. Movement. A low growl. A bestial form, sinking back into shadow. A whisper in its wake. A name. *His* name.

"Nathaniel?"

He didn't recognize the voice. Couldn't seem to remember where he was, or how he'd gotten there. In the ether beside him, something moved. The flickering impression of a slender, mustachioed man, beaten and shackled. There, but not. Nate peered around, squinting through the quiet gray oblivion. For a moment, he could've sworn he spied a mousy, bespectacled girl, peering right back through the murky shroud.

He felt dizzy. Lightheaded. He felt...

Memories of a dying ship. Emergency red lighting. Hazy neurotoxin. The languid, sickly acceptance of bleeding out.

Exsanguination.

The word sent sickening ripples through him. Twilight wavering.

Something was at work ahead, in a blazing cauldron of nebulous violet energies and showering sparks, stringing brilliant lines of starlight from here to there. A broad figure, clearly towering and yet bizarrely amorphous, its dark edges defying his brain's best attempts to categorize them. The more he tried to focus in, the less certain they grew.

"Not there," whispered that voice again, small and… mousy. "Over here."

Nate tried to pull his head on straight, focus, but it was like trying to blink away a thick, unmoving fog. There was something in that voice. A mental image. Something reminiscent of Tessa, and yet…

"Cammy," he whispered, gaping through the fog. "Cammy?"

There was nothing there. Nothing but a soft, tentative curiosity tugging at him from some undisclosed swath of the expansive nothingness, so soft and thin it was barely perceptible. Barely real. All of this, unreal. Cammy's presence…

Ahead, that writhing darkness had paused at its work, attention seeming to shift. Gravity itself, seeming to shift. Nate found himself holding his breath, though he couldn't say for sure in this place whether he had lungs or not. He sensed, on some level, that something was wrong with the thing's fantastical apparatus. Strained lines of light pulling tighter. Fraying in places. The cauldron sputtering, dimming like the car lights as the engine tried to turn. The darkness—the Archon?—reaching for something in the distance. Reaching.

A few of the brilliant lines snapped, overstrained. Resonant twangs and bursts of violet sparks. Something big happening. Something that kicked him through oblivion like a bubble slipped clear from the underside. Surfacing. Surfacing through turbulent waters. Boiling waters.

Surfacing to something that couldn't have been reality.

"WELL, I'LL BE DAMNED," Jaeger whispered to the quiet shell of the pod that should've been empty, as the wave that should've broken them instead broke itself *upon* them, parting down the center like the freaking Red Sea.

His heart hammered on, well past its healthy limits, the icy tendrils of imminent death still clinging to his frozen insides, eagerly waiting for reality to reassert itself, for the other foot to fall.

"My Lord has chosen wisely," offered his hulking Atlantean passenger, as

Jaeger craned around to eye the mysterious monument cargo that, against all rational odds, seemed to have just saved their lives.

Despite himself, despite everything, Jaeger chuckled at those words, and at the utter lack of fedora-wearing, knights-of-the-templar-crusading awareness with which the Round Table Atlantean had delivered them, sitting back there astride the most forward segment of their crumbled savior.

"You have chosen… wisely," Jaeger mouthed to himself, turning back to the display screens. He flinched as the writhing heart of nanoswarm condensed, regathering itself between them and the spire, and struck again.

Again, his heart leapt at the sight of rushing death. Again, the swarm split before them, sundered on the invisible edge of whatever the hell it was they were carrying in the trunk.

"Probably shoulda opened with the magic shield shrine maneuver, huh?" Jaeger thought aloud, on the back of a much-needed exhale. "Classic mistake."

If Tristan had anything to say to that, he kept it to himself—just like he'd been doing since Jaeger had found the Atlantean waiting in the escape pod, broad shoulders scrunched to fit in, and told him to get the hell out.

Stubborn bastard hadn't budged.

"Last chance to bail," Jaeger added now anyway, ostensibly to Tristan, as he began laying on the altitude, trying not to think of Carter's last words to him. Trying to convince himself they hadn't *been* the last.

"We go to fight for my Lord," Tristan replied, as if that were all that need be said on the matter.

Jaeger glanced back at the unwavering Atlantean, marveling at the single-minded devotion, the faith.

*She'd be proud, John.*

He took a deep breath. Unclenched his painfully tight jaw.

So many things that ought to have been said.

Best not to think about that now.

"Goddamn right, we do," he murmured. Then he punched it for the spire's peak, milking their modified escape pod for everything she was worth. The swarm roiled like an angry ocean before them, then around them. Engulfing them. Blocking out the nightmarish red sky. Jaeger held the pod controls steady, trying not to focus on the frantic nanite waves breaking against the field of effect all around them, switching patterns like a fighter desperately looking for an in.

Then a section of swarm opened ahead like an elongated barrel straight to hell, and disgorged a speeding missile straight at them. Jaeger registered the discrepancy just before it hit. Something about the way the speeding mass shuddered and dipped just shy of their invisible forcefield—like someone had killed the pilot. Like that pilot had been the only thing afraid of their magic rocks.

The rest continued right on, precisely as dumb ballistic bodies were wont to do.

Jaeger was distantly aware of his eyes widening, hands tightening on the controls, responding by instincts long past their prime. There was no avoiding it anyway.

A blur of motion as something flung itself across his chest. Tristan's shield arm, he noted thankfully, as the projectiles hit, ballistic nanostuff ripping through their pod's armor like nothing, ripping through everything. The Atlantean shield thrummed with impact against Jaeger's front. He sucked a sharp breath, angry fire needling through his unshielded legs. Felt Tristan holding tight to the crash couch behind him. Engines sputtering out with a whine of failsafe alarms.

His hands worked without thought, killing the power main long enough to reroute the entirety of their failing energy to their last two functioning thrusters, stomach lurching with the onset of freefall. He went with the motion as the swarm parted again, nudging the airfoils to twist clear of another speeding frag cloud. Kalders would've called it shit flying. And she probably would've had a point, he supposed, as the nanites ripped open their port side, ushering in howling winds, Tristan scrambling to keep his hold on the back of Jaeger's crash couch, breathing ragged.

"Knew I brought you along for a reason," Jaeger grunted, easing their wild rotation. The fire was spreading through his legs. The warmth of blood staining his tear-proof trousers. He didn't look. "You all good back there?"

More labored breaths at his back. Definitely not good.

"I will survive as long as I must," Tristan managed. "As will you, Colonel."

"Heh," Jaeger huffed, a feral, humorless grin stretching his lips to cracking. "Goddamn right, we will," he agreed, leveling them out as the swarm pursued them downward like a hungry animal. Then he threw the airfoils into position and kicked their last two thrusters into overdrive.

NINE HELLS BELOW, in the depths of Ginnungagap, Nate rose to the surface with a scream, raw flashes of pain and impossible visions searing through his brain. He tried to move. Yanked to a halt with a deep, sickening certainty that something was profoundly wrong. Hands grasping at blood-slicked metal. Something too twisted and obscene to process emerging from his body.

He gagged as it began to register. Retched coppery blood. Watched in horrid fascination as the fluid spilled down across the mess of his chest and abdomen. His torso unrecognizable. Splayed open in gory flaps. Defiled by the jagged mess of dark appendages that'd reached in, or exploded out, melding him to the Archon's superstructure like some perverse chimera. Draining his Light like a goddamn jump starter.

There was screaming. Maybe his. His hands and legs trapped. The freak-show apparatus shuddering with the intensity of the screaming, cracking at the seams where it adjoined to the superstructure. The pain, a disembodied mountain of sensation, terrible and yet somehow almost too physically outlandish to accept. Ex's voice inaudible. His presence thin and wrong.

Floating above it all, the Archon paid neither of them any mind, its mechanical attention focused elsewhere, elsewhere, on…

Darkness rose around him, threatening to consume him once again. Nate teetered on its edge, merciful emptiness calling to him with open arms, shock and sheer blood loss warping delirious thoughts.

A voice in the void.

A shudder, somewhere above. Somewhere far away.

He roused, mind grasping for some flicker of a vision he'd seen in a place somewhere between dream and reality. A deep growl shook the nearby shadows. A glint of feline eyes catching the stormy light of the superstructure, focused high above. Nate ignored the whiff of mechanized fear—it felt laughable in his current circumstances—and followed those slitted eyes upward, struggling just to stay conscious, feverish mind still grasping. A battered escape pod, punching into the spire, high, high above. Parting the swarm on some divine tide. Jaeger and Tristan, fighting for their lives inside. Fighting for him.

He hadn't imagined it.

The spire was in chaos.

He stared at the scene high above, watching across thousands of bizarrely warped kilometers as a small, stub-winged something came rocketing down the maw, the entire spire coming apart around it, throwing itself at the tiny pod like an enraged immune system repelling a foreign invader, the dark walls bulging and wobbling unsteadily as it passed, like an enormous esophagus trying to swallow something entirely too large.

Somehow, the pod sped on through it all, juking past wild clouds of nanite projectiles, taking hits, and pushing on anyway in a plume of dark smoke. Nate felt some facet of the Archon's will stretching through the spire walls, conducting the onslaught. Felt the bloody, nightmarish torture rack heating in his chest, sick tingles of his dwindling life pulsing from his body. He smelled blood on the air. His, and somehow, even across all that distance, theirs too. Nanite flechette ripping through the pod, killing the last of its engine systems. Tristan covering Jaeger with his disintegrating grav shield. Both of them covered in wounds.

Nate shifted, trying to reach for them on some helpless instinct—felt a give in his restraints that hadn't been there before. Ex there, somewhere on the murky periphery, fighting to break through from the other side. Something cracking. The Archon's focus centered elsewhere, on the pod, on...

There. Not just the pod. Not just intruders. Something else, aboard the pod. A bubble-shaped void, perceptible only in that same thin place where he felt the Archon's will stretching through the tower. Nate barely had time to perceive it before Jaeger blew the rear hatch panel, kicked out the airfoils, and spun the freefalling pod ass over teakettle. He caught a glimpse of stacked rubble, eyes widening as he recognized the shit-stained, weather-worn head of the Meyerwitz monument.

Then Tristan gave a mighty roar and smashed his fist into the back of his failing grav shield. The shield discharged in a thrumming rush, ripping itself to pieces, the resultant blast clearing the pod bay of its contents like so much chaff in the wind. Or like an improvised torpedo.

Below, the Archon blazed brilliant red and threw its glowing hands skyward, the roots of the spire shuddering into mass motion, seeking to close the way completely. Above, the payload sped on, unperturbed, splitting through the Archon's barriers like they were nothing, like they didn't even exist. Nate sensed the warhead riding at the center of that mass. Glimpsed Tristan crumpled in freefall against the back of the pod's pilot chair high above, Jaeger's face pinched in pain as he craned around to inspect their handiwork. Face bloody and grim. Eyes a little wide as he reached for something on the control panel, like he'd just realized what was coming, what he was truly about to do.

Time stood still as Nate realized too.

"Make it count, Kid," Jaeger whispered, voice rough with pain.

Then the payload detonated, Light surging like a newborn star, and the whole world caught fire with him.

CHAPTER 39

# ERUPTION

In an instant, everything was swept aside.

Rolling fire and screaming pain. The Archon's superstructure. The deafening boom of sound. All of it, gone.

Jaeger. Gone.

The thought hit like an angry thunderclap in the darkness. Too much, too loud, and too sudden to process.

Somewhere in a place beyond space and conventional reason, Nate howled and threw himself at the incorporeal presence of the Archon. Reality howled back in protest, bending between Nate's will and another's as they clashed on some level he couldn't understand. Bending until it snapped completely, and folded back into something more tenable to conscious perception.

He reeled in the strange, unfurling plane, searching for some bearing, some explanation of what the hell had just happened. Voluminous masses loomed overhead, little more than shapeless shadow. His left wrist was shackled, the chain disappearing ahead in a dense fog up to his knees. The breathless air hummed with displaced Light and a sinister charge, unmistakably alive, yet eerily still around him.

There were figures in the fog just ahead. The bespectacled girl from before, watching him with wide eyes, her hair done up in the same messy bun Tessa wore when she flew. Cammy, he realized in a rush. A stately Gorgon male stood beside her. He could only assume that was Kaldo, the persona of the *Kalnythian Wilds*. And there, towering over them all like a raging black cyclone, seemingly focused on the mind-melting, panoramic kaleidoscope of real space and swirling light beyond…

The Archon. Formless in this place. Endless.

Fucking dead.

"Nathaniel," Ex warned, from some muffled corner of awareness.

But Nate was already in motion, charging into the hellish winds of the Archon's storm, the world above licking frozen flames at the edges. A simple, unadorned longsword appeared in his hand as he went. He leapt forward, soaring across indeterminate space, blade coming alive with Light as he plunged in for the kill.

The Archon moved without moving, shapeshifting their labored reality before Nate's eyes. His shackled wrist yanked up short against the chains he'd forgotten were there, the darkness itself catching him by the throat. The hint of a silhouette rising from the chaos. The same dark figure from that night in the canyon. Nate heaved, fighting the construct's hold on reality as much as the chains themselves. Grim satisfaction as something gave way, and he caught the bastard by its shadowy wrist and ran his glowing blade right through its chest.

"Fuck you," he hissed, something vicious and animalistic swelling at the sight of his blade buried in the Archon's heart.

Then the silhouette vanished in a puff of ash and dust, only to be replaced by several more—three coming at him from the front. More shadow hands looping around from behind, yanking him down and back, away from the swarm. They all plunged into the fog together, just as Nate caught sight of another shadow figure furiously sawing away at something at the Archon's base. They hit hard, Nate throwing a hard elbow at his rear attacker, surprised to find himself breaking free.

He rose, slashing at the rest of the coming shadows, clearing the fog on a gush of azure energy, and—

"Nathaniel."

He followed the gruff croak of Ex's voice, unreality dilating in on the formless chaos of the Archon, where a hand was reaching out. He caught a glimpse of wild hair and wide eyes before the writhing darkness closed back in. Ex, battered to all hell. Reaching out. Wrist shackled just like his, Nate registered, as the darkness pulled his friend deeper. The chains—his chains, *their* chains—feeding into the Archon right where that damned little shadow spawn was still busily sawing away, hurrying to sever Nate and Ex's last binding links.

"No," Nate whispered, understanding striking as the sky caught fire in slow motion—strange hues of orange and ruby-violet. This place. This bond. The rushing tide of what was coming through that hazy panorama beyond the Archon's fog—a force unlike any protoswarm Nate had ever seen or heard of. All of it, hitting him the moment before the first bit of chain link gave way in a flash of sparks, and the rest of the shadows came crashing back in on him like an army of hungry wraiths.

"No!" he growled, the horde riding him into the fog, hammering down. The gnawing tug of the saw biting into his and Ex's last link nearby. His struggles futile, the horde clutching at his arms and legs, tying him hopelessly to spot. Ex crying his name somewhere far away. Fading.

"NO!"

The scream tore out of him like an explosion, fury given shape and sound. The air detonated—brilliant azure Light tearing through the shadows, obliterating them. And then he was on his feet. Lunging forward. Reaching for Ex.

He nearly made it.

The air thickened mere meters shy, time slowing. His body, slowing. Then the pregnant tension erupted with a torrent of gale force winds and godawful sound as the full force of the Archon's will fell on him like the freaking Eye of Sauron, thrusting him inexorably and irresistibly backwards. He scrambled to find some hold against it, bare fingers and toes clawing in the fog for some purchase, finding none. Sliding further and further away.

Then something small but firm pressed into his back, anchoring him in place.

Cammy, he registered with a flit of hope, floating there behind him like a feather on the wind, right beside a grim-faced Kaldo. Both of them small and laughably unimposing compared to the storm ahead, both of them holding their ground anyway.

"Hurry, Nathaniel," Cammy pleaded, her voice tight with the effort. Beside her, Kaldo seemed to add something more, but his voice didn't reach Nate's ears. Nate rounded back on the Archon, focusing on what he could control, clawing in the fog. He strained, teeth bared in a painful snarl, all of them pushing together, boiling with the effort. Shaking as they found the edges of their collective strength—and began to realize even that wasn't enough.

This thing. This goddamned relentless machine.

It drove on against them, unyielding. Untiring. Unmoved by the hateful scream that tore from Nate's throat as his grip began to slip, fatigue licking through his every inch. He felt the last link wearing desperately thin. Saw Ex's hand sinking into the fold, the Archon turning its indecipherable attention back to the deepening storm beyond, where thousands of light-years away and yet right there, the tip of its dark legions were just beginning to pierce the veil. Just beginning to step into the heart of Alliance space.

*Over*, Nate realized, watching in helpless horror as the last of the fight bled from his shaking limbs.

It was over.

He'd failed.

The Synth were coming.

There was nothing left to—

A furious roar shook the air, rolling over the howling winds, and something struck the Archon square in its swirling mass. A jet black blur of motion, ripping into it like a wild animal, grasping for something Nate couldn't perceive. It hardly mattered.

The Archon caught Myrr like an apathetic giant plucking up a petulant child. But not before Nate had torn to his feet and, bolstered by one last shove from Cammy and Kaldo, flashed across the last of the space between them. He smacked aside the last furiously sawing shadow figure and caught onto Ex's half-buried arm, clasping his friend by the forearm, preparing to heave as a submerged Ex clasped back.

The Archon bellowed a sound like colliding planets and swung for the fences, seeking to tear them apart.

Nate screamed right back and held on with all his will, stubbornly refusing to accept that any force in the universe, short of the Lady herself, could ever break the bond between them. He felt Ex holding right back. Felt their beliefs coalescing into one, bound by something far more than the strength of their individual fingers.

Then the blow landed, and they were rocketing across the murky dreamscape together. They hit with a strange lack of impact, Ex not bouncing to his feet so much as somehow just appearing there.

"Right, then," he grumbled, setting to curling their trailing chains methodically up along one forearm, like nothing had happened, and the galaxy wasn't preparing to come collapsing down around them. The chains began to glow as he finished the wrapping, melding seamlessly into his flesh. He looked to Nate. "Shall we try it together, this time?"

"Ex," Nate heard himself gasp. He could barely breathe in the blurry aftermath of the blow. Suddenly, he couldn't seem to focus on anything but the memory of Jaeger's face in those last moments, like it had been waiting there all along. Waiting for the first lull to come crashing down on him. Tristan slumped against the pilot's chair. The look on Jaeger's face. The words. His last words.

"I know, Nathaniel," Ex said, kneeling down beside him. "I know."

He was surprised at the depth of empathy in his friend's tone.

"But all we have to decide," Ex continued, offering his hand slowly, solemnly, "is what to do with the time that is given us. Yes, little hobbit?"

A flicker of dubious amusement, here in the deepest of nine hells. Ahead, the Archon blared something like fury at the turbulent aperture of an unfolding tenth hell—a mad vortex of light and sound, through which that incomprehensible force of destruction was trying to squeeze from half a galaxy away. The sight should've spurred panic. Urgent action, at the very least. All Nate could focus on was Myrr's limp form hanging in the Archon's grip. Body broken.

He felt a pang of pity for the creature he hadn't known or understood. Sympathy for it, and for Jaeger and Tristan, and for just about every other poor bastard in this universe, save for the heartless mass of death and destruction swirling ahead of them. He turned to Ex, who'd watched him through all of it, not sparing so much as a nervous glance for the catastrophe unfolding before them—like he was fully prepared to stand by and watch it all burn to the ground if that was what Nate truly wanted.

"Okay, Gandalf," Nate whispered, tears brimming over the deeper rage as he took Ex's hand. They pulled themselves up together, hands beginning to mend as one, the power surging between them, clean and pure. "Then let's kill this bastard for good, and make it count."

THERE WAS NO SNAPPING AWAKE, no coming to. Only a moment of disorientation as reality shifted shapes from what had been to what also was, and then Nate was back in the depths of the Ginnungagap spire, flying straight for the Archon through a maelstrom of raging nanoswarm and speeding rock—sword in hand, armor in place, ruined chest knitting itself together on a rush of searing Light as Ex sighed with the relief of coming home.

Home, to where it seemed it'd only been about two seconds since Jaeger's detonation.

A steady stream of debris still rained from the mouth of the greater spire above, punching through sections of dark superstructure like speeding meteors. The worst of the damage, though, had already been done. The sprawling nanite walls glowing red hot where they'd been struck by the explosion and its fallout. A thousand points of failure, groaning under the pressure of Ginnungagap. A frightening string of violent cracks and booms as the chain reaction took hold, and the entire superstructure began to collapse in earnest.

Nate had no idea what Jaeger had set off—how it'd yanked him and Ex into the twilight realm, and seemingly killed some part of the spire's regenerative mojo, to boot. He glimpsed in Ex's mind that there'd been a strange surge of Light on the blast, almost like a Beacon rupture, but there was no time to dwell on it. He raced for the Archon, determined to shut it down before it could try to squeeze its friends across the galaxy through its dying relay.

Ahead, the construct tossed Myrr's limp body aside and turned to meet them, non-face burning bright, the first hints of something like agitation in its movements—like they'd actually started to piss the thing off, at long last.

That was good.

*Good, indeed*, Ex agreed, with the same grim bloodlust.

Their first clash was deafening—the Archon catching his blade and all of his considerable momentum in its glowing hands with a blinding flash of ruby-violet, refusing to budge a centimeter. Nate didn't care. Couldn't care. Their surroundings paid the price for the construct's stubbornness, the shockwave of their impact ripping out like an explosion, tearing through everything around them. Nate abandoned his trapped sword and fought on, hammering the construct with one furious fist after another. It was like punching a condensed planet. Each blow spouting flares of reactive red energies and violent eruptions of displaced nanostuff. The Archon reassembling each loss like a rewinding clock, and fighting right back.

They soared through the onslaught of falling rubble, rising steadily as they fought, locked together in a relentless trade of earth-shaking blows. They'd nearly reached the top of the cavernous space when, more out of simple hatred than any real hope of fatality, Nate lunged forward and caught the construct around its broad neck region, squeezing its head in a savage bear hug. Twisting and straining. Some sick pleasure stirring as that expressionless ruby red non-face burned brighter, almost as if in alarm.

He yanked harder, determined to rip the damned thing's head off. Harder. Strange psychic whispers and unintelligible sounds greeting his ears like a mechanical plea, his armor practically melting where those glowing hands clutched at his arms, trying to pry him off. He yanked harder, the Archon's visage flickering with something he hoped to Christ was pain. He gathered his strength, preparing for one last heave—

And froze in shock as those ghostly features flitted into something like a human face.

Jaeger's face.

The image seared through him, stuck in time, sinking to the pit of his guts like a depth charge. Then Nate screamed, hot fury ripping from his bones, and blasted the Archon into the next universe. He reached out, preparing to launch after the bastard as the comforting weight of his sword snapped obediently back to his waiting hand from wherever it'd fallen. Something about the cloud of energy gathering around the Archon gave him pause.

The construct crashed through a falling superstructure column and pulled to a halt some several hundred meters away, hovering level with him over the collapsing wreck of its cavernous lair, positively radiating with building fury. Thrumming crimson waves of it rippling through its length, accumulating at the glowing ember of its chest before pulsing ominously back out. The air crackled around it. Limbs coming alive with strange glyphs and patterns.

For the first time since he'd come out swinging, Nate remembered what it was he was up against here—everything he already knew this thing to be capable of, and everything he didn't. And if it hadn't been pissed before… Now, the Archon looked ready for blood, as it blared a challenge that shook all of Ginnungagap and flashed forward on a burst of red light.

*It would appear we've pierced the veil,* Ex said. But Nate only half-heard as he flinched back for extra maneuvering room, trying to pretend like he'd *meant* to call the shield that'd just unfolded from e-dim onto his left arm. Trying to shut out the sudden and horrible reminder of what this thing had done to him the last time he'd gotten its full attention—the mess of blood and viscera still drying across his Light-mended chest.

He tightened his grip on his sword, gathering his strength as the Archon sped in.

Then a crack of thunder sounded, space warping, and something large punched into existence just above them. The *Crimson Tide*, some corner of Nate's brain registered, just before a copper blur came speeding out of the vessel and smacked the Archon hard enough to send it smashing through the spire chamber floor several kilometers below—moving so fast the thing might've actually punched clear through the crust on the other side of the planet.

For a second, Nate could only stare in wonder at the geyser of bright orange magma that replaced it far below, spewing in on violent planetary pressures. Then those thousand red hot points threw in the collective towel around the vast chamber, and the entire place erupted like a volcano with a thousand mouths.

"Your ship, Nathaniel," came the inordinately welcome sound of Iveera Katanaga's voice in his helmet comms, through the sudden shock of heat and pressure.

She was already moving, plunging for the quickly filling lake of magma far below. Nate blinked, only then fully accepting that this wasn't some hallucination—that the Gorgon actually had made it down here to the planet. Which meant...

*As I said*, Ex chimed, almost cheerfully. *Welcome back to Kansas, little hobbit.*

Nate blew out the breath he hadn't realized he was holding, relief flooding in along with the garbled comms activity of off-planet chatter. It was damned good to hear.

*Ah, yes*, Ex said. *How I've missed the chattering of the monkeys. Now, perhaps—*

"You'd best hurry, Nathaniel," came Iveera's voice in his helmet. She was already several kilometers distant, racing the rising tide of magma to a dense nodule near one crumbled superstructure pillar. He could vaguely sense Cammy's dormant presence there.

"The planet is becoming highly unstable," Iveera added, as if the fiery lake of doom and earth-shaking rumbles weren't proof enough. "Your crew will be—"

An enormous crack of sound clapped the cavern air, kicking up thick streams of magma from the swell. He felt it in his chest—deep and primal, like the planet itself was shaking loose old bones. It didn't seem to bode well.

"As I said," Iveera murmured, flaring bright emerald in the distance as she began excavating. Nate was already speeding down to join her, painfully aware of the growing seismic activity Ex had politely muted on the HUD. They both knew what was coming—suspected, at least. Luckily, Iveera made fast work of the Archon's impound nodule. By the time he pulled up, she was already coaxing the *Kalnythian Wilds* free from the residual tangles of aggregated nanostuff, the ship coming alive with her touch, relinquishing a subtle palor he hadn't even registered was there before.

The magma level was rising fast, additional jets punching through the nanite walls high above, raining fire down.

He hurried to the *Camelot*, anxious to get her shields powered up. Cammy's weak stirrings jabbed a pang in his heart. A few choice plasma blasts cleared the worst of the obstructions remaining from Iveera's once-over. He landed on the dorsal hull near the prow and laid a hand on his ship, surprised at how tender the action felt—how alive, the connection. He opened himself to her, letting his Light flow. Across the way, ministering to her own ship's health, he felt Iveera watching him, her faceplate clearing to reveal electric blue eyes, and an expression he hadn't realized he missed so much.

"It's good to see you, Iveera."

In their lithe armor membranes, her jin danced a few thoughtful pulses.

"Yes," she said, like she was almost as surprised as he was to find that she meant it. "Now—"

"Now," Malfar's deep Troglodan voice cut in, "perhaps we might set aside the pleasantries and focus on…"

The Troglodan Knight trailed off as another resounding crack split the cavern, pulling Nate's focus back to the quaking planet he'd almost forgotten to keep watching for whatever was coming.

"On that," Malfar finished, rather unnecessarily, as the first enormous appendage punched free from the glowing pool below, the entire cavern—maybe the entire planet—rumbling around it.

"Good to see you too, Malfar," Nate said numbly, as an oversized head followed, tearing free from groaning earth and searing magma, hissing smoke and ruby red fury.

"If I'm being honest," the Troglodan replied, "I could've done without."

*Ha*, Ex grunted. *Charming as ever.*

Nate was too riveted on the Archon, trying to wrap his head around the numbers Ex's sensors were feeding to his HUD. The construct had grown at least fifty times its original size since Iveera had smacked it halfway through the planet. It was still growing now, as it pushed higher out of the melting pit, colossal shoulders breaking clear, a rain of crumbling superstructure, collapsing spire walls, and deep Ginnungagap ore all gathering into it like a black hole drinking in mass.

"Your people, Nathaniel," Iveera's voice crackled over the comms, her jin gesturing upward, toward the surface. She spun away to atomize an inbound hunk of falling debris before he could answer. He wasn't entirely sure whether her words were a suggestion for him to send his crew help, or an invitation to get the hell out of there and see to it himself, but the proper course seemed clear enough.

"Go ahead, girl," he whispered to Cammy, eyeing the collapsing spire mouth high above as he stroked her hull, topping her off with as much energy as he could. He showed her the location in his mind as her shields came to full power. *Go get Tess and the rest of our people. Get them to safety.*

He felt the ship's reticence like an inward flinch of his own gut. *Who will get Nathaniel to safety?*

The spire cavern—maybe the entire planet—groaned all around them. It felt liable to tear itself in half any moment. Down in its hellish pool, the Archon shifted, rising up from the molten mess by the length of its now destroyer-sized torso, glowing arms still drinking in more matter, still growing, everything within several kilometers drifting in like the giant bastard had achieved its own gravity well.

*We've got this,* he told Cammy, giving her a gentle push as her engines came purring to life.

The *Camelot* lifted and turned, hesitating only a moment longer, then sped off to find their people, veering up for the mouth of the crumbling spire high above. Nate watched her go—watched her prow erupt with a lance of azure fury as she went, atomizing everything it touched, burning the way roughly passable, if not exactly clear. He watched his ship disappear into the smoking rain of detritus, blasting steadily away.

Then he turned back to the threat at hand—just as the cavern erupted with a head-splitting roar, and several thousand tons of reformed Archon came exploding out of the magma to meet them.

# CHAPTER 40
# TRIGGER FINGER

"Wait."

Somewhere far away, atop the high-rise edge of his own impending personal damnation, Pierce opened his eyes and gasped as the world came rushing back in. The *end* of the world, he'd been so damned sure, just mere seconds ago. And now…

Now, he took in the thinning red skies. Thinning like the mystical curtains of what-the-fuck-ever were suddenly receding, if not quite thrown wide. In the distance, the spire seemed to faintly tremble. The sound reached them several seconds later, like an ode to past mountain's collapse. Carter was watching him—she'd been the one who'd spoken, he realized. The one who'd just stayed his hand. And now she was watching with that freaky look she got sometimes, like her inner animal knew exactly what his had been fixing to do. What the old man had *left* him to do. He didn't begrudge her the look of calm disgust.

It was plenty fitting, he decided, as he dropped to his knees and puked his guts out.

Or dry-heaved, it turned out. Rather painfully. Pinched lungs and cold, clammy sweat. Faces and landscapes racing past his mind's eye—countless millions of abstract lives.

"Fuck," he whispered at the dry dirt, the stench of sulfur intermixing with the bile at the back of his throat. He eyed the singularity initiator switch in his hand, and had to stomp down the very real and very sudden urge to spring to his feet and hurl the thing as far away as he could.

Not a smart move with the kill switch to an entire solar system. Trisolar system. Fucking…

Carefully—very carefully—he slid the cover back over the trigger, reengaged the safeties. It was only as he finished that he caught the look on Carter's face.

"Didn't know you cared," she murmured.

"Fuck you."

He regretted the words the instant they left his mouth. The deadened look in her eyes, in her voice.

Jaeger.

Fucking stubborn old… Jaeger.

He glanced at Carter again, afraid of what he might find in her eyes. Afraid of what was liable to come crashing down on his own ass any moment here, even in the face of the fact that he'd honest to Christ just nearly killed them all.

Jaeger.

"Fuck."

He pushed himself up to his feet, acutely aware his hands were shaking. At the sound of boots crunching gravel to the right, he tried to pocket the initiator switch. Kalders saw the damned thing anyway, as she rounded into sight.

"The hell was that?" she asked, gesturing out to the expanse where she'd no doubt just seen their last "unmanned" bomb pod go jetting off prior to schedule. Her expression darkened as she did a double take on the initiator switch sliding back into Pierce's pocket.

"What the shit," she said, piecing it together before he could manage so much as a *fuck off*. She'd always been too damned smart for her own good. For her sake, Pierce almost wished he could've cured her of that particular ailment, at least for a moment, as those sharp eyes of hers traced from the kill switch, to him, to Carter. Back to him. He saw a flicker of the thought in her eyes—*He left it with a psychopath like you?*—right before the full implication of that thought landed. He *left* it. Full stop. Her eyes flicking back to Carter's muted face. Out to the now violently wobbling spire. Understanding dawning.

Pierce had never liked Kalders all that much. Never gotten along with her, at least. But that didn't make it any less horrible to see the realization hitting her—only helped it settle its weight down on his own black heart that much harder.

She turned back to him, eyes hollow, like she already knew.

"Where is he?"

Pierce opened his mouth. Tried to answer. Choked down a dry swallow instead.

"He went for Nate," Carter answered.

The sentence hung between the three of them with a kind of terrible finality. In the distance, the spire was coming down in earnest, now. Full collapse. It took several seconds for the first genuine thunderclap of sound to hit them.

Pierce tried to focus on the distant show. Tried not to stare at the simultaneous collapsing of Kalder's tough girl exterior right beside him—her breaths coming in ragged gusts, like she'd just had the wind knocked out of her. Mouth working soundlessly, trying to invoke some counter to the harsh reality of it all. The course she'd plotted. The plans they'd laid. The gusto with which she'd leapt to program Jaeger's updated evac routes into their remaining pods. A distraction. Still necessary for their survival, maybe. But a distraction, none the less.

He couldn't handle the brimming tears. The pathetic quiver in her jaw. He almost reached out to lay a hand on her shoulder.

"—the fuck is going on back there?" crackled a voice from the pod she'd just emerged from.

Ramirez. The away team.

They all traded a look, everything else forgotten for that one merciful moment as they processed that factoid, updating assumptions. Comms chatter beginning to spill in across the escape pod boards now. Chatter from new voices. Off-planet.

Fast footsteps rounding the shuttle.

"Holy shit." A frazzled Snuffy appeared, practically skidding in the gravel. "Holy shit! We did it! We—"

He drew up short at the looks on their faces, abruptly as if he'd smacked face-first into some invisible wall. The sigh left Pierce's lungs before he could help himself—an audible cue that now was absolutely *not* the time for this, even if the sound did confirm Snuffy's sudden darting suspicions.

"No." The mechanic looked between their faces. Looked for the fourth figure who wasn't there. Back to them, waiting for one of them to tell him otherwise. "No…"

"Sound the order, Snuffs."

To Pierce's surprise, it was Kalders' firm voice giving the orders.

"Everyone aboard the pods. We've gotta get airborne before—"

Pierce jerked in alarm, dropping into a ready stance before his rattled senses caught up enough to register it was hardly liable to do him much good. The crack had been breathtakingly loud. The quaking as sudden and violent underfoot as if the gods themselves had reached down and smacked the planet off its axis.

"Before something like that happens," Kalders finished, right as the ruby twilight clapped another sundering boom, and a great fissure split the dusty landscape, speeding straight for the courtyard.

They traded a microsecond of a look, then broke for the group at a sprint.

"That doesn't feel good!" a wide-eyed Lundquist announced as they rounded the pods and pulled up.

"They pay you the big bucks for this shit, Doc?" Pierce snapped, noting how quickly the same panic appeared to be spreading through the group—noting the great, deepening rumbles underfoot. Like the entire damned planet was having a nasty bout of indigestion. This earthquake was different than the ones they'd had earlier. Deeper.

No sooner did the thought occur than that racing fissure struck, and Pierce moved without thinking. It tore through the courtyard with a sound of grating earth, spewing dust and stone, shoving the very ground beneath their feet—an enormous maw opening at a rate that didn't seem possible.

It swallowed half the escape pods before he could so much as blink. Would've swallowed Lundquist, too, if a hand hadn't shot out and snagged the good doctor by the back of his shirt—Pierce's hand, he registered with some mix of surprise and detached satisfaction, as he hauled Lundquist back from the brink.

"Clearly," the doctor murmured numbly, still gaping into the chasm where their last-ditch escape rides had just vanished, "you've never seen an academic's paychecks."

Pierce glanced sideways at the doctor's blanched face—saw several others like it in the vicinity—and nearly let out a delirious chuckle. It might've been hilarious, if they hadn't just lost their last ride off of a collapsing planet. Beneath them, the planet quivered, straining the hair's breadth line of tension that seemed to have halted the fissure's expansion in its tracks. In the distance, something detonated.

Then the *Camelot* blasted out of the spire ruins like a bat out of hell, and came roaring their way.

"Take it up with the registrar later, Doc," Pierce growled, the urgency of his good senses crashing back in.

"But that's not even—"

Pierce just grabbed the glassy-eyed doctor and ran, lugging him bodily along, the chasm lurching back into violent motion like it'd somehow sensed it was about to lose a hearty meal. The fissure exploded wider, branching out. The courtyard devouring itself. Tearing the facility to pieces. All of it, collapsing in like an enormous sinkhole—like the entire planet was eating itself.

They ran for the blessed safety of the *Camelot*'s descending ramp, Pierce screaming for the others to hurry the hell up ahead of them, Lundquist just screaming. It was a blind chaos of panicked scrambling—Asgardians and Terrans and friends and foreigners all clutching and shoving at each other in their race to board the ship together. The ground giving way beneath Pierce's feet. The moment of terrible freefall before he hit something solid —knees and shins jarring on hard rock, bright pain as he ripped back to his feet, hauling Lundquist up from the sinkhole with him.

They staggered onto the boarding ramp just before the ground gave out completely. He thrust Lundquist roughly through the entryway hatch, whirling with the sinking certainty that they hadn't all made it. Icy barbs in his lungs at the flicker of golden hair disappearing in the deluge below. A terrible thought of Amelia. A worse realization as the ship veered clear of the collapse, and he felt the ramp pitching out from beneath him. A flash of nightmare skies and gaping depths—then something caught him. A blessedly strong hand clamping onto his wrist. Yanking him in so hard he thought his arm would tear off. It almost felt like it had as he smacked down to the deck.

He pushed himself up, dimly registering it had been an Asgardian who'd yanked him aboard. Barely made it to his knees before the hatch hissed shut behind them and Cammy laid on the juice. A chorus of disgruntled shouts, curses, and thumps as an entryway full of harried refugees went flying— inertial compensators bleeding off the worst of the *Camelot*'s organ-lique-fying acceleration, but still leaving more than enough to feel.

Despite everything, Pierce felt something like a moment of relief as he hit the bulkhead and a wide-eyed Amelia came crashing into his arms. Relief, shortly chased by the flicker of guilt that it must've been someone else he'd seen go down back there. Not Princess Elsa, he saw, scanning the packed entryway, spotting her rather composed countenance. Probably one of the Asgardians.

"Where is he?" someone groaned from the pile of tangled limbs and less-than-upright crew members, as Pierce peeled himself from the bulkhead and started pulling Amelia toward the bridge. He wasn't even sure who they meant: Jaeger, or Nate. The answer to both, though, seemed evident enough as the planet's surface crumbled in far below, and something in the depths of Ginnungagap bellowed a battle cry straight from hell.

CHAPTER 41

# EXPONENTIAL

"**S**weet Justice. What in nine hells did you feed that thing, Terran?"

All things considered—the mad, rock-blender cacophony of collapsing planet, churning magma, and howling atmosphere all around them—it seemed a rather impressive testament to Ex's tech that Nate was even able to hear Malfar's voice inside the sweaty confines of his helmet.

"Pretty sure it's feeding *itself* just fine," he growled back, lurching clear of what felt like a small continent of incoming debris. "But no, we can blame me. That works."

"Silence yourselves or keep your comms private, I care not," came Iveera's barely-calm voice over the line, "Either way, I'd prefer the next thing out of your mouths to be useful."

"Was kinda hoping *you'd* have the plan here," Nate admitted, atomizing another slew of tumbling Ginnungagap crust before it could assimilate into the growing colossus before them.

"What with my eons of experience at slaying Archons?"

*Lady's Beard, I do believe the Gorgon is being sassy*, Ex said—right before a speeding wall of rock smacked Nate halfway unconscious from behind.

He turned with a grunting effort and blasted clear of the obstruction, head spinning, body throbbing. "All I can tell you is that—"

Off in the distance of the quickly disintegrating spire cavern, the *Crimson Tide* opened fire in earnest.

"—That everything I've thrown at it has pretty much been useless," Nate finished, as the growing Archon—practically spanning the height of the enormous space, now, and easily outsizing all but the largest Alliance warships—phased harmlessly through the entire impressive array of death and destruction.

"Target appears to be in possession of advanced adaptive defensive capabilities," Malfar reported, with the professional efficiency of an ex-justicar describing a suspect's appearance.

"Like I said," Nate growled, as the giant Archon reared its head back and erupted with a countering tidal wave of roaring ruby energy. With nowhere to hide and nowhere to run, Nate threw his arms up, bolstering his shields as powerfully as he could and grimly accepting that this was going to hurt like hell—provided he was still around to feel the hurt at all.

Blinding light and hissing shields. Then the onslaught dimmed through his clamped eyelids, and something snagged him around the hips and shoulders like a full body harness—Ex coaxing his defenses down as the something squeezed breathtakingly tight. He opened his eyes just in time to recognize the faded orange ship hull smoking against his easing defenses— and the dizzying tumble of a jump into the strange reaches of q-drive space.

"Additionally, I'd prefer you didn't die *needlessly*, Nathaniel," Iveera's voice crackled in his helmet, as they dropped back into real space a blink of the eye later, and his charred restraints gave way, dumping him into zero g before recoiling indignantly. "Do refrain from cowering like an untrained child next time, yes?" she added, as he clung to the ship by startled reflex alone, watching the thick hull smoke venting past the shields into the endless black.

He released a pent up breath, gathering his bearings, and patted the *Wilds* affectionately on the underbelly. "I'll do my best. Thanks for the save."

They'd jumped to high orbit a few thousand kilometers outside Ginnungagap's failing atmosphere. Malfar's *Crimson Tide* blinked into real space a scant few kilometers away, venting off a similar nimbus of smoke. Far beyond that, dozens of Asgardian warships loomed, their blockade formation crawling with hundreds of smaller support craft, and plenty more on the way from insystem. Nate couldn't focus on that yet. Was too busy scanning the planet below, chest tight. He relaxed a touch as he found what he was looking for, Ex pinging the exact location: the *Camelot*, reading safe and fully loaded, climbing steadily out of Ginnungagap's gravity well by more conventional means.

He didn't have long to celebrate—or even to open a comms line—before Ginnungagap collapsed in full.

Even there, watching from the front row seats, it was almost impossible to wrap his head around the amount of mass in motion. The planet practically imploded, the crumbling sphere folding in on itself, great hunks of land and crust ripping free on catastrophic momentum only to come bending back around to extinction-level impacts as they failed to escape their dying planet's gravity.

"Jesus," he whispered, watching with a sheer, terrible awe that even Ex shared to some extent.

An entire world's surface, turned inside out in less than a minute.

Ginnungagap had hardly been a hospitable place. Certainly not a friendly one. But it had had a beauty of its own. A purity in the ferocious life that had called it home. And now, from that place of ferocious life, nothing remained but one ungodly apex predator, emerging first by one enormous, aggregated hand, then another. Something like a head followed, still forming as it pulled itself out of the chaos of its own creation. A planet-sized golem, rising from the ashes of the world it had just swallowed whole.

The comms pinged from the *Camelot*. Nate couldn't pry his eyes away as the thing stretched its colossal limbs, broad, bulbous chest coming alive with a smoldering red energy.

"Nate?"

"Tess," he gasped, latching onto that voice, using it to anchor himself back to the world where he was more than some awestruck bystander.

"Thank Christ you're okay," she said.

"Took the words right out of my mouth," he agreed, checking the *Camelot*'s position on his HUD—hardly in the clear, but at least still gaining distance at a good clip. "It's good to hear your voice, Tess."

"Well then here's another one, Romeo..."

"What the hell are we supposed to do about that thing?" Nate guessed aloud.

"Nailed it in one. Might have a suggestion, though."

"I'm all ears."

"Docs tell me we still have a few pieces of that monument stuff aboard."

"Monument stuff?"

"You didn't...?"

He read the hesitation in her voice. Sensed some deeper question lurking there.

"Something in that monument was... I don't know," she pushed on. "But there was—"

"A Beacon shard," Nate finished, remembering what Ex had felt in the moments before Jaeger's detonation.

"Yeah. And whatever it was doing in there seemed to be like... Archon kryptonite, or something."

He watched those moments replaying in his mind's eye. The way Jaeger's pod had seemed to weathered the storm in Nate's feverish vision of its spire approach, parting the swarm as if protected by the Lady's own divine hand. The load of seemingly worthless debris Tristan had blown out of the rear hatch along with the warhead. The look on Jaeger's face as he'd uttered those last words. The buried emotion in Tessa's voice now.

"That..."

*Explains a few pieces, perhaps,* Ex finished.

Nate only half heard. There were a million questions he wanted to ask. How they'd even realized there was anything special about the monument. How he and Ex had missed a freaking Beacon shard sitting right under their combined nose. Why Jaeger had done what he'd done. But there wasn't time for any of it right then.

Especially not as the Asgardian fleets opened fire with wild abandon.

"Oh shit," he muttered, as the hail of torpedos and plasma fire crossed the black sea of space.

"Oh, shit!" Tessa agreed, like she'd just caught sight of what was happening.

For a second, Nate could only watch as the first wave hit, a rapid string of detonations peppering their way across the Archon's enormous surface, spewing superheated clouds of scorched earth and slagged stone into space to no noticeable effect. Then the thing ate an entire cadre of antimatter torpedoes in a sizzling red flash, drinking them in as if any matter, anti or otherwise, would do for a snack. And that settled that.

"Get their C.O. on the comms and tell them to back off," he growled. "Until we have a plan, I don't want that thing going full—"

*Full aggro,* he was about to say, when the Archon flashed forward from the listing ruins of Ginnungagap with impossible speed, and obliterated half the Asgardian fleet in the blink of an eye.

"Get them the hell out of here!" Nate snapped. As if anyone could've. The rest of the fleet—those several dozen massive warships that hadn't disappeared in a single explosive flash—were already firing every thruster they had, pulling redline evasive maneuvers with all the speed of stirring icebergs, their entourage of support vessels scattering around them like schools of frightened minnows. Nate held helplessly to his perch on the *Kalnythian Wilds* as Iveera laid on the acceleration. Off in the portside distance, he saw the *Crimson Tide* angling around in kind, both of them clearly intending to engage.

On some level—the same one that couldn't even begin to comprehend how that much mass had just translocated itself across twenty-some-thousand kilometers in less than a second—he wasn't sure what the hell they hoped to accomplish with their quaint little Knightships. But they had to try. Or so he told himself, right up until the *Wilds* shoved him off with an unexpected jab of a manipulator arm.

"Give me space and get those ships clear, Nathaniel," was all Iveera offered by way of explanation. He might've been offended or indignant, had he still possessed the necessary faculties, but her meaning became clear quickly enough as the *Kalnythian Wilds* began to break apart, disassembling, changing in mid-flight.

"Malfar," she added, as the *Wilds'* transformation began to take shape, faded orange hull reworking itself into extending limbs, the entire ship seeming to grow on the fly, as if it were pulling significant mass and extra parts from e-dim, "prepare to unleash your singularity weapon."

"Too close to the sun," the Troglodan replied, admirably cool for the gravity of the request, and the full fleet being handily decimated in front of them. "System won't last a year. Might not even last a month."

"The system won't last an hour if we don't end this blackened thing," Iveera shot back. "The First Knight himself has already cleared the order. Unless either of you has a more viable solution…"

"Drive it into the sun," Malfar offered.

*Obviously*, Ex murmured.

"I intend to try," Iveera replied, as if she'd thought the solution equally obvious. Then she threw herself and her enormous *Kalnythian Wilds* avatar at the Archon, drawing its attention with an opening salvo that nearly dismembered one of its dreadnought-sized forearms.

"The Asgardians, Nathaniel," she added, flashing clear as the Archon reclaimed its limb with a flurry of reaching swarm tendrils, then fired back with an enormous ruby red blast and a swinging fist that might've cratered a lesser planet.

"And you, Ser Malfar," Iveera continued, strain creeping into her voice as the transformed *Wilds* danced back in around the colossus, blasting holes the size of city blocks. "This grav sling is hardly going to wind itself."

"Aye, Ser Katanaga," the Troglodan rumbled, with a clear note of begrudging admiration.

It was only by Ex's contextual markings on the HUD that Nate even perceived the grav traps and modified titanwire filaments she'd apparently been firing from the *Wilds'* magnetic accelerators as she went. He was too busy gathering his wits and gunning his thrusters to tease out what she was up to.

Then again, he wasn't all that sure what *he* was up to, either.

The Asgardians might've been warriors, but they weren't suicidal. Most of the fleet was either obliterated or already beating a full retreat, with few in-betweeners remaining, and the Archon could hardly be troubled to pay the Asgardian ships any mind at all, focused as it was on the comparatively small but impressively devastating Gorgon Knightship blinking around at ungodly speeds and peppering it with oversized craters like an overpowered yet ultimately ineffectual bug.

It wasn't hard to figure out where Nate should be throwing his weight.

He reached for Tessa's comms, thinking to set the *Camelot* on task clearing the stragglers. A flare of ruby brilliance and a sharp, sickened pang in his gut yanked him up short, as he shielded his darkened faceplate with a raised arm.

"Blackened hands," Iveera groaned over their combat channel, voice thick with pain.

Nate saw why a second later, first squinting at the HUD, then staring dumbly as the retina-seared afterimage began to resolve into a clear picture. The Archon had finally caught that blindingly fast bug.

The thing had slagged the better half of the *Kalnythian Wilds* clean out of existence.

"Iveera?" Nate gasped, staring dumbly at the listing remains of the ship, waiting for the Gorgon to brush it off and tell them she was okay. Tell them what came next. The new plan. Except most of the hectic trap they'd been stringing together had been slagged to shit, too, he realized. And as the Archon turned its massive head toward the distant wink of Asgard, Nate knew in his heart that there was no new plan. Not a damn thing they could do to contain its power. Nothing but—

"The singularity device," Iveera rasped over the comms. "Do it, Malfar."

"Very well," came the Troglodan's grave reply.

Nate relayed word to Tess via Cammy to get what survivors they could out of the vicinity and clear the hell out themselves. He teetered on the edge of the thrusters then, caught between rushing over to help the evacuation or sticking around to make sure Malfar's grav bomb found its way straight to the bastard's glowing red heart.

The *Kalnythian Wilds* shifted on his HUD, fairly quivering with the effort of trying to pull itself back together as the Archon drifted closer, silent and massive. Iveera silent on the comms as well. Nate made his call and kicked off toward his fellow Knights, not even a little bit sure what his plan was— only that time was short, Malfar's *Crimson Tide* speeding for the Archon's back at full burn, dipping beneath one massive swinging arm as it rounded on him. Juking a fleury of swarming nanite tendrils with more deft grace than Nate would've given the Troglodan credit for. Rolling clear of another furious column of ruby energy.

Nate drew up short of the *Wilds* as he registered the infinitesimally small something that'd split off from the *Crimson Tide* on his HUD at the ship's last maneuver. Ex confirmed it an instant later, zooming their helmet view in on the the unobtrusive little canister tumbling straight in for the Archon's glowing chest along the ship's original flight path, by all appearances just another minuscule bit of space junk.

It started like a more concentrated version of Ginnungagap's collapse— that luminescent red sun at the center of the Archon's torso simply imploding as the singularity device initiated. Nate watched in rapt fascination as the colossal Archon went rigid, unknown kilotons of ruby rock folding in upon itself instantaneously, distantly aware that it was over.

Distantly aware, in effect, that he'd just witnessed the beginning of the end of Asgard.

He felt sick.

There was good reason the use of singularity devices was explicitly forbidden anywhere near inhabited systems. There was no stopping it now. Even having left Jaeger with one of the doomsday weapons back down on the planet, he'd prayed it wouldn't come to this.

But at least the bastard was finished, now, once and for all.

"Burn in hell," he whispered at the convulsing planet of a titan, thinking, for one long moment, only of Jaeger.

*Nathaniel...*

He tensed at Ex's tone, eyes darting from the spectacle ahead to the highlighted readings on the HUD. Strange readings. Getting stranger. Some kind of gravitational anomaly like nothing he'd ever seen—not even back at Old Avalon, when the Clan Groshna war party had said to hell with the conventions and unleashed the singularity initiator they never should've had in the first place. On later review, that footage had been breathtaking in its own right. But this…

*What the hell's it doing in there, Ex?*

He felt Ex crunching the question. Was pretty sure he felt the gist of the answer, too, even before Ex finished his formal analysis. When his companion spoke, it was with a kind of slow, muted awe.

*I do believe it's trying to eat a black hole.*

No sooner had he said it than, several thousand kilometers away, the Archon set its massive shoulders, bracing like it'd just taken on some great weight, and Nate watched in disbelief as the collapsing vortex at the center of its chest simply snapped to a dead standstill—frozen in time like a photo negative of a dying star.

"Ex?" he whispered to the empty silence as, bit by bit, the very edges of that frozen anomaly began to squirm and vibrate free, flowing the wrong direction. Ex's voice was grim.

*I think we're going to need a bigger bomb.*

# CHAPTER 42

# AZMODEUS

"Why won't this thing just fucking *die?*" Nate growled, watching in helpless frustration as the shuddering edges of the black star at the Archon's core continued to reanimate in exactly the wrong direction.

*I believe I did tell you it's not technically alive,* Ex replied. *Still,* he pressed on, before Nate could snap back, *it's a neat trick, to be sure.*

They watched as Malfar's last ditch anti-matter potshots disappeared into the void, only to be absorbed and kick its unnatural expansion into overdrive.

*'If you can't beat them, join them,' and all that,* Ex added halfheartedly.

*This thing's about to eat an entire fucking system, Ex,* Nate pointed out, as the *Crimson Tide* cut its losses and circled back around to collect the drifting wreck of Iveera's slagged ship.

*Well, I'm at a loss, Nathaniel. You know I use humor to cope.*

Nate looked from the Archon out to the distant *Camelot* and the rest of the fleeing Asgardian fleet, practically smelling the panic in the ranks. Their world doomed. The very rule of natural law in doubt.

*Black humor, then,* Ex amended. *Egad. Sue me.*

"Never mind my ship," Iveera growled over their shared comms, voice rough. Nate spotted her a second later, crawling out from the wreck of the *Wilds* and waving off the *Crimson Tide*'s incoming tow. "We need to knock it off balance."

"Destabilize its defenses," Malfar said, like he was turning over the potential outcomes.

Nate was too distracted by the way the fleeing warships seemed to be slowing, slowing, beginning to drift back in, toward the Archon. Nate felt the pull too, then. Felt the panic building on his own distant ship.

"Overload its control before that black hole evaporates completely," Iveera concluded.

Control.

Something about the word snagged at Nate's mind, tugging him back. Something Lundquist had said about the nanoswarm's seemingly small size back on Ginnungagap. Something about what it seemed to suggest about the potential limits of swarm control. Of course, the sheer goddamn size of the colossus currently noshing down on a black hole in front of them seemed to throw that all out the window, right along with the baby and the bathwater. But then… maybe…

"Nate?"

Tessa's voice.

He hadn't even noticed himself reaching to open comms with the *Camelot*. He supposed he'd meant to find Lundquist, get a second opinion on the erratic mess of a plan suddenly attempting to form in his mind. Just as quickly, though, he realized there was as little point to that as there was time to dawdle. They'd crossed firmly into the land of unknown unknowns five exits back. Ex didn't even have a fair guess. And Malfar was already circling back around for another attack run on the dormant Archon.

Iveera was always telling him to trust his instincts, wasn't she?

"Tess," he said, making his decision, reaching to Cammy to begin the requisite adjustments.

"Yeah," she confirmed, sounding distracted. "You seeing this, by the way? Christ, am *I* seeing this?"

"Only if it looks like we're in trouble. But listen, there should be—"

He faltered, feeling it in his sideways stomach as much as he heard it in Tessa's sucked breath and the sharp upward shift of fleetwide chatter. Whatever the Archon was doing, the effect was peaking—half a fleet of capital warships suddenly caught in the swell, mighty engines straining against gravity, bleeding velocity. Even past his suit's compensators, Nate felt his organs shifting with the weight of it. Saw the nearest ships beginning to drift backward.

Then the *Crimson Tide* hit the Archon with a full spectrum barrage right in the side of the head, earning itself a brilliant ruby jab of return fire, and the field broke, releasing Nate's innards and the fleeing fleets all back into normal motion.

"Right," Tessa muttered under her breath. "Well, holy shit, then."

"Yeah," Nate agreed, fetching his bearings. Off in the distance, he spotted Iveera manually shoving her entire ship and its feebly sputtering engines off after the fleets before whirling and speeding off to help Malfar in person.

"Listen," he tried again, "there should be a small—"

"What the—" she murmured, apparently seeing what he already felt through Cammy.

"—a small slot appearing on your console," he finished anyway.

"No, yeah, hadn't noticed," she shot back. "Didn't like this beautiful layout of mine anyway. Follow-up question, though: Am I drunk, or is that thing *supposed* to be making a black hole its bitch out there?"

She was rattled. He heard it in her voice. And understandably so, all things considered. But even past the filtering on her mic, or maybe simply by merit of his mental connection with Cammy, he could feel that same insidious panic creeping through the *Camelot*'s bridge. Enough that he knew they needed to nip it in the bud.

"The slot, Tess," he said, simultaneously attempting to lay firing solutions with Ex and Cammy and also wondering who the hell he thought he was, coaxing *anyone* to get their shit together—much less the very same veteran who'd not so long ago found him floundering in a sea of his own hissy fits back in State College. When she spoke again, though, he heard the edge of control in her voice.

"Christ. Even in end times, it's all about the slot, isn't it?"

He felt the faintest tug of another creeping distortion beginning to build from where the Archon was sluggishly blasting and swatting away at the pestering Knights, attempting to maintain its fixation on its black hole dessert. Tessa must've felt it to.

"Fine," she pushed on. "How can I and my *slot* help you with… Hmm."

Nate roused from the final touches of his work with Ex and Cammy to figure out why she'd stopped speaking and saw she'd tapped Cammy's schematics, tracing the temporary path he'd just coaxed into existence through her innards, leading right to the capsule Cammy had just prepared in one of her port mag launchers.

"Well, I hate to disappoint you, cowboy," she said, apparently getting the gist, "but I'm all out of Granny's Magic Archon Killer Pellets over here. Unless you want me to lock and load my cheery disposition—"

"I need you to feed me one of those monument rocks."

"But—" A consternated huff as she turned that over, double time. "I'm not sure they're functional without Beacon juice, Nate. Christ, I'm not sure they're even functional at all. We don't even—"

"I've got it covered," Nate said. "I think. Just… Just stick it in the slot and let me handle the rest, will you?"

"Hoo! And me sitting here, thinking you'd never ask."

The comment sent a sharp flutter of *something* jolting through the already frantic bundle of nerves in his chest. He eyed the Knight v. Archon lightshow in the distance as Tessa snapped a few off-comms orders, muttering something in between about *end times*. Apprehensive impatience, more than any conscious decision, summoned a video feed on the HUD to show him what was going on back there.

"Well I'll be damned," Tessa said, as she came into view, flanked by a frazzled-looking Snuffy and Lundquist—and, to Nate's genuine surprise, an extremely shifty Vampire Bob.

"Looks like we've got the tip of the spear here, of all things," Tessa continued, inspecting the fragment Lundquist handed her. She glanced up as Nate allowed his holo likeness to appear over her console in miniature.

"Well, that feels kind of ironic," Nate said.

"Tell me about it," she said, touching the ancient stone to her brow in salute, then holding it over the custom receptacle with a questioning look. "You ready for all five inches, Mr. Knight?"

"Guess we'll find out."

"Nate…"

He wiped his face clear of whatever had crept onto it. "I'll be careful."

She blew out an *as-if* huff, narrowing her eyes. "Don't even think about it," she said, sliding the strange bit of stone home. It was only once it was in that she bit her lip, bravado wavering as she glanced around the bridge almost conspiratorially, and leaned in closer. "Just come back alive, okay?"

To his surprise, she clicked the line to standby before he could say a word.

"Guys," he said, toggling back over to Iveera and Malfar, and forcing himself to screw his head on tight. He began accelerating. "I think I might have something."

"How promising," Malfar rumbled.

"What do you need, Nathaniel?" Iveera asked, her tone less openly sarcastic but only slightly less strained by the heat of battle. It was easy to see why. Ahead, in the black grave of Ginnungagap, their battle with the Archon was intensifying, the construct's attention waking in full to the two

Knights blasting away at it. It seemed like a bad sign that the process at the core of its black star chest only seemed to be accelerating despite the fact.

Nate pushed his own acceleration higher, coming around to their planned heading. "Just keep that bastard's attention pinned down for a minute?"

Malfar just gave a vaguely incredulous harrumph, like *'the hell else you think we're doing over here?*

"Strike true, Ser Knight," was all Iveera said.

Only one thing left to do, then.

*All right, girl,* Nate thought to Cammy, laying the speed on in earnest now, giving his flight path freely to Ex's fine-tuning nudges. *Hit us.*

He felt her moving to comply—felt time stretching around them, space expanding out into that strange, mechanical flavor of abstraction it always acquired in deepening layers when he merged with Cammy. For a moment, the three of them were woven tight, three pieces of a whole, moving as one across thousands of kilometers—Cammy taking aim, Nate accelerating, Ex weaving the requisite construct down from e-dim. Crosshairs all aligning.

Then Cammy fired, and it all happened at once.

Fast as he was already moving, Nate actually saw the hyperkinetic capsule speeding up on his ass in the HUD rearview. He managed to avoid clenching, trusting in Ex and Cammy, and was rewarded a scant instant later with a blurring burst of acceleration that, even despite Ex's on-the-fly armor modifications, nearly tore his arm out of the socket. His eyes caught up an instant later, just in time to catch the capsule shedding off from the end of his weapon on a puff of tiny maneuvering thrusters, leaving behind its ancient payload. For a moment, Nate eyed the seemingly mundane bit of stone now tipping his impromptu spear, hoping to Christ and all his pals it was indeed something more than that.

And maybe it wasn't. And maybe *he* wasn't. "Guy thought he was a Beacon," they'd say at his closed space casket funeral, Iveera, Dalnak, and Zedavian Kelkarin all disappointedly shaking their heads in the back. The Merlin cackling like an old drunk at the sheer audacity of the thing.

Nate opened the tank anyway. Set his distant sights on the Archon's enormous red non-face and kicked the thrusters into overdrive. He dug deep, and let the Light shine down. And whether or not he actually came anywhere close to emulating the energy signature of a genuine Beacon, or even a shard of one, he didn't have the faintest clue. But the thing at the tip of his spear—whatever it was—drank it all up like an arid desert.

He flew on, approaching the Archon from behind, staggered by just how voraciously those unassuming five inches of arcane monument latched on, sucking up energy as fast as he could put it out. He felt Ex's surprise splashing against his own alarm, felt his friend's resolve as they wordlessly moved to adjust, striking a new balance between speed, shields, and keeping their new pet rock fed.

The shields dropped first out of necessity. Right about the same time the Archon caught scent of their approach, and began to turn—countless megatons of swarm and Ginnungagap's bones, whirling to swat him from space like the speck of a fly he was. Nate pushed on, vision darkening at the edges, trusting his gut. Trusting the Lady's grace. He felt her there, as he gave himself over to it. Her strength in his spear arm. Her Light in his veins, guiding him. He'd never felt it so surely.

Never seen such a breathtakingly gigantic arm moving so unbelievably fast, straight for him.

All that mass, just for him.

The word *pulverize* rang unpleasantly to mind, doubt catching on its syllables, jarring his resolve. Panic cresting at the sight of that rushing continent coming to crush him, screaming at him to budge.

Then a brilliant wall of white-hot energy split the black of space, ripping into the Archon's arm—a joint attack from Iveera and the *Crimson Tide*, some dispassionate observer noted in the back of his head—blasting clean through. Nate sped on, breathless as the gargantuan limb went racing past, close enough to shave and fast enough to liquefy his every organ. He ignored the rush of nanoswarm tendrils flooding out after it—to meet him or to recover the lost limb, he didn't know. He simply pointed the spear, throwing his everything behind it. Time stretching, bending on gravitonic dilation, then shuddering in hectic fits and bouts as his flight path took him a bit too close to whatever was happening in the Archon's black star heart.

In the last split second, he knew by the slow, searing pulses of light and the odd, muted *whoomph*s of half-sound gushing through what thin traces of atmos still clung to the Archon's gravity, that Malfar and Iveera were giving the exoconstruct holy hell back there. He also had some remote inkling that the spear seemed to be working, judging by the azure radiance flowing through it, and the thick trail of listless nanites scattering like so much space dust in his wake.

By that point, though, it hardly mattered.

By that point, he was moving faster than he'd ever moved under his own power. Arm and shoulder locked in place by some unbreakable combination of suit hardware, resolute muscle, and Ex's own grim spirit. By that point, in a very real way, he was simply along for the ride. A spear in his own right, wielded by the hand of the Lady.

Then the blazing aura at the tip of his spear met the fiery chaos of the exoconstruct's glowing non-face, and the world exploded in a blinding scream of pure, violent radiance. It engulfed him, ripping into him, overloading any coherent perception of worldly events until a deep, shuddering impact smacked him to a halt a brief instant later, and the onslaught of light receded. Even as fast as he'd been moving, he could scarcely believe he'd reached center mass of the Archon's continent-sized head so quickly.

But there, staring back at him from the shadows on the thrumming blade end of his spear, was the Archon. The *true* Archon—the same ruthless automaton who'd tormented him in the cave, jittering red false-face flickering in pale imitation of a stricken, wide-eyed human face.

*His* face.

Nate barely had time to register any of these facts—or the way the spear trembled in his hands, vibrations and heat building from the Archon's pierced chest—before the spear tip shattered in a burst of azure light, and the universe swallowed them whole.

He saw more than he knew what to do with, then. More than his mind could process. A raw, screaming rush of sight and sound, and something beyond words. Astral bodies soaring through spacetime, connected. An overwhelming multitude. Unbridled infinity, tearing through his mind. Another there with him. The swarms moving as one. Bright, mortal planets and mighty doorways quivering before them. The Light. The Light. The Lady's Light, and the Lady herself, weeping and ragged, beside herself in tatters. Reaching for him. Whispering his name, and another's. And through it all, another there with them. Through it all, he saw the Archon, and he knew the being more intimately than ever he could've, even as it'd torn into his flesh with its prying manipulators, baring his insides out.

*Azmodeus.*

The word reverberated through his brain, sending ripples through the scream of visions, and the construct snapped forward, gripping him by the throat, no longer just a construct. Something fuller, here in the miasmic shadows of this phantom place. Something infinitely more terrible. A force of nature, of darkness, clutching at his very soul, preparing to drag him down with it.

He took hold of those clawing roots, some dull part of him too shocked and fried to be afraid. Felt Ex solidifying beside him to help pry away yet more tendrils of darkness. He felt the unexpected strength in his hands, the afterimage of the Lady burning in his mind. The soft breeze of her voice whispering his name, and another's. Calling them back.

This wasn't real.

Not as real as the place where he'd just driven an arcane spear of Light through this blackened thing's heart, at least.

"Best show *him* that," Ex grunted beside him, struggling with two unruly handfuls of surging darkness.

Not real. The Lady's voice, whispering their name. Calling them back. The creeping weight of this phantom place, rolling over him, crushing his lungs until he couldn't breathe. Not real.

Not real.

And holding that thought firmly in place like a talisman against the darkness, Nate struck out and smote Azmodeus with a wordless cry, shattering the spell.

# CHAPTER 43

# AS THE KNIGHT FLIES

Mute, weary satisfaction filled Nate as the phantom place bent and broke all around them, collapsing the Archon's hellish scream down to nothing. They snapped back to real space with a disconcerting jolt, dark space and flashing weapons fire visible through the gaping wreck of a tunnel Nate had apparently blasted through the Archon's enormous exoconstruct head on the way in.

No sooner had he gained his bearings than that colossal exoconstruct shuddered with a full-body death rattle, and promptly began to collapse in earnest, succumbing to the hungry black hole still raging in its chest.

Succumbing too quickly, he registered, as whatever effect Azmodeus had exerted on the growing singularity likewise died, and Nate found himself suddenly ripping down a gravity well like nothing he'd ever felt, sucked along with the rest of the deluge like ice to the blender. He stepped on the gravitonics, lost for direction in the flood of collapsing matter, already too close to fight it. He felt Ex attempting to modulate the gravitational effects. Too little, too late. Nate bent their course, moving more on feel than by any visual cue, thinking to slingshot past the hole, break orbit from the hectic storm on the far side. But the fields were shifting too quickly, the mass piling on too fast.

He felt their course bending. A moment of terrible realization. An inane flashback to the first time he'd fallen off his bike at the ripe age of eight, and realized in slow-motion horror that there was nothing he could do before impact. No stopping it. No catching himself.

They'd stopped moving. Started drifting backward. Gravity twisting him around, stretching him out like some medieval torture rack. Fiery pain through his upper body, less pronounced in the legs. Nothing at all below the knees. He had to look down to make sure his feet were even still there. Nearly slipped up completely at the sight that greeted him.

*Hold on, damn you,* Ex growled, as Nate gaped at the bizarre spectacle of his unnaturally stretched legs, and the solid wall of pure, unfathomable blackness creeping up for them. *Only a moment longer, and—*

But Nate lost it, the pull growing too strong for his shocked body to resist.

They dipped frighteningly fast. Or maybe not at all. The signals were too confused—space and time, his entire body, all confused—but for the certainty that he was falling, one way or another, into oblivion.

Of all things, he thought of his parents in that moment, sitting in a silent stupor at the dining room table as Iveera broke the news to them over untouched cups of steaming tea, Copernicus sniffing curiously at the Gorgon's leg. He saw it clearly as if he were sitting there with them. Then the inevitable yanked him back to reality—where a copper-armored hand had just caught onto his wrist with bone-crushing strength.

Iveera.

He could've cried for relief had his lungs possessed the requisite air to do so. He didn't seem to be breathing anymore. That seemed concerning. But he was entirely more focused on Iveera. Too far away. Her arm strangely stretched. The space behind her *wrong* somehow. A short yet impossibly long corridor of darkness, capped on the end with only the faint hint of distant stars gone loopy and streaked to strange blurs far beyond. He felt—maybe heard—Iveera shouting something as tiny manipulators peeled from the armor at her wrist and darted down to his, melding them together, but it came out all wrong, all garbled and shifted. He tried to open his mouth, tried to tell her to say it again, and found he didn't have the strength to lift his tongue from the floor of his mouth, never mind the air to speak. He barely had the strength to close his own jaw.

*Ummm.*

His eyes moved like chalked Atlas stones under five-hundred gravities, shifting to where Ex's ghostly apparition had appeared riding the storm beside him, arms crossed, the slender fingers of one hand pinching thoughtfully at his pointy chin as he considered whatever he saw below them with a consternated frown. Nate toggled the HUD rearview in favor of looking back and inviting gravity to rip his tilted head off. His torso was already screaming as if it were about to tear clean in two, and—

*Wait. No, that's perfect!* Ex cried, with a victorious snap of the fingers. *Just like...*

*Just. Like. What?!* Nate growled through the mental equivalent of clenched teeth, eyeing the approaching darkness of the event horizon.

*Oh, never mind that,* Ex cooed, ghostly apparition elbowing into his side. *Just move over.*

He didn't quite register the meaning of those last words until Ex pushed deeper, moving in like he intended to go for full-on possession. Nate just set the heebie-jeebies aside and let it happen. He didn't know what his friend intended, but by that point it seemed enough of a miracle that Ex was even keeping his brain from liquefying.

*Jesus, take the wheel,* Ex agreed, prying open the armored fingers of Nate's clenched fist.

Above, Iveera was casting out her grav whip in strange slow motion, snagging an enormous and equally slow hunk of collapsing exoconstruct just before it sped up past Nate and went plunging into the blackness of the event horizon, dragging the whip with it. He felt a moment of panic for her, quickly washed out by the sight of his own freakishly distended legs reaching for the blackness of their own accord, and the indeterminate cluster of junk suddenly jettisoning out of Ex's e-dim stores to join it, tethered to their open palm by a heavily braided cable of titanwire.

He didn't understand what in the holy hell either of them were doing. Couldn't do much more than watch in morbid fascination as his warping legs distended too far, practically touching that unfathomable wall of blackness. The pain, oddly absent. Terror spiking like a wild animal in his chest.

He looked to Iveera, silently begging for help—utterly at her mercy. The look in her eyes, though, was plain enough.

*Break free now, or we both die.*

He set the rest aside. Felt Ex tensing alongside him in preparation. And then they all heaved, together. Iveera pulling with all her considerable strength. All of them tethered to the very black hole they were trying to escape, for reasons he couldn't comprehend. The stars blurred overhead. All of it spooling in a chaotic mess. He focused on Iveera. Focused on her slowly normalizing proportions, taking them as a sign that it was working —that centimeter by agonizing centimeter, they were winning.

Right up until Ex murmured a guilty, *Oops*, and it dawned on him that the other alternative was not that they were escaping, so much as that Iveera was being pulled in with them. He tried to hold that thought at bay. Tried to keep fighting.

Then Ex piped up with an uncertain, *This might pinch a little*, and pain blossomed like an ancient memory, something giving way down where his legs were supposed to be, right at the same time that an unexpected wallop of energy smacked into him, and Iveera's voice cried out with a strangely warped, "Now!"

Nate kicked the questions out of mind, and ripped away from the black hole with everything he had. Ripped away like a wild animal fleeing a trap. Leaving a part of itself behind. Pulled a thousand light-years across mere meters of space.

Something in that thought sparked sheer, bottomless terror. Flits of the Archon's visions flashing through his mind like bright red alarm lights, wobbling drunkenly as Iveera yanked harder, his thrusters firing absent his fading control. Something in the space brightening, darkening, kaleidoscoping in and out.

Something...

SPACE DECOMPRESSED. Exploded. Sprung into an endless abyss, dilating until, strangely enough, his reeling mind started to actually make sense of it again. Or to register it, at least. Sense... sense was harder.

He scanned for clues.

Stars and ships—a lot of ships, too many ships—and a dying sun. Iveera, hauling him along. Dull pain in his right knee, tight and throbbing, as they cleared the *Camelot*'s main ventral magseal, touched down to the deck. Something not right. Out of order. Seriously wrong.

He spilled out like a limp fish the instant she let go, the rest punching in on impact.

The Archon. The event horizon.

He'd passed out.

Flits of hectic visions. Death and destruction in the skies of—

"Iveera," he groaned, trying to push himself up. Struggling even to string two thoughts together. Odd that she hadn't caught him. Odd, the way she was standing there, looking, for all things, as if she were in shock.

"Iveera, the swarm," he choked out. Iveera didn't *do* shock. Needed to listen. "The relay. The—Vanaheim." He shook his head, trying to clear the floating haze of discombobulation, but it only made things worse. "Vanaheim… not a misfire. A test. It was—"

*It's too late, Nathaniel.*

"What?" He planted his hands and tried to push himself up to his feet, woozy and drained. The movement sparked more insistent fire in his right leg, head spinning with the urgent certainty that they needed to moved—needed to get to Yggdrasil. Dead Archon or not, it wasn't over. Except…

"Nate?" someone gasped.

He looked up, found the *Camelot*'s crew pouring into the cargo hold. Something wrong. Not just the looks of shock and open disbelief. Some ripple of detail.

"No, we have to—"

They were staring at him like they couldn't believe it. Beyond stunned.

"—the Archon's relay." He forced himself up, clamping a useless hand to his helmet and squinting through the blaring pain of his scrambled brain. "I think—I think it could've been—We need to get to—What?"

He couldn't ignore those looks. The open staring. The way Snuffy and Ramachandra had clamped their hands over their gaping mouths. The haunted look in Tessa's liquor-glazed eyes.

"We need to get to the Y-Sec relay," he heard himself whisper, even as Ex's words finally caught up to him.

"It's gone, Nathaniel," came Iveera's flat voice behind him.

The crew, staring at him. Those looks. Like they'd seen a ghost. Like he'd risen from the dead.

He turned to Iveera. Her back was still facing him, head bowed, jin drooped.

"Yggdrasil was destroyed weeks ago," she said quietly. "The relay, too."

"What are you saying?" He pulled off his helmet, feeling sick. Somewhere in the raw, aching vicinity of all this, he realized his right foot was missing, the boot filled by Ex's own hastily cobbled prosthetic, which his friend was currently darting to help his fried brain accept. Tor and Elmo had appeared at Nate's sides, like they fully expected he was about to eat deck for a second time. He clutched Elmo's arm for balance, feeling drunk. And that's when he saw it. Their clothes. Their faces. Washed and changed. Fed and recovered. Not the dirty tatters of the crew that'd just clawed their way off of a collapsing Ginnungagap.

"Someone tell me what the hell's going on."

They all watched him, seemingly unable to speak.

"We've been fighting our way out of that black hole for twenty-seven days, Nathaniel," Iveera said, turning to him with a look of weary, ashen defeat like he'd never seen on her before. "The Alliance has already fallen."

# CHAPTER 44

# CHAIN OF COMMAND

"I don't understand," Nate said, several hours later, as he leaned wearily back from the holo display, and the recycled Yggdrasian footage he'd watched too many times now. It was far from the first time he'd said those three words since Iveera had hauled him aboard the *Camelot*, and they were becoming less true with each passing iteration.

He understood perfectly well, by then, what'd happened.

Well enough for the parts that mattered, at least.

The mechanics of how he and Iveera had broken free back at the event horizon might've still escaped him. He'd been too dazed and exhausted to follow Lundquist's somber-yet-scientifically-giddy gibbering about mass transfers, and ergospheric negative energies, and how it was all beautifully in line with Sir Roger Penrose's predictions about how advanced civilizations might one day harness energy from black holes—how that might've even been part of what the Archon had been attempting with the black hole in its chest, prior to its destruction at Nate's hand.

None of it really seemed to matter.

The harsh facts remained.

Twenty-seven days wasted, trying to pull his condensed carcass out of a black hole. Days that, from his perspective, had passed in mere seconds. And in those seconds, they'd lost everything.

Time debt.

Two words Nate had somehow deluded himself into thinking he'd never have to overly worry about, thanks to whatever fancy geometrical grav field trickery let them key up the crusher drives without fast-forwarding centuries into the future every time. He still couldn't wrap his head around it. Didn't need to, to appreciate the general outcome.

The Archon Azmodeus was dead—or obliterated, at least. In a just world, that might've felt like a win. Yet here they were, sitting in one dark corner of an Alliance that was no longer reachable by any meaningful stretch of the word. The Y-Sec relay, gone. The *Forge*, gone. The Council. The Merlin. The very beating heart of the Alliance.

All vanished without a trace.

That was the worst part of it all. The uncertainty. The dull buzz of emptiness where there should've been some voice of command—someone telling them what to do, where to go, who to help. But there was nothing.

He looked around the common room, only then noticing that, for the first time since this unfortunate recounting of theirs had begun, none of the crew had even bothered trying to step in at his latest *I don't understand*. Probably, they heard it all too well in his numb, defeated voice. No more hiding in the safe folds of reflexive disbelief. Not after seeing the scattered footage of the fall of Yggdrasil for the seventh or eighth time. The sheer, unfathomable *size* of the megaswarm that'd rolled through the system, chewing up planets as easily as the Archon's exoconstruct had demolished those Asgardian warships. The Archon Azmodeus might've been obliterated, but the bastard had unquestionably opened the gateway to hell before he'd gone.

It had always sounded like something of an impossibility to Nate, the challenge of actually holding the Synth incursion at the outer rim when even the smallest invading protoswarm stood to proliferate out of control. But now…

Now, there was no stopping them. Not in any way Nate could see. Not with that much Synth presence loose in the heart of Alliance space. Or ex-Alliance space, as it were. No way to stop them. No way to even reach them, without the relays. And Iveera was nowhere in sight to tell him otherwise— not that she *would* have, had she been there.

She'd retired to her mending ship not long after hauling Nate aboard the *Camelot*. Retired to rest, she'd said. To think. But the defeat in her drooping jin had been all too clear. She'd said she didn't blame him for what'd happened. Said that there was no way he could've known how to effectively counter spacetime curvature of that magnitude on the fly, and that all evidence pointed to the sad truth that they would've already been too late to save Yggdrasil or the relay even if he had.

Case in point, on Iveera's orders, Malfar had abandoned the collapsing Archon and gone racing off for the Y-Sec relay the instant the alarm had come sounding in from Yggdrasil, and he'd still only just arrived in time to witness the final moments of destruction—and apparently to go plunging through the dying relay along with the tail end of that killer swarm, according to what scattered reports they'd gathered.

They still hadn't heard from Malfar, but something—some tenuous whisper of Light or faith—told Nate he would've felt it if the Troglodan had died in the jump. Maybe it was just wishful thinking.

Either way, he couldn't help but wonder, for the ten-thousandth time, how differently things might've turned out if he'd simply managed to see the Archon's true plan sooner. If it'd occurred to his thick-skulled brain that maybe, just maybe, it wasn't some misfire fluke of the Archon's device that'd "accidentally" scattered a fragmented protoswarm across multiple Y-Sec systems, but rather something more like a calibration of the thing's developing sights. Because what better way to open a door right into the enemy's backyard than to build one that didn't even need to physically *be* in that yard, but rather three or four plots over?

It all seemed so clear in hindsight. So inevitable.

Proxy Beacons and long-range relays. That damned arcane monument, sitting right under his nose all along.

Jaeger.

Nate swallowed, eyes stubbornly tracing to the empty armchair before he could stop them. Jaeger's chair. The one no one had even thought about sitting in, as they'd filtered into the common room. The worn gray fabric a palpable weight in his chest, on the room at large. No one had said his name since Nate had come to. Nothing but *the colonel*, and even that only sparingly. Like Jaeger's ghost was standing there among them and no one wanted to be the first to point it out. Or maybe it was simply that no one thought Nate was ready to handle the blame in the midst of everything else. And maybe they were right.

His gaze shifted to Tor standing vigilant watch in the corner, his thoughts flicking to Tristan. She'd refused to accept Nate's apologies for her partner's death. Had only insisted that Tristan had seen his duty through to the end, and that there was no higher mark of honor or fulfillment for a warrior of the Round Table. Duty and honor aside, though, Nate still couldn't help but wonder if she blamed him on some level for her compatriot's death, much as he feared the crew blamed him—and rightfully so—for Jaeger's.

The entrance of Amelia and Gendra the Gorgon to the common room dragged him back to the present before his mind could go spiraling down that particular wormhole again. The two wore an air that said they'd just been through another round of comms tag with the New Powers of Y-Sec, such as they were.

"They're... still wanting to speak with you out there," Amelia said, looking slightly apologetic about the fact.

"High King Kelkarin has made it quite clear he will neither leave til he's had word with you, nor wait much longer for an audience," Gendra added, her countenance slightly rankled.

"An audience," Nate echoed, eyeing the blockade of Eldari and Asgardian ships that'd apparently been at a tense standoff with the *Camelot* and her crew ever since arriving to find that Nate and Iveera had vanished in time. "I'm guessing those are your words, not his?"

Gendra, not seeming to gather that Nate didn't actually give half a shit about the perceived pecking order here, looked uncertainly to Amelia.

The Atlantean pinched her brow in that delicate expression that had once reminded him of Gwen but had since taken on its own life. "He... may have been referring more to his own, um, gracious offer of extending an audience to *you*."

"Gracious," Nate echoed absentmindedly.

"So I'm told," Amelia confirmed. Despite everything, there was a slight glint of amusement in her eyes. "At any rate, he's demanded your immediate presence aboard the *Celestari Imperiatus*. Though he did, um"—her lips quirked a little—"*graciously* consent that a holo link would suffice if absolutely necessary."

"'Can just smell the graciousness from here," Ramirez muttered, drawing a round of appreciation from the room, and a few additional jabs at the royal Eldari's expense. It was the first hint of any good cheer Nate had seen since coming aboard. He was too caught up in his own little world to appreciate it. Too preoccupied wondering how best to deal with this new, utterly inane wrinkle.

*King* Phaldissus Kelkarin.

High King, even.

How, in all the unfortunate piles of shit in the universe, that one had come to pass, Nate hadn't had a chance to ascertain, nor did he especially care to. Callous as it felt to think, if half of what he'd seen and heard in the past hour were any indication of the state of the rest of the galaxy, one questionably deceased Eldari royal hardly stood out of the mess, but for the fact that his puffed up successor floated here now, ostensibly trying to make as if he and his fleet could actually bar the way to a Knightship, if Nate should choose to leave.

What the golden prick hoped to accomplish with this fresh round of rabble-rousing, Nate couldn't say. No more than he could fathom how the hell he was supposed to care about the squabbles of politicos like Phaldissus after everything that'd, in his mind, only just happened a few short hours ago—the dead remnants of Ginnungagap literally winking Hawking radiation at them from a few tiny million kilometers in the rearview. He didn't have the energy to think about any of this right now. But as he looked to Elsa, and saw the somber shadow she tried to play off as a trick of the light, he realized he'd better find it all the same.

"Okay," he said, starting to stand, then deciding it simply wasn't worth it. His foot and shin—lost in Ex's so-called *little pinch* back on the event horizon—had already more or less regrown but were still partially aided by Ex's prosthetic and itchy as all hell.

Plus, Phaldissus Kelkarin was a dickhead, and Nate was in no mood to pay homage to a dickhead right then, royal or otherwise.

"Put them on, Cammy," he said, turning back to the wide holo display on the wall.

The ship chirped a cheerful affirmative, the holo display flicking over to a connection standby screen. *King* Phaldissus Kelkarin appeared a moment later, situated at the head of a stupidly opulent, gold pillared room that was more grand hall than ship bridge. To Nate's incredulous surprise—perhaps at the fact that he could even still *feel* surprised, more than at the spectacle itself—the glib bastard was actually mounted on that freaking griffin of his, the beast decked to the neck feathers in stylishly detailed battle armor.

"Your... majesty." He didn't really mean the words to come out so blatantly disrespectful in tone, but nor did he especially care once it'd happened. "I'm told you wished to speak."

Phaldissus only half seemed to hear him. There was a moment of confusion on the other end. Shifting and scrambling somewhere off-screen. Phaldissus was clearly displeased. Maybe at having been made to wait this long. Maybe at the apparently unforgivable fact that he had to turn his feathered steed a few measly degrees to come full center in view, or at the distraction of the grizzled, well-outfitted Asgardian who stepped into the viewing field a moment later, moving with a hesitancy that seemed at odds with her stern military countenance, and took her place on the lower platform of the High King's dais.

"Ser Knight," Phaldissus finally said, settling into place and drawing up to his fullest height. "You have much for which to answer."

Somehow, Nate had thought he'd been ready to grin and bear a few hot puffs of pompous posturing, but the sound of the High King's chiding voice chafed like sandpaper on open wounds, washing over unexpectedly raw nerves, conjuring unwelcome flashes of heat and violence until Nate found his clenched fists on the verge of trembling. Even as he stared up at that proudly held, shit-eating fashion statement of a royal visage, a part of him was back again in the depths of Ginnungagap, splayed open on the Archon's razor-sharp rack. Jaeger's eyes holding his across time and space. Lips moving silently.

"Tell me what you want," he said, somewhere far away.

On the display, Phaldissus' lips curled at his tone. "It is not what *I* want, Ser Knight, but what justice and honor demand. You and your kind are meant to serve the people, and yet here we stand on the doorstep of a doomed planet, with nothing to show for it. You have failed in your duties, Ser Knight, and in doing so have allowed this… abomination, this so-called Archon, to bring untold damages on the very Alliance worlds you were meant to protect. You must answer for these failures. The people of Asgard must be made whole once more."

"I didn't realize you were such a great friend of the Asgardian people."

It was only as he said this that the grizzled Asgardian—the Grand Admiral Darma Feldenborn, Nate realized, as Ex pinged the insignia and pertinent details to his retinal HUD—finally stirred on the lower portion of Phaldissus' dais, rousing as if she meant to speak. Phaldissus pushed back in before she could get a word out.

"The House of Kelkarin is friend to any who should find themselves trodden underfoot by the tyranny of those who'd carelessly lord their divine powers over mere mortals. You are well aware you have committed a punishable war crime, Ser Knight, in engaging the use of a singularity device in an inhabited system. Which is why I must demand, from the outset, your admission of guilt, and your full apology to the Asgardian people."

For a long moment, all Nate could do was stare.

An apology.

A fucking *apology*?

Words and curtsies for blood and destruction.

Jaeger's wide eyes locked to his.

Was he fucking serious?

"Anything else, your highness?" he heard himself ask, his voice rough and barely above a whisper, guts churning with disgust. Somewhere off to the side, he heard the crew whispering concerned words. On-screen, Grand Admiral Darma was eyeing Phaldissus like she'd already known he was a moron but couldn't quite believe just how stupid he was actually turning out to be. Even so, there was no sympathy as her golden eyes fixed back on Nate. Only cold rage bubbling beneath the surface. Nate had more than enough to match.

"I have assured the people of Asgard," Phaldissus replied easily, leaning forward in his saddle with a shit-eating *glad you asked* kind of look about him, "that you and your Order will spare no resource or expense in aiding their relocation to a planet of their choosing. To which end, I have already offered the Grand Admiral the full and permanent gift of the most prosperous of our unsettled exoplanets for the purpose of rebuilding that which was doomed by your hand, Ser Knight."

Again, the Asgardian admiral shifted as if she might speak. Again, Phaldissus pressed on before she could.

"Lastly," he said, leaning further over his mount, the first hint of real anger creeping onto his face, "you will immediately and unconditionally release Elsavataryllianna Priatus from your service, and return her to my custody. She is the rightful Queen of Aesirheim, lest Supreme Chancellor Priatus should see fit to rise from the dead in the coming days, and she is still my betrothed besides. You have no right to confine her to this continued charade of indentured servitude."

That said, the High King sat back in his saddle, as if that were that. List complete. Beneath him, his griffin mount shifted, picking at the golden dais with armored talons. The rest of those in attendance waited in dead silence, both on the *Camelot* and there in the grand hall of the *Celestari Imperiatus*.

"Justice and honor," Nate said quietly, too weary and sickened to even bother sifting through the multitude of self-serving hypocrisies and outright lies the Eldari royal had just spilled out like god's gift to the universe. "That's awfully noble of you, Phaldissus."

The High King straightened on his mount, clearly indignant to the max at the blasé use of his given name, but Nate was already pushing on.

"I'm sure this is all nothing to do with the fact that you suddenly find yourself among powerful potential allies in need of an endearing favor, or that—"

"How dare you—"

"Or that the *betrothed* of whom you so carelessly speak, the very same one you openly called an Aesir whore—"

"You dare—

"—and threatened with matrimonial dissolution barely a month past, just so happens to have overnight become the direct key to all the plunders of Aesirheim, and to your supreme rulership of the Eldari people."

"Silence! You insolent cur. How dare you impugn my—"

Nate rose to his feet with enough heat to give even the High King of Vanaheim pause.

"—my intentions," the so-called High King hastily finished, as if doing so could hide his flinch.

For a moment, the fire danced on Nate's tongue, yearning to come screaming out—to sear the flesh from Phaldissus' royal bones. To demand who the hell he thought he was, High King or otherwise, to demand *anything* of the Order Excalibur. Never mind that they'd all be dead by now, smashed to bloody Archon jelly, if Nate hadn't done what he'd done. Never mind that it wasn't even *his* singularity bomb who's steepening gravity well they were currently riding, but Malfar's. Never mind any of it, because none of it would've made the slightest difference. Not a single word of it worth voicing as he glared at that golden chin set high, and the nervous shifting of the griffin beneath him, betraying the so-called High King's own thinly-veiled nerves.

A sharp bark tore from Nate's throat before he could stop it. A dark, ugly sound that might've only loosely been called laughter. He didn't know where it came from. It took him by surprise as much as everyone else. Left Phaldissus glancing to his off-screen attendants, looking for some explanation as to what manner of madness he was witnessing.

Pathetic, this creature. This would-be tyrant.

"I'll think about it, your highness," Nate forced out, past the rising darkness.

Then he killed the connection.

Beside him, in the mental space that'd previously been relegated to sleep but seemed to be creeping more and more into conscious awareness, Ex's ghostly apparition chuckled and made a vulgar gesture at the blank display before shooting a concerned side-eye Nate's way. The rest of the room, the ones who were unquestionably physically there, eyed him much more openly in the tense silence, clearly wondering whether he'd been mentally fit to take a call of such weight so soon. Perhaps it was a fair question. But right then, Nate really didn't give a shit.

"Umm," Snuffy finally said, though he didn't seem sure how to follow up.

"What's that saying about poking bears?" Ramirez asked, almost conversationally.

"That one's no bear," said O'Sweeney, lounged back on one of the couches like she'd been watching a good drama. "Just a fussy golden peacock."

"A mounted peacock," Pierce pointed out.

"With lots of guns," Snuffy added.

As if in reply, the soft weapons lock alerts pinged, letting them know that the Eldari fleet had fired up a few preliminary targeting lasers. The room looked to Nate.

"Fuck him," he said, his gaze searching out Elsa.

"Hear, hear," O'Sweeney chimed, raising her mug in cheers at the edge of his peripheral vision. "That being said, though…"

As if on cue, Cammy chimed an incoming transmission alert.

"That… would be his highness' list of demands, I think," Amelia provided, checking the packet on her personal omni.

Nate kept his eyes on Elsa. She stared back evenly, almost challengingly, but there was something else there beneath the surface. Something that hadn't been there before. He couldn't tell what she was thinking. Had the vague impression that maybe she was still figuring it out herself. But between the lines, there was a tension there, like… like for the first time since they'd come together, she wasn't entirely sure what he'd do next. Like she was just then starting to question whether some part of him might've gone properly wild in the crucible of Ginnungagap.

He turned away.

"I'm going to speak with Iveera. Hold the fort here."

He looked reflexively for Tessa as he said the words, meaning to pass command to her, only to remember she'd slipped out while he'd been getting clobbered by everything he'd missed, wobbly on her feet and murmuring something about checking in on the bridge. At the time, he'd been too shell-shocked with everything else to think on it.

It was Pierce who spoke up instead. "And if King Dicknuts opens fire in the meantime?"

"He won't," Nate said, turning for the door.

But Pierce stepped forward, blocking the way. "And if he does?"

Nate noted the consternation on Pierce's brow, amplified a thousand times over—along with a good bit of anger—on Carter's face behind him. The medic stood by the door, arms crossed, looking like she was fully prepared to make an issue of it if he didn't slow down and explain himself.

"He won't," he said, starting to step around Pierce anyway—pausing as the anger surged back up and gripped him hard, fingers curling tight at the thought of Phaldissus Kelkarin's audacious golden throat.

"But if he does..." he added, thinking how easy it would be, after having tangled with Azmodeus, to tear through a few petty Eldari warships and take King Dicknuts by his titular jewels. He was a little unsettled at how alluring the prospect sounded. Even more so at the heat of the vitriol desperately longing to spew its way out of his mouth. He wanted to tell Pierce the manner of violent delights he'd wreak upon that royal bastard. The pleasure he'd take in doing it.

It wasn't him.

He let out a long breath, waiting til he believed it, then met Pierce's eyes.

"I won't be long."

# CHAPTER 45

# WAYWARD KNIGHT

"There's something you should see," Iveera said, the moment Nate cleared the magseal and set down to the *Kalnythian Wilds'* deck. It took him a moment of fruitless searching to realize she wasn't anywhere to be seen in the viny, floral stretch of the cargo bay.

"Bridge," came her succinct instructions, seemingly from thin air.

He followed the different but familiar path out of the bay and up to the main deck, a few bioluminescent vines tracing the way for him in soft blues and teals—responding, he wagered, more to Iveera's or the ship's subconscious than to any deliberate guidance on her part. Perhaps that also explained why the greenery felt so subdued around him, despite the seeming signs of nutritional flourishing. Like a great sadness had gripped the heart of the entire considerable on-board ecosystem.

For his part, Nate was just astounded any of it had survived its time on Ginnungagap, and the subsequent clash with Azmodeus. Then again—as he had to keep reminding himself—Iveera's shipwide greenery *had* had nearly a month to replenish itself since he and Iveera had nearly fallen into a black hole a few subjective hours ago.

On the bridge, Iveera had abandoned her Excalibur armor in favor of a plain woolen tunic and trousers. She sat cross-legged at the center of her ship's glowing control ring, her posture upright, meditative. He half-expected to find her eyes closed in meditation or deep thought as he came around in front of her, but she was simply staring out the forward viewport, unmoving.

It was only here, standing in front of her, that it finally occurred to him Iveera almost certainly could've made the entire mess of Phaldissus and his heckling fleet disappear far more effectively than he could've. Somehow, he hadn't thought to ask—was kind of surprised, now that he was here, that he had no desire to do so. The very fact that Phaldissus and his blockade had even thought to aim their displeasure at Nate rather than at the elder Knight on the scene told him that the Eldari peacock had probably never actually been looking to leverage any meaningful action at all, so much as to flex his influence, impress his watching supporters, and—maybe more than anything else—to stoke the fires and point all possible blame at the Excalibur Knights, positioning himself even more firmly as the post-collapse messiah to all of Y-Sec.

The entire damn spectacle just made Nate achingly tired.

He found himself settling down on the deck opposite Iveera almost before he'd consciously decided to sit. He drew his legs in to match hers, thought about saying something, and found the silence stretching. There was a certain comfort in Iveera's presence right just then that he was in no particular rush to break. Finally, though, she stirred and spoke.

"Malfar established contact."

Something about the way she said it, the way her jin shifted ever so slightly his way, as if attending to his reaction where her space-locked eyes were too busy to.

"He's alive," Nate said, though that much was already plainly obvious from her words.

"Through no small effort, it seems, after having jumped the C-Sec relay straight into the heart of the swarm. But he arrived in time to witness the Forge's final moments."

Nate sat up straighter, sensing the impetus of the juxtaposition between her curious jin and thousand-yard stare.

"It was as a scarce few among the scattered reports have already suggested," she said slowly, testing the words. "Though not, I think, for any reason they could've fathomed." Finally, she blinked, breaking her spell, and met his eyes. "The station was not overtaken by the swarm. As far as Malfar could tell, it fled on an anomalous surge of Light. By the Merlin's own hand, were I to guess."

"That's… Well, that's… good news, right?"

He honestly couldn't begin to guess. And neither, it seemed, could Iveera.

"Samael and the *Crimson Tide* are still analyzing the readings for any clues they might yield," she said, turning her gaze back to the infinite stretch of space as if she might find the answers out there. "You should know, however, that Malfar received a transmission from the Merlin just before the station vanished."

"Jesus. What did he say?"

Her electric blue eyes were grave. "Stay alive."

Nate frowned at those words, rubbing at his rough Ginnungagap stubble and waiting for them to open up and make sense—to deliver anything else but the empty, hopeless nothingness that spread through him like black ink the longer he sat with them.

"Stay alive," he echoed. "Stay alive for what? For how long? I mean... Where the hell'd they go, Iveera?"

But it was clear the Gorgon was either not listening, or merely uninterested in engaging in wild speculation on matters neither of them could possibly know. Nate let out a soft sigh, staring through the spot on the deck just in front of Iveera's crossed legs as his mind began to dance to its own fantasies anyway. Visions of the Forge dropping out of the Light like nothing had ever happened, a clean and tidy Merlin at the triumphant helm, sounding the cry to rally his Knights and the Alliance at large to his banner, and to the master plan he'd been harboring all along.

Except even then—even *if* everyone aboard Forge station hadn't died some horrible death, as seemed entirely possible, and even *if* the Merlin came back suddenly ready to do what he'd clearly, to date, held zero interest in doing—that all still left them with the awkward problem of a hopelessly fractured Alliance. Because whatever else had happened in the chaos, the Y-Sec relay was gone, as were the two C-Sec relays that had orbited the Forge, by all accounts. Not to mention the three Beacons that had been lost with them, and the unprecedented megaswarm now roaming free at the center of the galaxy, having chomped down on all that power. There was no magically fixing any of that.

He looked back up at Iveera, thinking to ask where Malfar had gone, what they should do next.

"I spoke with the Merlin," she said unexpectedly, her attention still distant. "Shortly after I made empathic contact with you back on Ginnungagap. I told him what was happening, as best I understood it."

"Why didn't you—What did he say?"

"He was drunk. He told me it wasn't an Archon. Said it was impossible."

"Impossible," Nate echoed, thinking of the drama back at Vanaheim, and the deeper, unerring denialism that'd gripped the Council and the Alliance at large ever since they'd returned from the Battle of Avalon over a year ago, spouting that the Synth had returned in full. "Seems like there's a lot of that going around these days."

"No longer."

"No. I guess not." He considered the Gorgon. "Iveera…"

She looked at him, electric blue eyes reticently softening to something open, yet assessing. He swallowed, uncertain what it was he even wanted to say. All of it inadequate to the magnitude of everything that'd happened. Pointless. He thought of Jaeger.

"I tried my best, Iveera. I really did."

The words fell out in a rush, plopping to the deck between them, woefully useless. Maybe worse than useless, some clinical part of his brain couldn't help but think, as it weighed those words with cold detachment, testing for veracity. That cold part of him wasn't sure what to believe.

Whether Iveera had any greater insight, he hadn't the faintest. She just watched him, looking… he didn't know what. Pensive. Uncertain. Troubled.

"You should consider your next moves," she finally said, uncrossing her legs and rising from the deck as if she'd decided she wasn't going to find whatever it was she'd been looking for out there. "There's no telling where the swarms will turn from galaxy's center, nor how our disparate factions will react now that the Council is lost."

The abrupt change of topic caught him off guard.

"I thought… I guess I figured we'd stick together," he said, starting to stand.

"To what end, Nathaniel?" she practically snapped, jin and eyes bristling with something very much like anger. The sudden burst gave him pause. But as quickly as it came, the heat bled away, her jin drooping back down with weary resignation. "There is very little a few well-meaning Knights can do to keep an entire galaxy safe from invasion."

He stood the rest of the way up, searching for something. Grasping for straws.

"But maybe… Maybe if the Merlin and the Forge come back…" he started, not really sure where he was going with it. Not even in his brightest daydreams did the return of the wizard solve any of this. For all intents and purposes, they were gone. To where, only the Merlin himself probably knew. Assuming the drunk bastard hadn't simply blinked the Forge straight into the supercluster at the heart of the galaxy.

*He would never*, Ex grumbled dutifully. But even he sounded a bit uncertain.

"Zedavian and Dalnak, then," Nate moved on, clutching for the next feeble straw. "They made the outer rim faster than should've been possible. If they can do it..."

"To ride the Light so fully is not a skill one merely acquires through the convenience of necessity and stubborn willpower. They have both had millennia to puzzle their way through the intricacies of the continuum."

"Then we rendezvous with Viktos. Ask Zedavian to meet us. Mount a..."

But he knew there was nothing to his words. No counterattack to be mounted. No clear target to even swing at. The Synth were everywhere now, outside and in. Nothing to stop them from picking at the neatly dissected bones of the Alliance from all sides at once.

"What about the Second Knight?" he heard himself ask, though he knew it was over. "The one no one talks about."

"No living being, save for Zedavian and the Merlin himself, has ever even seen Silas, Nathaniel. For all I know, the wraith perished millennia ago. And even if he hasn't, I see no reason why he'd suddenly elect to reneg on over two-thousand years of isolation."

She crossed her arms and faced him, her manner somber if not quite unsympathetic. "I do not have the answer you're looking for, Nathaniel. I'm not certain it exists."

Distantly, he felt himself rocking back on his heels as the words washed over him. It wasn't that they were particularly harsh, or even particularly unexpected. In truth, they were probably exactly what he needed to hear right then. But even so, he couldn't help but feel somehow... cheated. Like, after everything, he'd found himself at the butt end of some terrible galactic joke.

"How did it come to this?" His voice came out a whisper. "Why didn't the Merlin... I mean, he could've..." He waved a helpless hand. "Couldn't he? I mean, how the hell could it've been this easy? The most advanced civilization in the galaxy, and all it takes is one lucky shot to bring the whole goddamn thing down? Who the hell thought it was okay to prop a *Galactic Alliance* on top of a few measly gateways? How the—"

He caught himself then, hands raised, practically yelling by that point. Iveera watched calmly as he lowered his bladed hands, deflating, the last dregs of the burgeoning hissy fit bleeding from his system. Opening the way to good old shame and embarrassment.

"There are still the planetary q-junctions," Iveera pointed out.

But that only brought another bite of bitterness. Because without the relays, those q-junctions were little more than a system of factory-sized, galactic walky-talkies—a system that would do little more than enable the biggest, mightiest planets in the galaxy to scream bloody murder to one another as they died alone, unreachable light-years removed from their long lost neighbors.

"I said I'm not certain your answer exists, Nathaniel. But I'm equally uncertain that it doesn't."

He looked at her. "Is that supposed to be encouraging?"

Her jin gave the equivalent of a shrug. "It simply is."

"You haven't lost faith, then? You really believe this is all part of her plan?"

"You know the answer to that."

In truth, he wasn't sure he did, beyond the small detail that Iveera generally disapproved of such sloppy metaphysical concepts as "the grand plan." In all their talks of Lady's grace and the true duties of a Knight, Nate had never understood faith as Iveera seemed to see it. Not as some divine plan, or a test of one's beliefs—in the Lady, or otherwise. It wasn't even a question of free will or determinism, as far as he could grasp. It was something, he was starting to trust, that he was merely not equipped to comprehend. Not yet. Maybe never.

"It simply is?" he guessed anyway.

She shot him a look like he should've known better, but he saw something like a playful flicker in her jin. The closest thing to a playful flicker Iveera was capable of, at least. "What I believe, Nathaniel, is that divided or not, the remaining sectors will fight, if for no other reason than that of simple self-preservation. Perhaps it will be enough." Her face took on a speculative tilt. "Perhaps that megaswarm will simply wander too close to the supercluster, and do us all a great service."

He knew it was intended in jest, but even as exceedingly rare as that was coming from Iveera, he couldn't stop the sober shadow descending.

"They're not what everyone thinks they are, Iveera."

The ghost of a frown touched her brow, jin curling at the ends like she'd thought he might say something like that.

"I don't know what the Synth are," he pushed on, "but they're not mindless automatons. Not all of them, at least. The Archon, Azmodeus—"

Iveera actually shifted a little, as if the very sound of that name made her uneasy.

"Whatever it was," he continued. "I mean, I thought it was at first—an automaton. But there was something more inside of that thing. Something..." He touched uncomfortably at his all-too-recently healed chest, thinking of the rush of visions he'd had in those last moments of the Archon's non-life, lost for words to describe any of it. "I saw it, Iveera," was all he could think to say in the end.

She looked troubled as she turned that over. He felt her hesitance to accept what he was saying, but also some modicum of trust in his words— like she clearly would've preferred to disagree but knew she didn't possess adequate grounds on which to justly do so.

"They are the destroyers of worlds, Nathaniel," she finally said, her brow pinched, jin motionless. For a moment, she looked like she might say more, then she seemed to decide those words should suffice.

He thought about pushing the issue, but he couldn't see what good would come of it—now, or maybe ever. Because she was right. Whether Azmodeus and any other Archons out there were packing critical thinking skills or not, the Synth had to be stopped.

"I'm just saying maybe we can't count out the possibility that they're capable of more coordination than we thought."

"Perhaps you're right."

"So what do we do then? Where do we go from here?"

"There is..." Her jin rippled as she returned from some distant thought. "... Much chaos to undo in the proximal systems, if this sector is to have any hope of defending itself as an isolated entity. The situation on Vanaheim, in particular, must be... untangled."

"Tell me about it," he muttered.

"And that's not to mention the figurative mountains to be moved here on Asgard," Iveera continued, as if she hadn't heard him.

"I could help."

He wasn't sure why he felt the sudden need to point that out. Something in her words, or in the tone of her jin. Y-Sec, an isolated entity. Christ, there wasn't even an Yggdrasil anymore.

Iveera seemed lost in similarly dark thoughts of her own.

"You could," she finally said, focusing more closely on him.

He held her gaze, uncertain what it was she was looking for in him— only that it was something.

Then, to his surprise, she stepped forward and touched him, both with a gentle hand to the shoulder and, infinitely more shockingly, with a soft brush of her jin. The hairlike appendages cradled in around his face, surprisingly soft, and exuding warmth. More warmth than seemed possible. And beneath that warmth, a kind of peaceful, weathered sadness—so quiet, and yet so deep and aching that he found himself fighting back sudden tears.

*I should not pass so easily into your mind, Nathaniel,* came her whispered voice in his head. He barely reacted at all, lost as he was in the depth of her, and in the sudden certainty that it was no wonder at all that he sometimes struggled to understand what such a mind was thinking. It was haunting, and beautiful, and a thousand other things that couldn't even begin to be captured in the rueful smile that touched her lips as she withdrew, pressing her hand to his breast as if in farewell. "Something to work on, Ser Knight. For next time."

# CHAPTER 46

# BLACK HOLES AND REVELATIONS

Somehow, Iveera's words did little to soothe Nate's restless nerves by the time he returned to the *Camelot*. Especially not as he stomped up from the cargo bay to find Elsa gathering her bags, so to speak, in the main entryway as if expecting her ride to be there any minute.

"You don't have to do this," he said, before he could stop himself—before even checking in with Ex and Cammy to confirm that nothing had indeed changed with the blockade out there, and that no new transmissions had come in from the *Imperiatus*.

There'd been no word. No change. But Elsa just showed him a solemn smile, like she was waiting for him to realize how patronizing that sounded.

"I am the reigning Queen of Aesirheim," she said. "There is very little that I *must* do. And infuriatingly much that I most probably should."

"Yeah, well, I know I'm new to all this and everything, but I was under the impression an Envoy relinquishes any such titles, no questions asked, unless their Knight should choose to release them from duty."

Her smile took on a daring edge. "You would refuse the rightful Queen of Aesirheim, Ser Arturi?"

He searched her face, looking for some clue. "I might, if my Envoy asked it of me. I thought you wanted something else for yourself. Something different."

"My people need me, Nathaniel."

"You shouldn't have to marry that pompous asshole."

"You're very sweet," she said, slowly cocking one devious eyebrow, "but who said anything about marriage?"

"You're not…?"

"My people need *me*, Nathaniel. Not some fallow puppet on the arm of their would-be Supreme Overlord."

She watched him digest that, perfectly pleased to stand by and wait as his clunky brain attempted to maneuver the pieces into place. Pieces he was almost certain, at that moment, that she'd already thought over a thousand times by then.

"It occurs to me," he said slowly, tracing out the most immediately tangible of these new paths, "that the Asgardians could probably use a better friend than Phaldissus Kelkarin right about now."

"Oh, very much so," she agreed with an overly contemplative look, like she *hadn't* already thought this through a million times over. "One with ample resources to see to their relocation, no doubt. And now that I think of it, it mightn't be the worst of turns, were that aid to come from a known friend of Ser Nathaniel Arturi, no?"

Nate crossed his arms, though he failed to keep the grin at bay. "And if Phaldissus decides to take issue with all this?"

She looked almost blissfully amused by the question, and more than a little ferocious as she answered. "Then I genuinely cannot think of any Eldari more adequate to the task of eroding his public support than the one who spurned the Great King's matrimonial advances twice in a row."

He found his grin widening. "You really would've been an amazing Envoy, wouldn't you?"

She fairly beamed. "You have no idea. Now," she added, perking and turning to go, "I'd best finish gathering my possessions."

"Who are you waiting for, by the way?" he asked, eyeing the haphazard pile of her belongings.

"Wouldn't you like to know?" she called, not looking back.

"Elsa."

She paused and glanced back with a look of exasperation. His thoughts were elsewhere, idling on what fresh dick-swinging might be liable to unfold if the fleets of Aesirheim came rolling in to collect their queen, and on the rest of the plan that'd sounded like a match made in heaven, right up until he remembered the rest of the unfortunate details.

"The Asgardians," he said. "They did try to kill you, remember?"

"Did they, though?"

He frowned. "You found something on the attack?"

"Hardly. But... call it a hunch. And a deepening one, at that."

She waved the matter away as he opened his mouth to ask.

"Rest assured, you'll be the first to know, should I find anything of substance."

"Maybe you should stay with us, all the same," he said slowly, overly conscious of the growing unease creeping through his limbs. "Just a little longer." Erratic splashes of cold, attacking his insides out of nowhere. The quiet certainty that none of them were safe here. That none of them would ever be safe again. "I'd be happy to take you to Aesirheim, if you'd like. I'd... I'd feel better if you'd at least let me escort you that far."

His hands were shaking.

It was a small thing, but apparently not so small as to escape Elsa's notice. She looked up as he recrossed his arms to hide it, searching his face for some clue. He held her gaze, unsettled, and trying not to show it. Then she surprised him by striding right back up to him and leaning in to kiss him gently on the cheek.

"Do be careful out there, my brave Knight," she said quietly, cupping lightly at the kissed cheek with one hand.

He nodded, stuck for words, and watched her go, more than a little surprised to find he was actually going to miss her.

At least until she stopped and turned back again.

"On second thought... Would you terribly mind giving me a hand? I do have quite a large collection of rocks in need of hauling."

He blew out a chuckle, the black tension in his chest evaporating like smoke in the wind. "Don't you mean celestial bodies?"

"Well, we *will* see, won't we?" she said, looping her arm through his as he fell in step beside her.

IN THE HOURS following Elsa's departure, strange things began to happen around the *Camelot*.

By far, the most obvious was the unexpected but highly welcome dispersal of Phaldissus' royal blockade, shortly after a surprise visit from Iveera—and, to Nate's own surprise, from Elsa too. What the two of them must've said to High King Kelkarin aboard the *Celestari Imperiatus*, Nate could only guess at. For his part, he was still just trying to figure out when Iveera and Elsa had hatched this new alliance of theirs, and why neither of them had seen fit to mention it to him until the moment Iveera showed up at the hatch to collect her royal charge.

All that'd been left to do by that point was to watch.

So watched he had, as the two of them had broken the blockade, turning thirty-odd capital ships home for Vanaheim. Watched he had, as the Gorgon Knight and the Eldari queen then themselves set off aboard the more-or-less mended *Kalnythian Wilds*, bound for the high courts of Aesirheim. Watched he had, quietly resisting the stirring undercurrents of jealousy and self-pity—and maybe even betrayal—as Iveera and Elsa had vanished on him with little more than the dignified equivalent of a *see ya when we see ya*.

They must've had their reasons, he told himself. Neither one of them harbored him any ill will. He was almost certain of it. And yet there he remained, left behind by friend and foe alike. Adrift a few meager light-minutes away from the silent doom of the black hole that the Asgardians and everyone else seemed to have decided was his doing.

It was hard not to stare.

In the days since he and Iveera had fallen through that tightly-wound spacetime, dangerously close to gravitational oblivion, the black hole's pull had begun to make itself known on the closest of the system's three suns. Even in the past year of Alliance adventures, it was unlike anything Nate had ever seen—the mighty sun stretching for that orb of crushing blackness with its breathtaking tendrils of golden light, as if in hopes of going to live out the rest of its days as a fantastical accretion disk of fire and brilliant splendor around the growing black hole.

It wouldn't be so lucky, he knew. Nothing here would be.

It was strange, to see something so vast and powerful forced to yield and bend for anything. And yet there Ginnungagap's sun lay—dying, stretched to breaking, bleeding its radiance out to the simple yet inevitable rule of nature.

They needed to leave this place. Needed to leave behind that cursed black hole, and all its memories of Jaeger, and Tristan, and everything else. They could've set course for anywhere. He could've moved them with a thought. Yet the hours crept by, and still they lingered, no one quite daring to ask why, everyone silently agreeing to some awkward game of make believe busyness, even though there was next to nothing to be done. Everyone waiting for something. For *him*, Nate knew on some level.

Waiting for him to make up his mind, and tell them what came next. *Or not*, argued another scoffing voice from within. Because why should he think himself so high and important in their eyes after everything, when the air was still so clearly thick to choking with blame and heavy spirits? Perhaps it was merely an apology they were waiting for. Or perhaps a miracle. Because if Nate had come popping back to them after twenty-seven somber days, then maybe… just maybe…

He wasn't sure whose hopes were whose anymore. Only that the crew was in… he didn't quite know what. Mourning didn't even feel like the proper word. Not when they'd all had nearly a month longer than he'd had to get their heads on straight over all of it. There was sadness, absolutely. And mourning too. But it was a kind of soft death that seemed to have permeated the spaces between them. A listlessness given birth in the wake of Jaeger's absence. Their colonel. Their leader. Gone.

Just… gone.

It was too much to handle right then.

He needed to rest. Needed it more than anything.

He should've been exhausted. *Was* exhausted. About as exhausted as he'd ever been. And yet there was a complete lack of desire for sleep from his body. Maybe it was simply that Ex had more or less broken his brain's sleep signals for good by then, what with all the tinkering and the super sleep. But if he was being honest with himself, the real culprit was probably even more simple than errant physiology and adrenal overload. On some finicky level, it was even kind of obvious—the tricksy game of cat and mouse his own brain seemed to be playing with him, as if neither he nor Ex could see its little tricks, or the overwhelming tide lurking there just outside the light. Yet still he managed to put it off.

It was only when Cammy began her slow nighttime dimming around the ship that Nate finally gave in and retreated from the somber quiet of the common areas to the foreboding quiet of his quarters to perform the ritualistic farce of lying down to sleep. No part of him truly expected sleep to come, and no part of him was thusly disappointed.

For an indeterminate stretch of darkness, he lay there restless, thoroughly unable to get comfortable despite Ex's chemical nudges and Cammy's immaculate climate control. For his part, Nate just did his best to keep his racing mind busy with the small things, rather than the ones with real teeth. There was the small question of Tessa's continued absence from the crew quarters, for instance, and the many lingering oddities of Ginnungagap itself. There was the mystery of the odd droppings he'd found Snuffy puzzling over earlier in the greenery, and the fact that they clearly were not coming from the refugee snargladorf who'd taken to following Nate through the corridors like he was a walking slab of fillet mignon ever since he'd returned. There was the curious, slightly unsettling conjecture that Snuffy's mystery droppings must then have been coming from Bob's recessed alcove in the branches above, though none of them could've said what exactly the Ooperian had taken to eating.

There was the sudden piercing realization, lying in the darkness, eyes closed, that he still felt the Archon's unforgiving manipulator arms splayed out through his insides. That he was still there. Still hung out on the Archon's rack. Disemboweled. Draining. Dying. And there, staring him in the face—

He surfaced from the thought with a sharp gasp, disoriented, uncertain whether he'd been asleep or not. His pillow and bedding were drenched in sweat. He threw the blankets off, welcoming the rush of cool air on feverish skin, trying to push that last image out of sight before he could dwell on it. Trying, on some level, to convince himself he hadn't ever really seen it at all. But there was no point in pretending. Ex had already attested to what they'd seen, as Nate had driven that arcane spear into the construct's glowing red chest amid the bones of Ginnungagap.

His own face, staring back at him in ghostly ruby imitation.

Neither one of them had the faintest clue what it meant—whether it had been some form of reflexive mimicry, or deliberate psychological warfare. An attempt at communication. Blind random chance. Any number of unfathomable things.

Nate was in no mood to think about any of it.

*You do know I can give you something for the, ahh, discomfort,* Ex said.

"Feels like you already did," Nate murmured aloud, mostly just to kill the insidious silence.

*Something more, then,* Ex amended, not denying the allegations as Cammy not-so-discreetly opened the room audio to a pseudo-musical mix of gentle tones clearly intended to soothe.

At least he'd always have the two of them. His eternal companions, always here to lend him whatever support he might need, insofar as they could even begin to figure out what it was he needed—and that it *could* be delivered by a pair of disembodied synthients.

*Well, someone woke up on the wrong side of the sweat bucket.*

"Sorry," he murmured, mind already adrift again to Iveera's ship, and to Ginnungagap, and to what the hell Blackthorne had even been doing there in the first place—what she'd meant by that "Beware the Promethean" business, and how she'd known he'd find the *Wilds* there out of all the countless planets in the galaxy. How she'd known any of it.

He thought of something she'd once said aboard her ship—something about… what had she'd called it?

The endless dance. That was it.

He felt Ex's touch in his mind, sharpening his recall.

"I suspect it's all connected," she'd told him, back then—the strange, unshakeable pirate who'd showed up out of nowhere and dropped straight into his dreams. "It usually is."

The endless dance.

The Lady. The Knights. The Synth.

A galaxy at war.

Nate turned over, then sighed and sat up from the sweaty bedding completely. He hunched over the side of the bed, holding his face in his hands, mind turning. Jaeger and Tristan. Blackthorne and the *Wilds*. Azmodeus. The Promethean. A galaxy at war.

All connected.

The endless dance.

His mind drifted back to Ginnungagap, and to the note from their unknown Last LeFaye dubbing it by another name. New Avalon. The ghosts of New Avalon. He thought of the enigma of Myrr, and of the mad scientist who'd apparently created the creature. The same mad scientist who must've known at least something about whatever matter that monument had been forged from. And the same mad scientist who, Nate couldn't help but think, might well have in fact gone to Ginnungagap specifically *looking* for the dormant Archon, some ancient history past, for gods only knew what reason.

And then there was the matter of the monument stuff itself, and what it had done to the Archon's swarms. Not unlike whatever it was Nate had done to the nanoswarm that'd tried to hurt Tessa, back when the Myrr creature had ambushed them. Somehow, the connection hadn't even occurred to him until then. In the midst of everything, he'd all but forgotten about the episode of his swarm-killing battle cry.

*Isolated phenomena*, Ex answered, before he could ask.

*But similar*, Nate thought back. *Right?*

*Perhaps*, Ex admitted reluctantly. *Macroscopically.*

There was too much he didn't know. Too much even Ex didn't understand. And behind each and every gap in their knowledge, another world of unknowns waiting to knock them right back to square one—to teeter and totter until they didn't know which way was up.

*They are the destroyers of worlds, Nathaniel.*

He felt a tinge of uneasiness at the memory of Iveera's words. Some flickering thought of the cryptic corruption Mordred LeFaye had once struck into Nate's and Iveera's Excaliburs. An insidious moment's worry that, perhaps, there was some reason beyond rattled nerves that he still felt the phantom root of Azmodeus' manipulators splayed throughout his insides.

He thought of the vanished Merlin, and cursed the wizard. Thought again of Iveera and Elsa's practically casual farewell as they'd gone on ahead to meet with the Eldari high courts. Anger and festering abandonment. Betrayal that they'd left him here. That they hadn't seen what that thing had done to his insides. Hadn't bothered to look. Just gone on ahead. Or not ahead. Aside. Afar.

Elsewhere.

Elsewhere, where maybe he wasn't intended to follow.

Except he could nix that *maybe*, he knew. He felt as much in his aching bones, right next to the palpable pressure of his waiting crew. That infuriating little tingle, coaxing him along like some bastardized version of the itch before a sneeze. Except in this case... no handy, clear-cut climax.

No sneeze.

He sat back with a sigh, vaguely pining for a drink.

No sneeze. Just the empty, pervasive nothingness of the black hole hiding in the rearview.

*I think maybe you should talk to someone.* He felt Ex's ghostly apparition looking up at him from his workbench over in that between place—or that *higher* place, perhaps. Whatever they wanted to call it, the place no longer seemed to be respecting its previous boundaries between sleeping and waking, and the look on Ex's mustachioed face said it wasn't going away anytime soon.

Maybe he was losing his mind.

"The Lady *does* work in mysterious ways," Ex offered, drumming steepled fingers as he swiveled around to prop his shiny dress shoes up on the corner of Nate's bed.

"Just like our drunk wizard loved to say," Nate agreed. "Right before he went and abandoned his precious Alliance to slow, painful death by total Synth invasion."

"Now, now. I thought we'd agreed: no sniveling after lights out."

"Yeah, well..."

Nate stood, letting die the pointless stream of irritation and curses on the tip of his tongue. He didn't mean to call the cabin lights on. Certainly hadn't intended to summon that drink. Cammy, though, dutifully saw to both. He eyed the can of All-Day IPA she must've fabricated from some memory he'd subconsciously shared. A memory of State College. Of home. Except that word didn't quite gel anymore, did it? Hadn't for a while.

He crossed his arms, staring down the beer, longing for a sip and yet stubbornly resistant to the idea. Beside him, Ex stirred a tumbler of brandy he'd whisked out of thin air and held it up for a delicate *sniff-sniff* before glancing back to Nate like *shall we, then?* But Nate was stuck on something else now. A flitter of memory from the rush. A whispered word from the Lady, in the moment of unraveling before Azmodeus had broken. A name.

He looked at Ex, feeling it now even more fully.

"Caliburn?"

His friend paused mid-sip, conspicuously side-eyeing Nate before lowering his brandy with a peeved frown. "Hmmph," he finally grumbled in the back of his throat. Then he vanished completely.

"Hey," Nate said to the empty room. "C'mon, don't be like that. Cal."

*Don't you start with me, Nathaniel.*

*But that IS your name, isn't it? The proper one?*

*It is A name. And any name is but a name, proper or otherwise. I daresay I am not the same entity now as I was when that name, or any other, was bestowed upon me.*

Nate stared through the empty room, not entirely sure what the reticence was about, but not exactly displeased by it either. Somehow, the name hardly seemed cut out for his companion.

"Ex it is, then," he said, dropping it. Ex didn't reply, but he seemed quietly satisfied by the concession. For a second, Nate was too—almost like, in the simple agreement of a name, he'd scored some small victory.

It lasted all of two seconds before the real world came slinking back in with all its myriad issues.

He glanced at the bed and saw nothing but another puddle of racing thoughts and cold sweat in his future. Briefly, he reconsidered Ex's offer of *something stronger.* A nice, medically induced coma didn't sound so bad right about now. But tempting as it was, something told him that time alone was not going to cure what ailed him. The crew was waiting for *something*—be it his orders, or not. And whatever was working its way through him, whatever conclusion his mind was trying to arrive at, it wasn't going away on its own.

So, with a resigned sigh, he pulled a tunic over his bare torso and went to go stalk the halls in search of he didn't know what. *Space to think,* his mind reflexively offered—as if there'd been any appreciable lack of that back there in his quiet quarters.

Outside of those quarters, the ship was quiet in a way that had only partly to do with the subdued volume of nighttime conversation trickling through the corridors. He thought of Tessa. Wondered how she was doing since their unhappy debriefing in the common room, where she'd spent a few short minutes staring holes through him, like she didn't quite believe he was really there at all, before finally staggering out of the room.

He looked in the direction of her cabin, wondering what the past twenty-seven days had done to her, to all of them. Thinking to ask Cammy about it. Something thudded into the supposedly sound-dampened walls a few cabins closer, the sultry moan and muffled yet insistent thump-thump-thumping telling his sharpened ears that Pierce was, by the sounds of it, most likely decompressing with Amelia in there.

Nate cleared his throat and moved on, trusting his feet. Not for the first time, he found them carrying him to his favorite observatory on the far side of the ship gardens where Iveera had once made her temporary home, his mind already spooling up the well-trodden paths of what-ifs and useless blame that the sight—or non-sight—of the black hole so readily brought on. He felt Ex's thought currents—or maybe they were his own—gently tugging and nudging at the notions as he went, picking at the edges.

He frowned at the intrusion, if that's even what it was, and exchanged nods with a passing Snuffy. The gesture was mutually amicable, but also faintly haunted, as every move aboard the *Camelot* seemed to have been since he'd awoken twenty-seven days too late to do jack shit for anyone. It was hard not to see it in their every passing glance. They'd all had their time to mourn, to break it all down, play by play, over and over.

They didn't understand what he'd been through back there, down in the belly of the beast. How *could* they?

As he entered the greenery, the snargladorf sprang up from the cluster of shrubs where she'd apparently fallen to napping and started his way with a quivering, almost apologetic energy, as if she'd failed her duties in allowing him to wander unattended. He held up a hand, gesturing for her to stay, and the snargladorf relented, settling down reluctantly at first, then dropping her head back to the lush alien grass with a plaintive sigh. Somewhere in the hidden reaches of vines and leaves above, Vampire Bob gave a soft hiss, as if in commiseration. Two refugees of a lost world. Lost for good, this time.

He thought of Myrr, wondering, not for the first time, whether the flicker of guilt in his heart was at all founded—if maybe they could've helped each other from the start, if only he'd found a way to communicate with the seemingly savage creature. Preferably before it'd snatched and imprisoned most of his crew.

*Perhaps Myrr should have found the courage to simply ask for aid, if aid was what it desired,* Ex said, watching Nate with crossed arms from where he'd taken apparition beside the mouth of the greenery's burbling little brook.

*Which is to say maybe I should talk to my people about this shit before I accidentally eat a few of them in misunderstanding?* Nate asked, frowning at the thinly veiled jab.

Ex just shrugged as Nate moved on.

The point wasn't completely lost on him. He just needed time to think.

So easy to keep telling himself that. So hard to put his finger on what it was he was meant to be thinking about.

Maybe he should've opened up to Iveera more completely, told her just how deeply that thing had torn into him. Told her about the look in Jaeger's eyes in those last moments. If anyone could've understood, it was her. But then, he hadn't quite known himself just how rattled he'd been until he'd tried to lay down in a dark room alone. In reality, she'd probably seen it more clearly than he had when she'd touched him with her empathic abilities back on the *Wilds*. She'd seen whatever was lurking inside him. Seen it with six-hundred-plus years of life wisdom to which he wasn't privy. And she'd done as she'd seen fit.

She must've had her reasons.

Her, the Lady, and maybe even the Merlin. Hell, maybe even Azmodeus.

The endless dance. A galaxy at war. Everyone with their reasons.

It occurred to him that he, personally, was utterly *without* reason. A drifting cog, waiting for the teeth of fate, or the Lady, or anyone else to lock back into his grooves and tell him how to turn. And maybe that was it, right there. Maybe Iveera hadn't intended to leave him behind at all, but rather to set him free. Free to do whatever it was he needed to do. Of course, he didn't have the faintest fucking clue what that was. But he felt like maybe the universe was nudging him in a direction anyway, as he stepped into the observatory and found Emily Carter standing there.

The medic was staring out the wide viewport, arms crossed, rigid as ever. He hadn't seen the steel leave her posture since Iveera had dragged him aboard.

For one unadmirable iota of a second, he actually wondered if maybe he could simply slide back out of sight before she turned—if maybe she hadn't noticed him at all. Past that iota, it became evident she *had* noticed, and was waiting for him to do just that. To make like a tree, and bugger the fuck off.

Maybe it would've been the decent thing to do. Certainly, it would've been the easy thing. But all Nate could think of, standing there, was what Jaeger had asked him back down on Ginnungagap, while the others had slept.

*You care? Enough to do anything?*

He still wasn't sure what Jaeger had been trying to tell him through those questions—still wasn't sure he'd been trying to tell him anything at all, other than that maybe their people came first, always. The team first. Then the mission. And then, if possible, himself. Jaeger's Three-Tier Hierarchy of Leadership Priorities, Nate ventured, all too aware of the weight of Jaeger's ghost watching him from the corner of his mind.

Truth be told, Nate wasn't sure what the man would've wanted of him right then. He let out a long breath, all the same, and went to join the woman who, by his estimate, had probably loved Jaeger as much as she disliked Nate.

Carter didn't say a word as he stepped up beside her. Didn't even look at him. For a long while, he tried to find the right words. Then she surprised him, and broke the silence first.

"This is war," she said, her voice quiet, distant.

"I..." He wasn't sure what to make of that. He'd never figured out how to read her. But he thought he got the gist, anyway. "It wasn't in vain, Emily," he told her, turning to face her. "I want you to know that. If he hadn't done what he did..." He shook his head, choked off at the thought of it. "I just want you to know that I'm never going to let something like this happen ag—"

She moved fast. Grabbed him by the collar and yanked down before he knew what was happening, moving with clever leverages that short-circuited all his considerable strength and left him stooped down at her level. He could've straightened, then. Could've thrown her across the room. He stayed frozen. The look in her eyes was pure fury. He hadn't a doubt she would've punched him in the face if she hadn't known damn well she'd been trading a broken hand for little real damage.

"This is war," she growled, jabbing at his heart three times. "This. This in here." She shoved him back. "You remember this feeling, Arturi. And the next time you go flying us off into the piss—The next time you start thinking you've got it all under control..."

She took two hot breaths, as if preparing to spit pure venom. Then something died in her, and that fury receded, iron jaw and burning eyes melting down to something hollow and empty.

"You remember this," she said quietly. "You remember that the price we pay, it's not up to you in the end."

He stood there breathless, not knowing what to say. Wanting to defend himself. To apologize. But it was all worthless. Deflection and denial.

He straightened instead, standing tall as he met her eyes. "I'll remember."

She held his gaze, sizing up his words, and finally nodded, accepting his declaration if not quite applauding it. She turned to leave. Paused.

"He wanted it this way, you know," she said. Then she was gone.

He didn't know. Stood there for a long time after she'd left, not knowing. Not even sure he *wanted* to. Not all that sure about anything, other than that he needed to sleep. Needed to mend the gaping hole that lingered beneath the mended flesh of his chest and heart, festering with Azmodeus' dark spirit, and Jaeger's sacrifice, and a thousand other things he didn't understand.

He needed someone to understand.

Eventually, his feet saw their way to moving again. Something moving through him. Something *other*. Like his brain had kicked on the backup life support and gently pushed him aside to take the controls. He felt Death following him down the corridor. Felt Azmodeus lurking in the shadows. Told himself he'd take that coma now, like it or not. That everything would look clearer in the morning.

Except it wasn't his quarters that his feet had delivered him too, when he came to from his trance, reaching for the control panel.

A moment of hesitation. A muted sense that he shouldn't be here. Then his fingers brushed the panel, the door hissed open, and there she was.

"I didn't know where else to… I should've knocked."

Tessa watched him from the bed, where she sat propped up with pillows, an unlit tablet cast aside on the blankets beside her. It occurred to him that there must've been some reason she was awake at this hour, right around the same time it hit him that she hadn't been the only one doing the avoiding since his untimely resurrection. Since well before that.

He knew exactly what he'd come here for. And so did she, watching him from the bed, waiting for him to say it. Waiting like she'd be damned if she had to spell it out for him.

He wished she'd tell him, anyway. Wished anyone would.

He felt heavy, standing there in the open doorway. Felt dirty and torn. Death clinging to the air around him. The Archon's bloody rack spliced through his screaming insides. The crushing stretch of gravitation, tearing him to pieces, again and again. Here, in a tired quagmire of bad choices. There, in the searing flash of Jaeger's last moment, and in the friends he hadn't yet thought to call on the far side of armageddon.

"I know where we need to go," he heard himself say, surprised to find in that moment that he actually did. Surprised because the words only felt that much more like a betrayal in light of the fact—and because they weren't at all what he'd come here to say. He didn't need anyone to tell him that.

Tessa searched his face, weighing his words, looking, of all things, nervous as she bit her lip and reached for the blankets. "Tomorrow," she said, setting the tablet aside, drawing the blankets back. Watching him. Waiting. It wasn't a question.

He felt heavy. Felt dirty and torn. Lost for home.

Death at his back. Nothing but uncertainty ahead.

"Tomorrow," he agreed, his voice barely a whisper.

Then he stepped into the room, and closed the door behind him.

# EPILOGUE

## A STOIC'S GUIDE TO STOCHASTIC
## STOICHIOMETRY

The Trogarran heat was sweltering in the high noon sun. The smells of Troglodan musk and excrement mixing with those of sun-baked clay and the charred meats of the street vendors to yield something that might've been akin to what his distant ancestors had once known, on those occasions they'd left their fair city of Atlantis to walk among the mud-and-dirt squalor of the ancient Terran villages.

That, plus an extra point-six standard gees.

Calum Statecaste pulled his rough hood tight, feeling the added strain of the Trogarran gravity with each movement, and ensured the thin film of the ID scrambler was still activated and in place. There were reasons beyond the olfactory that he'd taken great pains to rarely make such meetings in person. But great pains were at no shortage throughout the galaxy at the moment, and extenuating times—not to mention skittish contacts—called for extenuating methods. Still, he decided, wrinkling his nose at the sight of the ramshackle grog house for which he was apparently bound, that hardly made any of this any less unpleasant.

The place was a shit hole.

Perhaps that was appropriate, though, given the nature of what he'd come here to do.

Not for the first time, he wondered whether the Lady or any other divine being would have words of reckoning for him, when all was said and done. Only time and context would tell. The Troglodans' holy Destroyer

370

godhead, for instance—represented in fearsome, fifty-meter high detail in the nearby town square—would no doubt be sporting the most turgid of arousals for Calum's audacious plans. Perhaps, Calum reflected with a wry grin beneath his scrambler, he would do well to visit the temple and convert while he was here.

But business first—aether take them all.

It was true that everything had changed. And yet so too had nothing.

He hadn't come all this way, hadn't fled the mother of all Synth invasions, just to lose his stomach now. He wouldn't have made it at all, had it not been for the timely warning from his dear Amelia Sundercaste, and her words of the great battle gone horribly wrong in the far reaches of the Asgard system. Fifteen minutes later, and his shuttle would've gone down with the entirety of Forge Station. Ten minutes later, and he never would've escaped the incoming wave of the swarms and made it out of C-Sec alive. The relay system had gone down galaxywide approximately thirteen seconds after he'd cleared the jump to G-Sec.

If anything, perhaps it wasn't the Lady's scorn he was incurring, but rather her grace. Perhaps it was *her* work he was doing here. Who was to say? Who, but the very Merlin who'd not only failed but blatantly refused, time and time again, to so much as lift a finger for the Alliance he had once —in a time none but his own loyal Knights now recalled—called his own?

No. Calum couldn't lose his nerve now. Not with the galaxy unraveling around them. Not with the brutal acts of violence he'd had to employ even just to get here, to the stinking streets of Trogarra.

It hadn't been an easy trip.

Chaos and uncertainty, all around. Spreading. Breeding.

Inside, the grog house was far cleaner than one might've expected, and yet somehow every bit as rank. Troglodans. Grunting, mouth-breathing, gas-spewing Troglodans. Belching and farting and drinking their grog by the buckets. A few off-worlders, too, here and there. Some of them—maybe most of them—shrouded like Calum. An illegal, scantily clad Gorgon slave moved in the large dangling cage at the center of the room, not quite dancing to the rhythmic percussions of the pulsing Trogarran drumbeat so much as obediently shuffling back and forth, like her survival depended on it. No one seemed to mind that her jin had shriveled along with her emaciated body, or that her blue eyes had faded and gone cloudy. This was not a place for appreciating the finer minutiae of beautiful things.

For a moment, Calum paused, and allowed some deep part of himself to burn with its righteous indignation. Then he calmly slid the lid back over that naive little fool of a boy, and began to scan the room more closely for his contact. Someday—perhaps someday soon—he'd have the strength to make it right. To make it all right. But until then...

There.

His contact waited at the bar, neon blue drink raised in greeting, grinning the way only a Satyrian could.

Slimy bastards.

Calum stowed his disgust right next to that naive indignation and all its noble friends, and set off through the raucous crowd. No one paid him any mind. Not in this place. It had been a different story out on the more respectable streets of the so-called Bone City. But here... Here, no one asked questions beyond that most universal of necessities: *for how much?*

An armored fortress of a treasury, in need of robbing? *For how much?*

A dearly beloved relative, in need of a mid-sleep strangling? *For how much?*

Illegal slave hands, and sex trafficking, and any other depravity one could dream of?

*For how much?* asked that shit-eating Satyrian grin, as Calum drew up to the bar, keeping his scrambled visage front and center, as if discretion was of any real concern here.

Someday, things would be different. But for now, he told himself, perhaps he'd do well to cease deluding himself that he was somehow any better than these cretins for the simple fact that he did what he did for the good of all. Or for the good of the empire, at least.

"Powerful tidings from the land of the golden gods," said his shit-eating Satyrian channel broker, likewise keeping it front and center as he gestured to the Troglodan barkeep for another round of his neon blue concoction. "Though"—the Satyrian shot a sideways grin Calum's way—"*though*, I have heard whispers on the net that *some* in present company mightn't be so inclined as to go shedding tears over any misfortune of Asgard's."

It was a minor irritation, that any such personal detail of Calum's inner life had managed to become attached to his shadow persona. Briefly, he considered making some pithy comment to disperse the notion. Pointing out, perhaps, that his lacrimal ducts would never again waste moisture on *anything*, save for what was strictly required to keep his eyes functioning. But that would only be another breadcrumb. A potentially narrowing clue to the possibility that he, the man behind the scrambler, had either been born to one of the physically toughened castes or, as was actually the case, had at some point paid for a full-scale genetic survival upgrade on a black market of another kind.

"I didn't come here for small talk, Dehvo," he said instead, keeping his scrambled face forward.

He felt the Satyrian studying him, all pretenses of discretion dropped, no doubt searching for any chink in his armor—any clue that might lead him closer to Calum's actual identity. Within the folds of his loose robe sleeve, Calum found himself rubbing together forefinger and thumb, by no means *intending* to activate the microdermal patch of gintari toxin there, but glad for its presence, anyway. Yet another black market upgrade—one of several —he'd accrued here and there for rainy days and extenuating circumstances.

There'd be no need to kill Dehvo the shit-eating Satyrian, now or probably ever. But it was a comfort to remind himself how easily he could, and quite untraceably so, at but the pinch and scrape of a finger.

"'Course not," the Satyrian finally said, turning back to his fresh drink with a frustrated air, sliding a second hyperblue drink flute Calum's way without a glance. "Business is business, and it's said the Promethean waits for no man."

Calum eyed the drink disinterestedly, not deigning to comment. In the mirror behind the bar, he scanned the grog house, not expecting any trouble, but alert nonetheless. Briefly, his eyes paused on that poor, swaying Gorgon. Dehvos was watching as he returned his attention to the bar. Watching like, even past the scrambler, the Satyrian had sensed the focus of Calum's gaze.

"Care to wet your appetite after the fact?" he asked, nodding to a few of the barely-dressed servers zipping around the place before settling, rather pointedly, on the emaciated Gorgon center of room. "That one's new. Ish. Be grateful for a break from the cage, I'd wager. For the right price."

"No, thank you."

Dehvo only barely seemed to hear him. "You ever touched tips with an empath, friend? She's good. Was training to be one of them Kalnythian priestesses before they nabbed her out on one of those backwater missionary affairs. Can you imagine? Bending the knee to the almighty one minute, only to—"

"I said no," Calum said—or maybe growled—far more heatedly than he'd intended. He was too disgusted with this place. Too disgusted with this peddler of vices, and with the creeping sparks of arousal tingling through him at the thought of having that sad, beaten Gorgon in some dark, dirty backroom. Of squeezing her to the edge of her once-noble life with the building pleasure of each thrust. He felt the sharp grounding of his nails digging into his palms. The ghost of Talie's memory, staring him in the face.

Fires on all sides. Chaos and uncertainty, even from within.

He must be stronger than that.

"Where is the emissary, Dehvo?"

"Fourth chamber on the right. *Promethean.*"

Somehow, the Satyrian packed more meaning into that single word than they'd exchanged in the entire conversation. It was a jab of controlled heat, a counter thrust of professional courtesy—or lack thereof. A slap on the wrist and a delectable bite of uninvited *knowing*, all condensed into four syllables. It was enough to tighten Calum's fists, even as it curled his lips in a kind of savage grin. Two animals of very different natures, momentarily acknowledging their begrudging respects for one another.

"Payment pending, then," Calum said, pushing back from the bar to go.

"Be still, my heart," Dehvo grunted, turning back to his drink and dismissing Calum from awareness with an impressive finality. It was good he did. Better that the Satyrian didn't clock the awkward transition as Calum readjusted his gait to the overbearing Trogarran gravity.

The last glimpse he caught of the Satyrian, before rounding past the rear corner of the bar, was of Dehvos plucking Calum's untouched drink from the polished surface and throwing it back in a single glug. Probably *not* poisoned, then. Though Satyrians did boast rather preposterous immunities to such things. Still. A curious creature, that Dehvos. Undeniably despicable. But reliably useful, too.

Calum turned his thoughts to the matter at hand, as he continued down the hallway behind the bar, passing beneath the sweeper hood and its armed Troglodan guards. They had the look of small-time thugs about them. Calum kept his focus ahead, paying no mind to the privacy chambers he passed on either side. He wouldn't have seen or heard much but incoherent buzzing if he had. That was the entire point.

At the fourth chamber on the right, he stopped and palmed the panel, requesting access. There was only a slight pause before the humming shroud dematerialized, revealing the small, dim booth and the shadowy figure situated within.

The emissary was not what he'd expected, but only insofar as he hadn't actually known what to expect.

To say the Svartalf appeared cold and deadly was merely to say that she was, in fact, a Svartalf. The dark elves of Nidavellir had always stirred a certain *something* in his nethers. Not uneasiness, exactly. Just, perhaps, an alertness to the presence of unerring threat. They were killers. Almost without exception.

The Svartalf at the table didn't look to be any different. The dark edges of her face sharp and hardened in the shadows. The unbroken blacks of her eyes unsettlingly deep as she turned his way. It was something about the eyes, Calum decided. Something far more alien in those empty black pits than even in the buzzing orange sparks of an Androtta's so-called eyes.

It certainly said *something*, he decided, settling across from her, that she hadn't bothered to hide her face behind a scrambler. He just wasn't yet certain *what*. Perhaps she was merely a puppet of a puppet, one whose masters had faith her lowly anonymity would pose no problem to them were she to be identified. Or perhaps she simply had no intention of letting him leave here alive, once their business concluded.

This one, very much unlike Dehvos the Satyrian, skipped the preamble and jumped right in before he had much time to worry about it.

"Unwise speak of such things, where Knight's planet concerned."

She spoke with the same harsh, guttural tones he'd come to expect in his few encounters with Svartalf kind—a broken, almost angry timber that always seemed to defy the translators' attempts at smoothing things out, grammatically or otherwise. Most Svartalfs didn't bother learning Common. They were too much outsiders. And an outsider was exactly what this one looked like as she spoke, dark eyes flitting around the booth as if the walls themselves might be listening. He might've wondered himself, if his own sweeper implants hadn't been reading clean across the board.

"I happen to know for a fact that it won't be a problem," he said, thinking of Amelia's latest update from the *Camelot*. "Not for quite some time, at least," he added, pulse quickening, despite everything, at the thought of Amelia herself, and at the way she'd edged him on when last they'd coupled, eyes wide, bloodshot, choking rough encouragement past the crush of his fingers on that perfect throat of hers.

"Speak plain, Atlantean. What you propose?"

"Not to imply any disrespect," he replied, chiding himself the moment's distraction, "but I believe you're asking the wrong question."

The Svartalf was impassive beneath her dark hood. It was only as the edge of her robe shifted that he noticed her slender fingers tracing the pale edge of a shadow blade beneath. He resisted the urge to twitch, to even think about reaching for his own defenses, limited as they were. The sweepers should've spotted the weapon. The fact that he was still alive seemed to suggest she merely wanted him to know that. A test, just like all the others. Just like the legendary pirate, daring him to flinch. Just like the impotent threats of that failure of a shiny imbecile Phaldissus Kelkarin, sitting on his throne of lies and patricide.

All of them pawns in a game they didn't even know they were playing.

The only question was whether he was, too.

"Enlighten," the Svartalf finally said, leaning back just a hair in the booth seating. He felt his genitals descend back down from his stomach as the brim of her cloak fell over the pale spectre of the shadow blade.

"The question you should be asking," Calum said, stowing all traces of uncertainty and leaning forward into the dim light, planting his hands well within throat-slitting range of the well-primed killer before him, "is what your kingdom will do first, once you possess your very own Excalibur."

# END B**OO**K THREE

# AUTHOR'S NOTE

## (AUGUST 12TH, 2021)

Dear Reader,

Holy f*ck.

If I had to pick any two words to sum it all up, those would seem a decent enough place to start. Shortly followed by a slightly less concise (and admittedly less crass), "I hope you enjoyed the story."

The experience of actually getting this here book written and into your adventure-loving hands was... well, quite the adventure itself.

Namely, this is the first book I've ever written whilst attempting to wrangle/raise/finagle our firstborn son, Ser Remington "Star-Lord" Mitchell, the 1st—He of the Winningest Smiles and the Fearsome Grabby-Grabby Hands...

Which is to say, the day-to-days of my quiet, contemplative writings this past year have been a bit, you know... not.

But hey! Life's grand. Remy is a beautiful, happy little goofball of a baby boy (or a 13-month-old toddler, at the time of this writing), and Marina and I couldn't be happier ourselves...

... or at least we totally *will* be, just as soon as we finish sorting out *another* whole host of major life changes. Chief among those being a pending (and logistically rather maddening) move to New Mexico, circa any day now.

But that's all a story for another time. (And probably quite an amazing/ultimately enjoyable one at that, lest I sound ungrateful about any of these big life changes at the moment.)

At the end of the day, while it seems on some level like everything has changed, I can't help but be amused as I glance back at the following passages from the Author's Note at the back of Nate's previous adventure, *The Black Knight*:

*Suffice it to say, this book was a beast to write—an entirely new challenge for me on several levels. (I say this fondly, and in the best possible meaning of the word "challenge.")*

*The Excalibur Knights universe is drastically more expansive than anything I've ever written before. (And holy wow if it doesn't just keep expanding with a life of its own the more I write!)*

— THIS GUY, CIRCA LAST TIME AROUND

I guess the punchline, here—the very same one that somehow escaped my notice, for the first several books of my career—is that writing books can be kinda hard, sometimes. Possibly most of the time (and especially amid such perturbations as global pandemics, first time parenthood, and cross-country moves).

But boy, can it all be a big ol' bundle of fun, too.

If you've made it this far, I can only hope you've enjoyed the adventure as much as I have, and I can't wait to share what comes next!

That said, if you're ready for more, I have but one recommendation for you today—and it comes with free gifts.

Normally, this would be the part where I list a link to pre-order the next book (*Homecoming: Book Four of the Excalibur Knights Saga... shhhh!*)... BUT, on account of all the wibbly-wobbly life changes and whatnot, I've decided to hold off on setting a pre-order release date.

Which means we need a way to stay in touch.

And hey, while we're at it, how about a way for me to give you some free Excalibur Knights bonus stories? And shiza, maybe a free Book One from each of my other (completed) series as well. Why not?

Fortunately, such a way exists.

(This is the way.)

Now, the words, "sign up to my mailing list" might not *normally* get you going, exactly...

But if you'd like to grab two exclusive Excalibur Knights special features, *Flight of the Huntress* and *The Last Good Boy*…

Not to mention score a whole bundle of other free goodies…

Not to mention stay up to date on Excalibur Knights news via occasional email updates in the lilting tones of Yours Truly…

Well… there's really only one thing for it.

Go to *www.lukermitchell.com/spoils-of-war-signup* and sign up to my mailing list today, friend! And prepare for good times ahead.

*(Alternatively, if you're already whole hog on the Excalibur Knights universe and/or my writing in general, I invite you to check out my Patreon at www.patreon.com/lukermitchell to find out how you can directly support the work and get unfettered access to EVERYTHING I write—including Patron-exclusive stories and more!)*

Whichever way you go, I hope you enjoy the adventure.

Now, I'm off to New Mexico—pending a few last Alliance-style hoops to jump through. (And on to plotting out Nate's next adventure, soon after that.)

Thank you so much for reading.

Onward,
Luke Mitchell

# ACKNOWLEDGMENTS

As usual, there's a long list of those to whom I owe thanks.

First and foremost, as mentioned at the outset, this book is dedicated to Rick, who was one of my earliest readers and who sadly passed away this year. I had the pleasure of exchanging many emails with Rick over the years, and he was always as kind and supportive as he was perceptive in his feedback. I'll always be glad for the exchanges we had. Thank you for that, Rick. And thank you to Drew and the rest of your family for allowing me to say one last goodbye.

On the note of family, it's never *not* worth reiterating that I'd be lost without the support of my wonderful wife, Marina. Thanks go this time to young Ser Remy, as well, for his endless babbles of wisdom and astute plot recommendations. (And to good ol' Mimi Mitchell, too, for wrangling the spud when Mom and Dad had work to do.)

Thanks, also, to my production team—Tom Edwards on the rocking cover, as usual, and Lisa Poisso and Rob Shores for general story wrangling and copy editing, respectively.

Penultimately, enormous thanks to the following Patrons, who directly support this work of mine every month, rain or shine:


*Mildred Ann Mitchell — James Mallison — Linda Lestha*
*Mark Frink — John Munson — Bartholomew Bacak*
*Bob Laughner — Simon Danner — Joan M. Combes*
*Janet Ober — Robert Stuart — Grant Wilson*
*Letcher Ross — Eldridge Newlin —Sharon Kenneson*
*Mary-Anne Mitchell — Andrea Johnson — Tony Tieuli*
*Toni Mcconnell — Steven Mathis — Howard Wolfgang*
*John Barnes — Lisa Hoffman — Ron Williams*
*Yaakov Bright — Aj Jain-Perkins — Debra Franklin*
*James M Blaine — Nicholas Ruppert — Daniel McNeese*

*Andrew Staples — Karl Hakimian — Faith Hakimian*
*Gordon Keller — Dan Andrews — Adam McIntosh*
*Sam Higby — Robert Poet — Dagmar Preusker*

You gentlebeings are the blessed wind to my authorship's funny little sails. Love and peace to each and every one of you.

*(Side Note: If you loved this book and would like to support more like it, hop on over to patreon.com/lukermitchell to learn more about the perks of becoming a Patron!)*

Finally, my deepest thanks to you, Dear Reader, for coming along for the ride. I sure do enjoy you spending this time with my work. Thank you. And here's to many more stories to come!

Cheers,
Luke Mitchell

# ABOUT THE AUTHOR

Not a llama. Mostly human.

Luke is a storyteller whose dreams include learning the ways of the Force, becoming a sentient robot, and maybe even one day growing up. Also, lots of zombies… Don't ask.

Oh, and that "growing up" bit? That was a lie.

After studying engineering science at Penn State and neuroengineering at Drexel, Luke finally decided to throw in the towel on building a working Iron Man suit and opted instead to simply make things up and write them down. Boy, is he having more fun now.

When he's not holed up in his writing cave trying to string words together, he can often be found powerlifting, video-gaming, reading, and/or drinking the darkest, most roasty beers he can get his mitts on. Sometimes all at once.

But you know what? That's enough about Luke. He's really not that interesting. Still, if you'd like to say hi to him for whatever reason, he'd probably be glad to hear from you!

Go to **www.lukermitchell.com/spoils-of-war-signup** to join up for fun emails, free books, and lots of other great deals and exclusive content you won't find anywhere else. (Content like the Excalibur Knights specials, *Flight of the Huntress* and *The Last Good Boy*, which you can read today by joining the list!)

~

Additionally (as you wish)…

Follow me on BookBub for new release alerts
*bookbub.com/authors/luke-r-mitchell*

Browse the rest of my published titles
*lukermitchell.com/books*

Join the Patreon team for digital copies of ALL of my work (past, present, and future) — and much more!
*patreon.com/lukermitchell*

Thank you for reading!